The
Traynor
Legacy

The Traynor Legacy

David Stinson

Five Star • Waterville, Maine

First Edition
First Printing: April 2005

Published in 2005 in conjunction with
Tekno Books and Ed Gorman.

Set in 11 pt. Plantin.

Printed in the United States on permanent paper.

Library of Congress Cataloging-in-Publication Data

Stinson, David, 1946–
    The Traynor legacy / by David Stinson.—1st ed.
      p. cm.
    ISBN 1-59414-285-8 (hc : alk. paper)
    1. Presidents—Election—Fiction. 2. Undercover operations—Fiction. 3. Intelligence service—Fiction. 4. Americans—Vietnam—Fiction. I. Title.
PS3619.T567T73 2005
  813′.6—dc22   2004029576

For

BECKY,
PRESTON,
LINDSEY,
and JACKSON

Acknowledgements

I would like to thank my friend and best-selling mystery writer, Carolyn Hart, for her advice and encouragement on this project and for sharing with me many of her contacts in the world of commercial fiction. I would also like to thank John Helfers at Tekno Books for taking the time to look at a manuscript submitted by an unpublished author, finding merit in the work and patiently leading me through the publication process. I was extremely fortunate to have Denise Dietz, author of over a dozen published works, as principal editor on *The Traynor Legacy*. I learned a great deal about fiction writing just by studying Deni's comments and suggested changes. She was instrumental in making the book better. Thanks also to my partners, Phil Hart and Dee Replogle, who graciously took the time to read and comment on an early draft of the manuscript, and to my wife, Becky, and our kids, Preston and Lindsey, who cheerfully slogged through numerous drafts, each time providing great suggestions for improving the story. Each of them contributed in a material way to the final product that is *The Traynor Legacy*.

PROLOGUE

21 July 1999—Monte Carlo

It was an easy shot for a man with Staley's talents. The high-resolution scope was filled with the swarthy, languid torso of Azbek Fahoud as he lounged shirtless in one of the white canvas chairs perfectly arranged on the afterdeck of Alexandrov's yacht. Fahoud was smiling and talking to someone just out of the picture. Staley was slightly curious about the other party to the conversation, but not enough to swivel the Austrian-made sniper's rifle off the target. It was almost noon in Monaco. Staley had been up and dressed for hours, watching and waiting for Fahoud to make an appearance on the afterdeck. The memorandum in the suitcase said that Fahoud always came out on deck just before noon to have a single glass of champagne—Krug Clos du Mesnil, of course. It was the only time he allowed himself the luxury of being outside the yacht's air-conditioned saloon, the only time he could breathe the hot Mediterranean air and feel the baking sun that reminded him of home. The memorandum said he never varied from the routine. It was a weak link in his otherwise tight security, but one that Fahoud had reportedly dismissed with a shrug. A year ago, he hadn't been so careless. These days, he felt invincible. No one would dare make an attempt on the most powerful man in the terrorism business.

Staley studied Fahoud through the scope. How could this man be an icon among his people? He was so obviously a fake—an agnostic, a pathological liar and, when it suited his purposes, a ruthless murderer. Yet millions of lives were shaped by his every word. Men and women had willingly gone to their deaths at the nod of his head. His constituents lived in squalor because of his selfish intransigence, yet at his direction they blamed others for their misery. Because of him, they had nothing. Because of them, he had everything.

His most recent jihad was in its second year and blood was flowing freely in three Middle Eastern countries. Peace was never an option; he had made sure of that. Despite his impassioned speeches, Fahoud had only one goal: personal enrichment and eventual freedom from the confines of the cause. Every vicious attack his organization sponsored attracted more financial support from the radical Muslim governments and their supporters around the world. The cash was received, accounted for and allocated by Fahoud personally. Part of it went for guns and training. Part of it went to a numbered account in Zurich.

Fahoud's five-year plan was simple. As soon as he had a billion dollars in various Swiss banks, he would fake his own death, change his appearance and disappear for a year, maybe two. Then he would resurface with a new face and a new identity, perhaps as a retired business executive in Tahiti or the Maldives. He was certain he'd love the islands.

All things considered, Staley judged it to be a good plan. He had done essentially the same thing by moving to Aspen in 1975, buying a small frame house on Hallam Street north of the business district and becoming a year-round resident of the mostly quiet mountain town. He had been frugal with the consulting fees he received from his only client, Brownstone Investments, and that, along with the modest amount he had inherited from Wallace and Marie, enabled him to maintain a comfortable but not extravagant lifestyle. And being a resident of a ski town in the heart of the Rockies made it possible for him to disappear for weeks at a time with no one giving his absence a great deal of thought.

Staley had never married, although he had considered the possibility once just after finishing his MBA, but things had not worked out. His profession did not lend itself to intimate relationships. He had always been a loner and that was probably the way he would end his days. He had lived a full and interesting life, but now he was ready to retire from what he still thought of as *the Service*. No more hurried trips to God knows where, no more forged papers and multiple identities, and no more working for Traynor. He was pretty certain that Wallace and Marie, his long-dead parents, would approve.

Hackler Michael Staley was born in Joplin, Missouri, on May 10, 1943, the son of Wallace Hacker and Marie Richardeau, who as a married couple had recently adopted the surname "Staley." Wallace and Marie had entered the United States illegally through Mexico only a few weeks before. The baby's given name, "Hackler," was a play on the common mispronunciation of Wallace's surname by the Maquis—the French underground fighters that had worked with Wallace in Normandy for almost eleven months before the young OSS agent suffered a near fatal wound in a violent confrontation with Gestapo agents near the town of Caen.

Marie Richardeau was second-in-command of the underground cell to which Wallace Hacker had become an advisor upon his arrival in occupied France in late March, 1942. Although it was unusual for a woman to hold a leadership position in a Maquis unit, Marie had earned the respect of the other members of the cell by her intelligence, judgment, and most of all, her proven capabilities in hand-to-hand combat and with weapons of all sorts, including the

German-manufactured Schmeiser machine pistol, the stiletto and the garrotte.

Marie was from an old and respected military family, her father most recently having served for four years—from 1935 to 1939—as the garrison commander of French forces stationed near the city of Dalat, in Indochina. It was during that tour that the young Marie not only learned and mastered the language of Indochina, but also learned about weaponry and about self-defense, soon becoming an expert in the ancient form of hand-to-hand combat taught by the local fighters.

She continued to study and hone her skills after returning to France in October, 1939, shortly after the German invasion of Poland. When the Wehrmacht attacked and promptly defeated the poorly prepared French Army in May, 1940, Marie immediately sought out and joined with other free-French patriots who dedicated themselves to the defeat and eventual expulsion of the Germans from French soil.

Although neither of them saw it coming, over the long weeks of working and fighting together, of planning and conducting guerilla operations right under the nose of the vast German forces occupying all of northern France, Wallace and Marie soon fell in love. Against all reason and the advice of those closest to them, and in direct contravention of standing orders issued to all United States Office of Strategic Services agents serving in occupied Europe, Wallace and Marie were married at two a.m. on July 4, 1942—Wallace picked the date—in a secret ceremony in the Abbey Church of Saint Ouen in Rouen.

Eight months later, in an ambush based on an informer's tip, the Gestapo killed or captured nearly all of the members of Wallace and Marie's unit near the Pegasus Bridge in Caen. Because Marie was in the late stages of an unexpected pregnancy, she was not part of the operation. Wallace was one of only two survivors of the ambush. The other, an old man who had lost his entire family in the war, dragged a badly wounded Wallace into the reeds lining the canal and held him there until the Germans had gone. He then went to find Marie and, between the two of them, they managed to move the unconscious Wallace to a nearby barn where they tended to his injuries.

With Wallace still recovering from the wounds sustained in the shootout with the Gestapo, and their underground unit having been decimated by the ambush, Marie decided that their only hope, and the only hope of survival for their unborn child, lay in leaving France and finding a new life somewhere safe, perhaps to return again if necessary once things were sorted out.

She first made a visit to the outbuilding near an abandoned farmhouse not far from Caen where she recovered all of the money she had stashed there at the start of the war, most of it in English pounds and American dollars. Then, traveling at night to avoid the Germans and leading a mule-drawn cart carrying her wounded husband, Marie headed south, hoping that she could keep Wallace alive long enough to find medical care somewhere along the way. On the second night, she found the man she had been looking for, a Resistance contact in Flers who was an old friend of her father. He had heard of the ambush in Caen and was surprised to learn that there were any survivors. Upon hearing Marie's story and seeing that she was pregnant, he offered all the help he could summon to assist her in getting herself and Wallace—whom he did not know was an OSS agent—to safety.

At the friend's urging, a local doctor tended to Wallace, removing two German slugs from his body before treating and sewing up the wounds. A day later, when word came that the Gestapo were closing in once again, Marie's contact convinced another member of the local cell—a baker who was believed by the Germans to be harmless—to drive Marie and her wounded husband to Saint-Nazaire on the coast. There, they arranged passage on a small commercial fishing boat heading south to San Sebastian in northern Spain. Once in neutral Spain, they were safe.

After a short period of recuperation for Wallace, he and Marie decided that they could not go back to France. Marie's due date was just weeks away and there was no way she could receive proper medical care while constantly on the run. As for the period following the birth, Wallace could not bring himself to take Marie and their newborn child back into the violent world in which they had lived for almost a year before the ambush. There really was only one alternative and that was to find some way to get back to the United States so that the baby could be born on American soil as an American citizen. Although it meant desertion from the OSS for Wallace and abandonment of the Resistance movement for Marie, they decided to do whatever was necessary for the safety of their child.

Two weeks later the couple booked second-class passage on a barely seaworthy Moroccan steamer and eventually made it to Tampico, Mexico. From Tampico they traveled north to Matamoros and finally to Brownsville, Texas, where Wallace used his OSS training to hijack a new identity from the local death records and forge a passable driver's license and Social Security card issued in the name of Wallace Staley.

Traveling in a stolen car with modified plates, the Staleys made their way north, finally settling in Joplin, Missouri, where they rented an old house and moved in just in time for Marie to see a local doctor and make final preparations for the birth of their child.

When Marie saw that the newborn was a boy, she told Wallace that she wanted the child to have a name that carried with it a part of his hidden past. So she decided to call the baby Hackler, the name she had called Wallace the first time they had met and the name by which Wallace was known among the Maquis.

"One day," Marie told Wallace, "he will be told the entire story. He must know his past and how he came to be here. We will teach him our ways and our skills, so that when the time comes, he will be prepared for whatever he has to face in his world. We owe him that, Wallace, and we will see it done."

And so, Hackler Staley was raised with considerably more intensity than a normal child. When the time was right, Wallace taught him how to train his body to develop strength and stamina, how to hunt and fish, how to move undetected in the forest, how to think beyond the obvious and how to deal with the unexpected. Marie taught him languages—French and Indochinese—and the oriental martial arts style she had learned in Dalat. The boy was an eager and quick learner, and he made his parents proud.

Hack Staley grew to be tall and strong, a good student and an exceptional athlete, yet he remained modest and self-effacing, never seeking the limelight and always holding something back so as to not draw attention to himself. It was Wallace and Marie's way, and it became his way as well. Almost a half a century later, it was still his way.

Staley unconsciously recalculated the shot as he studied Fahoud through the scope. He then checked his watch. It was about time. Fahoud continued to sip his champagne

15

and laugh. *He's boasted many times that he was prepared to die for the cause. Now he's going to do just that.*

Fahoud had made a serious mistake in getting mixed up with Alexandrov, the most notorious and internationally visible of the Russian mafia dons. Every good intelligence service in the world had a copy of Alexandrov's list of merchandise for sale, and they all knew which of those items most interested Fahoud. The connection with Alexandrov signaled the real possibility of the introduction of nuclear weapons into the Middle East melee. That was an escalation that would not be permitted.

Evidently the new head of the Agency had made the decision that Fahoud should be eliminated before a deal with Alexandrov could be closed. That had surprised Staley. He didn't think Charles Rathmann had that kind of backbone.

Traynor had notified Staley in the usual manner that there was an operation in the works that needed his immediate attention. There was nothing pressing on Staley's calendar—there rarely was these days—and since this *was* his job as the only independent contractor providing specialized "consulting" services to Brownstone Investments, Staley initiated standard pre-mission procedures by traveling to Canada where he contacted Traynor and received final instructions in the manner he and Traynor had worked out years before. When he found out who the target was and where, he confirmed the engagement. He loved the Cote d'Azur, particularly Monaco, and he didn't mind being the one to take Fahoud out of the lineup.

Staley's modest hang-up bag was packed and leaning against the wall in the little hallway that led to the door of his room. The black Andiamo suitcase left by his unseen contact lay on the bed. Someone else's clothes were neatly folded in the main part of the suitcase, which was closed and zipped. The other part, with the pre-cast plastic forms specially designed to hold the disassembled rifle and tele-scoping tripod, was open and waiting.

Staley walked to the open doors leading to the balcony just outside his spacious room, but stopped short of step-ping outside. The Hermitage was a wonderful hotel with luxurious rooms and splendid service, and conveniently sit-uated just a half a block from the Monte Carlo Grand Ca-sino. Staley had requested a harbor view and since he, under the name François Villon, was a return guest known to be generous with the staff, his request was granted.

The French doors on the south side of the room opened out onto a wide balcony with a fine cut stone railing. There were large urns and potted plants on the balcony, along with some chairs and a table for reading or private outdoor dining. Just below the balcony were the beautiful grounds of the Hermitage, with meticulously cut grass and flowering shrubs of all colors and sizes. Just beyond the grounds and to the left was the famous tunnel that during the Monaco Grand Prix seemed to shoot brightly painted formula one cars down the hill to the harbor level and then into a sharp left turn at the bottom. And directly to his front was the picturesque harbor, with its perfectly shaped rock walls and towered entrance on the east side, just below the Grand Casino.

Alexandrov's yacht was anchored on the south side of the sheltered harbor, near other vessels of its class but not quite its size. Only the Sultan of Brunei's yacht was larger, and it was noticeably absent, probably put out to sea to avoid the appearance of any business or social interaction with Alexandrov and his guest.

Staley estimated the distance to the yacht to be about five hundred meters, which was perfect since the memo-randum said the weapon had been zeroed to five hundred meters—probably no coincidence. The package had contained detailed information about sighting this particular rifle with this particular suppressor, and he was confident that the information was totally reliable. He had bet his life on Traynor's penchant for perfection many times in the past and had never been disappointed. All he had to worry about was the wind, and it was a perfectly calm morning. The flags were limp, even those atop the castle that towered above the southern end of the harbor. It was time to get started.

Speaking fluent French with an accent faintly resonant of Normandy, Staley called the bell desk, "This is Monsieur Villon in room 207. I need a bellman immediately please. I am checking out and have transportation waiting."

Check-out time was only a few minutes away and Staley had to catch a certain chartered bus bound for the international airport at Nice. It was scheduled to leave at noon. Timing was critical now. He had to make the shot and get clear before the Monaco authorities fully grasped what had happened and shut down the Principality.

Staley turned back to the sniper rifle, securely latched to the top of the tripod that stood in the middle of the room, well back from the open French doors. He quickly took up a shooting position, put his eye to the scope and once again looked into the smiling face of Azbek Fahoud. Staley wrapped the silk cloth provided in the suitcase around his shoulders and tucked it into the neck of his white dress shirt to ensure there would be no powder residue on his clothes.

Now! He pulled the trigger, wincing at the louder-than-expected noise as the high-powered rifle coughed against the suppressor. Even so, no one could have heard the shot outside of Staley's room. He immediately got the scope back on the target. Fahoud's head was listing to the right and there was a black spot where his left eye had been. Blood was splattered on the back of the white deck chair. Staley fired again, this time a little lower. The round impacted just below Fahoud's Adam's apple and drove him back against the chair. No need for additional confirmation. Fahoud was dead.

Staley quickly disconnected the rifle from the tripod, twisted off the scope and placed it in the form in the suitcase specifically molded for the sight. He broke the rifle down just as quickly and placed the three components in their spots in the suitcase. Next came the tripod, its thin, high carbon steel legs collapsing to less than a foot-long bundle. He wiped everything down with the silk cloth and tossed it in the case as well. He then closed the suitcase and latched the hidden compartment so that it would not be noticed without considerable inspection and could not be opened except by someone who knew exactly what he was looking for.

He checked his watch. One minute thirty since the shooting and two minutes since he called for the bellman.

Staley quickly closed the French doors and picked up a can of what appeared to be a popular aerosol deodorant. He sprayed the contents around the room—a neutral air freshener to dispel the light odor of the specially manufactured charge. He placed the suitcase near the front door of his room and hurried into the bathroom where he rinsed his hands, face and the exposed part of his neck with a light solvent that had the texture and essence of an expensive aftershave. He slid the deodorant can and the aftershave bottle into an inside pocket of his hang-up bag. There would be no scientific evidence of his recently having fired a weapon.

As he was finishing up in the bathroom, there was a knock at the door. Staley checked his watch—not quite four minutes since the call. He smiled at the efficiency of the bell staff. He had counted on it and they had come through.

Still no sirens or other noise from outside. Fahoud's security detail was probably in a panic, trying to figure out what had happened. Alexandrov's people most likely were nervous too, wondering if their boss might also be a target, and if so, whether the shooter was still around.

Staley opened the door for the bellman and made conversation in French with the young man while he loaded the two bags on a handcart. Staley looked around the room like an anxious traveler making a last minute check to see if he had left his airplane tickets on the nightstand or a pair of socks in the closet.

"Sorry for the rush, but I need to check out and make the charter." Then looking at his watch, "I have noon. What about you?"

"*Oui monsieur,* noon exactly." An alibi, if needed.

Staley led the way down the wide, sumptuously carpeted and beautifully furnished hallway, then around the corner to the small elevator. Because his room was below the street level entrance to the hotel, Staley had to take the elevator two floors up to the main lobby.

He walked across the elaborately decorated lobby and directly to the front desk.

"Checking out, please. Monsieur Villon in 207."

Now there was a siren outside; a police car passing by. No way of knowing where it was headed.

The pretty, young desk clerk smiled at Staley. She remembered him from when he had checked in several days earlier and from the couple of times he had come to the desk to ask for change or a non-existent message. She cleared his account with the American Express card on file, then handed him the folio.

"So nice to have you with us once again, Monsieur Villon. I hope you enjoyed your stay."

"Thank you. It was very pleasant and the hotel was wonderful, as always." Then his best smile. "And people such as you, mademoiselle, make it a pleasure to be here and a pleasure to return. Au revoir." Another alibi.

Outside, Staley found the bellman preparing to load his luggage in the small, comfortably appointed coach that was waiting to take Staley and several other guests to the airport in Nice, just thirty minutes or so away. He glanced at the passing traffic and looked further up the street. There was still no commotion, no police activity.

Staley watched as his hang-up bag and the Andiamo suitcase, with a small red ribbon tied to the handle, were placed in the luggage compartment underneath the bus. There were several other bags in the compartment and other passengers already in their seats, most with their heads in magazines or newspapers. They took no notice of Staley and offered no conversation. He evidently was the final passenger to board. The driver closed the door as he walked back to find a seat in an empty row.

He settled into a window seat on the right side of the coach. As the bus pulled into the crowded street, he made a production of being busy, working on his Palm Pilot, apparently checking for appointments and updating personal information on contacts made during his visit.

The bus wound through the streets of Monaco, stopping a few times for traffic and once for some minor construction. Still no commotion. Staley wondered if anyone had called the police. Maybe Alexandrov's crew had some cleaning up to do before allowing the authorities to roam freely on the yacht.

The bus finally reached the highway for the upcountry

route to Nice. They picked up speed while the air conditioner blew a chilly mist over the heads of the preoccupied passengers. Staley looked around casually to see if he could spot the contact. He or she could have been any one of five or six different people. He stopped looking; he didn't want to know.

Thirty-five minutes after leaving the front door of the Hermitage, the small bus pulled into the Nice International Airport. Earlier that morning, Staley had made a reservation on a Delta flight to New York, connecting with an Air Canada flight to Quebec, Monsieur Villon's home, according to his passport and other identification documents.

The bus stopped twice before reaching the Delta departure area, and each time the driver assisted the exiting passengers in retrieving their bags from the under-coach compartment. When the driver announced the Delta gates, Staley walked forward and down the steps onto the curb. The luggage compartment was open. Staley picked out his hang-up bag and quickly scanned the remaining luggage for the Andiamo suitcase the bellman had loaded on the coach at the Hermitage. It was gone. But an identical black Andiamo suitcase remained, this one without a red ribbon. One of the early departing passengers had claimed the suitcase containing the rifle just as described in the memorandum and had left the suitcase Staley had brought with him from Quebec. It was the same procedure Staley and the unknown contact had used to swap suitcases upon his arrival in Nice. He could not identify the contact and the contact presumably could not identify him.

Secrecy and anonymity had been a way of life for Staley since he was a child. It had been drilled into him by his father and reinforced by his mother. He kept everything he did, everything he knew, to himself. No one really knew Staley.

He never let anyone get that close, not even Traynor. It was the reason he was still alive after all these years.

The line to purchase tickets for business class was relatively short and Staley made good time clearing the lobby. He collected his boarding pass, checked his bags and made his way through passport control. He then took the glass elevator up to the Delta business class lounge where he relaxed with a glass of very dry Chablis and some roasted almonds. Everything seemed to be on track.

Staley busied himself reading the current month's edition of *Le Monde Diplomatique*. He checked the twenty-four-hour news channel from time to time, but still no word of the shooting.

Time passed slowly. He almost expected some kind of special security check—maybe a closer look at each passenger or a search of luggage. They *had* to know about the assassination by now. Maybe they would send in a canine unit with dogs trained to smell the residue of a fired rifle. If the solvent worked, that wouldn't be a problem.

When it was thirty minutes to the scheduled departure time, Staley first visited the restroom, then took the glass elevator down to the main lobby. He loitered for a minute among the duty free shops, apparently examining watches and expensive wines, but mostly checking the crowd for faces that looked out of place. He had an uncomfortable feeling that something was wrong. Rationally, that was highly unlikely. *Relax. There are no holes in the exit plan. You're just getting too old for this.* Traynor had told him that almost no one in the Agency did field work past the age of fifty. Staley was fifty-six.

He was halfway to the gate when he saw them—two French policeman and two men in civilian clothes. They were standing beside a support pillar near the gate, out of the way but obviously looking for someone. *They couldn't be looking for me. There's no connection, no way they could have figured out this soon where the shot had come from and who was in the room. No way they could have tracked me to the airport so quickly. No way they could know what I look like or where I'm going. Unless, that is, they had help.*

An old concern resurfaced. For the past twenty-eight years, Staley had placed his life in Traynor's hands. *Could anyone, even Traynor, be trusted forever?* Yes. Staley was certain of one thing: Jonathan Traynor would never give him up. *But what about the Agency?* There were too many politicians running the show these days, men like Charles Rathmann, and it was axiomatic that politicians could not be trusted. And then there was the fact that Traynor was getting on in years. *Maybe he'd given in to bureaucratic pressure to disclose the details of the operation.* Unlikely, but it could happen.

There was always the lingering possibility that it would end like this. The Director of Central Intelligence would contract for Traynor's special services, would cause him to send an unknown field agent out on a high profile job and then arrange to have the agent eliminated, terrified of the possibility that someone would uncover the connection between the operation and the Agency.

But Staley also knew that whoever implemented the decision to give him up would never allow the police in any country to take him alive. He knew too much and the drugs were too good. No one could go to their grave with a secret if a sophisticated intelligence agency wanted answers. If the French police up ahead were really there for him, then someone wanted Staley dead—not in custody and not subject to interrogation.

Despite his misgivings, Staley continued on toward the

gate. His pulse and blood pressure had not changed at all. His demeanor was that of a business traveler, nothing to arouse suspicion. He had been in too many tight spots to let something like this cause him to panic.

Business class was boarding, so Staley approached the flight attendant stationed at the doorway and handed her his boarding pass. She looked at it, then glanced at the waiting men and nodded.

The two men in plain clothes walked toward Staley, the uniformed officers in tow. One of the plainclothes officers spoke.

"Monsieur Villon, could we have a word with you please?"

They spoke in English. Staley looked at them with surprise, as though seeing them for the first time. His cover was as a Canadian, so speaking English was not a giveaway. But he was from Quebec after all, so he affected a French accent.

"Yes, I am Monsieur Villon. What do you want—what can I do for you?"

"Will you come with us please?"

The uniformed officers looked tense—Staley guessed they were real cops. The plainclothes guys were cool and calm—probably special operations. Good plan.

"This plane is about to leave and I must be back in Quebec tonight. What is this all about?"

One of the plainclothes operatives took Staley's elbow, firmly guiding him away from the gate. Staley concentrated on looking confused while half-heartedly trying to pull his arm away from the agent. But inside, his mind was churning, evaluating every possible exit, trying to determine how he was going to get out of the airport after disposing of these four. None of them had a weapon drawn, and he was pretty sure he could take them all out in a matter of seconds. If he was going to do anything inside the airport, he knew he would have to act quickly.

The other special ops agent sensed what Staley was considering and stepped away a few feet, his hand inside his jacket. The one with his hand on Staley's arm said quietly, "Please, Mr. Villon, we know who you are. Do not start something in here. You won't make it to the door."

What does that mean, "We know who you are?" Do they believe I am Villon, the assassin, or do they really know? How could they?

Staley made a quick assessment of the situation and decided the agent was right. Starting something inside the airport would be risky, especially with the plainclothes operatives alert to some kind of escape attempt. And besides, he did not want to kill the French cops. In order to take all four of them, he would have to be fast and deadly. If he was still alive when they got out of the airport, they would probably split up. The special ops team would want to ditch the police. After they were gone would be the best time to make a break. He thought he knew some people in Nice that might help him. He tried to remember how to find them.

Still in character, Staley looked back and forth between the officers, the picture of a man victimized by a case of mistaken identity. He intended to remain passive until they got out of the airport.

"I don't know who you are or what you want, but I need to be on that plane. Can you assure me that if I go with you, I'll still be able to be in Quebec tonight?"

One of the uniformed cops finally spoke up. "We can give you no such assurance, Monsieur. Please, come with us quietly and we will explain everything."

"Someone will have to get my luggage. I have bags on that plane."

"Yes, Monsieur, we will take care of your luggage."

Staley allowed the plainclothes agent to hold him by the elbow as the small group of men walked out of the airport. Staley acted embarrassed, as would a business traveler who had been mistakenly pulled off a flight by the police.

As they cleared the door of the terminal, the agents guided Staley to the left, toward a parking area reserved for official vehicles. There was a white van parked close to the curb. It had some kind of government markings but it was not a police unit. The sliding door on the passenger side of the van was open.

As they walked toward the van, the agent on Staley's right pulled his hand from his pocket and jabbed a needle through Staley's sleeve and into his upper arm. He felt a warm rush throughout his body as he tried to pull away, but the agent had a firm grip. Staley turned his head and looked at the agent. There was no reaction whatsoever.

Staley expected the lights to start going out any second, but nothing happened. He had never been drugged before so he didn't know what to expect. *Maybe it was just a tranquilizer—something to make me easier to handle once inside the van. I've got to do something before whatever that was kicks in.*

He looked for an opportunity to break free. The traffic in front of the busy airport was barely moving and there were hundreds of people trying to load, unload, park and check baggage. The crowds would help. Staley was certain he could find a way to get out of the airport if he could survive the first twenty seconds after making his move. The tough part would be getting away from the security detail. He did not want to kill the cops, but if that became absolutely necessary in order for him to escape, he was prepared to do so.

The driver of the van turned toward Staley as the plainclothes agent guided him toward the side door. Staley could see a Russian-made Makarov automatic in the driver's hand, just hidden by the armrest. This was getting more and more difficult.

There was a police car behind the van, and the two uniformed officers broke off from the rest of the group and started walking back to the marked car. Staley had figured it right, but he was going to have to do something before getting into the van with the special ops detail. Wherever they were going, he probably would not survive the trip.

As he started to step into the van, continuing to protest but at the same time looking for an opening to disarm the driver, Staley felt a strong push from behind. Both of the plainclothes agents started shouting in French.

One said, "Look out," and the other, "He's got a gun."

Everything came together for Staley in a heartbeat. His captors were creating a scene to cover whatever was about to happen. It was now or never.

Carrying the momentum of the push from behind, Staley dove into the van and lunged for the Makarov, his quickness startling the driver. With his right hand, he grabbed the barrel of the small automatic, pulling it free. At the same time he kicked backward with his left foot, dropping one of the agents with a blow to the solar plexus.

But before he could make another move, the other agent standing outside the van fired twice at point blank range. The impact of the gunshots knocked Staley forward onto the floor of the van, his head hitting a metal box under the seat and creasing the side of his skull. He knew he had been shot twice in the back, and it was bad. He tried to turn against the shooter, but he couldn't move. He was helpless and paralyzed. *It was a setup—it had to be. Did they get to Traynor?*

Staley lay face down on the floor of the van. He was

alone—no one was coming to his aid. He could hear commotion outside and could feel the life draining from his body. He had been shot before, but not like this. He couldn't move a muscle and breathing was becoming more of a chore than he could handle. He was suddenly very cold. The sounds from outside became distant and hollow, hard to understand. He was floating, his lungs on fire and his heart working hard to keep the blood flowing.

Staley's last thoughts were about Wallace and Marie as the inevitable blackness closed in from the corners of his vision. Finally, he let go. The pain was gone.

PART I
1970–1971

1

TRAYNOR

April 1970—Washington, D.C.

It was late Friday afternoon on a cool April day in Washington. With the passing of the spring equinox, the days were growing longer and the grass was beginning to take on the bright green hues that previewed the annual renewal of summer. The cherry blossoms were in full bloom and the nation's capital was crowded with tourists. All the best restaurants were packed; it was hard to get a table unless you were a regular. Long lines of sightseers snaked around the museums and monuments on the Mall. The seat of government was alive and everyone wanted their share of what it had to offer.

Up on the Hill, Congress was in session and down Pennsylvania Avenue, the President was in the residence. The business of government was being conducted everywhere—indoors and out, in richly appointed offices, in smoke-filled hallways, in overpriced hotel rooms and at wrought iron tables outside trendy cafes. There were new ideas to be explored, new laws to be passed, new treasures to be found, new obstacles to be overcome, new money to be made, new power to be won.

But for one man in particular, the change of seasons in Washington was of little significance. The attractions that brought many to the nation's capital held no interest for him. His focus was outside the mainstream, in a world that few knew anything about and fewer yet would ever enter.

Jonathan Traynor sat alone at the kitchen table in his magnificent old house on a tree-lined street in the heart of Georgetown. His bad leg ached, as it sometimes did when troubling thoughts occupied his active mind. He unconsciously rubbed the deep scar under his trousers as he watched the shadows lengthen, then overtake the room as they did every day when the sun dropped behind the stone fence that separated his house from the neighbor's next door.

Traynor was not thinking about the crowds on the Mall or the busy restaurants, or the cherry blossoms, or the stirring of life brought on by spring. His mind was thirteen time zones away in Southeast Asia. There it was perpetual summer. Young men—a good number of which had been trained and led by Traynor in earlier postings—were still there, still fighting, just trying to stay alive long enough to finish their tour and come home.

Traynor had spent almost two years in South Vietnam before being seriously wounded and medevac'd home near the end of his second tour. Although that was four years ago, in times of deep introspection Traynor's mind always wandered back to Vietnam. It ate at him that he was out of the war while others were still there fighting.

It bothered him more that Johnson's war continued to rage on while everyone with any sense knew that it was lost. It had not been lost on the field of battle but in the Oval Office of the White House and in the halls of the Senate Office Building. It sickened him to think about the American soldiers still fighting in Southeast Asia, the chance for victory having been ripped from their grasp. But even so, they continued to fight, marking time in a lost cause while the politicians fumed and fumbled. Something needed to be done to get the troops home.

Traynor was not a large man, a trim 165 pounds and just under six feet in height, but he had a presence that all who met him noticed immediately. He walked with a slight limp due to the wounds he had received four years earlier while commanding a combat brigade with the First Cavalry Division near the little village of Bong Son, located in the northern part of Binh Dinh Province, South Vietnam. The limp, combined with his prematurely gray and thinning hair, gave him the appearance of being at least a decade older than his fifty-two years. But his eyes were bright and piercing, and anyone who knew Traynor also knew that behind those sparkling eyes was a brilliant and driven man, a man who had lived his life on the edge and whose passion had never ceased to burn. At least until now—now all of that was at risk.

The old grandfather clock in the living room ticked loudly as he continued to wait, slouched in a wooden armchair next to the round oak table, his bad leg stretched out to one side. His right hand flexed periodically with minor spasms as he absentmindedly scratched behind the ears of the old terrier standing patiently alongside. Just as with his limp, the tremor in his fingers was a visible remnant of the wounds that had nearly killed him and then had driven him into forced retirement.

As usual, Traynor was alone. He didn't mind being alone; it was the life he had chosen. He had always had the energy to ignore the loneliness by occupying his mind and his time with matters of importance. But that was becoming increasingly more difficult. Now he was alone and tired. Tired of the boredom, tired of the tedium, tired of not being able to contribute in a world that cried out for action and leadership. They should not have forced him to retire.

It was an unnecessary waste of a valuable asset. He had a lot of good years left and nothing to do. The inactivity was driving him crazy.

Despite his repeated offers and inquiries, it was clear that the Army was not going to take him back. He was medically retired and that was it. He was an old soldier with a strong will and a desire to continue his career—*some* kind of career—but there was no opportunity in sight. For the first time in his life he was depressed and he didn't like it. Not one damned bit.

Traynor was disappointed that he had not had the foresight to see this day coming. *Poor planning,* he thought. *I used to kick people in the ass for poor planning. Now look at me.*

But he had not given up just yet. He had one more card to play. He had formulated a plan, an entirely original plan unlike anything ever considered before. It was his brainchild. He had thought through all the issues, worked out all the details, planned the required staffing and arranged for the necessary funding. And then, just two days ago, he had presented it to the only man in the world who could accept it and bring Jonathan Traynor back into the fold. The proposal he had made in that meeting was his last best hope.

Traynor unconsciously scratched the dog and watched the clock, waiting for the phone to ring. As he sat there, he thought back over the past few years and where he might go from here. *Hell, maybe this is what it's all been about. Maybe this is where I'm supposed to be and what I'm supposed to do. I guess I'll find out soon enough.*

Traynor had been medically retired from the Army in 1967 after failing to completely recover from the wounds received that morning near Bong Son. After a short period of rest and recuperation, he decided that despite his forced retirement, he was not ready to quit just yet. There was more to be done and he needed to find a way to stay involved. He was enthusiastic at first, confident he could find a job suited to his particular abilities and his extensive experience. He was not anywhere near ready for the elephant's graveyard.

It was not a matter of needing a job or a source of income. Traynor had never come close to spending his monthly check from Uncle Sam. For twenty years he had sent money each month to his older brother Harmon, who was in the investment banking business, just as their father had been. Harmon had invested Jonathan's money in a mix of stocks—a small percentage in a few speculative stocks that Harmon followed closely—and in bonds, government securities, and the occasional private venture capital opportunity. Jonathan had received a statement from Harmon every month for the first couple of years, then told his brother not to worry about statements, just keep the account and take something for himself once in a while as an investment advisor's commission. Jonathan gave Harmon a general power of attorney to handle his financial affairs and Harmon gladly did so, his only regret being that due to a severe asthmatic condition, he could not serve in the military. Harmon viewed his taking care of Jonathan, the family warrior, as satisfying, at least in part, his service obligation.

When Harmon died from a sudden heart attack in 1965, Traynor learned two things. As a result of Harmon's investments on his behalf, Traynor was a reasonably wealthy man in his own right. And, because Harmon had no other family, he had left his entire estate, valued at over eight million dollars, to Jonathan.

Jonathan was overwhelmed by Harmon's success, his generosity and his lifelong stewardship of Jonathan's finances. He had never told Harmon just how much his love and support had meant over the years, and now Harmon was gone.

For some unexplainable reason he felt like he had to stay connected to Harmon, so shortly after his separation from the Army, Jonathan moved into the old house in Georgetown. Harmon had purchased the house just a few months before he died. It was where he planned to spend his retirement years. And because of that, Traynor made the same commitment. He decided that the house in Georgetown would be his home as well. The memory of Harmon would always be there with him.

Traynor had excellent contacts in the Pentagon and early on he worked those contacts regularly, always looking for an opportunity to get back into the game. He made the rounds as often as possible, most of the time for lunch, sometimes hosting or attending a dinner party. A few of his old friends, and some of the new ones that he had carefully cultivated, encouraged him to try to come back. Several of the senior people near the Chief of Staff put in a good word for him—a recommendation for reactivation and assignment to a headquarters or planning staff. But the civilians running the show would have none of that. Traynor was retired and would stay that way. He was an old soldier and his time was past.

Far sooner than he would have expected, his sources started drying up. Duty assignments changed, old friends rotated out to new jobs, new officers he did not know filtered in to take over the jobs with the best access to the senior decision makers. Traynor lost contact with his "class"—the guys most likely to help him. While sympathetic to his plight, they had their own problems to deal with: new assignments, new responsibilities, new commands or, for an unlucky few, unexpected retirement of their own. The senior officers closest to Traynor who remained at the Pentagon became increasingly disillusioned, constantly complaining about lack of funding, about the oppressive bureaucracy, and most of all about the fact that our government had lost credibility around the world due to the manner in which the Johnson administration had elected to conduct the war in Vietnam. They often asked Traynor why he would even *want* to come back, since in their view, things were going to hell in a handbasket.

Despite his discouragement, Traynor continued to work the system, trying to find some way to put to good use his years of training and experience.

Johnson's surprise announcement in March of 1968 that he would not run for reelection that fall was welcomed with enthusiastic, albeit quiet, affirmation at the Pentagon. He had cost the military dearly. It would take time to recover, provided the new administration had the sense and the ability to turn public sentiment in favor of the military instead of against it.

Traynor continued his efforts to get reinstated in the Army throughout 1968, but without success. When the Republicans won the White House in November of that year, his enthusiasm was rekindled with the hope that somehow the new administration would implement policies that would make a man of Traynor's talents desirable for re-employment by the Army, or *somewhere* within the Department of Defense. But those hopes soon were dashed.

While the new administration under Richard Nixon evidenced some improvement, it was not enough to make an appreciable difference. America's foreign policy was being dictated in the streets and on television rather than in coherent long-term strategy sessions in the Departments of

State and Defense. While Nixon was tougher than Johnson, political expediency remained the order of the day. America was becoming a paper tiger, unable to project its influence around the world because no one really believed that we had the moral courage to do what needed to be done in those areas where evil was a way of life and oppressive governments quickly extinguished every spark of freedom. At home, soldiers returning from a year of fighting in Vietnam were being spit on by protesters and reviled by the media.

It was a dismal picture, and after a while Traynor gave some consideration to simply staying in retirement, out of sight and out of the mainstream.

Then one day in the fall of 1969, Traynor was invited to lunch by an old friend who at the time was the Army's senior intelligence officer. At the luncheon he met several other people also involved with the U.S. intelligence community, including a man introduced as the Assistant Deputy Director for Operations of the Central Intelligence Agency. Traynor immediately liked the CIA man, and found himself wondering if the Agency might be able to use a worn-out cavalry officer. The meeting became even more interesting as they talked over coffee while sitting on the veranda of the golf course clubhouse just south of Annapolis, looking out over the gold and red colors of the Virginia countryside.

The discussion was frank and disconcerting. The Agency had so much to do. There were important matters to be investigated and dealt with in China, North Korea, the Soviet Block countries, the Middle East, Latin America. But conducting operations in those areas and elsewhere around the world was becoming more and more difficult—not due to the enhanced capability of our adversaries, but rather because of the almost disabling restraints continuously imposed by a new breed of politicians here at home. Arbitrary limitations on overseas operations, disclosure of covert operations' budgets and constant reporting made running an effective intelligence operation almost impossible. Every decision was made with concern for how it would look if uncovered by a Congressional investigation.

It was clear that the liberals in Congress really did not want a "secret" intelligence organization; they wanted a hand in every decision and a first look at every operation. Most of them had never been to war, had never risked their own lives or seen the blood of others spilled for the preservation of democracy. But they did understand the value of television coverage in furthering their careers, and what better way to get it than by going after those in the government who operated for the most part in secret.

The most vocal critics of the Agency—the Congressmen and Senators whose primary interest was their own visibility— were the least informed. They had no idea that without the ability to operate outside the lines, to employ men who lived in shadows to gather information and those devoid of moral conviction to fight the close-in dirty war of espionage, the Agency could not function effectively. And if the nation's most important intelligence and counterintelligence agency couldn't function effectively, the inevitable consequence would be catastrophic. The Central Intelligence Agency was under attack from within the government, and the attackers were being praised for it in the liberal press. They either did not understand, or they just did not care.

And then there was the ever-increasing problem of the so-called "investigative journalists"—a new generation of media hounds whose only goal in life seemed to be uncovering governmental secrets. They were becoming a terrible nuisance, always looking for a story without regard to the harm such disclosure could do to American lives and American interests around the world.

The CIA man was convinced that an intelligence and security service could not operate in an environment in which there were no secrets. It was clear that American interests abroad and at home would suffer the consequences of government in the sunshine in a world where those who followed the rules would inevitably lose.

By the time the luncheon was over, Traynor had seriously begun to consider the idea of going to work for the CIA. It was a trap he had not run for a couple of reasons, not the least of which was the fact that he had no experience in the intelligence business and was uncertain if there was anything he could bring to the table as an analyst, or even as some kind of non-professional manager, within the Agency. More importantly, he had no contacts within the Agency, and without a contact, he knew it would be next to impossible to find a position there. He thought he probably ought to just let it go. Finding a responsible job with the CIA was a real long shot.

Nevertheless, Traynor left that luncheon meeting incubating an idea that had sprung into his mind even as the CIA man had explained the new problems faced by the Agency. It all seemed so simple to Traynor. It was an idea that if implemented would give the CIA the ability to conduct absolutely untraceable, and totally deniable, covert activities that would be unimaginable under the current system. The value of such a capability in the cold war would be inestimable to the Agency. He wondered if he was the first to come up with the idea. Surely someone else had seen the same possibilities. Maybe the idea he had in mind was already in play.

Without anything more pressing to do, Traynor worked

on the project through early winter. By January, he had a pretty good outline of the plan, how it would be implemented, how it would be funded and how it would be kept off the books. The more he worked with the plan, the more he became committed to its plausibility.

There was just one problem. Traynor knew he would never have the opportunity to present his idea to someone who could make the decision to further pursue the matter without compromising the security of the entire proposal. The new organization he envisioned would work only if its very existence were kept totally secret from all but a select few of the highest ranking executives in the Agency, and the possibility of Traynor ever getting the opportunity to make a presentation at that level was very unlikely.

Then in late January, 1970, the director of the CIA resigned unexpectedly and President Nixon appointed a new director, a Washington insider named Sanders Colburn. It was the break Traynor had been hoping for but never dreamed would come to fruition.

Sandy Colburn had attended Dartmouth College and had graduated at the top of his class in 1941. Believing that war was likely, he had immediately attempted to join the Navy, but was turned down because of a chronic heart condition that was discovered during his induction physical. Being unable to serve in uniform, Colburn volunteered for government service in whatever capacity might be suitable for a man with his educational background and family connections, and finally wound up working for the Office of Naval Intelligence. He spent the entire war in Washington, D.C., reviewing intercepts and assisting in the direction of naval intelligence operations in both the European and Pacific theaters of operations.

While Colburn was securing his position as a civilian employee with the Department of the Navy, his best friend and college roommate joined the Army, went to OCS, and had just been commissioned as a second lieutenant when the Japanese attacked Pearl Harbor on December 7, 1941. His best friend's name was Jonathan Traynor.

Colburn and Traynor had a lot in common from their Dartmouth days. Besides being roommates, they had both been smallish guards on a football team that was not quite as good as the Ivy League school normally fielded. They became close and leaned on each other for support during two-a-day practices in the late summer heat, through the beatings they took playing both ways in games where the team often lost by several touchdowns, and fighting through the painful injuries each suffered but neither would acknowledge to the coaches or trainers. They were friends in the classroom as well, each having a high regard for the intelligence and hard work of the other while always engaged in a good-natured competition for the best grades. They learned a great deal about themselves during those years—about being tough, both physically and mentally, about moral courage and about maintaining a commitment.

It was a bond that still lit up their smiles on the rare occasion when they happened to bump into one another. While they had been in touch only a few times since college, their friendship had weathered well and was still strong. Despite the years, each of them continued to believe that they could always count on the other when the chips were down.

When Traynor read about Colburn's appointment to be the new director of the CIA, he just sat in his chair, grinning from ear to ear. It was an expression that few people who knew Jonathan Traynor had ever seen.

Traynor decided to wait at least ninety days after his

friend's appointment before contacting Sandy Colburn. During that time, he worked on and refined the plan. He kept coming back to the issue of deniability. If the Agency could find a way to do the all the dirty and disagreeable things that were essential to the conduct of an effective foreign intelligence service—especially field operations—without exposing the origin or details of such activities to Congressional inquiry or public examination, its effectiveness could be enhanced dramatically. That was the crown jewel of the service Traynor would offer and that was the way he would sell it. The real value would be in the fact that the Agency could effect whatever result was needed in any situation in which American interests were at stake without regard to political considerations. It would in essence be the perfect weapon for a truly effective intelligence organization.

But, of course, the key to the entire project would have to be an unquestioning belief by Sandy Colburn in Traynor's ability to perform whatever tasks might be assigned and in his absolute commitment to secrecy. Traynor thought he could make a convincing case to his old friend on both issues.

Finally, Traynor made the call. He knew it would not be easy gaining access to Colburn, even on the telephone. So rather than push the matter during the initial call, he simply left a message with the Director's secretary, telling her that he and Colburn had been roommates at college and that he would appreciate a call from the Director whenever he had a few spare moments. It was just the right touch, and within an hour, Colburn called back.

"Mr. Traynor?"

"Yes."

"Please hold for Director Colburn."

Twenty seconds passed, then a familiar voice, "Jonathan?"

Effecting a very formal tone, Jonathan answered, "Yes, Mr. Director. Congratulations on your appointment."

"Thanks, Jon, good to hear from you," Colburn replied with a smile in his voice, "and you can dispense with the 'Mr. Director' business."

"Just kidding, Sandy," Traynor said. "As a matter of fact, I was just sitting here wondering if you have any idea what the hell you're doing down there? I remember when you couldn't figure out who to block on tailback sweep."

Before Colburn could reply, Traynor had second thoughts about his irreverent treatment of his old friend. "Sorry, Sandy, I probably shouldn't have said that. I'll bet your calls are taped, aren't they?"

Colburn laughed, "That's okay, Jonathan. As usual, your comments are insightful. There's not much levity in this job, you know. And by the way, the answer is 'no' to both of your questions. I *don't* know what the hell I'm doing and the calls are not taped."

Both men laughed at the openness they shared.

For the next ten minutes, Traynor and Colburn caught up on each other's recent past, the two of them not having talked for almost five years. The conversation was completely informal, with the same one-liners and familiar expressions they had used during their college days, some thirty years before.

Funny, Traynor thought, *how some things never change.*

When Traynor steered the conversation back to the present, specifically about Colburn's recent appointment, the tone became more serious. Yes, he was enjoying the new position, but it was extremely time consuming and the decisions were more difficult than any job he had held before. There were geopolitical consequences to almost every significant move the Agency made overseas, and with the ever-increasing unrest here at home, domestic political considerations associated with every action. Colburn clearly loved what he was doing, but found it more complicated that even he could ever have imagined.

Traynor took that opportunity to open the door.

"Sandy, I'd like to ask you a favor."

"Sure, Jon, what is it?"

"I know this is going to sound completely nuts, but I've been studying the Agency for some months now. With all the free time I've had while trying to get used to retirement, I've had to focus my attention somewhere. Anyway, I've been working on a proposal that I'd like you to take a look at. And Sandy, I want you to know that I started on this long before your predecessor resigned or there was ever any mention of you being nominated to serve as Director of the Agency. So while the initiation of the project didn't have anything to do with your appointment, the fact that I may get the ear of the Director certainly does."

There was an ominous silence on the other end of the line. Traynor's request was an imposition, an undisguised attempt to take advantage of an old friendship. He hoped Sandy Colburn would understand that he would not have asked for a meeting to talk business unless the matter were very important.

"Sure, Jonathan. Let me check my calendar and I'll have my secretary call you back with some dates and times. Will that be okay?"

"That'll be perfect, Sandy. And thanks. I think you might find what I have to show you quite interesting. But if you don't, that's okay too and no harm done. And by the way, I don't want you to think that this meeting will constitute payback for the dinner you owe me at Billy Martin's.

You haven't forgotten that have you? I can almost taste the soft-shell crab right now."

Colburn chuckled, "No, I remember, and I *do* plan to buy you dinner one of these days, just as soon as I can find the time to get out of here at a reasonable hour. See you soon."

Two hours later, Colburn's secretary called back and a time for the meeting was agreed upon. It would be six-thirty a.m., two days hence. For the first time in a very long time, Traynor was excited and just a little bit nervous. He had become completely sold on his idea, and he hoped he could sell it to his old friend.

The early morning meeting was held in the Director's office at Langley. After some brief preliminaries over a cup of coffee, Traynor outlined the concept then started backfilling with details, all the time focusing on the key point: why a totally deniable and anonymous team working outside the confines of the Agency would be so useful to the CIA.

Colburn clearly was stunned by the audacity of the proposal. It was obvious he thought the idea implausible, its implementation unimaginable, but he gave Traynor the benefit of the doubt and allowed him to continue. Jonathan had counted on being heard, and despite his apparent misgivings, Sandy Colburn did not disappoint.

Traynor knew that Colburn had been appointed as Director of the Central Intelligence Agency for several reasons, an important one of which was his adeptness in accomplishing difficult tasks without becoming a political liability for the administration he served. The proposal, if implemented, would not only put the administration at risk politically, it would also violate the Agency's charter and nearly every federal statute, regulation and directive governing the conduct of the Agency's business. The fact he had taken this meeting would cast Colburn in a very unfavorable light if the subject of the discussion were even made known to the press. Jonathan realized that he was asking his old friend to risk his political future, maybe even his freedom, but Jonathan had convinced himself that the potential benefits of his plan justified the risks. Sandy Colburn was smart and savvy. Jonathan was confident that Colburn would make his own assessment of the risks, independent of their lifelong friendship. At least he hoped that would be the case.

To Jonathan's great relief, Colburn listened patiently and without interruption, and then began to ask questions, hypothetically of course. Each time Colburn identified a specific problem with the plan, Traynor had the answer. Still, Jonathan could tell that his friend wasn't anywhere close to being sold.

Traynor pressed on. Setting aside for a moment the illegality of such an operation, there was the critical issue of funding. The Director pointed out that regardless of the stories in the popular press, it was nearly impossible to really hide substantial funding for black operations. But Traynor had an answer for that as well. He told Colburn the story about how he had amassed a rather substantial personal fortune and about how his income far exceeded his needs. He did not require a monthly paycheck from the government. And best of all, he could bankroll most of the operations he had in mind from his private funds. Traynor had no family and no heirs. He told Colburn that although it sounded trite, he'd prefer to reinvest his assets in the future of America than pay millions in Federal estate taxes upon his death.

Traynor made the case that he could work as an independent contractor, without specific direction or oversight from any lawfully constituted agency of the U.S. government and outside the restrictions imposed by Congress or the President, and that he would work without compensation or reimbursement of any kind. His offer was to handle, free of charge, any matter that required prompt and decisive action but for which the government of the United States, or at least the CIA, needed deniability.

After a while, Jonathan could sense that Sandy Colburn was starting to seriously consider the proposal. The Director acknowledged that on occasion, political considerations caused the Agency to take or refrain from taking certain actions in response to a particular threat to national security that intelligence professionals inside the Agency believed to be ill-advised. Traynor helped Colburn envision an arrangement whereby the Agency could appear to be following documented orders and Presidential directives, while at the same time proceeding to accomplish what *needed* to be done through the efforts of Traynor and his team. The Director seemed to buy in. Jonathan knew he'd made considerable progress when desirability was conceded and feasibility was on the table.

They talked for almost two hours, then Colburn ended the meeting by saying that he would need some time to think about all they had discussed. As they parted, he promised to give Traynor a call before the end of the week.

It was getting late, and Traynor still hadn't heard anything. He checked his watch. The sun was down now and he had switched on the overhead light in the kitchen. The glare of the old fixture made the room even more lonely, more austere.

Traynor knew that if his old friend was going to call, it would be today. If he didn't call, that meant the proposal had been rejected and that Sandy simply did not want to discuss it any further. Traynor worried that he had gone too far in taking advantage of their friendship to gain access to Colburn. Maybe he shouldn't have done it. Maybe the idea was crazy and he was grasping at straws, trying to keep his hand in, trying anything to avoid the inevitability of retirement. Maybe he should just let it go.

But no, it wasn't a mistake. He was *certain* that this was the right thing to do.

Just then, the telephone rang.

"Jonathan?" the familiar voice asked.

"Yes, Sandy. Good to hear from you."

"Are you interested in continuing the discussion we had earlier this week?"

Traynor's stomach knotted with excitement, the first time that had happened in a very long time. "Yes, I'm very interested in continuing the discussion."

"Do you recall the cabin where we had drinks and dinner about ten years ago?"

Traynor remembered quite well. Colburn had just sold his consulting business and had bought the cabin in the mountains of northern Maryland as a very private retreat.

"Yes, I remember."

"Can you meet me there Sunday at around noon? I'd like to further discuss the matter we talked about Wednesday morning."

"Certainly. I'll see you Sunday."

Colburn's voice became very serious. "Jonathan, there's one other thing. I'll be alone and I want you to come alone. No one, and I mean *no one,* is to know about our meeting or the substance of our discussions. If anything about this matter should ever become known, then any further communications between us will be impossible. I'm sorry to have to say that, but I want to ensure you understand how important this is to me. Are those terms acceptable to you?"

"Sure, Sandy. As a matter of fact, I wouldn't have expected anything less. Thanks, and again, I'll see you Sunday."

The meeting between the two old friends in the secluded log cabin just southwest of Westminster, Maryland, resulted in the formation of one of the most important alliances in the history of the intelligence community. There was no record of the meeting and neither party took notes. The agreement reached between the two men was forged over coffee and sandwiches, and later in the day over a cold beer on the back porch of the cabin, and sealed with a handshake that carried with it a lifetime commitment to secrecy and personal loyalty. The deal struck there was monumental in proportion, but from a historical standpoint, it never happened.

Two weeks later, the Director surprised his staff and the administration by announcing that Jonathan Traynor, a retired Army colonel, had accepted the post of Special Assistant to the Director, reporting only to the Director himself. Inside the Agency, the word leaked that Traynor had been an old friend of the Director at Dartmouth, and that since his forced retirement from the Army, he had been trying to find a position with the government to supplement his retirement pay.

Everyone accepted Traynor as a personal confidant of the Director. Although it became generally known that Traynor had no real experience in the intelligence business, he was regarded by the senior staff as a satisfactory sounding board to assist the Director on closely held matters. No one begrudged the Director the privilege of a little well-intended patronage. By the same token, no one really expected Traynor to do anything, and from all outward appearances he did very little in the job.

But this was the CIA, and appearances were sometimes deceiving. From that point forward, Jonathan Traynor and Sanders Colburn carried out one of the great deceptions of all time, one that neither of them ever expected to be made public.

2

STALEY

September 1970—Washington, D.C.

Hackler Staley opened the black wrought iron gate and walked up the concrete steps of the dusty brownstone located on a quiet street in the heart of Georgetown. He was immediately taken with the understated elegance of the old three-story structure. It was obviously a very expensive home in a very exclusive part of the District. Some residue from the early morning rain was puddled in a low spot on the small porch. The afternoon paper soaked up moisture as it lay at a cocked angle against the side of the house. A dog barked from inside.

Staley stood quietly for a moment and checked the address against the scribbled note he pulled from his pants pocket. Colonel Traynor apparently had done pretty well for himself. He hadn't bought this place on his Army retirement pay.

As Staley rang the bell, he wondered again why he was here, why the Old Man wanted to see him. He also wondered how the Colonel knew he would be in Washington this particular weekend. Staley was naturally suspicious of coincidence. He often found the source of an apparent coincidence to be a well-considered plan. He knew that his former boss was retired from the military, but was he still working for the government? Staley had not seen Jonathan Traynor for over four years. What did the Colonel know about Staley and what did he have for him, or was this re-

54

ally just a visit to renew an old acquaintance?

Traynor had been Staley's brigade commander during his first tour in Vietnam. Hack Staley had gone to Vietnam in 1966 as a brand new second lieutenant right out of Officers' Candidate School. He was assigned to the 1st Cavalry Division, then operating in northern II Corps, and immediately was thrown into the action. After three months in country, he had outlasted all of the other junior officers in his unit and would have been made company commander if he'd had just a little more time in grade.

Staley first caught Traynor's attention by the consistent praise he received from his company and battalion commanders. He was known for always being the first trooper out the door in an insertion, the first tactical unit leader to take the initiative when the stakes were high, and the last man out when his company was in trouble. He led from the front and he always accomplished the mission, without complaint, qualification or excuse. But he always did it his way. And while his way was sometimes remarkably unorthodox, it usually turned out to be the best of all possible alternatives. Traynor had followed Bravo Company of the 1st Battalion on several operations and had seen Staley at work. His performance was exemplary, his reputation well earned. The Old Man soon realized that Staley had something special. He was a natural at leading men in combat. And best of all, he seemed to thrive on it.

Traynor singled out Staley as the best young lieutenant he had ever seen. He was tough and loyal—first to his men and then to his superiors—and was absolutely fearless under fire. And that made him somewhat of a legend among the troops. They were better soldiers because of Staley, and they knew it and respected him for it. Somehow he kept them alive—at least most of them—during some of the toughest fighting of the war. They became as protective of him as he was of them.

Partly as a result of Staley's outstanding performance, the Old Man sometimes suggested to the 1st Battalion Commander that Bravo Company take the lead on a particular mission, knowing that Staley's platoon would be on point. That's why Staley was there that morning just east of Landing Zone English when a large NVA force ambushed the lead elements of the battalion as they kicked off the operation code-named Tiger Shadow.

As usual, Staley was on the first lift in. The NVA allowed six ships to land in trail on the paddy dike they were using as a landing zone. Then all hell broke loose. The enemy had to know what was coming; the ambush was well prepared and well executed. The sky troopers on the ground were immediately in serious trouble.

Upon learning that Bravo Company was pinned down in the landing zone, the Old Man ordered the pilot of his command and control helicopter to take him up over the action so that he could offer whatever assistance his troops on the ground might need. When casualties started piling up faster than they could be evacuated, Traynor turned his command and control aircraft into a medevac ship. On the second trip into a hot LZ to pick up wounded soldiers, the slick was shot down and the Colonel ended up on the ground, side-by-side with the lead elements and Lieutenant Hackler Staley.

After an hour of continuous engagement, including artillery and helicopter gunship support, the Old Man ordered the battalion to withdraw to the south. Bravo Company was told to remain in place as long as possible to cover the withdrawal. Staley repeatedly tried to get the Colonel to pull back with the other troops, but he refused to do so, saying that he would remain behind with the rear guard. After fighting a successful holding action for almost thirty minutes, Bravo Company was ordered to withdraw under the cover of friendly artillery fire. Staley ordered his men out, one squad at a time, while he held his ground with a few hand-picked troops to cover the platoon's fighting withdrawal. Against Staley's strongest possible objections, Traynor insisted on staying behind with Staley and his men.

Staley, Traynor and two other men held the last position until the remainder of the company was clear, then made a run for it. A platoon of NVA regulars chased them through the reeds and paddies while artillery rained down on their position. Halfway to safety, both Staley and the Colonel were hit—Staley with an AK-47 round clean through the fleshy part of his neck and the Old Man with wounds to his chest and right leg.

Staley went down, gathered his wits about him and took inventory. He was badly hurt and bleeding down the front of his jungle fatigue blouse, but he knew that he had to go on or they were both going to die. The Old Man was aspirating blood from the hole in his chest. Staley placed the Colonel's field dressing on the wound and cinched it tight with his belt. If it held, the Old Man had a chance. If not, he would bleed out in just a few minutes.

Faced with no alternative, Staley stood up, emptied his M-16 at the advancing NVA, tossed the Colonel over his shoulder and started running toward friendly lines.

Later, Staley did not remember how he had made it to the aid station. Some of the troops at the perimeter of the blocking position said that Staley had come running straight at them through a hail of bullets, carrying the Colonel over his left shoulder, stopping occasionally to turn and fire the

.45 in his right hand. He ran past them and on toward the medics, screaming for people to get out of his way. He was covered in blood. People tried to help but he wouldn't stop. No one believed that he would make it, but he did make it. He carried the Old Man all the way back.

The last time Staley saw Colonel Traynor was at the aid station on the north bank of the An Lao River where Staley had dumped his badly wounded CO after carrying him almost a kilometer across the Bong Son plain. Shortly after getting the medics to pay attention to the Old Man, Staley passed out from loss of blood. He was treated at the aid station and then hospitalized in country for almost a month before returning to duty.

When he had left Traynor at the aid station, draped over a dirty field cot, Staley was pretty sure the Old Man was going to die. Blood was bubbling out of his mouth, the right side of his chest was torn open with broken and splintered ribs sticking out at odd angles and his right leg was mangled above the knee. Traynor had literally been shot to pieces.

Three months later, Staley heard that the Colonel had been shipped to the U.S. hospital in Japan, a place where they sent combat casualties that appeared to be hopeless. But surprisingly, the Old Man had pulled through. Almost six months later he was returned to the States, but soon thereafter was forced to take a medical retirement. Staley heard about it when he returned home. He had intended to visit the Old Man several times, but never got around to it.

Soon Staley was back in Southeast Asia with other matters to attend to. In some ways it seemed impossible that it had been four years since he had seen Colonel Traynor; in other ways it seemed like a lifetime ago. His duty assignments had taken some interesting turns since that first tour with the Cav. Staley was no longer an officer on a career path. He was in a class by himself now, a specialist, an asset that was deployed only for special operations, a shadow. The Old Man probably would be surprised to know all that Staley had done since last they had met, but Staley had no intention of telling him. He had no intention of ever telling anyone.

Someone pulled back the curtain at the edge of the front window. A moment later a much older looking Traynor opened the door, stared at Staley as though appraising his fitness, then offered his hand with just a hint of a smile.

The young man standing in the doorway had the look of a soldier who had seen too much combat. He stood six feet tall with dark hair and broad shoulders. His face was thin and gaunt. Traynor remembered the steel blue eyes that were hard and missed nothing. Staley was at least ten pounds lighter than the last time Traynor had seen him, but still appeared to be in top physical condition. The Colonel had expected nothing less.

"Captain Staley, good to see you. Please, come in."

Traynor stepped back and out of the doorway, his eyes briefly taking in all that could be seen near the front of the house. Staley recognized the habit—he did the same thing every time he opened a door.

Staley walked into the darkened house, stopping in the foyer while waiting for the Colonel to take the lead. The Old Man's terrier barked once, smelled Staley's trousers, then ambled back into the kitchen.

"Nice to see you too, sir. How have you been?"

Traynor motioned for Staley to follow him into a small but magnificently furnished living room, probably called a "sitting room" at the time the house was built. There were old leather chairs, antique tables, a large fireplace with an ornate Chinese screen of heavy bronze, a glass-fronted bookcase with dusty, leather-bound books, and two polished teak end tables holding large ceramic lamps topped with unusual oriental shades. Staley thought he recognized them as Thai. There were old English hunting prints on one wall and an original impressionist painting over the fireplace. An ancient Persian rug covered most of the dark wood plank floor. A grandfather clock ticked loudly in the corner. It was a comfortable room, one that reflected the personality of the sole occupant of the house.

"I've been well, thank you." Then, motioning to one of the cracked leather chairs, the Old Man said, "Have a seat."

Staley waited for Traynor to be seated, then followed suit.

There was no pretense, no small talk. The Colonel took a worn file from the end table between them, opened it in his lap and got directly to the point.

"I suspect you're wondering why I looked you up and invited you here."

It was a rhetorical question that Staley did not feel obliged to answer.

"I remember you as a fine officer with unusual leadership skills, more than a normal amount of courage and remarkable good sense," Traynor continued. "Your record with the Cav after I was medevac'd home is impressive too."

Traynor looked down at the file. "You refused a battalion staff assignment and eventually took command of Bravo Company. I don't know how you managed that with all the career captains looking for a command slot. You received several citations for heroism under fire and a letter of commendation from the division commander. Your Officer Efficiency Reports were exceptional, the narrative in each one describing a very mature company-grade officer who never failed his commanding officer, never failed his men, and never lost sight of the mission. All in all, you did an excellent job."

Then looking up, the Old Man added, "My successor was as fortunate as I to have you in the brigade."

With only a hint of a smile, Staley said, "Thank you sir, I appreciate that."

Traynor flipped more pages in the file. "You were wounded twice more in combat"—he looked up and smiled—"after our little problem there at Bong Son." And then with his head back in the file, he continued, "But you never left your unit for more than two days, returning the second time with a bandage on your left thigh that had to be changed once a day for two full weeks. You probably could have milked that into a ticket home, you know?"

Traynor looked expectantly at Staley, as though waiting for a comment. Staley did not like the idea of anyone, even the Colonel, making him the subject of a research project.

"Well sir, I've never found Army records to be particularly accurate."

Traynor continued undeterred, again looking at the file. "You rotated home in June, 1967, and immediately volunteered for Special Forces training where you graduated first in your class. Upon completion of that course, you asked a special favor of the commandant of the SF school, who had come to know and respect you during your time there, and the commandant helped you get immediate orders for a second tour in Vietnam. You arrived in country just in time for the Tet offensive of 1968.

"Because you speak fluent Vietnamese, you were assigned to a special operations team headquartered just north of Pleiku in the central highlands. There you recruited a group of Montagnard tribesmen to join you in conducting covert operations on the Cambodian side of the border. Those operations were highly successful and resulted in a significant and continuing interruption of the enemy's ability to resupply and reinforce its units operating in South Vietnam, thereby causing the NVA a great deal of discomfort throughout the spring and early summer of that year."

Staley was stunned. There was no way Traynor could have found out all that information without unrestricted access to some very classified files. He thought he could count on one hand the people who *ever* had knowledge of his operations in Cambodia during the spring of 1968, and he knew for a fact that a couple of those men had been killed in action that same year. He started wondering what else Traynor might know about him. There were some things about his past, particularly about his family, that no one knew and no one was ever supposed to know. Wallace and Marie had drilled that into him from the time he was just a child.

"In late June, 1968, you took a team into the A Shau Valley to conduct reconnaissance in advance of a planned major offensive in that area. Of the eight men who went into the A Shau, only two walked out again some ten days later. You and a PFC named Gonzalez. The details of that operation were never recorded. The files contain only your after-action report and a statement from Gonzalez who, incidentally, is now a Staff Sergeant and is back in South Vietnam with a Special Forces A Team working in I Corps."

Staley never changed his expression, but smiled inwardly thinking about Gonzalez. He was one tough kid who never gave up, even when the VC had them surrounded and everyone on the team was hit. Staley and Gonzalez had helped each other crawl through the dense jungle to get away from the ambush site, then both of them had passed out from their wounds. Staley was the first to regain consciousness. He eliminated the VC that were closing in on their position, then tended to Gonzalez. The two of them had literally leaned on each other as they walked for days to clear the area. *So Gonzalez had made E-6 in record time, huh? Sounded like someone at the promotions board finally got something right.*

Traynor continued, "You insisted on remaining at an in country hospital rather than take a medevac out. Two months later, you were back in action, this time running three- and four-man patrols along the DMZ and west into Laos. You extended your tour of duty for an additional six months specifically for the purpose of continuing the secret cross-border operations. Over a period of almost a year, your teams provided I Corps headquarters the best available intelligence on NVA activities along the border and across the Ho Chi Minh Trail. During that time, you worked directly for the I Corps G-2 who was your OER rating officer and the only senior officer with whom you had any direct contact, a matter of security that you evidently insisted upon."

Traynor looked up from his notes. "I'm surprised George Wilkinson accepted that condition, Captain Staley. You must have made a pretty good pitch for him to have gone along with that kind of arrangement."

The statement was in the nature of a question—another that Staley did not feel compelled to answer. He remained quiet, politely waiting for Traynor to continue. More than thirty seconds passed in silence, then the Old Man got back into the file.

"In late August, 1969, you rotated back to the world, but only for three months. Then you went off to Europe to participate in an experimental, joint forces commando training program with the British and the Germans. Yours was the first and only graduating class. The program was scrapped shortly thereafter due to insufficient funding and a general lack of cooperation between the sponsoring countries."

Traynor looked up again. "Seems like no one wanted to give away their secrets to their allies. I can understand that. It was a foolish idea to begin with."

Again, Staley remained silent. The commando project was a miserable failure, just as he had expected it would be. He had resisted the assignment, but certain people in the Pentagon wanted ten of our best to go, and someone had insisted that he be among the ten. He never knew who his rabbi was on that score.

The Colonel read over a few more documents, then closed the file. "The remarkable thing about all of this is that for the most part, your *official* personnel file is devoid of any details with respect to any of these assignments. By looking at your records Captain Staley, one would think that you were just another young officer who had seen some action and had come through it quite well, much like any number of other officers we've sent through the meat grinder these past six years. Do you know where I found most of this material?"

Staley was amazed at the accuracy of the information the Colonel had recited. It had always been his intention to remain anonymous—to serve without being noticed. But it looked like he had gone too far—done too much too soon. Wallace and Marie had warned him time and again to be inconspicuous. Evidently he had failed. He desperately wanted to know who could have compiled such a complete dossier and what else might be in it, but his outward reaction toward Traynor was one of confusion and surprise. He had to answer the Colonel's question.

"I have no idea where you came up with that material, sir. Nor can I verify the information. As a matter of fact, it's just the opposite. I suspect there's been a mistake somewhere. My first tour in Vietnam, part of it with you, was pretty routine, mostly the same as any other young infantry lieutenant. And my second tour was a cookie-cutter trip for a Special Forces captain right out of school. I did my job and that was pretty much it. The rest of that stuff's probably the product of somebody's imagination, although I can't figure who would've put together such a story."

Traynor stared approvingly at Staley. He was just what the Old Man had expected, completely composed with just the right balance of modesty and gee-whiz. And, he was a damned convincing liar. Traynor had not shaken him at all with these stories that no one was supposed to know. It had taken him weeks of going through files at the Pentagon and at the Agency, looking for just the right man for the arrangement he had in mind. At the end, he had tentatively decided on Staley. This interview had sealed it. Staley it would be.

"No, Captain Staley, it's all true. And I suspect there's much more that no one knows about you. But that's okay with me. I've decided that I want to offer you a job."

Staley did not want to hear any more. He just wanted to get this over with. He didn't know what Traynor was up to or how he'd gained access to some highly classified information, but on-the-level job offers usually were extended in a command office on a military post, not in a retired colonel's living room. He began to wonder if the Old Man was into something illegal. He decided to set the stage for a rejection.

He'd listen to what the Colonel had to say, then graciously decline. He wanted to be back in Missouri by the next morning.

"Thank you, Colonel. I appreciate your interest in me, but I'm about ready to finish up my commitment and get out of the Army. I've been thinking about going back for an MBA, *if* I can get into grad school."

He rose to his feet. "So I don't think I'd be interested. I have other things on my plate. But thanks for inviting me here and it was good to see you again."

Staley walked the few steps to the Old Man's chair and thrust out his hand in an effort to end the meeting.

Traynor looked at Staley very carefully, trying to read the young man's motives in choosing to end the discussion—whether Staley really wanted out or if he was just uncomfortable with the ambiguity of the situation. Traynor needed a few more minutes to make his case. He felt that Staley could be trusted to keep a confidence, perhaps the most important confidence Traynor would ever relate to anyone. He had decided that Staley was the one. If it would not work with Staley, maybe he would just abandon the project. But he had come this far. He had to give it a try.

Without getting up, and completely ignoring Staley's outstretched hand, Traynor said in a quiet and pleasant voice, "Please sit down, Captain. I want to tell you some things that are more highly classified than anything you have ever been exposed to before, information that cannot under any circumstances leave this room, and then I'm going to ask for your help in a job that will involve a lifetime of service to your country. If after listening to me you decline, I'll be very disappointed, but I'll understand. And either way, whether you accept or decline, I'll expect you to never say anything about our meeting to anyone, and I do mean *never.* I'm very, very serious about this. Do you understand?"

Staley was many things, but at heart he was a twenty-seven-year-old man with a desire to get on with his life. He had reached the conclusion that his usefulness in the military had run its course and that he needed to explore other alternatives. At the same time, he remembered his family background and his upbringing. He remembered all the things Wallace and Marie had gone through to make his life possible and the values they had taught him. With all that in mind, the invitation from Traynor was too interesting to ignore. He decided to hear more.

Staley gave the Colonel an appraising look, then turned and sat back down in the soft leather chair.

"I don't know what you have in mind, Colonel, and I doubt that I'm the right man for whatever job you're talking about. But I am willing to listen, provided we have a clear understanding of the ground rules. If I don't have an interest in the job or don't believe it's something I want to do, I want you to assure me that I can walk away from here without any permanent consequences. I don't want the Army to suddenly find some way to keep me in for the next twenty years, and I damned sure don't want to have to be looking over my shoulder every time I walk down a dark street or try to find my car in a parking lot."

Staley's tone changed noticeably before making the next statement. "Because I can assure you, sir, that if any of that happens, I will be very disappointed, and that will not be a good situation for me or for whoever else may be involved. I want you to understand that, as well."

With the implied threat, Traynor could hear a coldness in Staley's voice that reminded him of the capabilities of the man described in the file lying in his lap. It was the first time since the interview began that Staley had revealed a hint of his true character. The Old Man was sure he had made the right choice.

"I understand completely, Captain Staley, including your reticence to engage in this conversation in these unusual surroundings and with the kind of secrecy I'm suggesting. If I didn't have complete confidence in your ability to maintain the confidentiality of what I'm about to tell you, I wouldn't have raised the discussion to this level. There will be no adverse consequences to you if you chose to decline, but I doubt you will decline."

"Okay, Colonel, I'm listening."

Staley sat quietly as Traynor told an astounding story. Coming from anyone else under other circumstances, it would have been hard to believe. But Staley had an intuitive sense about people and that intuition told him that Traynor was serious and on the level. Intending no commitment whatsoever, he listened to the Old Man's story. At the end he accepted the job, and with that acceptance, his life was changed forever.

3

COOPER-CHURCH

26 December 1970—Gaithersburg, Maryland

It was snowing harder again. The wind had picked up considerably since he had arrived almost a half an hour earlier. Staley sat nursing a draft beer, occasionally checking his watch while waiting for Traynor to show. It was three-thirty in the afternoon and the shabby pizza parlor was almost empty—just a group of loud, long-haired teenagers in one corner and a poor-looking family with three small kids at a booth near the door. Staley could not imagine too many people going out in a storm like this the day after Christmas.

The cheap colored lights strung around the walls and the dirty plastic wreaths placed at irregular intervals between the V-shaped, floor-to-ceiling windows were frayed and worn. Fake garlands hung here and there from the crosspieces supporting the ceiling tiles. Despite the decorations, the place did not seem too festive, especially in the fading light and bitter cold of late afternoon. The whole scene would have been pretty depressing if it had not been for the jukebox. Someone was playing the Mamas and Papas.

The fat guy with the dirty apron who had seated him came by to check on him once again. He introduced himself as "Ronnie, the manager," as he rested his elbow on the back of the booth across the table from Staley and tried his best to be friendly.

"Can I get you something else, maybe a small pizza or a salad?"

"No thanks. I'm waiting for someone. He'll be here in a few minutes."

Ronnie offered a smile. "Probably still full from that big turkey dinner yesterday, huh? You live here, or in town to see family?"

Staley looked up. He didn't like questions from strangers, but the guy appeared to be harmless. "Neither. Just driving through. Stopped to see an old friend." Then with a dismissive smile and gesturing toward the ceiling, "Figured we could both find a place with a big plastic guy on the roof holding a pizza."

The manager nodded cheerfully and then walked over to check on his other customers, wiping off a couple of tables on the way.

Staley looked back into his beer. Since he had no family anymore, Christmas meant nothing to him. He thought about his parents. Wallace had been gone for some time, Marie just a few years. Without family, there really wasn't much to do on Christmas. Driving halfway across the country on Christmas Day was better than sitting at home alone.

Even so, he was surprised that Traynor had called him on Christmas Eve with instructions to meet him two days later at a rundown restaurant over a thousand miles from home. Whatever the Old Man had in mind must be pretty important. Staley had already received two monthly retainer checks from his new employer, a company called Brownstone Investments, which he knew was owned indirectly by Traynor. Evidently this was to be the first mission in his new job, working secretly for Traynor on projects that were never to see the light of day. He was anxious to get started.

The fact was, he didn't have anything better to do. Following the agreement he had reached with Traynor, Staley had allowed his military commitment to expire and had signed out of the Army at Fort Belvoir, Virginia, on October 10, five years to the day after his arrival at Fort Benning to attend Officer's Candidate School.

For the past two months, he had been living in the old farmhouse just south of Joplin, the place he and Marie had moved into after Wallace had died. He was still getting settled in, trying to decide if he would stay there or move back into town, or maybe somewhere new like California, or perhaps Texas. He was alone and could pretty much afford to live wherever he wanted, especially with this new job.

While the pay was not particularly important to Staley, he thought Traynor was very generous in offering to double the amount of his base pay and allowances as a captain with over five years of active duty service, and to reimburse him for all of his travel and living expenses while working on an assignment. Traynor also promised to award future consulting fee increases—Staley thought of it as salary—at the same rate as if Staley had stayed on active duty and been advanced with the top five percent of his officer class. Staley could not have matched that compensation package in any job he was qualified for in civilian life. But the pay was not a major factor in his decision to accept Traynor's offer. Staley had never spent all he had earned from the Army. And there was the money that Wallace and Marie had left him. He could live on that for a while if need be.

After his initial meeting with Traynor at his Georgetown home, Staley had met with the Colonel on two other occasions to talk more about the nature of the work he would be doing, the level of logistical support he could expect, how they were to communicate in the future, and how often

Traynor might require his services. In every case, he was satisfied with the answers.

As for the details of the work, Traynor was completely candid. He never tried to glad-hand, never tried to hustle, never tried to minimize the fact that in most cases, Staley would be operating outside the law and with no traceable connection to the United States government. In fact, Traynor made it very clear that the absence of any connection with the Agency or the government would be the most important aspect of every mission Staley would be assigned. He would be working alone, without a safety net or backup. He would be completely on his own and, if caught, he would be a man without a country.

Staley accepted it all with a clear understanding of what he was getting into. In some way, he knew that if Wallace and Marie were still around, they would hate the fact he had given up a normal life for this kind of work, but they also would be enormously proud that he was doing something important and that few other people *could* do.

Staley was surprised at how comfortable he was with Traynor, how much he trusted him and how quickly. Part of it was his understanding that Traynor had, by bringing Staley into his confidence, exposed himself and the man he had described as a lifetime friend, the Director of Central Intelligence, to expulsion from government service and possibly criminal charges. By telling him the whole story, Traynor had placed an enormous amount of trust in Staley, and in part because of that, Staley had come to trust Traynor in return. It would be the most important element of their relationship.

The metal and glass door to the restaurant swung open and a cold wind blew in, along with a dusting of fresh snow. Jonathan Traynor stood just inside the doorway, pulling off his gloves and looking around the restaurant as though searching for whomever he was to meet. But Staley knew the Colonel was examining every person in the room to ensure there was no one there who might recognize him. The obvious point of meeting here was anonymity.

Traynor nodded without expression when he spotted Staley across the room, walked to the booth and sat down heavily, as though out of breath.

In a voice loud enough for someone nearby to hear, Traynor said, "Nice to see you, son. Sorry I'm late. Wish the weather could have cooperated a little better."

He extended a hand. Staley reached across the table, took the Colonel's hand and shook it warmly, as he might have greeted an old friend of the family.

"Good to see you, sir."

Ronnie the manager sidled up to the table, constantly wiping his hands on the dirty apron tied around his waist. "Can I get you some coffee or a beer? How about a menu?"

Traynor ordered coffee, Staley another beer. They told Ronnie they'd hold off on looking at a menu.

They made small talk until the drinks came. At about that same time, a pimple-faced teenager feeding the jukebox opted for a Doors album. The resulting noise was a welcome cover for the conversation that was about to take place.

Traynor got right to the point, talking in low tones under the din of the jukebox.

"Hack, do you know what the Cooper-Church Amendment is?"

Staley thought a minute. "Yeah, I think so. Isn't that the law that Congress passed in a huff after Nixon invaded Cambodia last spring—says American troops can't fight outside South Vietnam?"

"That's correct. Evidently it's tying a few hands in theater, but they think they're going to be able to live with it because it doesn't affect the bombing. No restriction on the activities of aircraft or aircrews."

"Yeah, well I can't imagine that it's keeping the special ops guys from jumping the fence just as often as we did a couple of years ago. Surely no one's taking it that seriously?"

"No, they're still running special ops, cross-border recon, snatch and grab, that kind of stuff. But it does mean that we can never send ground troops across the border again on any kind of acknowledged mission."

"Okay, so what? Does the President want to invade Cambodia again?"

Traynor looked up from his coffee and directly into Staley's eyes. "No, Laos."

Staley was surprised. "Are you serious, Colonel? We're really going to go after the NVA in Laos? That's a new twist. Has somebody decided that we should try to win the war?"

"No, it's not *that* good. In early February, the ARVN," meaning the Army of the Republic of South Vietnam, "is going to invade Laos just west of Khe Sanh in northern I Corps. They're going to attack west along an axis centered on Highway 9 and advance forty clicks to the town of Tchepone. The idea is to cut the Ho Chi Minh Trail and interdict supply trains for as long as possible, then pull back to the border with the possibility of reoccupying if the NVA reestablishes significant traffic on the Trail. While that sounds good, there's one problem. Because of the Cooper-Church Amendment, we can't send advisors with the maneuver elements and we can't send in blocking or reaction forces to stop a counterattack or exploit an advance."

Staley remembered his experiences with the ARVN. "Colonel, you know as well as I do that the ARVN will never be able to hack it in Laos without Americans shoulder to shoulder with them on the ground. Even with our tac air leading the way, they'll be the ones that will have to close with and destroy the enemy, and I'm not sure they've got what it takes to do that."

Traynor was silently pleased once again with his choice of Staley. He thought the young man's assessment of the situation had a lot of merit, mainly because it was his assessment as well. It was amazing to him that the decision-makers at the Pentagon had not come to the same conclusion. Or maybe they had and this whole operation was just to prove a point. But that was not the issue for the two of them.

The Colonel continued. "Here's the tough part. Even though we can't send in ground troops, the ARVN units invading Laos will be principally supported by U.S. Army aviation units—air cavalry units, assault helicopter units, heavy lift units, aerial rocket artillery units, medevac units, the whole works—and by Air Force and Navy tac air. Cooper-Church doesn't keep aviation units, even Army helicopter units, from flying across the border. It just prohibits ground combat forces across the border."

Staley thought about that for a minute, then said sarcastically, "Well I'm sure the poor sons-a-bitches who get shot down supporting the ARVNs will make every effort to not end up as ground combat forces. We wouldn't want the Congress to get upset."

Traynor did not react to the sarcasm. "This operation is going to be very tough on the aviation units supporting the ARVN across the fence. Estimates are that we could lose more aircraft in one week than we normally lose in two months on the South Vietnam side of the border. If that happens, and I *do* agree with *that* assessment, then the aircrews that find themselves on the ground will have to rely on ARVN units to find them, secure them and get them out.

"Let me ask you this, Hack, would you want to rely on an ARVN unit to get *you* out if you were on one of those American aircraft shot down in Laos? What would the prospect of having to rely entirely on an ARVN rescue do to your morale? How would you feel about continuing the mission the first time one of your buddies went down and no one went in to get him out?"

Staley gave serious consideration to the Colonel's questions, even though they were almost rhetorical. He was glad someone was thinking far enough ahead to see the problem. This was all starting to come together. Someone wanted a deniable American presence in Laos to rescue downed aircrews. Sounded like something right up Staley's alley. He knew the area and he had policed up a couple of downed pilots across the fence in '68 and early '69. It was just a question of how, and he figured the Colonel was coming to that part.

"So," he said, "we've got to come up with some way to get an off-the-books American unit in position to go into Laos and pull out the downed crews, is that it?"

"Not exactly. There are going to be a lot of guys down over there. There's no way we can keep an *American* rescue unit secret. The prohibition on the use of American troops is absolute, and no one is willing to ignore the restriction. It would be a career-ending decision for any commander to send G.I.s across the border, even to recover downed aircrews. *And,* from a political standpoint, the administration couldn't stand the heat they'd get from Congress. The word from the White House is that no American will be on the ground in Laos, *period.*

"Obviously, both General Abrams and General Westmoreland registered strong objections to sending Army aviation units across the border without the availability of a reliable search and rescue unit. But the White House wouldn't budge. So here's the compromise someone came up with. There's a unit attached to the ARVN First Infantry Division called the Hoc Bao Company. Ever heard of them?"

"Yeah, the Black Panther Company. They're supposed to be a pretty good outfit, but I'm not sure they have the leadership or the inspiration to risk their lives for a bunch of Americans who are completely surrounded in 'bad guy' land."

"I agree, and so does the brass. So they've come up with the idea of supplementing the Hoc Bao with mercenaries. We're talking Cambodians, Laotians, Thais, Filipinos, even some Chinese Nungs. The deal is that the U.S. government will pay hard currency for recovered aircrews. The hope is that financial incentives will spur the Hoc Bao to respond much the same way American forces might in a cross-border rescue operation."

Staley considered the proposal. "That might work, but the problem with mercenaries is always leadership. I've worked with them—unless someone is kicking them in the ass, they don't always react the way they should."

"Exactly. But when the suggestion was made that American special ops guys be tasked to participate with and advise the Hoc Bao, the civilians in the White House killed the idea. They are deadly serious about this Cooper-Church Amendment business. They're not going to put an American on the ground in Laos with the Hoc Bao. Period. End of discussion."

Staley studied the condensation on the side of his glass, then drained the last of his beer. He was already thinking about how he was going to run the operation.

"Well, sir. It sounds to me like what we need is a mercenary to join the Hoc Bao and lead the rescue missions across the fence."

Traynor managed a tight smile. "That's a very astute observation. Here's the plan. I'll use CIA contacts to ensure that a former French Army officer, an ex-captain named Jack Delon, will be taken on by the Hoc Bao. It will be made known that Captain Delon has had extensive training and experience with an elite French special forces unit called Commando Hubert. His specialty will be the recovery of friendly troops from occupied territory, having been involved in many such operations while working in Algeria.

"All of this will, of course, be bought and paid for in advance by a Saigon businessman who has done a few jobs for the Agency in the past and who has important contacts inside the South Vietnamese military. But this time, our friend will be given the contract through a blind who will be working for me. He will be led to believe that Captain Delon recently was discharged from the French Army under less than favorable conditions and is in a bit of trouble with the civilian authorities in France. He's simply looking for a place to hide out for a year or so, while continuing to earn a decent living at the only job he knows. It's not the best cover story in the world, but it should work. By the way, how's your French?

Staley wondered how Traynor knew he spoke French, or if he was just guessing. "I can probably get by."

"Well, you may not have to use it, but it might come in handy if someone gets inquisitive."

Traynor continued, "I will have your identity papers for

you day after tomorrow. I think we can use a current file photo for the passport. You will leave the United States on January 2, as Hackler Staley, for a pleasure trip to Hong Kong. There you will become Jack Delon. You will immediately make your own way into Saigon where you will contact the Adjutant of the ARVN First Infantry Division, mentioning Mr. Tranh—that's our contact's name. If everything has been arranged as expected, the Adjutant will see to it that the Hoc Bao offers you a job.

"You will stay with the Hoc Bao until the operation in Laos is over. You will then either leave under agreeable circumstances or desert. You will make your way back to Hong Kong, become Hackler Staley once again and return home."

Staley played it out in his mind. It might work, but it was a hell of a lot of trouble to go to just to get in position to do something secretly that the United States government should have been doing in the open. He wondered if future projects for Traynor would be this convoluted.

When Staley didn't immediately respond, Traynor asked, "Do you think you can do this?"

Staley twirled his empty beer glass on the table as he considered the proposition, making damp circles on the red-checkered oilcloth. He then looked up at Traynor.

"Yes, sir. If you can get me there and into the Hoc Bao, I can do it."

"Good. One more thing, Hack. There never was a Commando Hubert officer named Jack Delon, at least not that I could find in the archives. The Hoc Bao shouldn't go to the trouble of trying to verify the story, not with what they're being paid. But some inquisitive American intelligence officer or, God help us, some reporter, might take an interest in you if you give them the opportunity. So stay with the

Hoc Bao, away from U.S. Army units and away from the press. Don't talk with anyone from the outside world and avoid all notoriety. Pay attention to where the reporters and the photographers are located. The last thing we need is a picture of you on the cover of *Newsweek* hauling some wounded pilot off a medevac ship or returning to base camp on the South Vietnam side of the border with a Huey full of Hoc Bao troops."

"Shouldn't be a problem."

"By the same token, you're going to be there to recover downed American pilots, and that means you may have to spend some time with some of them. Don't get familiar with them. Always maintain the French cover identity. You're nothing more or less than a French mercenary who happens to be at the right place at the right time. It's okay for you to speak English, but you may want to color it with a French accent. Don't get chummy with the guys you pull out of the bush. They'll want to thank you and be your best friend—you know how that goes—but you've got to stay away from them. Get them out, then don't ever see them again. Got it?"

"Yes sir, I got it."

"Now listen to me. You may think I'm crazy when I say this, but all things considered, this should be a relatively simple assignment. To some extent you're going to be impersonating yourself. It's a job and a theater with which you're very familiar. If this works, the next project likely will be something entirely different, perhaps something where you will have to make up a persona and act a role. Or perhaps you will have to conduct an entire operation while remaining undetected in a hostile environment. This will be good training for the harder missions to come. I want to know how it goes and what kinds of problems you encounter. We're both going to have to learn from this one."

"Yes sir, I understand. I'll be in touch."

Traynor looked across the table at Staley, studying him as one might a trusted lieutenant being sent into battle for the first time. The future of the entire project was now in Staley's hands.

After a moment of silence, Traynor got up, put on his coat and walked to the door. He looked outside while pulling on his gloves, and just before leaning against the metal bar on the glass door, he nodded at the manager.

"Doesn't look like it's letting up any. Guess I'll give it a try." And with that he opened the door and slipped out into the snow.

Staley didn't even glance up as the chill wind again blew into the restaurant. He was already back in Vietnam. He sat there quietly for a few minutes, thinking about the mission, then ordered another beer.

4

LAM SON 719

21 March 1971—Khe Sanh Combat Base, South Vietnam
Staley lit a cigarette as he walked away from the Hoc Bao
bivouac site and toward the southwest perimeter of the bustling combat base at Khe Sanh. He was dressed in faded
South Korean tiger fatigues with worn French commando
boots. Cocked to one side and pulled down over his forehead was a faded green beret. On his right collar point was
the subdued rank insignia of a U.S. Army captain, on the
left the crossed rifles of the infantry, and on his right sleeve
was the distinctive black panther patch of the Hoc Bao. The
name tag above the right pocket of his fatigues was smeared
and faded, completely unreadable.

His trousers were secured tightly around his legs with
strips of raw black linen and his mottled uniform was
stained from shoulder to boot-top with the white residue of
dried sweat and the ever-present red clay of Khe Sanh. He
was wearing U.S. Army web gear on which was hooked a
French Army canteen, a K-bar knife and a .45 caliber automatic in a thirty-year-old soft leather holster that appeared
to match the boots, surely the remnants of a uniform last
worn in Algeria or French Morocco. An AK-47 assault rifle,
the weapon of choice of the VC and NVA, hung from his
left shoulder, the muzzle pointing down and behind him.

His long black hair broke over the collar of his fatigue
blouse and a thick black mustache covered his top lip and

drooped down on both sides of his mouth to just above the jaw line.

Despite his western appearance, rank insignia and green beret, it was obvious to anyone who knew anything about the United States Army that this soldier was not an American Special Forces officer. Quite the contrary, he looked like a mercenary, even to someone who had never actually seen a mercenary. That was exactly the impression Staley intended to convey.

Staley had made it to Saigon just after the first of the year, taking the route he and Traynor had discussed. Upon his presentment at the ARVN First Infantry Division rear area headquarters, he had been greeted by an unctuous lieutenant colonel who said that he had heard a great deal about Captain Delon and was sure they could use him in the Hoc Bao Company. It was obvious that someone had been paid off.

The lieutenant colonel was surprised and pleased that Captain Delon spoke both English and Vietnamese fluently, since bilingual officers were always useful in obtaining materiel from the Americans. While extra combat supplies and equipment enhanced the prospects of survivability in the field, they also offered a nice opportunity for certain South Vietnamese officers to add to their personal bank accounts by trading the goods on the black market. It was a way of life in Vietnam and Staley had come to accept it, and besides, graft was the reason he had been accepted into the Hoc Bao with sufficient rank to lead a special recovery platoon. It was also the reason that from the very first moment he arrived, very few questions were asked about his past.

While the mercenaries that comprised the Hoc Bao initially had been reluctant to accept Staley's presence, and more importantly his leadership, after a few weeks together they slowly began to gain confidence in his demonstrated knowledge and experience. Remaining totally in character in his Captain Delon persona, Staley was ruthless in his dealings with any man that failed to comply immediately with his orders in the field. He beat one unfortunate Thai nearly to death for openly challenging his leadership on a training mission. The man was hospitalized and eventually sent away. Staley did not know where and, quite frankly, he didn't care. The Thai soldier was one of the ones Staley had been watching. The guy was a troublemaker and had deserved the punishment. Being able to make an example out of him fit nicely into Staley's plan to solidify his legend among the Hoc Bao.

Just as Traynor had predicted, in late January the Hoc Bao were moved north along with the First Infantry Division for participation in the invasion of Laos and were assigned the primary mission of recovering downed American aircrews across the border. While First Division Headquarters was located several kilometers away, the Hoc Bao were sent to Khe Sanh and placed under the operational control of the commander of the recently reinforced U.S. Army 2nd Squadron, 17th Air Cavalry, which was given general responsibility for reconnaissance, gunship and emergency lift support across the entire front.

Khe Sanh, the site of the famous siege where thousands of Marines came close to being wiped out by a determined NVA force in early 1968, was located only twenty kilometers south of the demilitarized zone that separated South Vietnam from its communist neighbor to the north and ten kilometers from the Laotian border to the west. Khe Sanh was the principal staging area for the Army of the Republic of South Vietnam—the ARVN—invasion of Laos.

The operation had been kicked off on February 8 when

the lead elements of the ARVN First Armor Brigade, covered by a U.S. Army air cavalry recon team, crossed the border into Laos just west of the abandoned village of Lang Vei. The stated objective of the operation, code-named "Lam Son 719," was, as Traynor had indicated, to cut the Ho Chi Minh Trail all the way from the Laotian border to the town of Tchepone, some forty kilometers to the west.

Lam Son 719 had been one of the most closely guarded secrets of the war. In order for the incursion to be effective, the North Vietnamese Army—or NVA—had to be taken completely by surprise. It was essential that the ARVN armor, infantry and airborne infantry units drive straight through the NVA fortifications along the Trail, interdict traffic southbound on the Trail and destroy the infrastructure that for years had been the principal avenue for resupply of the Viet Cong and NVA forces operating in the south.

During the first few days of the incursion, the ARVN met little organized resistance. They succeeded in establishing two firebases on hilltop positions ten kilometers north of the main axis of advance. Both firebases first were reconned by air cavalry fire teams comprised of light observation helicopters and Cobra gunships and then softened up by U.S. Air Force and Navy tactical fighter-bombers. When the areas were cleared, the ARVN troops and artillery units were inserted by U.S. Army twin-rotor Chinooks and assault helicopter company aircraft.

Two ARVN Ranger outposts were successfully established to the north of the northern firebases to provide early warning of a large-scale enemy attack and to serve as a base camp for recon and screening missions. Again, those outposts were reconned and cleared by U.S. aviation assets and the South Vietnamese Rangers inserted by Army helicopter units.

By the third day of the invasion, the ARVN First Armor

Brigade had advanced west along Highway 9 almost halfway to Tchepone. But again, all advances were based on American aviation support. The ARVN had not made a move without U.S. Army air cavalry fire teams screening ahead and on the flanks of the advancing column, providing close-in air support whenever needed.

Along the southern end of the advance, the ARVN First Infantry Division, carried by U.S. Army helicopter units, established a string of landing zones and firebases along the escarpment overlooking the Sepone River. Each of the LZs served as a base camp for the next advance, and all were totally dependent on U.S. aircraft for protection, movement and resupply.

Things had gone fairly well during the first few days of the incursion. There were losses, of course, including dozens of American helicopters. But for the most part, it appeared that the operation had a chance of being successful. Initially the NVA were not committed to opposition in force and had taken no offensive action to stop the ARVN advance. By late February, however, that had all changed.

First the Ranger bases fell, one at a time but in quick succession. Then the NVA launched a full-scale armored attack against the northern firebases and they both were overrun. The ARVN were stopped dead in their tracks on Highway 9 and soon took up a totally defensive posture.

As the tide turned against the ARVN, American aircrew casualties grew at an alarming rate. The combat environment in the air over Laos was the worst faced by U.S. Army aviation units at any time during the war to that point. Aircraft were being shot down one after another, and the extraction of American aircrews was becoming a major concern, just as Traynor had predicted.

By the third week of March, the rout was on. The ARVN

were in full retreat, their only remaining objective being to get out of Laos with as many units intact as possible. The incursion had failed miserably. The NVA were on the verge of completely eliminating the First Armored Brigade and two brigades of the ARVN Airborne Division, and were it not for those American aviation units that had been given and bravely performed the task of protecting and rescuing the South Vietnamese, it would have been a slaughter of the first magnitude.

During the first six weeks of the incursion, the Hoc Bao had proved themselves well suited to the task of recovering downed aircrews across the border and had performed remarkably well in carrying out the mission. Sometimes they would go in at night, find and secure a downed crew, then bring them out the next morning, all right under the NVA's nose and without firing a shot. Other times they would have to fight their way from the landing zone to the crash site, find the crew and then disappear into the jungle for a day or so until they could be picked up. There were as many stories about the amazing things the Hoc Bao had done as there were missions across the border. They were every bit as good as advertised.

During that same time, the men of the Hoc Bao Company learned not only to respect and fear Captain Jack Delon, but also to trust him. He never had to give an order twice and no one dared question his authority or his judgment. He was fanatically loyal to the men who accompanied him on the dangerous missions they ran inside Laos. Several times he risked his own life to bring them all home, and that did not go unnoticed.

Captain Delon became the toughest and best of the Hoc Bao, and his men were committed to follow him anywhere. As a result, his team's record in recovering downed aircrews was nearly perfect. Delon never passed on a mission, never came home without results and never left a downed pilot or one of his own men across the border. He either brought them home alive or recovered their dead bodies, but he would not leave them in Laos.

Because of that record, Captain Delon and the Hoc Bao were revered by the American aircrews. Some of them had seen the Frenchman at Khe Sanh, some had been rescued by him across the border, but none of them knew anything about him. All they knew for certain was that if they went down, the Hoc Bao, and maybe even the Frenchman himself, would soon be there to police them up and get them out. When it came to suiting up and going back across the border each day, whether flying insertion missions, recon or gun support, that assurance made all the difference.

Staley, now Captain Jack Delon, looked up and behind him at the familiar *whomp whomp* of an Army Huey passing overhead on short final for a hot approach into the aid station pad about two hundred meters away near the southwestern perimeter of Khe Sanh. The red cross painted on the side of the olive drab helicopter clearly marked it as a medical evacuation aircraft, but even from this distance, Staley could see the battle damage on the bird. The medevac ships had been coming in regularly all day, each one carrying dead and wounded ARVN soldiers and, occasionally, American aircrews, casualties of the barely organized withdrawal of ARVN forces from Laos.

He turned and continued to walk down the perforated steel plate runway toward the U.S. Army air cavalry unit that he had found hospitable a few weeks before. They had decent coffee and were more than willing to share it with him without asking a lot of questions. He enjoyed being among the pilots, listening to their conversations and reflecting on what it was like to be part of a real American combat unit once again. After more than two months with the Hoc Bao, the mercenary cover was wearing thin. This morning more than most, he needed a good cup of coffee and chance to relax.

But before he had made it halfway there a Vietnamese sergeant named Vinh, one of his men from the Hoc Bao, shouted his name then ran to catch up.

The sergeant saluted sharply. "Dai uy Delon," he said, using the Vietnamese term for captain, pronounced *die we,* "it is requested that you return to the briefing bunker. We have a task."

Staley shook his head in resignation. *More guys on the ground—I'm getting sick of policing up G.I. bodies. When are the dinks going to finally get the hell out of Laos and take the heat off the American pilots and crews? I told Traynor the ARVN couldn't hack it. This whole operation is bullshit.*

Speaking Vietnamese, Staley answered calmly, "Thank you, Sergeant Vinh. I will come immediately. Get the men together and ready to go."

After sending his sergeant on his way, Staley grasped the receiver of his AK to keep the muzzle from bouncing against his knee, then started jogging back to the Hoc Bao area. He had taken his team across the border so many times now that it no longer held any fear for him. His only concern was getting the aircrews out alive. Too many good men had died. He thought about the Americans that might be down just now. If they could stay alive until his team arrived on station, chances were good they would survive. It was his responsibility to get them out. He had done it before and he would do it again. Nothing was more important.

Staley picked up the pace and ran on toward the briefing bunker.

5

PHANTOM DOWN

21 March 1971—North of Highway 9—Laos

Berman couldn't believe that anything could hurt this badly. He lay back against the fallen tree and tried to collect his thoughts. His left side and chest were on fire. The pain was becoming unbearable. He was afraid to look at his left arm, knowing it was torn to shreds. He was certain that at least two of the 14.5-millimeter anti-aircraft rounds that had ripped through the cockpit of his F-4 fighter/bomber had taken most of it. He had no feeling in the arm at all. What remained could not be more than a bloody stump. But he was not quite ready to deal with the loss of an arm. He had to get his mind working. He had to fight this. He wasn't ready to die, not just yet.

He thought about his weapons system officer—the backseater in the Phantom he'd flown out of Da Nang just an hour and a half earlier. *Where's McGowan? I wonder if he got down okay?*

Berman could taste something vile in his throat. He was nauseated and about to vomit. A random thought of the breakfast he had eaten at the Officers' Club just a few hours before suddenly made him sick. He hated to vomit. He couldn't get his mind off of those greasy eggs and potatoes.

He closed his eyes and replayed the mission. Close air support for an ARVN armor column trying to make it back across the border. The NVA were closing in with tanks and infantry. The ARVN were on the run. The NVA had to be stopped.

He remembered the frequencies they had been given during the briefing and his reminding McGowan to double-check the avionics since they had had some trouble with the radios in his aircraft the day before.

They had taken off from Da Nang and climbed to 20,000 feet enroute to the target area. A forward air controller had been on station and had marked the target, a large force of NVA armor moving down from the hills above Highway 9 to engage the retreating ARVN. He took his sequence and started down, his wingman on his left and in attack spread. McGowan called the target, although Berman couldn't see anything but jungle and the gray clouds of scattered explosions on the ground.

He started in on the run—high explosive snake eye bombs and napalm. The ARVN needed some good iron on the bad guys and he was going to give it to them.

Then came the tracers, the .51s and 14.5s. He had seen the bright green and red tracers before, had attacked through that kind of stuff before. No big deal; they either hit you or they didn't. He couldn't worry about that. He just wished that McGowan would keep his mouth shut this time. He always bitched about making low runs into the anti-aircraft fire.

He had just pickled the snake eyes when a stream of 14.5-millimeter rounds came tearing through the cockpit. It all happened so fast he couldn't believe it. Then came the realization that he was hit and going down. They were on fire and had to punch out. He screamed at McGowan, "Eject, eject, eject." He realized that he couldn't reach the ejection handle with his left hand. His left arm was useless, hanging limp and covered with blood.

What's McGowan doing? Why hasn't he punched out? Maybe he's hit.

Just as the aircraft started rolling uncontrollably to the right, Berman managed to get a good grip on the ejection handle and started pulling. At the same instant, he heard McGowan blast out of the seat behind him. Both chutes were in the air at the same time, drifting down into the jungle. It was extraordinarily quiet after the noise inside the cockpit and the frantic fight to control the aircraft long enough to bail out.

He remembered hitting the ground—hard. He blacked out then, probably from the pain in his left arm and chest. When he came to, he was stretched out in dense under-growth, his chute pulling unmercifully on his shoulders. He popped the quick release and ran for about thirty yards before collapsing. He blacked out again.

Some time later—he wasn't sure if it was seconds, minutes or hours—he came to again. With great effort he took off his helmet with his right hand and pulled himself over against the fallen tree. He wondered how long he had been down and who might be coming for him. The NVA had to have seen his chute.

He remembered that he had a .38 strapped across his chest and he pulled it free, allowing it to fall to the ground beside his right hand. He wasn't sure what damage he could do with the pitifully inaccurate revolver, but he decided that if they came for him, he was going to make an effort to take a few of them with him.

Berman sat there for several minutes, trying to gather his strength and take inventory of the damage. He had been hit in the right leg just below the knee. The wound burned like a bee sting but wasn't bothering him too much, although he could feel the blood running down into his boot. He touched his face and then looked at his hand—it was covered with blood. His right eye seemed to be swelling closed.

Finally, he summoned the courage to turn and look at his left side. The sleeve of his flight suit looked like it had been through a shredder. While he still had a hand and a forearm connected at the elbow, all he could see was raw meat, bone and bloody tissue. His entire left side was soaked with fresh blood. He rolled his head away from the carnage and vomited down the right side of his flight suit. The finality of the situation sunk in. He was going to die. He fought the dimming light for a few seconds, then acquiesced and passed out.

McGowan lay face down in the thick green foliage, his heart racing as he listened to Vietnamese voices not more than thirty meters away. They had to be NVA, and probably looking for him.

He had ditched his chute as quickly as possible and had run toward the spot where he'd expected to find Berman. *That damned glory hound! If he hadn't insisted on being a hero, we wouldn't be in this mess. I told him a hundred times to stay up and make high speed bomb runs when we know we're gonna get triple A, but the ignorant asshole had to be a big shot and take it down to the deck, low and slow. If I make it out of here, I'm never flying with that son-of-a-bitch again.*

After a few minutes, the voices became more distant. McGowan cautiously moved forward. He had lost his .38 revolver and just about everything else in the ejection. He hadn't made it down with anything but the gold-plated cigarette lighter Senator Winston had given him for working on his 1968 campaign. He needed to find Berman and figure out a way to get the hell out of here. Berman was good in tough situations. He was a by-the-book jerk, but he knew what he was doing.

God help me if he's dead. I don't know how I'm going to get out of this by myself. I shouldn't be here in the first place. I'd like to throttle Winston and his damned daughter for getting me into this mess. Shit!

After what seemed like an eternity, McGowan found what had to be Berman's chute, tangled up in the underbrush. But Berman wasn't still attached—he had popped the release and taken off. That was good news and bad news. The good news was that Berman was alive, which meant that McGowan probably would not have to try to get out on his own. The bad news was that Berman was nowhere to be seen. *If that son-of-a-bitch has left me behind, I'll kill him!*

McGowan tried to remember his escape and evasion training. The first thing was to get away from the crash site immediately and find a place to hide, at least until the first group of searchers had cleared the area. He had done that. Then he should try to contact the surface-to-air rescue, or SAR, team and find a spot for a pickup, but how? He remembered once again with dismay that he had lost his survival radio during the ejection. He had to do something. One thing was for certain. The longer he stayed on the ground in enemy-controlled territory, the greater the chance he would be caught or killed.

I've got to get out of this damned jungle. I've got to find Berman, get his survival radio and make contact with the SAR team. They're probably up there right now, trying to find us, trying to contact us. Why did I have to lose that damn radio? If I had it now, I'd be on my way out of here.

Then he saw it. There was fresh blood on the tropical plants that covered the floor of the jungle. It had to be Berman's. He'd been hit and had crawled away from the site.

McGowan got the general sense of which way the blood trail was leading and followed it through some almost impenetrable undergrowth. He knew he was making too much noise, but he had to find Berman and get the radio. That was the only way they were ever going to get out of this alive.

McGowan broke through into a small clearing and there he saw Berman. He was lying against a rotting log with his head down and tilted at an unnatural angle to the right, almost as if his neck were broken. His eyes were closed as though he were asleep. His face looked like a prizefighter who had been beaten to a pulp. The right leg of his flight suit was soaked with blood. His right shoulder and sleeve covered with vomit. But the really hideous sight was the place where his left arm should have been. McGowan could see that it was almost completely gone. There were jagged bone fragments, torn sinews and strands of exposed muscle from his shoulder down to what remained of his left hand, and there was blood everywhere. At first glance, McGowan was certain that Aaron Berman was dead, and with that realization, he panicked. *Oh my God, no! What am I going to do now?*

He scrambled over to the body and roughly tried to locate the carotid artery on the left side of Berman's neck. The pilot's skin was gray and cool to the touch. He stunk from fresh vomit and McGowan gagged, nearly throwing up himself.

As he groped for a pulse, Berman took a breath. The unexpected movement caused McGowan to jump back in surprise, then redouble his efforts to determine if the pilot was really alive. He continued to feel for evidence of a heartbeat, finally locating a barely discernible pulse, although it was rapid and weak. Energized by the discovery that

Berman was not dead, McGowan grabbed the pilot by the front of his flight suit, fighting off almost debilitating revulsion and fear.

Whispering loudly, he said, "Berman. *Berman.* Can you hear me? Wake up, you bastard!"

Aaron Berman opened his eyes, squinted at the shape before him then smiled weakly. It was enormously difficult to remain conscious, but the sound of a friendly voice had tapped his ever-dwindling supply of adrenaline. He tried to speak.

"Bob." McGowan hated to be called "Bob"—he always insisted on Robert—but Berman frequently called him "Bob," just to upset him.

Berman slurred his words, "I don't think I can move too well. You're going to have to . . ."

He never completed the thought. His eyelids slowly fell and his head rolled to the right as he passed out once again.

McGowan leaned into his pilot and put his ear to Berman's chest. His heart was still beating and he was still breathing, although the breaths were shallow and each one seemed like it would be the last.

McGowan thought about what Berman had said—that he didn't think he could move. *What am I supposed to do now? Should I try to help Berman or just get the hell out of here?*

He dug around in Berman's survival vest until he found a sterile bandage; each pilot carried only one and McGowan had lost his in the ejection. He tore open the package and used the sterile gauze to wipe off Berman's face. The injuries there were superficial.

Then he looked at the wounded man's shattered left arm. He had no idea how to apply the bandage to the mangled arm in a manner that might accomplish something, so he pulled Berman's right pants leg up above his knee and wrapped the field dressing around the seeping hole in the pilot's calf. It was all McGowan could think of to do.

McGowan sat back and considered his situation. One thing was for certain, Berman was never going to get out of this jungle on his own, and McGowan didn't see how he could possibly carry him out. And he damned sure wasn't going to wait here until Berman finally stopped breathing. Berman was going to die. It was just a matter of time. There was no point in McGowan being killed or captured just so he could sit here with his unconscious front-seater—no point at all.

He caught a glimpse of something on the ground beside the injured pilot's right leg. It was Berman's .38. McGowan picked it up and stuffed it into the pocket of his flight suit.

He then checked Berman's survival vest. The pocket size emergency radio was still there! He turned the volume all the way down then switched it on. As he increased the volume, he could hear traffic on the emergency channel. All hell was breaking loose, but he knew they were looking for him and Berman. Both members of the F-4 crew had punched out with good chutes. Someone would have seen it and they would be doing everything possible to find them right now. He was certain they would send someone in to get him, if he could just tell them where he was.

He resisted the impulse to key the radio and simply start talking. He had to figure this out. There was no way to get Berman out on a jungle penetrator, or even himself for that matter—not here, not now. They would have to get to an area where a rescue helicopter could land and pick them up. He couldn't carry Berman through the jungle to a landing zone—they be spotted for sure by the NVA. He ran through all the alternatives.

I could leave Berman and try to make it out on my own, but

97

what if someone finds him? If I leave him, I'll have to tell everyone that I couldn't find him. They'll either suspect I didn't look for him—that I panicked and ran—or that I left him. What if the NVA finds him and somehow he survives? Or even worse, what if a rescue team finds him and he talks? Would he remember that I'd been here? It would be obvious that I'd left him. How will I explain the fact that I lost my survival vest bailing out and somehow ended up with Berman's radio and .38? Maybe I can get past that. Who would know?

McGowan sat back and thought about the lie he was about to manufacture. It had to be good and it had to be plausible, absolutely beyond question.

As he sat there, he looked down and realized that he had Berman's blood all over his flight suit. *Damn! How am I going to explain the blood? Should I try to cut myself with something?*

McGowan finally concluded that he could deal with just about any anything except the possibility that Berman might live long enough to be captured or rescued. If he left him and Berman lived, McGowan would be in serious trouble. The shame and humiliation would follow him forever. He couldn't risk that.

He sat there looking at Berman for a long time, trying to decide what to do. He heard aircraft overhead, the distinctive sound of the A1Es. The Spads were up, the surface-to-air rescue team in place. Somehow he had to act before the opportunity was gone.

It took him nearly fifteen minutes to decide on a course of action and then to work up the courage to follow through on what he had concluded was the only feasible plan. During that period he tried several times to bring Berman around, but there was no response. Berman was dying. There was no question about it. There was no point in him dying too.

The rationalization sold itself. He knew what he had to do.

He removed one of Berman's dog tags from the silver chain around the pilot's neck. He left the other in place as he had been instructed in survival school. He then went through Berman's pockets, although he could not bring himself to scrape off the vomit and blood that covered most of the front of the pilot's flight suit. He took his billfold and some military payment certificates, a map with some grease pencil marks and frequencies and some other papers. He tried to remove a college ring but couldn't get it off.

When he was finished, he raised the .38, pointed it at Berman's head, and from a distance of less than five feet, he winced and pulled the trigger.

The injured man's head snapped back; he rolled off the log and lay still. It was over for sure now—Berman was dead. *It's probably the best thing I could have done for him,* rationalized McGowan. *He was going to die anyway. At least the NVA won't get him.*

With the echo of the .38 still ringing in his ears, McGowan jumped up and started back the way he came, through the thick underbrush and toward the road he knew was some distance to the south. The gunshot would attract attention and he wanted to get well away from the scene before making his first call on the survival radio.

6

RESCUE

21 March 1971—North of Highway 9—Laos

The barely discernible sound of a single gunshot caused Staley to freeze in his tracks. It wasn't close, probably not within three hundred meters, but it meant that someone was shooting at someone else, and that meant trouble. Without looking back, he signaled with his left arm for the men following him to get down.

Two U.S. Army Hueys had inserted Staley's team in a clearing just north of Highway 9, in an area known to be thick with NVA positions. It was the closest reasonable landing zone to the spot where the Air Force forward air controller had spotted the chutes of the two F-4 pilots.

They had taken plenty of fire coming in, mostly AK and other small arms, but no one had been hit. The aircraft had taken even more fire climbing out. Staley had come to admire the guts of the Huey pilots. They never wavered on a mission like this. When someone was on the ground, they put the Hoc Bao in just as close as possible to the site, without regard for the dangers of getting in and out of the LZ. They were brave men.

Now that they were in place, it was up to Staley and his team to find and rescue the F-4 crew. The FAC said they had two good chutes, so it was likely that both men were still alive when they hit the ground. Keeping them alive on the ground and getting them out was the Hoc Bao's specialty.

The single gunshot was a mystery. It wasn't an AK or an SKS—certainly not an M-16. It sounded more like a pistol, but the jungle could do funny things with sound, especially over long distances.

Staley turned, slowly and quietly, to look at his men. They were completely invisible in the undergrowth. *Good work.*

After a minute of complete silence, he rose and gave the signal to move forward. Staley had the point, as he always did on these kinds of missions. It was a matter of self-preservation.

The small unit crept ahead slowly, moving as one man, silently sliding through the jungle like a snake, disturbing nothing. Staley sensed, more than heard or saw, something to his right. He gave the signal for his men to stop and cover.

He checked out everything within sight. Broken plants, scarred trees, the smell of last night's fire. He knew the signs. It meant recent NVA activity very close by, probably a bunker outpost.

That was bad news. If the airmen were still alive, they should be up ahead. There were NVA soldiers between his unit and the downed crew.

Staley turned and caught the attention of Sergeant Vinh. Using hand signals, Staley directed Vinh to take three men and swing around to the right, taking a track parallel to the main force. Vinh nodded, then disappeared into the undergrowth.

Staley waited approximately thirty seconds, then raised up and started the remainder of the men moving again, slowly but inexorably forward. Silent. Silent. They seemed to move between the branches, sliding under the tropical plants without breaking a stem, gliding over the ground cover without leaving a trace. Their passing was barely noticed by the birds and insects that kept up the familiar background chatter. They were all but invisible.

Despite their stealth, the Hoc Bao moved at a deliberate pace through the jungle, ever advancing on the site where the chutes had been spotted from the air. Staley thought they should be just about there. He started scouring the trees and branches overhead for signs of the brightly colored parachutes, hoping he didn't find one with a body hanging from the risers.

Then he heard it, maybe fifty meters ahead. Someone was talking on a radio. It had to be one of the pilots. Staley winced and gritted his teeth in exasperation. If he could hear the pilot, so could the NVA he knew were nearby.

He gave the signal to his men to move more quickly. They picked up the pace, making slightly more noise and compromising their principal advantage—the ability to remain undetected in the midst of enemy soldiers. But they had to take the chance. They had to get to the pilot before the bad guys got there.

McGowan knew it was time to make radio contact with the surface-to-air rescue team. He thought he was far enough away from Berman that anyone looking for the source of the gunshot probably would not have tracked him this far. He took out the small RT-10 survival radio and keyed the mike.

"Rescue aircraft north of Highway 9, Socket Two-One Alpha on guard. Over."

McGowan's spirits soared when he heard the immediate response.

"Socket Two-One Alpha, Sandy Lead. Over."

"Sandy" was the call sign universally adopted by the

coordinator of each surface-to-air rescue operation, usually a senior officer flying a Douglas A1E Skyraider. It was confirmation to McGowan that the SAR team was in place.

"Sandy Lead, Two-One Alpha is on the ground and in good shape. Can you get a fix on my beacon and pull me out? Over."

Up above in the Skyraider, also called a "Spad" by the men who flew them, James Callahan, the forty-two year old Air Force colonel who was Sandy Lead on this particular SAR, rolled his big single prop airplane over on its side, staring down below as though he could see through the jungle.

Colonel Callahan took a deep breath before answering the youngster on the ground. *Why the hell don't they teach these shit-hot jet jockeys guys how an SAR is handled?*

"Negative, Two-One Alpha. We can get a fix on your beeper but not close enough for a jungle extraction. The Jolly Green," meaning the rescue helicopter that would actually go in for the downed crew, "will need more than just a signal to get a visual and they will definitely need a visual for the pickup. Are you near the site where we spotted the chutes? Over."

"Two-One Alpha, that's affirm. How are you going to find me? Over?"

"We'll find you, son. What is the crew status? Are you alone? Over."

Berman's call sign was Socket 21. By using the call sign Socket 21 Alpha, McGowan was indicating that he was the weapons systems officer, the back-seater. The SAR leader wanted to know if the pilot of the aircraft was with him.

It was do or die time for McGowan. Once he started down this road, he could never go back.

"Rog, I am alone. My driver was injured in the ejection

then killed by the NVA on the ground. He is KIA and not recoverable at this time. Can you guide me to the pick-up point?"

"This is Sandy Lead. Just find a secure place and stay under cover for a while. We have a recovery aircraft inbound for the pick. You'll have to guide them in. There is also a South Vietnamese recovery team on the ground heading in your direction. If they get to you first, they'll get you out. Do you roger, over?"

"Ah, roger that, Sandy. But hurry if you can, there are bad guys all over the place down here."

"Roger. I'll call you when we have something for you. In the meantime, stay under cover and keep the volume turned down on your radio. Out."

McGowan was sitting near the edge of a small clearing, huddled against the base of a tree. He turned the volume down on the survival radio and waited. They knew approximately where he was; they would eventually find him. The SAR guys had a reputation he knew he could count on. They would get him out, he was sure of it. He just needed to stay put and avoid any contact with the NVA until the time came to haul ass.

He had just decided to crawl around the tree to find better cover when something caught his eye; movement in the bushes across the clearing. His heart raced as he slowly pulled the .38 out of his flight suit pocket and tried to steady it with both hands.

Just then an NVA soldier, wearing a khaki uniform and pith helmet, stepped into the clearing, his AK-47 pointed directly at McGowan. McGowan froze. If he shot and missed, the NVA soldier would kill him. He lowered the pistol and cowered against the tree. He knew he had no chance. He was either going to be killed or captured.

The enemy soldier waved his rifle at McGowan, directing him to move into the open. The soldier opened his mouth to speak, but no words came out. Instead, his head snapped back abruptly, he dropped his rifle, and his body became as limp as a rag doll. As his knees buckled to the ground, McGowan saw directly behind the soldier a small man dressed in dark fatigues who at that moment was twisting a thin knife into the side of the NVA's neck and lowering him to the ground.

The silent execution of the NVA soldier happened so fast that McGowan didn't realize he was being rescued. He was paralyzed with fear, hardly aware that he was still holding the .38. Without warning, someone reached around him from behind, grabbed his wrist with one hand and removed the pistol with the other. McGowan offered no resistance.

McGowan turned and stared into the face of a rugged-looking man with a thick, droopy mustache—maybe American, certainly not Vietnamese. McGowan started to say something, but the man stopped him by quickly cupping his left hand over McGowan's mouth. The stranger then pulled McGowan backwards into the jungle, careful to not make a sound. McGowan resisted at first, then realized what was happening and allowed the strong Caucasian to pull him back and down into the vegetation.

The man held McGowan motionless for two full minutes, his hand pressed hard against McGowan's mouth. Then a Vietnamese soldier appeared beside them, wearing the same tiger fatigues as the one who had killed the NVA across the clearing. He whispered something and the man holding McGowan nodded his head. The other soldier withdrew and disappeared into the undergrowth.

More than three minutes had passed since the rescue had first started to unfold. There wasn't a sound in the jungle, other than the birds and insects, which carried on as though nothing had happened.

Staley leaned close to the lieutenant's ear and whispered, his voice heavy with a French accent.

"I am Captain Jack Delon. Although you cannot see them, my men are all around us. We are here to get you out."

The terrified officer nodded his head enthusiastically, his eyes wide with excitement.

Staley continued, "I am going to remove my hand now. You will say nothing until I advise you it is safe to speak. You will then speak only when you have my attention and you will whisper as I am doing now. If I hold up my hand, you will stop speaking immediately. Do you understand these instructions?"

McGowan looked into his rescuer's steel blue eyes, hesitated briefly, then nodded.

Staley removed his hand, then smiled reassuringly. In a whispering voice, still thick with the French accent, he said, "I am sorry, Lieutenant, but your loud talking on the radio attracted an enemy patrol. My men have killed three NVA soldiers within fifty meters of where we sit. We must remain still and quiet until we are certain there are no others nearby."

McGowan, his eyes wide, simply nodded in the affirmative, then sat back, waiting for additional instructions. He was duly impressed with the Frenchman. This was not a man to be taken lightly.

Ten minutes later, a small Vietnamese soldier wearing sergeant's stripes eased up next to the Frenchman. McGowan had not heard him coming and the sudden presence of the tough-looking sergeant startled him.

Staley and Vinh spoke briefly in Vietnamese, then Staley

turned to the downed flight officer and said in a low voice, "We are secure now. We will move out and head south to the road. There we will be picked up by a helicopter."

Staley pointed to the bloodstains on the front of the man's flight suit. "Are you wounded?"

Forgetting himself for a moment, McGowan blurted, "No, I'm not hit. I'm fine. Let's just get the hell out of here."

Staley was confused. "What happened? Whose blood is this?"

"I'm the weapons officer on an F-4. It's my pilot's blood." Then pulling out his survival radio and changing the subject, McGowan said, "Look, there's an SAR taking shape upstairs. I need to call the lead and let him know what's going on."

Staley nodded. "Please, keep it as quiet as possible, and if I raise my hand, turn the radio off immediately."

McGowan acknowledged with a shake of his head, then whispered into the small radio.

"Sandy Lead, Socket Two-One Alpha. Over."

He adjusted the volume down to a barely audible level as the SAR leader answered.

"Two-One Alpha, Sandy Lead. We thought we'd lost you, son. What's your status? Over."

"This is Two-One Alpha. I've been secured by the recovery team. We'll be moving out momentarily. These folks have another ride coming. Thanks for being there, Sandy."

"Good to hear that, Two-One Alpha. Have you recovered Two-One?"

Oh, shit. Why did he ask that? I wonder if the French captain heard that, or if he did, whether he understood the question.

"Ah, negative, Sandy. The situation will not permit that at this time."

Upstairs in the Spad, Jim Callahan did not like that answer. If there was a way, he wanted to recover the body of the dead pilot. He had a Jolly Green inbound and the rescue jumpers would not hesitate to go in, even for just a body.

"Ah, Two-One Alpha, if you can give us a mark, the Jolly Green can make the extraction. I don't want to leave one of our guys on the ground, over."

McGowan just wanted to get away. *Damn the Spad jockey!*

"Sandy, Two-One Alpha. I don't think I can get back there and these guys want to move out, over."

Callahan still didn't like it, but he wasn't there on the ground. Maybe the site was surrounded. Maybe the NVA had taken the body. He didn't know all the facts and it wasn't his call. He made a note to follow up after everything calmed down. Something didn't feel right about this one.

After a few seconds' consideration, Callahan replied, "Ah, roger, Two-One Alpha, we are breaking station at this time. Good luck. Sandy Lead, out."

Staley had heard the entire exchange, and he didn't like what the Air Force lieutenant was saying either. Staley never varied from the principle that you did not leave people on the ground, alive or dead.

Maintaining the French accent, Staley asked, "Where is the other pilot? How did you get his blood on your uniform?"

McGowan decided he needed to come up with a reasonable explanation, or this Neanderthal was going to ruin everything.

"Captain Berman was hit by ground fire before we punched out. We landed a couple of hundred meters apart. I immediately made my way toward where I thought he'd come down and eventually I found him. He was unconscious, badly wounded and bleeding to death. I bandaged him up as best I could, but I'd lost just about everything in the bail-out and there was not much I could do for him, other than make him comfortable. I sat there with him, waiting for the NVA, but they didn't come.

"I knew the surface-to-air rescue team would be looking for us, so after a while I took Berman's emergency radio and tried to find a place where I could talk without making too much noise. I figured I'd have to carry him out. No way he could have ridden out on a penetrator.

"I was about fifty meters away, just getting ready to call the SAR, when I heard a shot. I crawled back to the spot where I'd left him and watched while two NVA soldiers picked through his pockets. The bastards had murdered him, shot him while he was unconscious. He didn't have much on him. I'd already taken his dog tags, map, frequency card and personal items, just to ensure they didn't get lost. I couldn't believe what I was seeing. I wanted to kill them, but all I had was the .38 and they had rifles.

"Aaron was hurt real bad. He wasn't going to make it anyway, but they still shouldn't have killed him.

"After I thought they'd gone, I tried to get back to him, to see if there was anything I could do. But as soon as I stepped into the clearing, I heard the NVA. They hadn't gone. They saw me and I started running. Then I hid until you found me."

The story sounded sort of right, but something about it bothered Staley. He looked at the lieutenant. The guy was either telling the truth or was an accomplished liar.

But regardless of whether or not the story was true, Staley was not going back to Khe Sanh without the body of the dead pilot.

"Can you lead us to the body? We will take the dead pilot back with us."

McGowan hadn't counted on that. He looked around the dense jungle as though trying to get his bearings. "I don't know for sure where he is. I just ran. I could have been running in circles for all I know. I was just trying to get away from the bad guys. I'm not even sure how far I ran. There's no way I can lead you back there. I'm sorry as hell, I mean, you know, the guy was my friend. I want to recover the body, too. I just don't know where to begin."

Staley thought a minute. Taking the lieutenant with him on a search of the jungle would be impossible. He would probably get them all killed. It was better to send him back.

The Frenchman called the tough-looking sergeant over and they began to speak quietly in Vietnamese. McGowan wished he knew what the hell they were saying. He wanted badly to get out of there.

Finally, the Frenchman turned back to McGowan.

"I will take three men and go to look for the body of your pilot. Sergeant Vinh and the remainder of my men will take you back to the pick-up point and will call the helicopter for extraction. If you want to live, you will do exactly what Sergeant Vinh tells you to do. He does not speak English well, so pay close attention to his hand signals and stay very quiet. He will get you out."

The Frenchman then extended his hand and smiled, "I'm glad you made it, Lieutenant. I hope to never see you again under these circumstances. Au revoir."

McGowan accepted the handshake and smiled back. "Thank you, Captain. I'm in your debt. If you're ever in Da Nang, stop by and I'll buy you dinner."

Then McGowan remembered the .38. "Ah, Captain, I'd like to have my .38 back."

Staley pulled the weapon from the waistband of his jungle fatigues. He thumbed the cylinder open and checked the load. Five of the six chambers were full, as was the custom with pilots. But one round had been fired—the one in the firing position. Staley turned the .38 up on its side, tapped it lightly and emptied the cartridges into his hand. He put them in his pocket, snapped the cylinder closed and handed the pistol back to the lieutenant.

"You will not need your sidearm. My men will not fire a weapon unless there is no other choice. They will not want you to have a loaded weapon while in their care. Please put the pistol away and do not take it out of your pocket. If a firefight becomes necessary, other weapons should be available. Trust Sergeant Vinh."

McGowan took the .38 and put in back in the pocket of his flight suit, thankful that the Frenchman had not asked about the empty cartridge.

Staley then nodded to Sergeant Vinh, who tapped the Air Force officer on the shoulder and led him off into the jungle. Staley collected the three men who would be going on with him and they fanned out, following the instructions conveyed by Staley's hand signals. In less than five seconds they melted into the jungle, without a trace and without a sound.

It took them almost forty-five minutes to find the pilot. It was just as the lieutenant had described. The man was lying at the edge of a small clearing and obviously had been badly wounded before having been executed by the NVA. His left arm was a mass of mangled tissue and coagulated blood, his face was scarred and bloody and he had a field dressing on his right leg. The lieutenant's story was starting to bear out.

Staley remained motionless and watched the clearing for several minutes while his men screened out in all directions to ensure there were no NVA soldiers nearby. When they had reported by hand signals that all was clear, Staley approached the body. He could see no alternative but to carry the dead pilot out on his shoulders.

He expected to find an AK-47 wound in the man's chest since that was how the NVA likely would have executed the unconscious pilot. But there was no such wound. Instead, there was deep scar on the left side of the pilot's head, running from his eyebrow to a point in his short black hair, just above the ear. Blood from the wound was still trickling down the side of the pilot's face and on to his flight suit. An AK hadn't made that wound.

As he leaned over to pull the body toward him, grasping the front of the pilot's flight suit, he realized that the man was breathing. *How the hell could this guy still be alive?*

Staley pulled the injured pilot away from the fallen tree, gently laid him on his back and began to administer basic first aid. The wounded man was breathing, although the breaths were shallow and labored. The airway was clear and most of the bleeding had stopped, except for the gash on his forehead. Staley was certain the pilot was in shock, but under the circumstances he really did not have the capacity for dealing with that. He would just have to do the best he could.

Staley took the first aid kit from his web gear and starting treating the visible wounds. He cut off the left sleeve of the man's flight suit and discovered that while the arm was mangled and probably would be lost, the pilot's body had somehow reacted to the trauma by stopping the bleeding on its own. Staley wrapped the damaged arm with gauze and secured it tightly at the shoulder with Velcro straps used to bind wounded soldiers to a field litter. The bindings would surely cut off all circulation to the arm, but they would also stop any further bleeding.

He rewrapped and re-secured the field dressing on the pilot's right calf. That wound would not be much of a problem. A piece of shrapnel, probably part of the airplane, had gone clean through without too much damage to the leg.

The face wounds were all superficial, and the bleeding there had stopped as well.

The troubling wound was the one to the man's forehead; the deep scar was obviously the result of an injury more recent than the others. The blood there was still fresh and the tissue inside the scar was still bright red and oozing. It was as though the man had been shot right where he lay, and not that long ago. But Staley was certain he had not been shot with an AK. It looked more like the bullet had been deflected by the man's skull and had followed the path of least resistance around the side of the skull until it exited above the ear. An AK fired from close range would not have done that. It would have killed the pilot for certain.

Staley continued to work on the pilot while thinking about the head wound. He then thought back about the lieutenant's story of how the NVA had come and killed his front-seater. He looked around the clearing for signs that NVA had been there. No NVA shoe or sandal prints, and no AK brass. There was no evidence of enemy soldiers being there at all.

Staley held his hand under the pilot's head and tried to give him some water. The captain choked at first, then swallowed one sip, then another. The pilot barely opened his eyes, looked at Staley and smiled thinly.

"Thanks, Bob," he whispered.

"How are you doing, Captain?" Staley asked. He wondered if the wounded man had any internal injuries. If so, he probably wouldn't make it.

"I'm fine," the captain answered weakly. "I just need a little rest." He closed his eyes. "What time do we take off?"

"Try some more of this." Staley gave him a few more sips of water, which he drank more enthusiastically this time.

"Thanks. I . . . I can't stay awake."

Staley gently placed the captain's head on the soft ground, then sat back and tried to decide what to do. The pilot was badly injured. Staley doubted that he would survive being carried back to the pick-up point, but there were no good alternatives.

Staley noticed something in the right sleeve pocket of the wounded man's flight suit, covered with dried vomit. It was a gold Cross pen. He took it out and examined it. *The NVA wouldn't have left that pen.*

He then checked the pilot's other pockets. In his left breast pocket, saturated with blood and thick pieces of gray tissue from what used to be his left arm, was a small pad with a spiral binder at the top. Staley flipped through the pad. There were personal reminders, briefing notes and other scribbles, along with some radio frequencies. It was the kind of notepad many officers carried to write down things they needed to remember from day to day. *No way NVA soldiers would have missed that pad. Even if they couldn't read English, they'd have taken it because of the radio frequencies.*

The frightened lieutenant's story was starting to come apart. *What the hell happened here?*

Staley began retracing his steps, remembering the position of the pilot's body when he had first come into the clearing. The wounded man's back was against the log and his body was laid over to one side. He had probably been lying against the log when he was shot.

Staley slid over to the log and immediately found what he was looking for—a hole where the bullet that had creased the pilot's skull had imbedded in the dead wood behind him. Staley pulled out his K-Bar knife and dug the flattened slug out of the soft wood. It was small and light gray in color—a pistol round, definitely not AK. *But the lieutenant said they had rifles. Only NVA officers carry a pistol.*

Staley remembered that just before handing the .38 back to the lieutenant, he had checked the cylinder. One round had been fired. The lieutenant had not offered an explanation.

Staley also remembered the single shot he had heard in the distance while they were looking for the downed crew. *What happened here?*

Suddenly it became clear. The lieutenant had found his front-seater, realized he could never get him out and that if he stayed with his partner, the lieutenant himself would likely be killed or captured. So he had decided to kill the pilot and escape on his own. That had to have been it. *The son-of-a-bitch shot his pilot to cover up his own cowardice in leaving him to die.*

Staley was furious. He wanted to get the lieutenant. He wanted to beat the hell of him, then bring him before a court martial.

But then he realized that that was never going to happen. Unless the pilot was able to make it back and could re-member enough to press charges, the lieutenant would walk. The only way to make the charge stick would be for Staley himself to testify, and he could never do that. He could not carry off the French mercenary charade in a court martial proceeding and Americans couldn't be on the ground in Laos.

Having no other choice, he decided to describe the matter in detail in his final report to Traynor and let the Old Man take whatever action he deemed appropriate. Unfortunately, Staley didn't know the lieutenant's name. But that was okay, Traynor could find out easily enough. He would have to leave it with Traynor. Traynor would know what to do.

The Following Morning—East of FSB Aloui—Laos

"Dustoff Three-Four, Panther One-Six. Over." The heavy accent was even more pronounced on the scratchy FM radio.

The copilot of the medevac helicopter, a young warrant officer on only his third mission into Laos, looked over at the pilot and pushed the floor button to key the intercom.

"Did you hear that, Ron? That guy sounds French. Are there French troops working this operation?"

Without responding to his copilot's question, the experienced dustoff pilot answered the transmission from the ground. He had picked-up Panther One-Six before and knew the Frenchman was a mercenary with the Hoc Bao, and one tough-looking son-of-a-bitch.

"Panther One-Six, Dustoff Three-Four is low level west on Highway 9 about five clicks east of Aloui. Do you have us in sight? Over."

"Dustoff Three-Four, this is Panther One-Six. Negative tally at this time, but we are about two clicks east of Aloui, so you should be close. I will pop smoke in the road. Land on the smoke and we'll be there."

"What's the situation on the ground? We have a couple of gunships with us if we need them. Over."

"We are not in contact at this time, but there are NVA nearby. You should plan for the LZ to be hot. I say again,

116

assume the LZ will be hot. We have five for pickup including a WIA who needs immediate attention. Over."

"Three-Four, roger. Understand five for pickup. We'll have the guns work out on both sides of the road as we come in."

"Roger, Three-Four. Popping smoke at this time."

The medevac pilot strained against his shoulder harness as he looked down the road to his front. They were only fifty feet above the trees that lined the sides of the road, staying below the envelope of the large caliber anti-aircraft weapons that were ready to greet any aircraft operating above one hundred feet. Ahead he could see bright red smoke billowing up from the center of the dirt track known as Highway 9.

"Panther One-Six, Dustoff Three-Four. We have cherry smoke in the road."

"Three-Four, One-Six. Confirm red smoke."

As the medevac pilot set up for a high speed, straight-in approach to the smoke, he turned to the inexperienced copilot, who was still trying to figure out what was going on.

"Pay attention, newbie, and follow me through. This could get ugly fast. The good news is that the guy on the ground knows what he's doing. Let's get 'em in the aircraft and then get the hell outa here."

As he watched the flight of three helicopters approach from the east, Staley thought about the past eighteen hours. He couldn't believe the pilot was still alive after all he had been through.

Staley had been reluctant to move the captain at first, and since there was no sign of the NVA patrolling in their direction, he had decided to take a chance and leave the badly wounded pilot right where he was until Staley could get more liquids into him and allow his body to stabilize. The guy had one hell of an immune system, or whatever it was that enabled him to fight the loss of blood and the infection that had to be working on him.

Just before dark, Staley had moved his small group about five hundred meters to the east, well away from the spot where his men had killed the three NVA earlier in the day. Although they had hidden the bodies well, the soldiers eventually would be missed and someone would likely come looking for them. Staley wanted to be a good distance away when that happened.

In the middle of the night, the captain became delirious and started to cry out. Staley had to hold his hand over the man's mouth, almost suffocating him. But he had no choice. If the NVA found them with the wounded man in tow, they would not make it back.

When the captain became so uncomfortable with pain that he could not lie still, Staley reluctantly gave him an ampoule of morphine. That calmed him down, but Staley then had to watch him all night, giving him small sips of water and keeping a cool cloth on his head.

Two hours before dawn, Staley moved the group once again, this time in the direction of the road. It was a two-kilometer walk, and carrying the wounded man made stealthy movement through the underbrush much more difficult.

Halfway through the trek, the point man came across an NVA position, including log bunkers billeting twenty or thirty men. The small group of rescuers had to backtrack almost three hundred meters to avoid arousing the sleeping enemy soldiers. They then turned and made a wide arc to the east in order to get back on course.

Just before sunup, Staley found a spot near the road

where he decided to stop until the extraction ships were inbound. It was completely covered in thick, green undergrowth, and the men were careful to avoid the ever-present danger of poisonous snakes in the heart of such deep foliage. But it was a good spot to hide. The NVA probably wouldn't look for them that close to the road.

At 0620, he motioned for his Chinese corporal, a squat but enormously strong man at least ten years Staley's senior, to bring the radio close by so that Staley could make the call. His transmission was answered immediately, and within a few minutes a medevac ship with gun cover was in the air.

Staley watched from below the low-hanging branches of a hardwood tree as the slick approached with two heavily armed Cobra gunships flying alongside.

The medevac pilot called, "Three-Four's on short final to the smoke. Get ready to haul ass One-Six."

As the medevac Huey flared for landing in the road, the Cobra gunships opened up on both sides with rockets and miniguns, the sound drowning out the *whomp, whomp* of the rotor blades of the approaching aircraft. Staley had not heard any fire directed at the medevac and knew that the gunships were simply laying down suppressive fire.

He pulled the still-unconscious captain across his shoulders in a fireman's carry and ran to where he expected the helicopter to touch down. His men followed him out, covering the underbrush on both sides of the road.

The Huey flared to bleed off forward airspeed, its nose high in the air and its tail nearly touching the ground, then tilted forward and landed smoothly on the dusty road. The medic in the back of the aircraft helped Staley load the Air Force officer onto the floor of the cargo bay, then yelled for everyone to get on board. The remaining Hoc Bao clambered aboard with great dexterity, their weapons still pointing outside the aircraft, ready to take on any new threat.

The medevac ship, after being on the ground just a matter of seconds, rolled forward on its skids and took off at full power. After clearing the trees, the pilot of the Huey banked his aircraft hard to the left and headed back east toward Khe Sanh, staying low to avoid the anti-aircraft fire.

Upon reaching Khe Sanh, the medevac ship landed at the aid station pad on the southwest side of the combat base, at virtually the same spot from which Staley had taken off almost twenty hours earlier. Several medics and an officer that Staley recognized as a doctor ran to the helicopter and pulled the captain onto a stretcher. Staley jumped down and watched with interest as one medic quickly started an IV while the doctor checked vital signs and then carefully started unwrapping the blood-soaked field dressings.

Staley felt like he had a stake in the wounded pilot. He wanted to be sure the captain was still alive when he left. When the doctor told the medics to carry the stretcher into the surgery tent, Staley quietly wished the young man well, then turned and walked away.

Behind him he could hear more aircraft taking off, heading west into Laos in an attempt to cover the failed ARVN incursion. *More brave young men heading out into harm's way, and for what?*

Staley was tired. He slung his AK-47 over his left shoulder as he walked back to the Hoc Bao bivouac area. Things had gone from bad to worse in this operation. Bad enough we had G.I.s getting killed across the border to save the retreating ARVNs. Now we had Americans shooting other Americans to save themselves.

He thought about the saying he had learned from Wallace years before. *You can only be responsible for the things you can do something about.* At this point, he couldn't do anything about the ARVN incursion into Laos, and he couldn't do anything about the cowardly lieutenant who had tried to kill his pilot, but he could do something about the men he would be sent to recover tomorrow and the day after that and from then on until this operation was over. That was the best he could do under the circumstances, and it would have to be enough.

7

TRANSITION

December 1971

By December of 1971, much had happened to the men who were involved in the rescue of Captain Aaron Berman and First Lieutenant Robert McGowan following the shoot-down of their F-4 Phantom in southeastern Laos on March 21 of that year.

On April 2, just two weeks after leading the surface-to-air rescue mission to recover Captain Berman and Lieutenant McGowan, Colonel James Callahan was shot down while covering the rescue of another F-4 crew just west of the Laotian border. His wingman reported that the A1E Skyraider piloted by Colonel Callahan took several hits from two of the three 14.5-millimeter anti-aircraft guns that had been set up to ambush the rescue team. Colonel Callahan apparently suffered debilitating wounds and was unable to respond to calls from his wingman and the pilot of the H-53 Jolly Green Giant recovery helicopter on the scene. His Spad went inverted and crashed into the jungle just north of the Sepone River. There were no survivors. He was reported missing in action, but presumed dead due to the eyewitness accounts. His questions about what really had happened on the morning of March 21 were never answered.

When Captain Aaron Berman arrived at the aid station at Khe Sanh, his blood pressure was 60/30. The doctor who met the arriving medevac and administered initial treatment thought there was very little chance he would survive. Berman was given an immediate blood transfusion and a broad range of antibiotics in an effort to stabilize his condition. Later that day, a field surgeon performed an interim procedure on the pilot's left arm to permit closure of the wounds and avoid further complications. Berman had suffered a fractured skull and a concussion from the bullet wound to his forehead, which limited the treatment regimen since the doctor was uncertain of whether or not the patient had a more serious brain injury, perhaps a life-threatening blood clot. The wound in his right calf, which required thirteen stitches to close, became infected and initially did not respond to the antibiotics. That wound had to be reopened and retreated.

After almost two full days at the aid station, the doctor decided that Berman was stable enough to be moved to a rear area facility. He was flown by medical evacuation helicopter to the hospital at Quang Tri where he remained for two weeks, unconscious the entire time. It was during that stay that his left arm was amputated just below the shoulder. From there he was transferred to the Air Force hospital at Clark Air Force Base in the Philippines for further recovery and treatment.

After a while, his physical condition began to improve, but he was severely depressed upon discovery of the loss of his arm. Berman had no recollection of the events of March 21, after initiating the bomb run that resulted in his aircraft being shot down. He did not know until a month after the incident that his weapons systems officer, First Lieutenant Robert McGowan, had survived the shoot-down and had been rescued.

Berman remained in the Philippines until late September,

at which time he was transferred to the United States Air Force Medical Center at Keesler AFB, Mississippi, to begin his rehabilitation. It would be a long road back for Aaron Berman.

After his rescue from the jungles of Laos by the Hoc Bao, First Lieutenant Robert McGowan was debriefed in Quang Tri, then returned to his unit in Da Nang. There he was debriefed a second time. He recalled in the second debriefing how he had remained beside Captain Berman's unconscious body, his .38 at the ready, while the NVA came looking for them. He reported how he had held Berman close and kept him quiet as the first team of NVA searchers passed within twenty meters of their location. The blood on McGowan's flight suit, Berman's blood, made the account all the more convincing.

As the story circulated among the various units at Da Nang, McGowan became somewhat of a celebrity. He was recommended for a citation and eventually was awarded the Silver Star for gallantry in action. He even received a Congressional commendation at the instigation of Senator Winston, his old friend and mentor. The fact that no one was able to fully corroborate his story was lost in the enthusiasm of his commanding officer to ensure that his pilots and aircrews were well taken care of when it came to awards and decorations. No one had the time or the inclination to follow Berman to the Philippines to get his side of the story, and months later when he was finally capable of giving an interview to an officer investigating the incident, he confirmed that he could not remember anything after his aircraft was hit.

In November, 1971, McGowan rotated back to the United States and took advantage of the customary thirty-day leave to visit Senator Winston and his daughter Sarah. On Christmas Day of that year, Robert McGowan, Vietnam veteran and war hero, and Sarah Winston, daughter of Senator Randolph Winston, were formally engaged to be married. The evening of the engagement party, Senator Winston assured McGowan that he wouldn't have to be concerned about going back to Southeast Asia. The Senator had arranged for McGowan to complete his remaining military obligation at Andrews Air Force Base near Washington, D.C. Robert and Sarah would take a nice but modest house in Alexandria, Virginia, where they could be close to the Senator and McGowan could learn all that he needed to know to get started on a promising career in politics.

By the end of the first week of April, 1971, the unsuccessful and costly ARVN incursion into Laos was over. Khe Sanh was abandoned and all U.S. Army aviation units were redeployed to their respective base camps. The Hoc Bao was returned to the ARVN First Infantry Division and, eventually, transported back to Saigon. Consistent with the plan he and Traynor had discussed, Staley asked for and was given a release from the Hoc Bao, and two weeks later he made his way back to Hong Kong. There he once again became Hackler Staley and, on May 10, 1971, he returned to the United States.

Staley furnished Traynor a full written report of his activities while working with the Hoc Bao during Lam Son 719, including recommendations for aircraft utilization, tactics and downed aircrew recovery operations while operating in a high threat environment. He also described, in detail, a few specific incidents he had witnessed while engaged in rescue operations across the border, incidents that he believed worthy of follow-up by someone at the Pentagon. The most important of these, at least to Staley, was the attempted murder of an Air Force captain named Berman by his weapons systems officer, whose name Staley did not know. Along with his report, Staley included a plastic bag with the slug he had pried out of the dead log near the wounded pilot and the handful of cartridges he had removed from the weapons officer's pistol, along with the pilot's Cross pen and spiral notebook.

Traynor acknowledged receipt of the report but that was the last Staley ever heard of the matter. He understood that to a great extent, Traynor's hands were tied. There was no safe way to pass along the information in Staley's report without revealing that an American, or someone working for the Americans, was on the ground in Laos during the incursion. While the information Staley provided was important, it was not worth the risk of blowing the operation, which had been carried off without even a hint of suspicion.

During the last half of 1971, Staley received and successfully carried out one additional mission for Traynor. It was only a two-week assignment, but it was exceptionally important in that it involved a necessary action that directly contravened stated U.S. foreign policy. Traynor was delighted with the result and with the manner in which Staley approached and carried out the mission. It was the beginning of what both men expected to be long and mutually satisfactory relationship.

In December, 1971, with Traynor's approval, Staley submitted an application to attend the University of Missouri Business School at Columbia to start an MBA program. Traynor suggested the school because there was a retired colonel on the admissions committee who owed Traynor a favor from years before. Staley was surprised when his application received early consideration and was approved. He was admitted for the semester beginning in the fall of 1972.

Having nothing pressing to do in the meantime, Staley moved home to the old clapboard house just south of Joplin, Missouri, where he spent his days working around the farm, exercising, reading and waiting for another call from Traynor. He soon realized that from that point forward, waiting on the next call from Colonel Traynor would be the most important thing in his life.

Staley completed his course of study and received his MBA in December, 1973, with an emphasis in finance. Traynor attended the graduation ceremony. The next day, Staley left for South America on a mission that would prove to be one of the most dangerous of his career.

PART II
1999

8

RATHMANN

14 July 1999—Washington, D.C.

Retired Army Colonel Jonathan Traynor, looking all of his eighty-one years, sat quietly across the desk from Charles Q. Rathmann, the Director of Central Intelligence. Despite his passive demeanor toward the Director, Traynor disliked Rathmann intensely. He was a typical political appointee—extremely intelligent and a shrewd politician but with no practical experience and wholly unqualified for the job; a bright amateur in a position that demanded depth, commitment and a multi-dimensional understanding of international affairs. How Rathmann had made it past the Senate Select Committee on Intelligence was just about as baffling to Traynor as how Bill Clinton had managed to get re-elected in 1996. The world was changing. Traditional values and common sense were becoming outmoded. The MTV generation was taking over.

As Traynor sat there, sipping hot tea and waiting for Rathmann to gather himself sufficiently to be able to respond to Traynor's startling report that the operation was already in progress and could not be called off, he thought about all the times he and Sandy Colburn had sat across from one another like this, thinking and planning, orchestrating events that most observers never knew were influenced by the Agency. Those had been the good days, the *really* good days.

* * * * *

The arrangement between Jonathan Traynor and the CIA had worked exactly as Traynor and Sanders Colburn had envisioned when giving life to the project in 1970. Traynor served as an advisor to the Director and made suggestions where he thought appropriate, but he never pressed Colburn to reach the conclusion that deniable action was needed to deal with a particular problem. But when the cards fell that way, Traynor was given the job of making things right. The object of each engagement was results and that was what Traynor delivered. He worked entirely on his own and outside normal channels. He was never required to report the specifics of the missions he conducted or the identities of the men who worked for him. Colburn trusted him to maintain the strictest confidentiality and Traynor never let him down.

Just as promised by Traynor in his initial sales pitch, a totally deniable instrumentality of the Agency was found by the Director to be invaluable in accomplishing those tasks that could not be undertaken in the glare of public scrutiny. Although he held a titled position, the depth of Traynor's relationship with the Agency was known only to the Director.

Unfortunately, Sandy Colburn's tenure as the Director of Central Intelligence did not survive the political firestorm that followed the Watergate debacle. He tendered his resignation in early 1975, and it was reluctantly accepted by Gerald Ford. According to the polls, a majority of Americans, then paranoid about any secret governmental agency in any way identified with the Nixon administration, suspected that the CIA had provided support to the White House in managing the much talked about cover-up. Concerned that his continued presence would result in irreparable harm to the Agency,

Colburn decided that he should go.

The resignation of Sanders Colburn as Director of Central Intelligence had a serious adverse impact on the vital national interests of the United States, both at home and abroad. Had the truth been known, instead of calling for his resignation, the country would have rallied around Colburn for his brave and selfless actions in the aftermath of Watergate. But Colburn was not about to defend himself with the details of the work he had done following Watergate and during the investigation of the cover-up, some of it known only to Colburn, Traynor and a young man named Hackler Staley. Instead, he did the honorable thing and quietly withdrew from public life. Sometimes going down with the ship was part of the job, especially in the intelligence service. So, Sanders Colburn resigned.

Before leaving office, Colburn spent several hours with Traynor discussing whether or not to bring the new Director in on the secret of Traynor's activities on behalf of the Agency. The new Director designate, who had not yet been confirmed by the Senate, had a reputation for toughness and honesty. He had spent the previous twenty years as a diplomat. But before that he'd held several jobs in the intelligence community, including a brief stint with Naval Intelligence during World War II, during which time he had made the acquaintance of the young Sanders Colburn. Colburn had not worked with the man for almost thirty years, but based on his recollection of their prior dealings and the uniformly favorable comments received in Colburn's private investigation of the appointee, he decided they should trust him. Traynor agreed.

It turned out to be a good decision. By the time Charles Allan Reece was formally confirmed by the Senate, he had already faced a serious international crisis and in connection with that problem had given Traynor an assignment that carried on the tradition established by Colburn.

Under Reece, Traynor continued in his role as Special Assistant to the Director of Central Intelligence, although with not quite the same level of comfort he had had with his lifetime friend, Sanders Colburn. But nevertheless, Reece and Traynor worked together well and effectively.

Reece's tenure as Director of the CIA lasted only three years, at which time the process was repeated of trying to decide whether or not to bring the new Director into the circle and attempt to continue the project. Reece and Traynor were well aware, as was Colburn in making the same decision years before, that the more people who knew about the special operations unit, the greater the risk of exposure.

It was in connection with briefing the second Director-designate that Traynor came up with the idea of advising the new appointee about the availability of Traynor's services, but not disclosing any prior activities. Since there were no files, there was no institutional memory of the missions Traynor had conducted on behalf of the Agency. And because almost every mission assigned to Traynor involved serious violations of Federal law, no outgoing Director had any interest in making known the Agency's involvement in the missions conducted by Traynor during that Director's tenure. Making sure there was never a record of any Traynor-run operation made it possible for Jonathan to continue with his work.

Despite inquiries by several Directors over the years concerning the names and backgrounds of the men who worked for Traynor, that information was never disclosed. In fact, only one man actually worked for Traynor, and that was Hackler Staley. From the very beginning, Staley's identity was carefully protected by Traynor. Non-disclosure of any information concerning his operatives was an essential, although sometimes unpopular, condition of Traynor's engagement. Traynor knew that Staley would not accept any assignment without the assurance of total anonymity, and moreover, Traynor wanted to ensure that if he went down, he would not take Staley with him.

Keeping both Traynor's connection with the Agency and Staley's identity secret was an ongoing problem, especially on those missions where Staley required outside assistance. But Traynor always figured out a way to wire around the problem. Any logistical support that Staley needed on an operation was performed by free-lance operatives hired by blind intermediaries engaged by an offshore Traynor entity. The support personnel were given incorrect or misleading information concerning Staley and had no idea that they were working for Traynor or, indirectly, for the CIA. Security was breached only twice in all the years they had worked together, and Staley had handled both of those situations on an impromptu and permanent basis.

By 1999, Traynor had for almost thirty years conducted clandestine intelligence and special action operations around the world with the knowledge of only the then-serving Director of Central Intelligence and Staley. During that entire time, Traynor never failed to carry out an assigned mission and never requested direct Agency assistance to get the job done.

Traynor had been requested to relinquish the title of Special Assistant to the Director of Central Intelligence shortly after the Iran Contra affair, in order to create greater separation between him and the Agency, but he continued in essentially the same role as a special consultant for intelligence matters. As each new Director came and went, knowledge of the operations conducted by

Traynor was the most closely guarded secret of the job. No Director ever rejected the opportunity to use Traynor's services and none ever went public with information concerning the relationship, for two very good reasons.

First, each Director quickly realized that Traynor offered an invaluable service to the country that likely could not be duplicated by utilizing on-the-record Agency personnel. An asset like Traynor was something that every intelligence chief had at the top of his wish list but few ever saw materialize. It would have been crazy to blow the whistle on Traynor. He was just too valuable, and besides, exposing Traynor would have by necessity implicated the Director who had given him the illegal assignments.

Second, while none ever gave voice to the concern, every Director after Charles Allen Reece secretly feared Traynor. His dedication to the job and his demonstrated ability to carry out difficult missions without hesitation and in absolute secrecy were truly remarkable. He had proven that he was both willing and capable of undertaking any project that he believed was in the best interests of America, including, when necessary, assassination. No Director was really certain how far Jonathan Traynor might go, or what the men who worked for him might do, if Traynor were exposed. For some, that concern became a significant consideration in their decision to punctiliously observe the rules set out by Traynor for maintaining the confidentiality of the relationship.

So, Jonathan Traynor, his role with the CIA still a mystery to even the Deputy Directors of the Agency after twenty-nine years of service, continued to function in the capacity he and Sanders Colburn had discussed that spring morning in 1970 in the mountains of northern Maryland. And partly because of that relationship, by 1999 the United

States had become the most powerful and influential nation on earth, without serious challenge, even from its traditional Cold War enemies.

But Bill Clinton's March, 1999 appointment of Charles Rathmann had complicated things to the point that Traynor had considered more than once bringing the entire operation to a halt and retiring. Rathmann was preoccupied with self-importance, a politician whose principal objective was preserving his position and enhancing his personal status.

Immediately after their introductory meeting, at which the outgoing Director briefed Rathmann on the role Traynor *might* play in carrying out the Agency's business, Rathmann secretly took the unprecedented step of bringing someone else into the loop. While Rathmann appreciated the potential benefits of having a totally deniable resource solely at his disposal, he also was concerned that he might need some cover if a Traynor-run operation went wrong.

So without seeking the advice of either the outgoing Director or Traynor, and without informing either man of what he intended to do, Rathmann decided to share all the information he had learned about Traynor and the services he offered with the senior minority member of the Senate Select Committee on Intelligence, Senator Robert J. McGowan.

Rathmann's unchallenged confirmation as Director was due principally to effective behind-the-scenes lobbying by Senator McGowan, who for undisclosed reasons had been the obscure politician's chief supporter. Following the near-unanimous vote of confirmation by the full Senate, McGowan made it clear to Rathmann that he expected something in return for his unwavering support, and in this case that *something* meant current, non-public information concerning the Agency's activities, because in Washington politics, information is the currency of power. Rathmann understood the trade and committed himself to faithfully carrying out his responsibilities to the Senator.

The first Traynor mission approved by Charles Rathmann was the assassination of Azbek Fahoud. Reliable intelligence sources reported that the world's most notorious terrorist had made arrangements to purchase a nuclear device from the Russian mafia. After being briefed by Rathmann, the White House directed the CIA to "interdict" the transaction, without specific instructions or authorization concerning how the Agency might proceed. However, the National Security Advisor made it clear that the receipt by Fahoud of a nuclear weapon would be unacceptable to the United States, either now or in the future, and that the CIA was charged with ensuring that eventuality did not occur. Faced with these orders, Rathmann determined that targeting Fahoud personally was the only logical course of action; however, because of his international visibility and his position as the political leader of a well-recognized group in the Middle East, the United States government could not openly, or even covertly, be involved in eliminating Fahoud. Feeling boxed-in, Rathmann turned to Jonathan Traynor.

Traynor studied the evidence against Fahoud and reviewed the intelligence briefs. The following day he advised Rathmann that the pending transaction with Alexandrov would never occur. He also advised the Director that Fahoud would not be in a position to arrange another. Rathmann acknowledged Traynor's report, thanking him for his assistance.

A week later, after the mission was already in progress, Rathmann disclosed the details of the Fahoud matter to his patron, Senator Robert McGowan, including the direction he had received from the White House and his engagement of Jonathan Traynor to handle the matter.

McGowan was incensed that Rathmann had commissioned the assassination of a foreign national to someone with direct ties to the Agency, and he told him so in a lengthy diatribe rife with criticism of the Director's judgment. Secretly, McGowan was even more incensed that Rathmann had had the incredibly poor judgment to bring McGowan in on the project.

McGowan could not allow himself to be in any way associated with the Fahoud operation. Even his knowing about it would be damning if something went wrong. So he did the only thing he could think of to avoid possible adverse consequences. He directed Rathmann to call off the mission. It was too risky.

Rathmann, who had originally been so certain of the course of action he should take, was now confused. The instructions from the White House had been clear: stop the delivery of the nuclear device and make sure the threat would not resurface again later. He was obliged to do *something,* but perhaps he had gone too far in engaging Traynor to kill Fahoud. Maybe there were other ways to comply with the orders he'd been given. Maybe he had acted too hastily. McGowan probably was right. No, he *was* right. It was time to tell Traynor that the mission had to be cancelled.

Rathmann left a message for Traynor to see him first thing the next morning. The meeting got off to a very poor start.

"Thank you for coming in so early, Colonel. I wanted to bring you in on my decision regarding the Fahoud matter just as soon as possible. I've given the matter further consideration and decided that it would best be handled by our operations group. Let's just forget our discussion of this matter a few days ago. Please do not take any further action."

Traynor was dumbfounded. In all the years he had worked with the various directors of the Agency, nothing like this had ever happened. Barely maintaining his composure, he said, "It's too late for that, Mr. Director. As H. R. Haldeman once said during the days following Watergate, 'Once the toothpaste is out of the tube, it's very difficult to put it back in again.' The operation we discussed is in progress. There are several people involved, all working in a blind environment with only the principal operative having ultimate knowledge of the objective. It cannot be stopped with a phone call. It cannot be stopped at all."

Rathmann became animated. "What do you mean it can't be stopped? You set it up, you can stop it. Call off the mission, Colonel, and I mean *now*."

Remaining impassive, Traynor replied, "You have no idea what you're dealing with, Mr. Director. The complexities of matters such as these are well beyond the depth of your experience. Accept my word for it. I seriously doubt that I am capable of bringing the operation to a halt, for any reason, no matter how important."

Then, with a squint of his hard gray eyes and a hint of curiosity in his voice, Traynor asked the critical questions. "*Why* do you want the project stopped? What has happened to change your mind? Has there been a security leak, or have your orders been changed? What am I missing here?"

In an obvious state of vexation, Rathmann buckled. "I've discussed this matter with a trusted advisor, a man who's been around this town for a while and whose judgment I value. He concurs with me that this is not the right way to go. I acted too quickly. The operation must be called off."

Traynor leaned forward in his chair, stunned by

Rathmann's admission. "You did *what?* With whom did you discuss this matter? This is of utmost importance, Mr. Director. I need to know! *Who?*"

Rathmann lowered his eyes and said in a quiet voice, "Senator Robert McGowan. He's a brilliant leader and can be trusted to maintain a confidence. He thinks we should proceed differently and I agree with him. I've brought him in on several other matters over the past few months and his advice has always been right on target. I think he's right this time too."

Traynor's blood pressure hit the red line. It was the worst possible news. *McGowan, of all people! Rathmann's a fool, and a dangerous fool at that.*

His eyes boring into Rathmann, Traynor asked, "Have you told him about me, about my availability for deniable operations? Surely you haven't disclosed that, have you?"

Rathmann squirmed, "Well, yes, I've told him some of it."

"What do you mean, 'some of it'? Do you not recall our agreement that my relationship with the Agency was to remain absolutely confidential, that nothing about our relationship was ever to be disclosed outside the two of us? Have you breached that agreement, Mr. Director?"

"As I said, I've told him some of it. I've told him that which I believe he needs to know in order to provide the input I need when seeking his advice. Keep in mind that I have no information on any operations you might have conducted for the Agency in the past, Colonel, so there is nothing about you to tell, other than, of course, your potential involvement in pending matters. He did mention once that he was aware of some vague whisperings concerning you, that you had a somewhat *sinister* reputation. But you know that's meaningless."

Traynor just stared at Rathmann, obviously incensed at

the Director's flagrant violation of what Traynor understood to be an iron-clad agreement.

The silence became uncomfortable. Rathmann tried to
rationalize what he now realized was a major miscalcula-
tion. "Listen, Colonel, the Senator is my friend and a
source of wise counsel, and he most likely will be the next
President. I think it's fair to assume that he can be trusted
with highly secret information."

Traynor looked away and shook his head in resignation.
"You have no idea of the harm you may have done." After a
few seconds, he turned back to Rathmann. "Nevertheless,
the Fahoud operation is on, and neither you nor I nor your
friend Robert McGowan can stop it."

Rathmann slipped off his reading glasses, closed his eyes
as if in pain and tightly pinched the bridge of his sharp, thin
nose between the thumb and forefinger of his right hand.

Traynor leaned back in the deep leather chair fronting
Rathmann's desk, picked up the fine china cup from the
side table and sipped his tea. He could almost hear the
wheels grinding in the Director's head. The politician had
no idea what to do next. He had been completely surprised
by Traynor's unequivocal statement that the cancellation
order was too late and there was no way to stop the independent agent now enroute to carry out the mission. The
Director of the CIA was completely lost, his lack of experience in intelligence matters bubbling to the top.

While Jonathan Traynor continued to sit quietly, his outward appearance once again calm and totally composed, inside he was seething. That Rathmann had disclosed to
McGowan—*McGowan* of all people—knowledge of Traynor
in general and of the Fahoud mission in particular had sealed
it for Traynor. His relationship with this Director and with
the Agency was over. Fahoud would be the final mission.

Finally, Rathmann stopped pinching his nose, opened his eyes and replaced his glasses. He had made a decision.

"Listen, Colonel, I have an appointment in about ten minutes that I need to take. Can you meet me back here at one o'clock? We'll decide what to do at that time. In the meantime, see if you can come up with some alternatives for stopping the operation."

"That will be fine, Mr. Director," Traynor said tightly. "I'll see you at one, but I don't expect to have any alternatives. As I said earlier, these kinds of operations are very difficult to set up and cannot be cancelled with a simple phone call. The contract *will* be completed."

Traynor rose and started for the door, and just before reaching it turned and said, "I'm very disappointed with the way you've handled this matter, Mr. Director, *very* disappointed."

The tone of that comment caused chills to run up Rathmann's spine. He too was secretly afraid of Traynor.

Traynor grasped the brass doorknob and started to open the door, then turned slightly. Not looking directly at Rathmann, he added one final comment. "The Fahoud operation will be my last for the Agency. After this one, I'm through. I only wish I could leave our nation's senior intelligence organization in more capable hands. Good morning."

Before Rathmann could answer, Traynor slipped out and closed the door.

9

MCGOWAN

14 July 1999—Washington, D.C.

Senator Robert J. McGowan was sitting at the large mahogany desk in his office in the Hart Senate Office Building. He was looking over some recent polling data when Hazel Farnsworth, his long-time secretary, buzzed in.

"Senator, CIA Director Rathmann calling. Do you want to take it?"

As the senior minority member of the Senate Select Committee on Intelligence, McGowan often had official business with Charles Rathmann, the Director of Central Intelligence, but more often than not these days, the two men spoke off the record with respect to matters that should not have been discussed by the Director with anyone—even a ranking member of the Committee.

Off to the side of the large blotter that filled the work space in front of McGowan was a draft of a canned speech that one of his staffers had prepared for the Senator's upcoming trip back home, the annual one where he drove around the state and talked with constituents in courthouses, shopping malls, corner drug stores, union halls and high school gymnasiums.

McGowan was a man of the people, or at least that was his image. His speech had to have just the right touch of concern for the status quo, enthusiasm for the future and dedication to the issues that would make a difference. The

144

draft on his desk was pitiful—a really poor effort. McGowan often wondered how the hell the people that worked for him ever expected to get anywhere in politics if they couldn't write a speech that closed the sale. He seemed to be the only one who had the right touch, and remarkably enough, even those staffers that had worked for him for years could not quite master the art. It was frustrating and time consuming, but he believed that one day soon, all the hard work would reward him with the top job—the one he had been thinking about and planning for since the seventh grade, when he had won his first election to the student council.

McGowan was absolutely convinced that some day he would be the President of the United States. People had been commenting for years that he just, "looked presidential." He was fifty-seven years old, had the face of a men's fashion magazine model, was in excellent shape and had close-cropped gray hair that reminded people of Jeff Chandler. Whatever "charisma" is, he had it.

It was said that visitors in the Senate gallery could feel the electricity when he walked into the chamber—even those who could not see him immediately because of their position in the back rows of the gallery were reported to have felt it. The lights at a cocktail party seemed to brighten wherever he circulated among the crowd. People were attracted to him everywhere he went. Even in a pair of jeans and a dirty sweatshirt while working on a charity home renovation project, he had an aura that made people want to see him, want to be around him, want to listen to whatever he might have to say. Women threw themselves at him unashamedly, although he had dealt with that problem by carefully maintaining a perfect marriage. His popularity cut across all age brackets. From the rap music crowd to the

AARP, McGowan was the man.

An aging senator from the Deep South had said it best in an interview with *Newsweek*. Robert McGowan was the best politician anyone in Washington had ever seen. He was strong on all the right issues and innovative when sitting on the fence, finding merit in conflicting positions without angering either side. He had no flaws, no weak points, no vulnerabilities of any kind.

And that was not by accident. McGowan had been working to perfect that image for as long as he could remember.

Hazel Farnsworth was probably the only person who could get away with pressuring her boss on anything. Right then she needed an answer.

"Shall I tell Director Rathmann you'll call him back, or do you want to take the call?"

McGowan really did not want to talk with Rathmann that morning, but it was a contact that had to be nurtured and cultivated. Further analysis of the polling data could wait, as could rewriting the speech.

"Yeah, I guess so," McGowan sighed. "Put him on."

McGowan waited for the click, signifying that the connection had been made.

"Morning, Mr. Director. What can I do for you today?"

"We have a matter of some importance over here that I'd like to discuss with you in your capacity as the senior minority member of the Committee. If convenient, I'd really appreciate it if you could come over during the noon hour, maybe twelve-thirty or a quarter 'til one."

Rathmann's presumptive arrogance always annoyed McGowan. He did not appreciate being summoned by anyone, not even someone holding the high office of Director of Central Intelligence. But having Rathmann in place at the Agency was part of McGowan's long-range plan, so he needed to handle the matter more cordially than he felt about the intrusion.

"Any chance we could put this off until tomorrow or the next day? I'm busier'n hell this afternoon."

"Actually, we need to do this today, before one o'clock. It's a very important matter of national security on which I need the benefit of your thoughts. I'll explain when you get here. Can you possibly make it?"

McGowan checked his calendar. He had a scheduled vote on some environmental legislation right after lunch and a three p.m. meeting with some folks who wanted to form a political action committee to support his rumored presidential campaign. He could miss the vote—the measure was sure to pass and his record on the environment was as pure as the driven snow—but there was no way he could miss the meeting with the money people. Senator Winston had once told him, "Son, you can tell everybody in the world to kiss your ass, *except* the minorities, the labor unions and people who want to give you big money. They're the ones who'll make or break your career in this town."

Rathmann seemed insistent, and it was important to McGowan that he continue his close working relationship with the Director, so he agreed.

"Certainly, Mr. Director. I'll clear my calendar and see you around twelve-thirty. But I'll have to be back here no later than two-thirty or so."

"Thanks, Senator. That will be more than enough time. I appreciate it. See you at twelve-thirty."

When Jonathan Traynor was shown into Director Charles Rathmann's office at one p.m. that afternoon, he was stunned to find United States Senator Robert J. McGowan seated in the black leather chair opposite the Director's desk. The Director had broken yet another of the cardinal rules that Traynor had made clear to him during their very first meeting. Discussions between them were never to take place in the presence of others. There were to be no exceptions to that rule. *None*. Rathmann continued to disappoint.

Traynor had never met McGowan, but he recognized him immediately. McGowan was a national figure, much more than just another senator from an unremarkable midwestern state. He was gaining popularity and rumor had it that he most likely would be the Democratic candidate for President of the United States in the 2000 election. According to recent polls, McGowan was the front-runner of all the unannounced candidates. It was assumed that if he ran and won the nomination over the incumbent vice president, McGowan probably would win the general election as well.

For reasons known only to him, Traynor despised McGowan. But that was not the issue right now—the issue was the possibility, suggested by McGowan's presence, of discussing the Fahoud operation with an outsider, and a political outsider at that. Even though Rathmann had told him that the Senator knew all about the Fahoud operation, Traynor had decided that he would not discuss the matter in McGowan's presence.

Trying his best to avoid the encounter, Traynor nodded apologetically to Rathmann and said, "I'm sorry, Mr. Director, I thought you were alone. I'll come back later."

"No, come in, Colonel. There's someone here I want you to meet."

"I really can't right now, I have something that requires my attention. I'll . . ."

The Director cut him off, and with a confident smile said, "Come now, Colonel Traynor, have a seat. I suspect you recognize Senator McGowan. I want you to meet him. And besides, we do need to continue our discussion of the matter we started on this morning."

Traynor was furious, but stepped inside and closed the door. It was obvious that McGowan's presence had given Rathmann some backbone. The Fahoud matter *was* going to be discussed.

The Senator stood and offered Traynor his hand. The old man ignored him and sat down in the easy chair far removed from Rathmann's desk. McGowan retreated to his chair, surprised at the old man's reaction. Most people wilted in the presence of Robert McGowan.

He nodded at McGowan. "Senator," he said flatly.

Traynor's normally blank face evidenced his disdain for the man. He remembered in great detail the story Staley had told him about the F-4 crew his Hoc Bao unit had recovered in Laos during the final days of the 1971 ARVN incursion. And he remembered the file he had put together on the young first lieutenant Staley had suspected of attempting to murder his wounded pilot. After all these years, even Staley did not know that one of the men he had rescued that day in Laos, one of the men who owed his life to Staley and to the Hoc Bao mercenaries he had illegally led across the border, was Robert McGowan, the man most likely to become the next President of the United States of America.

Although Traynor had all the facts, he had never taken any action against McGowan, and at this late date, he probably could not do so. While he had hard evidence against McGowan in the form of the spent slug, the matching cartridges and other evidence assembled by Traynor after the fact, he had no eyewitness testimony. In view of the illegal nature of the operation being conducted by Traynor and Staley at the time that evidence was collected, the veracity of the case against McGowan surely would be called into question. And perhaps more importantly, prosecution for the attempted murder of Aaron Berman, if it could be proven, probably would be barred by the statute of limitations.

Still, the issue of McGowan's treachery had simmered inside Traynor for years. He had never been able to let it go, especially with McGowan's gradual rise to political prominence over the past two decades.

McGowan could sense the animosity coming from Traynor, but he had no intention of being cowed by this old man. He smiled an insincere smile and said with a hint of sarcasm, "Well, Colonel Traynor, it's a pleasure to meet you at last. You're rather like a ghost, you know. I feel like I'm in the presence of one of the great spies of all time."

McGowan had no use for Traynor or the super-secret James Bond nonsense the morons at Langley had used for years as an excuse to spend American tax dollars. And he certainly had no use for state sponsored assassination, even of a master terrorist like Fahoud. If it became known that McGowan knew about the Fahoud operation and did nothing to stop it, his political career would be in serious jeopardy.

While the Senator was pleased with the inroads he had made in co-opting the Director of Central Intelligence, it was not without a price. Now that he was privy to many of the operations being conducted out of Langley, he had to be careful that nothing occurred that was outside the law or that could harm him politically if it wound up on the front page of the *Washington Post*.

Based on the results of three nationwide polls secretly

funded by the prestigious Winston Foundation, McGowan had decided to make cleaning up the CIA a major issue in his political platform. That was part of the reason he was so instrumental in selecting the current director. McGowan was publicly committed to stop wasting tax money on field agents and, instead, to focus on enhancing the capabilities of the Agency through technological advancements. The days of assassinations, clandestine meetings and one-time pads were over. It was time to get rid of the dead wood and rebuild America's intelligence agencies in the image McGowan had in mind. Technology would lead the way. Computers did not take bribes and could not be persuaded to change sides. No more spy scandals. It would sell at the polls. No one could convince him to the contrary.

Traynor could hear the sarcasm in McGowan's voice and it made him all the more angry. God only knew how much Rathmann had told McGowan about the Fahoud project. Probably everything. The good news was that the Fahoud mission was the first undertaken for Rathmann, and in keeping with historical precedent, Rathmann had no knowledge of the operations conducted by Traynor in the past.

Traynor's anger and his disdain for the slick Senator were evident in his quiet, raspy reply. "I'm not a spy, Senator. I never have been. My career was in the military. The men who work for me these days simply handle the occasional unpleasant matter here and there, when and as requested by the Director. They are the ones who stand ready to accomplish whatever needs to be done. I'm just a facilitator."

McGowan could not resist a little verbal jousting with the crusty old bastard. "Who *are* these men who work for you, Colonel?" Then looking at the Director, "I'd like to meet them, maybe find out something about their backgrounds. Do you suppose they are the kind of men the

American people would want acting on their behalf?" Then looking back at Traynor, "Are you certain they are in fact acting on America's behalf, Colonel, or are they just mercenaries, paid thugs?"

Traynor realized that McGowan had been called in by Rathmann to intimidate Traynor and take charge of a situation that Rathmann had allowed to spin out of control. McGowan's sharp words were intended to put Traynor on the defensive. It was almost amusing.

Rathmann doesn't believe me. He thinks that McGowan will be able to pressure me into calling off the Fahoud operation. These two have no idea what they're dealing with.

Then it occurred to Traynor that this was going to be the meeting he had secretly looked forward to for years. He had recently discovered within himself the broad range of emotions that normal people routinely experienced. He regarded it as a disappointing side effect of aging, something that could not be avoided and that perhaps made him unsuitable to continue in his present position, even if Rathmann had not made doing so quite impossible. In that moment, staring at Robert McGowan, he could feel his self-discipline slipping away. It was an unpleasant experience.

And so, knowing he should remain passive, but unable to sit quietly in the presence of a man he had despised for almost thirty years, Traynor answered, his anger just below the surface. He leaned forward in his chair and virtually spit the words at the Senator, "Believe me, Senator, the men who have worked for me over the years are owed a great debt of gratitude by this country. The American people would be proud to know their story."

He then added, "Unlike the stories behind many of today's very visible politicians, including some who have aspirations for high office."

The implication was clear. It was a direct attack on McGowan. The Senator was not used to being talked to in such a manner.

"Is that so, Colonel? Then why not give me the names of your agents and I'll tell their story? I've always suspected that these so-called 'black' operations, if known, would bring great shame on America. Tell us, who does your dirty work?"

Suddenly aware that his idea for a meeting between Traynor and McGowan was a rapidly developing disaster, Rathmann said, "Please, gentlemen. There is no need to go down this road any further. There is another matter that we need to discuss and resolve. I've asked Senator McGowan to join us in order to obtain the benefit of his counsel. Can we proceed?"

But Traynor would not let it go. He looked McGowan straight in the eye and said quietly but with no hint of trepidation, "Let me be very frank with you, Senator. I don't like you and I don't trust you. And I have good reason. I know more about your past than you might suspect. And believe me, you don't want what I know to ever see the light of day."

And then, almost as an afterthought, Traynor added, "And as for your political aspirations, I'm confident you have neither the courage nor the integrity to serve this country as its President."

McGowan was speechless. No one had ever questioned his character before, not *ever*, and no one had had the nerve to speak to him in that manner since he was a first-term Congressman. He was an all-American hero, a decorated veteran of the Vietnam War, a perfect husband and a loving father, and a model public servant. He had faced all kinds of difficult challenges in his political career and had come through each with flying colors, and in most cases an enhanced following. McGowan's record was squeaky clean and he knew it. *What in the world could the old man be talking about?*

He stood up and towered over the frail Traynor. He could not let that statement go unchallenged, even in the privacy of the Director's office.

"I don't give a damn who you are or what you've done, Traynor. Or what you claim to have done or what you claim to know. No one talks to me that way. It's a matter of honor with me, something you obviously know very little about."

Remaining seated, Traynor responded sharply, "Oh, that's where you're wrong, Senator. I know a great deal about honor, and about bravery, and about service to this country. And I know something about caring and taking responsibility for my fellow man and the kind of sacrifice that evidences that caring. And I also know a brave man who's worked with me for almost thirty years, one of those men who's done America's 'dirty work' as you call it, and he knows more about honor than you'll ever know. But more to the point, because of that brave man, I know about you, McGowan. I've often wondered if I should do anything about what I know. I'm still considering that option."

McGowan was stunned by Traynor's answer. For the first time in years, he felt a twinge of fear in the pit of his stomach. "What are you talking about, Traynor? What do you think you know and what does one of your henchmen have to do with me?"

Traynor considered his next move carefully. Quietly he said, "Mr. Director, would you mind very much leaving me alone with the Senator for just a moment? What I have to say to him would best be said in private."

Rathmann was angry with both men and did not appre-

154

ciate the suggestion that he leave his own office. But with a nod from the Senator and in deference to Traynor, he rose and walked to the door. "I suppose you know that I don't like this, but I'll give you five minutes. I'm going down the hall to check on something. I'd appreciate it if you'd settle this amicably before I return."

As soon as the door was shut, McGowan spun on Traynor. "Let's have it, Colonel."

"Does the date 21 March 1971 mean anything to you, Senator?"

Of course it meant something to him. It was a date he would never forget. It was the most terrifying day in his life, one he was sure he would never survive. But he did survive, and the official account of that action had been the springboard that had launched his entire political career. He had accepted the recognition and adulation first with relief, then with pride. His story—how he had found and treated his wounded pilot and stayed with him until being routed by an overwhelming enemy force—had been written up in *Time* and *Newsweek* and he had been labeled a hero. His celebrity had propelled him into the limelight and he had made the most of it—first the state legislature, then several terms in the House, then on to the Senate.

Despite his intelligence, his charisma and his effectiveness as a legislator, throughout his career he had been known first and foremost as a war hero. While he could take full credit for all the success he had achieved in every elected position he had ever held, at the root of it all was the 1971 incident on the Ho Chi Minh Trail. It had been his ticket to the big dance. But despite his remarkable rise to power, McGowan knew there was one thing that could bring it all down. It was the dark secret of the horrible thing he had done that day in Laos—a secret that McGowan had

155

resolved to take to his grave.

And now, Traynor seemed to be indicating that he knew something about the events of that day. *How could he possibly know anything? No one else was there! Berman couldn't have told anyone. Sure, he had survived, but he didn't remember anything.* McGowan had checked up on Berman several times in the years after the crash. Berman's report was clean. It squared with McGowan's story.

But nevertheless, the fear of exposure tightened the Senator's throat as he fought to remain calm. "Sure, I remember the date. I was a first lieutenant in the Air Force, flying out of Da Nang in the northern part of South Vietnam. As you probably know, I was a weapons systems officer—the back-seater—in an F-4 Phantom configured as an attack aircraft. That morning we were flying close air support for the South Vietnamese Army during their invasion of Laos. We were holding it right down on the deck, trying to keep the NVA tanks off an ARVN unit about eight miles west of the border. The situation was desperate. The troops on the ground were in big trouble. We had to get down low and slow in order to be effective."

McGowan had a distant look in his eye as he easily recalled the narrative in the citation for his Silver Star. The words came with practiced sincerity.

"As we banked around a hillside on our first bomb run, an NVA anti-aircraft gun ripped through our Phantom. Both engines spooled down. We had fire lights on the panel and warning horns going off in our helmets. The pilot, a captain named Berman, was hit bad. I helped him through the emergency procedures and we both ejected. We hit the ground about two hundred meters apart. I fought my way through the jungle and found Berman. He was bleeding to death. I made a tourniquet for his arm, or what was left of it, and administered first aid. He was in terrible pain and finally passed out. I was sure he'd never wake up.

"I stayed with him as long as possible, but I realized I'd have to get help for him soon or he'd die. I took my .38 and scouted the area, in case there were any NVA close by. When I felt it was okay to leave him, I moved out to try to find an open area to call for help on his emergency radio. Mine was lost in the ejection. I heard a noise and went back to investigate. When NVA soldiers came into the clearing, I thought about trying to take them on, but there were too many of them and I had only six shots. Before I could take any kind of decisive action, they shot Berman. They shot him in cold blood as I watched from the bushes. There was nothing I could do.

"I managed to slip away into the jungle. A short while later, a rescue team of mercenaries hired by the Vietnamese to recover downed flight crews found me. I told them where to find Berman but they wouldn't let me lead them to the spot where he had been shot. I was sure he was dead, but it was important to me that we recover his body. Part of the rescue team went to find Berman and the others led me out. The mercenaries called in some Army helicopters. They picked us up and took me back to Khe Sanh for debriefing. That was pretty much it."

"Nicely recited, Senator, but that's not quite the way it happened, is it?"

"Of course it is. What the hell are you talking about?"

"I think it was more like this. Yes, you and Captain Berman were flying the mission, just the way you described it, and you were shot down just the way you described it. And you found the wounded Captain Berman just the way you described it. But that's where the story gets a little fuzzy, don't you think?"

"It's not at all fuzzy to me, Traynor. It happened just the way I said. Surely you can't dispute it. You weren't there and neither was anyone else. What's your game here?"

Traynor gave McGowan his best icy smile. "No, I was not there, Senator. But a young man who had just started working for me *was* there. He's the one who led the rescue team that was inserted to pull you out and he was the one that eventually found Captain Berman and got him out as well. You *do* remember the young Frenchman, do you not?"

McGowan felt a cold chill on the back of his neck. He'd thought the Frenchman was probably dead. He'd never heard another thing about him after the rescue. *Where could he be now? But so what? He couldn't know anything. Could he?*

"Sure, I remember him. If it hadn't been for him and his mercenaries, I wouldn't be here. But I don't understand. His story, if truthful, should corroborate my account of what happened."

"Not exactly, Senator. You see, according to the Frenchman, you abandoned Captain Berman. You left him for dead. And when the rescue team found you cowering in the jungle, you were less than cooperative in directing them to his location. After my associate found Captain Berman, he realized why. Captain Berman had been shot all right. Shot in the head. And although the wound was made much later than the wounds incurred as a result of the anti-aircraft fire, it was not inflicted by a North Vietnamese Army AK-47. Rather, it was made by a .38 caliber revolver, the personal weapon carried by Air Force pilots, just like the .38 you had in your possession when you were found by the rescue team. Incidentally, the Frenchman found the slug that creased Captain Berman's head in the log where he had been resting before being shot and returned that slug to me. Lab analysis conclusively identified it as a .38 slug, U.S.

military issue. The very same ammunition the Frenchman removed from your pistol before returning it to you.

"You may recall that before returning your .38 to you there in the jungle, the Frenchman emptied your .38 and in doing so, found that one round had been fired. The firing of that single round was never part of your story, Senator, and I know why. You see, all of the evidence taken together leads to only one conclusion. It was not the NVA that shot the already wounded and unconscious Captain Berman. It was *you*."

McGowan was sick. But he had been in enough tough spots to not let it show.

"How *dare* you make such an accusation? That story is absolutely preposterous and totally untrue. You're basing all of this on a thirty-year-old report from some French mercenary? Come on, Colonel. That's never going to fly and you know it."

"No, Senator. I'm absolutely certain that it's true, and I've got the spent .38 slug, the matching cartridges from your pistol and some other very interesting physical evidence to prove it. The young man you remember as the French mercenary is the most honest and trustworthy of all the men I've ever worked with in this business. The special position he held with the team that rescued you was his first assignment for me and he's been with me ever since. Because of what he discovered that day in Laos, he submitted a special report on the mission. It was very detailed and very thorough and I followed it up with my own investigation.

"The inevitable conclusion was very clear. *You* shot Captain Berman. You shot Berman to save your own life and you abandoned him in the jungle to rot. And then, to make matters worse, you tried to divert the rescue team away from his position, not even having the decency to see to it that his body was recovered.

"Now, Senator, I don't care if you have some lame excuse as to why you shot your wounded pilot that day in Laos—maybe you've rationalized it in your own mind to the point that you believe what you did was acceptable behavior. The fact is, I don't want to hear your story. It's too late now to try to explain. You've built a career on a lie. You're a fraud, McGowan, a liar and a fraud. Instead of basking in the limelight, you should be seeking forgiveness and reconciliation—from the American people generally, and *specifically* from Aaron Berman."

McGowan sat very still, glaring at Traynor, trying to decide what he might be able to do to control whatever damage the old man might cause.

Traynor, sensing what was running through McGowan's mind, broke the silence. "But there is a bright spot. I've had this information for a very long time now Senator, and to this point I've never seen any compelling reason to make it public. I'd probably have to trade information on years of covert activities just to bring you down, and quite frankly, up to now you haven't been worth it. So long as you simply spin your ideology before the cameras and posture here and there in the Senate, the story of your treachery can remain undisclosed."

Traynor then leaned forward to emphasize his next point.

"But I cannot allow you to become the President the United States without the country knowing the true story. Who knows? Maybe the people of this great nation won't care. They've ignored reprehensible behavior in a President before. Your friend in the White House is evidence of that.

"So, my advice to you is this. Before making any decisions

with respect to your political future, I'd suggest you consider the likelihood that not only will you not win the presidency, but you may never be able to run for public office again."

McGowan was struck dumb. All he could do was stare at the old man, hatred glistening in his eyes.

Traynor braced himself to his feet, slightly unsteady from the exertion. He started toward the door, then stopped only a few feet from McGowan. He looked the Senator squarely in the eye and said quietly, "Give it some thought, McGowan. In the meantime, stay out of my way and out of my business with the Agency. The less I have to think about you, the better off you'll be. Good day."

With that he walked to the door, opened it and slipped out into the anteroom, leaving McGowan standing in the middle of Rathmann's expansive office, his features drawn and his complexion uncharacteristically pale. McGowan ran his fingers through his perfectly groomed hair, trying to digest all he had just heard, wondering if anything would ever be the same again.

When Director of Central Intelligence Charles Rathmann returned to his office a few minutes later, he found Traynor gone and Senator McGowan waiting for him.

By that time, McGowan had recovered his composure and was already working on a plan for how to deal with the problem. "I listened to what Colonel Traynor had to say, Charles, and formed only one conclusion. He's completely lost his mind. For some reason, he's threatened to ruin my political career by spreading lies about my military service unless I stay out of Agency matters. I believe the old man perceives me as a threat of some kind, although I can't understand why. I know he's had some value here in the past, but I'd be very leery of the Agency having any further dealings with him. He's too old and too unstable to continue to have access to highly secret information affecting this country. You've got to do something about him, Charles."

Rathmann quickly agreed. Traynor had challenged the Director's authority in refusing to cancel the Fahoud operation and then had threatened Rathmann's most powerful patron. The old man was nothing but trouble. Rathmann decided that he needed to get rid of Traynor as soon as possible. McGowan was the man he had to get along with if the Agency was going to be well-funded and protected from excessive Congressional intrusion. And, if the polls were accurate, in eighteen months McGowan very likely would be sworn in as the next President of the United States. The Director enjoyed his position with the Agency and hoped to hold onto it for a while, at least until something better came along. Traynor was becoming an impediment that he could not afford. The old man had to go.

Unfortunately, however, the Fahoud mission was still on the table and that was the immediate problem. Rathmann tried to console McGowan, hoping he could find a way to call off the operation before they were all tarred.

"I agree, Senator. Traynor's relationship with the Agency will terminate as soon as the pending mission is completed. Which brings me back to the reason I asked you to come over here today. Traynor says it's too late to stop the operation against Fahoud."

McGowan was not pleased. He didn't trust the CIA to do anything right, and he damned sure didn't want to be associated with an assassination—especially not with Traynor involved.

"I suggest we let the matter go forward," Rathmann continued. "As distasteful as the means might be, the world will be a better place with Fahoud gone. To my knowledge, no Traynor mission has ever been linked to the Agency, so I think we should allow the operation to proceed, if for no other reason than to get the Colonel out of our hair."

McGowan tried to buy time as he considered his next move.

"I don't know, Charles. Is there *any* possibility of tying the Fahoud matter to you personally, or to me for that matter?"

Rathmann had to decide quickly whether or not to lie to McGowan. He knew that if he lied, McGowan would never trust him again. Maybe Traynor had told McGowan that he knew the Senator had been briefed on the Fahoud matter? Maybe McGowan was just testing him? He decided that the downside of telling the truth outweighed the risk of being caught in a lie.

"The only possible connection would be through Traynor himself, and I don't believe he would ever compromise one of his own operations."

"You mean Traynor knows that I've been briefed on the mission?"

"Yes, but I don't think he'll be a problem."

McGowan closed his eyes and shook his head. Rathmann was an idiot.

"I'm confident he won't go public with the information," Rathmann said. "His self-imposed ethics would never permit it. There's no way he'll disclose anything or he'll put his own people in jeopardy and risk damaging the Agency. He won't do that, no matter what the cost."

"Do you have any idea who Traynor uses for these kinds of jobs?"

"Well, let me think. He told me during our first meeting, the one where I was introduced to Traynor and his potential usefulness was explained, that he has only one field agent with whom he maintains an ongoing relationship, and that that man has been with him for a very long time. Traynor said that the field agent is only a contractor and has no idea that Traynor is doing the Agency's bidding. If that's the case, and I have no reason to believe otherwise, there's no way Traynor would ever tell him of my or your knowledge of the matter. Therefore, I suspect that Traynor is the only connection back to the Agency or to me. And indirectly, I suppose, to you."

McGowan looked away, considering the damage that Traynor might be able to inflict on his presidential bid.

Rathmann continued. "So, I suggest we permit Traynor's agent to finish the mission, allow Traynor to retire, and then move on to other things. It will be in all of our best interests to get this matter behind us and get Jonathan Traynor out of our lives."

McGowan was not prepared to accept that scenario. He was afraid Traynor would never be completely out of *his* life. Something had to be done about the old man. But first, he had to deal with the Fahoud mission. He could not allow it to go forward with his implied blessing. He was worried about Rathmann. If things started going south, Rathmann would not hesitate to implicate McGowan.

For the record, he had to strongly object to the Fahoud mission, just in case the details of this meeting ever became public. Traynor had said he could not cancel the operation. Nevertheless, McGowan's best strategy was to make a formal demand on Rathmann that the mission be called off. Then he then could safely work behind the scenes with Rathmann to try to stop it without incurring any responsibility should they fail.

In the midst of that analysis, something struck a chord with McGowan—something Rathmann had just said. *What was it?* Oh, yes. Traynor had told Rathmann that he had only one field agent with whom he maintained an ongoing relationship. In their private meeting, Traynor had told McGowan that the Laos mission was the first the Frenchman had undertaken for Traynor and that he had been with him ever since. The logical conclusion to be drawn from those two statements was that the Frenchman was the one he had sent to kill Fahoud.

McGowan's mind was spinning with possibilities. His preoccupation with Traynor was suddenly overshadowed by thoughts of how he might eliminate the Frenchman. He could deal with Traynor at any time. But the Frenchman was a different story. His only lead to the identity or location of the Frenchman was the Fahoud operation. For a brief period of time, he knew where the Frenchman was going to be. If he could find a way to deal with the Frenchman first, and then eventually silence or discredit Traynor, the potential threat posed by the only two men who knew anything about the unfortunate incident that had occurred almost thirty years earlier in Laos would disappear.

Rathmann seemed convinced that the Fahoud operation could not be called off. Perhaps it would be better if the assassination were successfully completed. At that point, McGowan would have all the leverage with Rathmann he would ever need. Imagine, the Director of the Central Intelligence Agency authorizing a public assassination on the sovereign soil of another country, and then going forward with such a plan after a senior member of the Senate Select Committee on Intelligence had intervened and given him explicit instructions to call it off. Faced with the prospect of that information being made public, Rathmann would do whatever McGowan suggested. *Especially if it involved eliminating the agent that had conducted the operation.* Charles

Rathmann should be more than happy to accommodate McGowan's desire to permanently eliminate the Frenchman. That being accomplished, it would not be out of the question for Rathmann to then take care of Traynor as little more than a loose end.

Because his ultimate objective required completion of an operation that he had to openly and forcefully oppose, McGowan had to be very careful in his handling of Charles Rathmann.

He finally responded to the Director's last statement. "Well, Mr. Director, I must say I strongly disagree. As I stated when this matter was first brought to my attention, I do not condone assassinations by this Agency, even the assassination of a person as despicable as Azbek Fahoud. That continues to be my position on the matter. You must cancel the operation and you must do so in a manner that does not adversely implicate this Agency. So the question is, how do you plan to stop Traynor from going forward?"

Rathmann finally began to realize that he was being hung out to dry. "I can *try* to stop it, Senator, but I'm not sure where to begin. Traynor won't do it and I don't know who his contacts are. You need to keep in mind, Senator, that trying to stop the mission might create more risk of exposure than going ahead with it."

McGowan made a steeple with his fingers and bounced them against his chin, as though deep in thought. But inside, he was elated. Rathmann was going right down the path.

"Well let me suggest this. You have the capability of monitoring Traynor's telephone calls, do you not? And pulling his phone records for the past month or so? And perhaps even searching his house for private files? Why don't you do that and see if you can find out who the field agent might be? And after you get that information, maybe action can be taken to intervene and stop him. It's a long shot, but better than doing nothing, especially if you ever have to explain the Agency's unfortunate involvement in this matter."

Rathmann stiffened. "Phone taps and break-ins by officers of this Agency against U.S. citizens inside this country are illegal, Senator. The Agency has no authority to operate inside the U.S. You know that. Are you suggesting I involve Agency personnel in illegal domestic activities?"

McGowan feigned an eruption of his rarely seen temper. "Oh for God's sake, Rathmann, face the facts. You've already screwed up by giving Traynor the go-ahead when the matter was first brought to your attention. I'm not suggesting you do anything illegal per se, what I'm suggesting is that you do whatever is necessary to bring this harebrained scheme to an end and save yourself a lot of grief down the road. What's worse—hiring a hit man to kill a private citizen in a friendly foreign country or conducting domestic surveillance operations related to a matter that involves a critical issue of national security? You have to understand, Charles, that in the last analysis Jonathan Traynor presents a greater threat to this Agency than any you've faced since your appointment as DCI. And you might want to consider how a threat to the Agency impacts you personally. Up on the Hill, it's very difficult to distinguish between the two. The Director usually goes as the Agency goes. I'm certain you understand that."

Rathmann did not respond. He just sat there, staring vacantly into space.

McGowan waved dismissively at the Director. "Make up your own mind, Charles. But I'm telling you that if responsibility for this assassination finds its way back here, I'll have no hesitation in stating publicly that I opposed it and that I strongly urged you to stop it. It will be just you and

Traynor. You're going to have to make a choice."

Then in a more kind manner, McGowan added, "Look Charles, I'm just trying to help you. You're a capable guy and I like you. And one of these days I might be in a position to work with you directly as a part of a new administration, maybe with you in this office, maybe in another. But I can't do anything about this Fahoud matter and I can't do anything to minimize the risk posed by the Agency's association with Traynor. You're going to have to solve those problems on your own. You need to keep in mind that if the Fahoud operation goes forward, Traynor will always have something that he can use against both you and the Agency, and that will not be a good situation."

Rathmann was sick. He wished he that had never met Traynor, never accepted the outgoing Director's suggestion that he might find Traynor useful some day. He also wished that he had never told McGowan about the Fahoud matter. He thought he was buying friendship with that most valuable of all commodities in Washington: information. But he had been wrong. By the same token, McGowan was right about Traynor. It was now up to Rathmann to figure out a way to stop the mission to terminate Fahoud. He would have do whatever needed be done to find Traynor's agent and stop him. And he also would have to consider taking action to remove Jonathan Traynor as a threat.

The Director looked directly into McGowan's eyes. "I understand, Senator. I'll do what I can to bring this matter to an end before it goes too far."

McGowan smiled his approval. "That's great, Charles. Listen, for the record, I want this Agency to be an institution that the American people can be proud of. We can't afford any more of the kinds of operations that have been run by Traynor. I want you to make sure this doesn't happen again and that Traynor really does retire. I'm counting on you."

"I think we see things very similarly, Senator. I believe we should be able to work together for a long time."

McGowan rose to leave, and in doing so offered his hand to Rathmann. "Call me at the office if you hear anything that I should know about."

"I certainly will, Senator. Have a good day."

While driving back to his office, McGowan convinced himself he had done everything he could to drive Rathmann in the direction of neutralizing both the Frenchman and Traynor. He had to make sure that neither of them could ever pose a threat to his upcoming campaign or his presidency.

He was certain that he could count on Rathmann to find and deal with the Frenchman, more likely after the Fahoud operation was completed than before. Rathmann *had* to realize that it would be in the Agency's best interest to eliminate Traynor's hired assassin. That point had been well made.

Traynor would be more difficult. Despite McGowan's implicit encouragement, Rathmann would be reluctant to take any direct action against the old man. Perhaps Traynor would be a problem that McGowan would have to solve on his own. Maybe a way could be found to discredit Traynor. Perhaps something in his past would provide an opening. On the other hand, maybe Rathmann *could* help. He had the most information and the best available means. It was not a pleasant prospect. McGowan had never been involved in that sort of thing, but he knew that it happened in politics all the time. Traynor must not be allowed to interfere with Robert J. McGowan realizing his destiny. The country needed him, needed his leadership, needed his vision. Sometimes distasteful things had to be done for the greater good. This was one of those times.

10

THE WEASEL

17 July 1999—Washington, D.C.

Wes "the Weasel" Ratowski waited in the shadows just inside the gate that connected the driveway to the back yard of Jonathan Traynor's old Georgetown home. From this position he could cover both the gate and the door from the detached garage into the back yard. He checked his watch. It was eleven-fifteen p.m. Toby had told him that according to his source, the old man would be home by midnight. Wes unconsciously tugged the rawhide thong that attached the heavy leather sap to his right wrist. He was ready to do a number on the old man, just like Toby said.

Toby Markham had given Wes five days to come up with the money he owed Toby, or the Weasel was a dead man. Wes had figured his only chance was to skip town—maybe go back to Newark and see if he could get lost among the old crowd. But Toby had warned Wes that no matter where he might run, somebody would find him. Twenty large was a lot of money, even to a high roller like Toby. With only five days to raise the money, Wes had no choice *but* to run. He didn't have the twenty grand and there was no way he could get it in time.

When Toby collared Wes the day before in his apartment, Wes had thought it was all over. He had been in the process of packing up to leave the District for good when Toby stopped by. It didn't look good that the Weasel had all

170

of his clothes on the bed and was stuffing them in an old duffle bag when Toby walked in. Wes had been scared to death. He was sure that Toby had come to collect the money or take it out of his hide.

But he was wrong. Toby had come to see the Weasel a day early to give him a chance to earn his way out of the debt. All that Wes had to do was wait for some old man in the back yard of his house, take him inside and beat him up—*really* beat him up bad—break some bones, break some ribs, bust his skull, stuff like that. If the guy happened to croak, okay, but what Toby really wanted was for the old guy to be out of commission for a long time. "ICU" was what Toby had said. He wanted the old man to end up in the ICU.

It was a pretty simple tie-up. Better some old man take the gas than Wes. But Toby was insistent about one thing. It had to look like a robbery, not a hit. That was important. The good news was that Wes could keep anything he took from the old man's house, except for books, papers, that kind of stuff. All of that was to be left alone.

The Weasel bought in. Twenty large was a pretty big score for an easy job like this. He always thought that down deep inside, Toby liked him. Of course, Toby was probably getting more than twenty grand for taking the old man down. That was okay with Wes, just as long as he was off the hook.

Jonathan Traynor had spent the day tying up loose ends. He had made a new tape for Staley and secured it in the customary manner. He had been doing this same thing for years, and in all that time, Staley had never listened to a single tape. It was Traynor's continually updated fail-safe plan, a way to ensure that important current information would always be available to Staley in the event of Traynor's untimely death.

It took him over an hour to describe his recent encounter with McGowan and the manner in which Rathmann had betrayed his trust by bringing McGowan in on Traynor's activities for the Agency, including the Fahoud operation. He referenced other materials previously prepared and set aside for Staley describing in detail the background of the McGowan matter, including the initial report Staley had filed with him in 1971, the physical evidence Staley had collected, a summary of the lab reports, and the narrative of Traynor's own investigation tying it all together. Without providing specific direction, he concluded that part of the tape by admonishing Staley that Robert McGowan must never be permitted to become President of the United States.

He then brought Staley current on all open matters—matters he would want Staley to be aware of or attend to if this were his last communication concerning the work they had done together over the years.

At the end of the tape he reiterated the details of what he considered to be an untenable situation with Rathmann and McGowan. Finally, he expressed his belief that he was now such a threat to McGowan's political future, and by extrapolation Rathmann's future as well, that they might take some action against him.

After finishing the tape and handling some routine personal business, Traynor had slipped on a sport coat and driven down to a small restaurant at the sailing marina just off the George Washington Memorial Parkway. It was an old favorite: fresh seafood, good wine and a quiet atmosphere with excellent service and interesting views of the many boats in the harbor.

He treated himself to crab cakes, Dover sole with new potatoes and a half bottle of Cakebread Sauvignon Blanc. He finished the meal with a cup of coffee and a glass of Far Niente Dolce, his favorite dessert wine.

It was almost eleven p.m. when he left the restaurant and the marina, having stopped to look at two new sailboats he had not seen before.

He pulled into his driveway at eleven-twenty p.m. and decided to leave the car out for the night rather than put it in the cluttered, free-standing garage just behind and to the left of the main house. He was relaxed but tired, ready for a good night's sleep. He locked his two-year old BMW with the remote button on the key, then walked around the car to the wrought iron gate into the back yard.

Wes heard the car door close and the click of the doors locking, then the quiet squeak of the gate as the old man pulled it open and shut it gently from the inside. His hands were sweaty. He always got sweaty when he was about to get into something heavy. He wondered if he ought to go ahead and kill the guy, so he couldn't be identified. He had never killed anyone on purpose before. There was just that one time when a kid he had sold some product to tried to knife him and Wes had shot him. It was a clean shot; it didn't bother him too much when it was over. But that had happened unexpectedly. He hadn't had time to think about it. He hadn't planned to kill the kid. This was different. He was lying in wait. He was going to beat up some old man, maybe beat him to death. Wes's hands suddenly started to shake.

Traynor closed the gate into his back yard and walked toward the house. He had taken only two steps before he realized that he wasn't alone. He looked to his right just as the leather and steel sap, filled with lead shot, crashed down on the side of his head. He wasn't in a position to deflect the blow and his reflexes probably wouldn't have been quick enough anyway. His knees buckled and he fell onto the concrete sidewalk.

Wes leaned over the old man, and when he saw him trying to get up, he hit him again—this time across the shoulders. Toby had been very specific. Wes had to get the old man into the house, take care of business inside, then leave him there.

Traynor lay face down on the sidewalk. He knew he was in deep trouble. This *might* be a violent robbery, but he didn't think so. It had all the marks of an Agency-sponsored contract. McGowan could be behind it, but probably not. More likely it was Rathmann. McGowan wouldn't have the nerve to get involved in something like this.

Traynor knew that he had to remain calm. He had to keep his composure or he wouldn't survive.

Wes leaned over the old man again, this time grabbing him by the back of his sport coat and pulling him up.

Quietly he said, "Look, pal, I jus' want your money, your jewelry, 'lectronics an' other shit like that. You go along wit me here or I'm gonna have to hurt ya real bad. Ya know what I'm sayin'?"

Traynor played along, biding his time.

He put as much fear in his voice as he could muster. "Yes, yes . . . I understand . . . please, don't hit me again."

Wes helped the old man up, then pushed him toward the back door.

"Open the door, an' don't yell or anything like that, or I'll have ta take ya out, you know what I'm sayin'?"

"Yes, okay. Let me get my keys."

Traynor found his keys and opened the door. He would

have only one chance to free himself. He knew what was in the house. The moron trying to be a tough guy didn't.

After opening the door, he stopped and turned slightly toward his attacker.

With a quiver in his voice, Traynor said, "Please stand still for a minute while I turn off the alarm."

He reached across the counter and punched in the alarm code. But as he brought his hand back from the panel, he felt in the dark for the bottle of merlot he knew was standing on the counter. He had left it there last night after dinner. As quick as he could and with all the strength he could muster, Traynor spun around and crashed the half-empty bottle into the side of his attacker's pitted face.

The intruder fell against the doorjamb and yelped as the bottle broke, cutting him across the cheek. At the same time, Traynor lunged forward and opened the drawer next to the refrigerator where he kept a loaded .45 caliber automatic. He searched frantically in the dark for the pistol. The drawer was cluttered—placemats, hot pads, a flashlight. Finally, the cold steel of the heavy .45. He found the grip, pulled the pistol free and started to turn. But it was too late. His attacker landed a vicious blow to the back of Traynor's head, driving him to the floor. After two more blows, he lost consciousness.

The Weasel continued the savage beating. When he tired with the sap, he kicked the old man in the ribs until he heard a loud crack, then kicked him a couple of times in the face, just for good measure. His instructions were to put the guy in the ICU, but he'd lost his temper. *The old son-of-a-bitch shouldn'ta hit me with that damned bottle. Toby'll understand when I tell him what happened.*

Wes found a dishtowel, wet it in the kitchen sink and held it on the gash in his face while he removed the old man's wallet and watch. He then ransacked the house, making it look like a robbery, just as Toby had instructed. He didn't find much, but he took a few things—some cash from the old man's dresser, some silver and a small television set that ran on a battery and would fit on the dashboard of a car. Some of the old man's stuff was pretty cool, but he couldn't take it all. And besides, most of it would be hard to fence.

The robbery was cut short by Wes's need to take care of the wound on his face. He went back into the kitchen and found another clean towel to hold against his cheek. He couldn't believe the old man had done that to him. *The crazy old bastard. I hope I killed 'im.* The Weasel stared down at the old man, then kicked him hard on the side of the knee to see if he would groan. Wes had seen that in a movie once.

The old man didn't make a sound and he didn't look like he was breathing, so Wes was pretty sure he was either dead or would be before anyone found him. The Weasel remembered that he was supposed to make it look like a burglary, not a hit. He cocked his head and looked at the body. *Yeah, that'll work.* He decided he was pretty good at this kind of stuff. Maybe Toby or somebody else would use him for one of these numbers some other time.

Wes the Weasel took one last look around, then left by the back door and walked the half block to his car. On the way he called Toby on his cell phone to tell him the job was done. Toby was pleased.

Across the alley from Traynor's driveway, a slight man wearing a black windbreaker waited in the shadows for Wes to finish the assignment. The man had never met Wes and was certain that Wes was unaware of his presence. The man watched as Wes closed the gate and walked east down the alley, holding a towel to his face. After a few minutes, the man slipped quietly into Traynor's back yard. The door to the house was open. He cautiously stepped into the kitchen and saw the old man lying on the floor in a pool of blood. Satisfied that the job had been completed as ordered, he retraced his steps, latched the gate and walked out the other end of the alley, unseen and unheard.

Two hours later on the other side of town, Toby Markham sat in his apartment, sipping a cold Rolling Rock and looking at the pile of crisp one hundred dollar bills lying on the coffee table. He had just finished selling a kilo of cocaine to a big time distributor from Maryland who had traveled to D.C. to make the connection.

Toby was distracted by a noise in the hallway. He listened for a minute but wasn't sure he'd heard anything at all. Then there was a light knock at his door. He scooped up the pile of bills and hid them under the cushion on the threadbare velvet couch. He picked up his 9-millimeter and walked to the door.

Whoever was outside knocked again, louder this time.

Toby turned sideways and leaned against the wall. The door had a viewer but he wanted to know who was knocking before he stood squarely in front of it.

"Yeah, who's there?"

A voice answered quietly, "It's me, the guy that hired you to do the job tonight. We need to talk."

Toby had received half of the twenty-five grand the guy had agreed to pay. He was anxious to get the rest of the money. Maybe the guy had it with him.

Toby looked through the viewer and saw the same nicely groomed, middle-aged man he had met two days earlier in a bar a couple of blocks away. He was wearing the same black windbreaker he had worn that night. *Who the hell wears a windbreaker in July?* The guy had said that Toby had been highly recommended by a street dealer Toby had known for a long time. Toby had made a couple of phone calls from the bar. The guy's story had checked out. But he was such a wimp. The whole deal had something to do with his ex-wife's family.

Toby unlocked the door and opened it. Before he could say a word, his visitor raised a silenced automatic and fired it directly into Toby's forehead at point blank range.

The impact carried Toby's lifeless body back into his apartment where he fell to the floor in a contorted heap. The man stepped through the door and closed it, then searched the apartment. He found almost fifteen thousand dollars in cash, including the stash of one hundred dollar bills under the sofa cushion.

After pocketing the money, the man opened the door, checked the hallway and slipped out, quietly closing the door behind him. He casually walked down one flight of stairs to the ground floor and out into the street. The crime scene looked just like he had intended it to look—another drug deal gone bad.

Traynor awakened in unfamiliar surroundings. He suddenly realized he was in a GP medium tent at the aid station at Bong Son, lying on a cot. His body was wracked with pain. His head ached so badly he could hardly think. His legs were numb and he was having trouble breathing. Probably took an AK round through the chest, *he thought.* Maybe another in the back or hip. No feeling in my legs.

There were medics and doctors all around him,

*working feverishly on other wounded soldiers. He knew
the injured men were his troopers. He recognized a few of
them, including some he thought had been killed in action
weeks or months before. He could hear the guy beside him
moan in pain.*

*More wounded were being brought in every minute, all
of them on stretchers. Near the back of the tent he could
see a pile of olive drab body bags. Two faceless medics
were lifting bodies into the body bags, zipping them up
and carrying them outside. Jonathan watched with detached interest as they put Harmon, his brother, into one
of the body bags. Somehow he knew Harmon was dead,
but he couldn't remember why Harmon was in Vietnam.*
When did he get here? How in the world did he get
hit?

*Traynor's throat was dry. He needed a drink of water.
He tried to get someone's attention, but no one would
listen. Finally one of the docs came over and looked down
at him. The doctor held Jonathan's wrist and frowned as
he felt for a pulse. He then lifted Jonathan's eyelids,
shining an Army issue flashlight into his eyes. "Looks like
this one's gone," he shouted to the medics. "Bag him and
tag him."*

*A jolt of fear surged through Jonathan as he realized
the doctor had just pronounced him dead. He tried to
shout, "Hey, I'm not dead—I'm just hit," but nothing
came out. He tried to move, tried to get up, but his body
wouldn't respond. He tried to raise his arms to show the
doctor he was alive, but he found that he couldn't move
them either. In fact, he couldn't move a finger.* Maybe I
am dead, *he thought.* Maybe this is what it feels like.
After all, it's about time, isn't it?

Then Jonathan saw a VC soldier slip into the aid sta-

tion tent. It was all so strange. For some reason, no one else saw him. He was wearing black silk pajamas and a conical straw hat, and he carried an AK-47 assault rifle. The VC was thin, had sunken cheeks and a look that expressed something between fear and determination. He walked silently in a crouch, moving among the injured soldiers, bashing in their heads with the stock of his rifle. Jonathan again tried to cry out, but he could make no sound, attract no one's attention.

While he lay there helpless, watching the VC soldier kill his wounded troopers, the medics came and lifted Jonathan off the cot and carried him toward the back of the tent and the waiting body bags. He had reconciled himself to the fact that he was dead. Death held no fear for him now. But then he saw Hackler Staley, lying unconscious with a bloody bandage on his neck and an IV in his arm. Somehow Traynor knew that Staley was alive. Then he remembered that it had been Staley who had carried him back from the ambush and into the aid station. He remembered being hit and he remembered Staley picking him up and carrying him back through the lines as he fought the NVA soldiers who had tried to stop them. He figured that he must have passed out, but Staley had made it.

With greater determination that he had ever summoned in his entire life, Jonathan willed himself back into the world of the living. He had to get the medics' attention, had to let them know that Hack Staley was in trouble. If he didn't do something, the VC soldier would kill Hack. He would never see it coming. Jonathan mustered all of his remaining strength and tried to scream, fighting to stay alive. If it was the last thing he ever did, he had to help Staley . . . had to warn him . . . somehow.

★ ★ ★ ★ ★

The closer Jonathan came to being fully conscious, the more he felt the searing pain. It took him several seconds to realize that he was lying face-down on the floor in his kitchen. Something had trickled down his cheek and pooled under his nose. The left side of his face was stuck to the varnished wooden floor. He recognized the sweet copper scent of blood. He could taste it in his mouth.

The house was dark. The only brightness in the room was the dim glow of night from the window above the sink. A piece of broken glass lay inches from his right eye. He remembered the attack. He knew he had been badly beaten. He also knew that he had to be careful before making any noise, so he lay there listening, ensuring his attacker had gone.

The house was quiet, except for the ticking of the grandfather clock in the living room. After a minute, Jonathan tried to move. Perhaps he could drag himself into the other room. He quickly discovered that his legs were not going to respond. They were broken or paralyzed. He managed to pull his right arm out from under his body. He had some strength left there, but not much. Just continuing to remain conscious took a tremendous effort.

He braced the palm of his right hand against the floor and pushed hard, trying to roll over onto his back, but before the half-turn was complete, his momentum was stopped by the wall of cabinets lining the old kitchen. He rested his head back against the space between the cabinet and the floor and pulled his left arm free. He could feel his heart racing, working very hard to keep the blood moving in his battered body. He was listless and faint, having a difficult time keeping his eyes open and focused. The effort of turning over had caused him to break out in a cold sweat.

181

He knew he didn't have much time, that he'd never be able to move very far.

Jonathan struggled to reach the inside breast pocket of his sport coat. He found the cool plastic case of his cellular telephone. He felt for the Power button and pressed it. The glow of the liquid crystal display screen was an enormous relief. At least he could call for help. But that would have to wait. There was something he had to do first, if he could just think of it.

Yes. It was Staley. He had to warn Staley.

If Rathmann was willing to go this far to get rid of Jonathan, he'd definitely go after Staley next. But Rathmann was smart enough to know that the odds would be against finding the assassin before the mission was completed. Therefore, he most likely would have agents shadowing Fahoud with instructions to watch for an assassination attempt and then find and eliminate the shooter as he made his getaway. Staley would never expect a reaction team to be in place. Jonathan had to warn him.

He considered his next move very carefully. Whoever found him would find the cell phone too. There would be an easily accessible record of any number he called. He had to warn Staley, but he had to do it in such a manner that no one would be able to figure out who he had called or why. After a minute, he realized that there might be a way. He remembered his discussions with a friend the previous year about a new procedure for making an untraceable call to a particular person should the need ever arise. He worried that his information might be out of date. His friend had died six months ago. *Is it possible the protocol is still in effect, that the number is still active?*

Jonathan pressed the Clear button and again illuminated the dull silver screen on the small Nokia handset. The time appeared in the upper right-hand corner. It was almost one o'clock. He had been unconscious for over an hour. He did the time zone arithmetic and found the timing of his call to be perfect. He wasn't sure if it would work. Would the man he hoped to reach answer? If he did answer, would he help? Jonathan had no choice. He had to try.

Lying immobile and badly injured on the floor of his Georgetown mansion, Jonathan scrolled through the cell phone directory until he found a particular four-letter identifier. He had selected the letters of the identifier at random, so that anyone checking the directory would have no clue as to the identity of the person being called. When the number came up in the LCD screen, he pressed Send. After a forty-second delay that seemed almost interminable, a connection was made and a tone chimed twice in rapid succession. Continuing as instructed almost a year earlier, Jonathan spoke the name of the man he was trying to reach. Ten seconds later an unfamiliar voice answered with words he did not understand.

11

ETIENNE'S

19 July 1999—Washington, D.C.
Robert McGowan sat transfixed at his kitchen table, the
steaming cup of coffee in his right hand suspended halfway
between the table and his mouth. It was the article on page
six of the *Post* that had grabbed his attention.

RETIRED ARMY OFFICER NEAR DEATH AFTER
BEATEN IN ROBBERY AT GEORGETOWN HOME
Colonel Jonathan Traynor, U.S. Army (retired), was
found beaten and apparently left for dead Sunday
morning in the kitchen of his upscale Georgetown
home. Traynor, 81, had lived in the fashionable
neighborhood for over thirty years. Police were asked
to check on the retiree by an unnamed business associate who reported that Traynor had failed to attend a
rare Sunday morning meeting and did not answer his
telephone. A District police unit responding to the
call found the rear door of the house open and entered
to find Traynor lying on the kitchen floor, unconscious
and badly beaten. According to police spokesman
James Altwyler, robbery was the apparent motive of
the break-in. The house had been ransacked, but
since Traynor lived alone, police were unable to
determine what might have been taken. Police specu-
lated that Traynor had been accosted as he returned

home for the evening and entered his back gate. Neighbors were questioned but none reported hearing anything unusual during the time the assault likely occurred. The elderly victim was beaten so badly that only prompt action by an emergency react team saved his life. Traynor was taken to Walter Reed Hospital where he was admitted to the intensive care unit and listed in critical condition. Doctors have refused to comment on the victim's prognosis. In a brief statement released late last night, Altwyler said that the matter was under investigation but no suspects had been identified.

It had been only five days since the tumultuous meeting in Rathmann's office.

Could this be a coincidence or is it something Rathmann cooked up to stop the Fahoud operation and, at the same time, solve the Traynor problem? Could he have acted so quickly? Would he be willing to go that far?

McGowan could not resist the temptation to find out. He picked up the portable phone lying on the antique washstand beside the breakfast table and dialed Rathmann's main office number. An operator answered and after only a few seconds on hold, put the call through. McGowan was not surprised to find the Director in his office, even at this early hour.

"Good morning, Mr. Director."

"Good morning, Senator. What can I do for you this morning."

"I just read the article in the *Post* about Colonel Traynor. Have you seen it?"

"Yes, I have. As a matter of fact, I've taken a personal interest in the matter. You know how close we were. I saw

Jonathan on Friday afternoon and he was doing fine. I can't imagine someone beating an old man nearly to death in his own home, especially not in that neighborhood. It's a sad commentary on our society."

Well, thought McGowan, *that's a gold-plated bullshit story if I've ever heard one. Either this call is being recorded or there's someone in his office. In either case, it won't trouble me to go along.*

"I agree. I feel really badly. You know how much I respect the Colonel. Do you know anything more about his condition?

"No, but at last report he had not regained consciousness. I've left specific instructions for the hospital to call my office if anything develops."

"Good. Let me know if you hear anything that won't be in the papers."

"Certainly, Senator. By the way, do you have lunch plans today? There are a couple of budget items, things we touched on briefly last week, that I'd like to discuss with you before making a decision one way or the other."

He wants to talk about Traynor or the Fahoud operation, but not in his office or over the telephone.

"Yes, I can do that. How about Etienne's? Say around twelve-thirty?"

"That would be perfect. See you then."

As he hung up the phone, McGowan started wondering whether he had underestimated Charles Rathmann.

Did the meek little bastard have the guts to go after Traynor? If so, did he find out anything about the Frenchman? This should be interesting indeed.

The luncheon crowd at Etienne's, a well-known midday spot for Capitol insiders, was light for a Monday. As usual, the proprietor was present and personally greeted his distinguished guests. Etienne still owed McGowan for help with an immigration problem that had been settled ten years earlier. The middle-aged restaurateur never forgot what his friend, the Senator, had done.

Etienne led Rathmann and McGowan to a booth near the back of the restaurant that was angled for minimum visibility from the main room. Rathmann's security detail settled in for lunch at a front table while waiting for their boss.

The two men exchanged pleasantries while ordering. As soon as the waiter left the table, Rathmann turned to the business at hand.

"Senator, I recall that you were interested in any information we might uncover with respect to one of Colonel Traynor's associates. I believe I might have something for you."

"Is the information reliable? Should I ask how you came by this information or would that be a matter for which I do not have a need to know?"

Rathmann studied his hands as he picked a fleck of pepper from the linen tablecloth. Looking up, he said, "I believe the information to be extremely reliable."

Allowing himself a tight smile, Rathmann added, "As to how the information was obtained, that was the fortuitous result of the tragedy that occurred to Colonel Traynor. You see, when the colonel failed to show up for a meeting we had scheduled for yesterday morning and I was unable to reach him by phone, I had a member of my staff call the D.C. police and ask them to check his home. The newspaper article pretty much relates what happened next, except that an Agency team arrived at Traynor's residence shortly after the responding police units. They identified Traynor as an intelligence consultant. Our team remained on site while the police worked the crime scene. At our insistence, the investigating officers permitted our people to take a first look at Colonel Traynor's files and papers. A potential matter of national security, you understand."

It was obvious that without expressly admitting that he had been behind the operation, Rathmann was taking credit for the attack on Traynor and the subsequent search of his home for information regarding the Fahoud operation and Traynor's operative. McGowan made a mental note: Rathmann might be tougher than he appeared.

"So what did you find? I can't believe the old man had everything laid out for the world to see."

"No, actually there was very little evidence of the Colonel's avocation, mostly housekeeping paperwork and memorabilia from his days in the military. Remarkably, he didn't even have a computer, so there were no computer files to copy, no hard drives to scour. But there were a few scraps of information here and there that, with the benefit of certain other information known only to you and me, filled in some blanks with respect to a matter in which we are both quite interested. And, under the guise of ensuring there were no other loose ends, our team made some follow-up inquiries—telephone records, credit card purchases, other records accessible with the right computer equipment and expertise. Those inquiries revealed other facts about Colonel Traynor's activities over the past few months."

"Okay, so again, what did you find?"

"At first, nothing. But our people brought back to Langley for further examination a blank notepad that was found on Colonel Traynor's desk blotter. It is common procedure these days to examine the top sheet of any tablet or notepad found at a crime scene to see if it is possible to pull up indentations of handwritten notes. Evidently, Traynor *had* taken notes on the pad and then destroyed the page on which the notes had been written, as I suspect was his custom. Fortunately, our lab was able to draw out and highlight the indentations on the unused top sheet of the pad, thereby making Traynor's notes readable. The notes included certain dates, which we know to be the dates Fahoud intends to be in Monaco to meet with Alexandrov, along with certain shorthand codes that clearly are unique to Traynor and that we will never decipher. The important thing about tying these particular notes to the Fahoud/Alexandrov meeting is the fact that on the same scrap of paper there is the name of a luggage shop which we now know, after more intensive investigation and computer research than you can possibly imagine, is in Montreal, Canada. We don't know the importance of the luggage shop to the overall puzzle. One of our men is on the way up there right now to see what he can find out. But next to the name of the business is the letter 'V' which, we believe, is likely to be an initial. Next to the initial is more doodling that looks like this."

Rathmann handed McGowan a scrap of paper on which he had written: Q, N —> M—7.14.

"While there are a number of possibilities, we believe this to be a travel itinerary and date. 'Quebec, Nice to Monaco, July 14.' While we cannot be sure, it is possible the letter 'V' is the first or last name of the contractor's alias. The 'Q' could refer to the Province of Quebec, which of course includes Montreal, or it could refer to Quebec City. If we are correct in all of these assumptions, Mr. 'V' left Quebec for Monaco five days ago for the purpose of killing Azbek Fahoud. The early travel date may be the reason Traynor stated that the mission was already underway and could not be stopped."

The connection with Quebec made perfect sense to McGowan. If "V" was the Frenchman, predominantly French-speaking Quebec would be a logical place for him to live in North America while continuing to work for Traynor.

McGowan needed to convey that information to Rathmann without being too obvious. He squinted his eyes and looked away, as though deep in thought. Then, turning back, he said, "Something Traynor said last week in your office fits right in with the lead you have on this 'V.' He said that his most experienced field operative was French, a fellow he recruited years ago, and that the Frenchman was still with him. I think you can narrow the search by advising your agents that 'V' most likely is French or French-Canadian."

Rathmann made a note of the suggestion.

McGowan continued, "What else did you find at Traynor's house?"

"There was one other matter that has me a bit concerned. He was found unconscious with his cell phone lying beside him. We obtained the call records and found out that Traynor placed a call at approximately one a.m. to a number in Milan, Italy. The number was registered to a bicycle shop of which there is no record. The address for that particular number on file at the local telephone exchange does not exist. Nevertheless, the call *was* connected and lasted for about three minutes. We can only speculate that the number was on automatic forward and rolled over to another destination. But if so, we don't know where. We're still working on that idea. The Italians are trying to be helpful, but they seem to be genuinely confused. At this time, we have no idea who he called or why. But making that call must have been more important to Traynor than seeking medical attention. He completed the overseas call before trying to call for help. He evidently passed out before he could finish dialing 911."

McGowan frowned as he considered that bit of information, then asked, "Anything else?"

"Just some random bits of information that we haven't yet tied together."

"That's pretty thin, isn't it?"

"Yes, it is. But we're still checking. For example, we found that over the past three years, Traynor made several telephone calls to Canada, five of them to numbers in Quebec Province, all of which were public phones. I think that's quite interesting. And, we found a record of Traynor having sent a Federal Express package to a Mr. Delon at a motel in Montreal on July 12, one week ago. That date ties nicely with what we believe to be the travel itinerary. Unfortunately, Delon is a dead end. He never checked into the motel, just waited for the Fed Ex delivery van and stopped in to pick up the package. We intend to have an agent visit the motel to see if anyone can give us a description.

"So, right now that's all we have to go on and we're following up both leads. If we can find a man, possibly French or French-Canadian if your information is correct, with the initial 'V' who flew from somewhere in Quebec to Nice on the fourteenth, and then can trace him to Monaco, we'll likely have Traynor's man. If we can find him before the Fahoud operation is completed, which by the way is highly unlikely, we'll alert the Monaco authorities and ask them to hold him for us without disclosing the reason, which they will undoubtedly do."

McGowan's expression questioned the Director's intention to involve the Monaco police.

Rathmann explained. "The time is too short for us to plan and conduct direct Agency operations in the Principality without substantial risk of things blowing up in our face. It is a very small country. The political repercussions of our agents being discovered while working illegally in Monaco would be disastrous. If we do not locate this 'V' while he is in Monaco, and before he takes action against Fahoud, then our people will find him after he leaves Monaco, while he executes his escape plan. That is when he should be the most vulnerable. We will take him at the first opportune moment."

McGowan considered all that Rathmann had told him.

"If the 'V' initial is correct, I'd think you could track him easily enough. Surely running the passenger manifests on the flights originating in Quebec and connecting with flights arriving in Nice can't be that difficult."

"It wouldn't be if we wanted the direct assistance of Canadian authorities or didn't mind leaving a few footprints in a rough computer search. But in the interest of maintaining confidentiality, we're going a bit slower. Remember, if 'V' is caught after shooting Fahoud, we do not want there to be a record of us looking for him days before the operation. That would require a whole new round of explanations. Also keep in mind that we have only one initial to work with, and we don't know if it's a first name or a last name. But despite all the uncertainty, the good news is that we know where the target is going. If we don't find him before the job is completed, we'll find him after it's finished."

"Okay," McGowan agreed. "What else?"

"We are trying to find out more about the telephone call Traynor made to Milan. You should understand, Senator, that having a working telephone number that for all practical purposes does not exist is not a simple operation. In addition to sophisticated technology, it requires a great deal of planning and maintenance. That particular number has been listed on the Milan exchange for almost two years. Monthly bills have been sent to a post office box and routinely paid during that time, and yet no one seems to be able to tell us who really owns the number. Jonathan Traynor is a resourceful man. He has been involved in clandestine operations for a long time. My guess is that he set this up years ago and it's some kind of emergency notification protocol. But once again, at the present time we don't know who he called or why."

"What do the agents know who are working on this matter?"

"Nothing definitive. As for our interest in Traynor, they have been told that Colonel Traynor has either held a position with or served as an intelligence consultant to the Agency since 1970 and that we need to ensure that his incapacity or death will not result in the exposure of vital intelligence information or potentially embarrassing revelations concerning Agency operations. They have no idea what the data they've assembled means. As for the hunt for 'V,' they've been told he's a contract agent who at one time worked for us but now works for the highest bidder, that Traynor was following his activities in connection with a matter we have been investigating for some time and that we need to locate and neutralize this 'V' just as soon as possible.

"It's very plausible and no one has raised an eyebrow. I'm handling the really sensitive matters personally."

McGowan considered all that Rathmann had said, then asked, "Bottom line, what do you think your chances are of finding Traynor's agent?"

Rathmann answered without equivocation. "We don't have a lot of hard evidence, but what we have is promising. Other than the notepad we found on his desk blotter and the few, probably inconsequential, mistakes with the telephone calls and the Fed Ex package, Traynor didn't leave a trace of any operation he's ever conducted. It's almost as though he hasn't done anything for the past thirty years but stay home and watch soap operas. The man really did a marvelous job of maintaining security. No wonder he's been so effective. But I believe we'll find the assassin. It's just a matter of time."

McGowan wished that Rathmann had a more concrete lead. Although his people apparently had found some good information concerning the Frenchman's travel plans, and Rathmann himself had developed a good cover story for eliminating him, they still had not identified the man and could not be absolutely certain that they would ever find him, even *after* the assassination of Fahoud. Perhaps the Agency would be able to track him down, but if they missed him and Traynor were to die, the Frenchman might show up some day on "Good Morning America" and tell his incredible story in the middle of the presidential campaign. McGowan cringed at the thought. They *had* to find the Frenchman. Whether it was before or after he killed Fahoud was not that important anymore. McGowan had covered his tracks on the Fahoud operation. The Frenchman had to be found and eliminated as soon as possible.

Just then one of Rathmann's bodyguards approached the secluded table.

"My apologies for interrupting, Mr. Director, but I need to speak with you for a moment."

Rather than ask the reason for the interruption, Rathmann guided the agent to a rear corner of the restaurant, out of sight of the other guests. After a brief conversation, he dismissed the agent and returned to the table. Rathmann waited a moment, then leaned forward in a conspiratorial manner and said quietly to McGowan, "An interesting bit of news."

"Anything I should know about?"

"Yes, actually. We have an update on Traynor's condition. The attending physician advises that the Colonel is extremely weak and that his vital signs are decaying steadily. They are beginning to believe that he may not regain consciousness."

"Will one of your people remain with him?"

"Yes, at all times. We have alerted the hospital staff and the police that we are very concerned about what information Colonel Traynor might reveal if he begins speaking in a state of delirium. No one is to talk with him without an Agency official present."

"Good. If he regains consciousness, please let me know."

"Certainly, Senator."

The unexplained call still troubled McGowan.

"Who do you think he called in Milan, Charles? Any indication that it could have been the Frenchman?"

"As I said, we have no indication one way or the other, although I suspect the person he talked with was not physically located in Milan."

McGowan thought for a moment. "Can you get some help from the NSA? Maybe they can trace the call."

"I seriously doubt it, and besides, they'd want specific information as to why we want them to go to all that trouble. We're better off not getting the NSA involved."

McGowan closed his eyes, and with his elbows on the table, rested his chin on the steeple created by the fingers of his large hands. For a moment he was back in the jungles of Laos, looking at Aaron Berman, raising the pistol and firing into his bleeding face. *This has got to end. That was twenty-eight years ago. It should mean nothing now. I'm not going to let Traynor or his hired thug ruin my life.*

He opened his eyes and saw the curious, concerned look

on Charles Rathmann's thin, angular face. He realized he would have to continue to nurture Rathmann, continue to encourage him and continue to hold out the promise of greater things to come once the Traynor matter was put to rest.

McGowan gathered himself and smiled, turning on the charm that had made him America's most promising political superstar.

"You're doing a great job with this, Charles. Please keep me informed, especially anything about this 'V' . . . the Frenchman. Also, let me know if Colonel Traynor regains consciousness."

"Certainly, Senator. Thank you for your support."

The two men rose, shook hands and walked together out through the front door of the restaurant. Etienne picked up the tab.

12

VILLON

21 July 1999—Fairfax County, Virginia/Washington, D.C.
McGowan awakened with a start to the ringing sound generated by the chip in the portable telephone on the nightstand beside his bed. It was his private line—the one very few people knew about. He looked at the lighted face of the nearby clock—six-thirty a.m. Too damned early for anything but a very wrong number or a very important call.

Doing his best to sound alert, McGowan answered the phone before the third ring.

"Hello?"

"Senator, it's Charles Rathmann."

The Director's voice was clear and confident. Something was up and he wanted McGowan to know that he was right on top of it.

"Good morning, Mr. Director," McGowan said, sighing deeply. "What do you have for me?"

"I just happened to be near your house and thought if you were up I'd stop in for a quick chat."

McGowan checked the clock once again. *What the hell is this all about?*

"My God, Charles, it's six-thirty in the morning. Can't it wait a couple of hours?"

"Well, it probably *could*. But it involves the matter we discussed day before yesterday, something in which I know you're keenly interested."

197

It has to be the Frenchman. They've found him.

"Certainly, Charles. I was awake anyway. I'll go in and start a pot of coffee. Knock quietly on the front door when you get here. No point in waking Sarah."

"Fine, then. I'll see you in a few minutes."

McGowan had barely enough time to visit the bathroom, put on a robe and close the door to his bedroom when he heard a soft knock on the front door. He stopped mid-stride, walked into the front hallway and peered out. He could see Rathmann standing alone on the porch, illuminated by the post light just beyond. If the Director was accompanied by his normal security detail, they must have remained in the car. McGowan opened the door and stared curiously at Rathmann, who in his odd way stared back without speaking.

"Come in, Charles."

McGowan closed the door and led his visitor into the well-appointed living room of the luxurious home. McGowan sat in a plush upholstered chair, crossed his legs under his silk robe and motioned for Rathmann to park himself in a companion chair separated by an antique French provincial table.

Rathmann sat down and leaned back in his chair, a tight smile on his thin lips.

"I *am* sorry to bother you at this hour, Senator, but there are two items I thought you'd like to know about as soon as possible. I didn't think it appropriate to discuss these matters on the telephone."

"If it's about Traynor or the infamous 'V,' that was probably a good idea. Continue."

"First, early this morning the team investigating the Traynor notes identified a possible suspect. You were right about him being French. That bit of information helped in the search. A Mr. François Villon left Quebec City on July

13, not July 14, as Traynor's note indicated, and flew to New York on a one-way ticket. Since the itinerary started on July 13 and did not connect with another flight, they assumed he was not our man and disregarded the 'V' match. Later, after hitting a brick wall with other prospects, we decided to check earlier departures and subsequent connections for individuals passed in the first sort."

McGowan smiled at the pronoun switch from "they" to "we." Rathmann's people must have come up with something solid or he would not be taking credit for the breakthrough.

"We discovered that Mr. Villon left New York on July 16 on an Air France flight to Nice. He purchased a one-way ticket so we do not have any return flight information. The following day he checked into the Hermitage Hotel in Monaco. We're still working on background, personal information, *et cetera,* about Mr. Villon and expect to have more by this afternoon. But I'm fairly certain now that he's the one we've been looking for."

"How can you be so sure? Have you followed-up all the other leads? I'd think there'd be any number of possible suspects if you include subsequent flights leaving for Nice within a week after arrival in New York."

"You are correct, Senator, except for one additional fact that I learned just a few moments ago while on my way to the office. That fact was the real reason for my asking to meet with you at this unusual hour."

"And what is that?"

Rathmann glanced at his watch, then looked up.

"About forty-five minutes ago, Azbek Fahoud was shot to death while sitting on the sundeck of Alexandrov's yacht in Monaco harbor. It was an assassination by a person or persons unknown. At the present time, Monaco authorities have no suspects in custody and no idea where the shots came from. Have you ever been to Monaco, Senator?"

McGowan paused for a few seconds as he digested the information, then answered Rathmann's question. "No, I haven't. Why?"

"The Hermitage Hotel is situated just above the harbor. There are many rooms in the hotel that have an unobstructed view of all of the yachts at anchor in the harbor. It would be a perfect hide for a long-range shot with a high-powered rifle. It appears to me that François Villon is our man."

McGowan's mind was in high gear. He had harbored some small hope that the CIA would find the Frenchman and stop him *before* he had a chance to kill Fahoud. Now that Fahoud was dead, killed by an Agency-sponsored assassin, he had to ensure there were no tracks to suggest CIA involvement. He did not relish the thought of having to rely on Rathmann to keep him out of it. But he still wanted the Frenchman, and he wanted him dead.

"Okay, Charles, now listen very carefully. The fact that you were unable to find the assassin *before* he completed the contract makes everything a little more complicated. There is obviously nothing the Agency can do now to stop what Traynor started." McGowan conveniently overlooked that fact that it was Rathmann himself who had engaged Traynor to do just what had just been successfully accomplished—the elimination of the world's leading terrorist.

"But you have to ensure that nothing about the operation is tied back to the Agency. At the same time, we need to find the Frenchman and take whatever steps need to be taken to ensure he doesn't do anything to compromise the integrity of the Agency or the United States government. Are you with me on this, Charles?"

"Yes, Senator, one hundred percent. Although we have a team in Monaco, there are a number of reasons why we cannot at this point take any action to apprehend Villon there. We've already discussed some of those reasons. By the same token, it might be risky for us to attempt to take him into custody anywhere in Europe. We probably couldn't do that anyway since there isn't enough time to put an operation together. Our best hope is that Villon, or whatever his name is, gets out of Monaco and out of Europe without being arrested. There might be some in Europe who'll want to give him a medal for killing Fahoud, but more likely than not if he is arrested in Monaco or by the French authorities, they'll act offended as hell and press him pretty hard to find out who he's working for, and that could lead to Traynor."

Rathmann paused to allow McGowan to catch up, then continued.

"I'm betting he's on his way out right now, probably going back to Canada or maybe even coming to the United States. At this moment we're checking passenger manifests and ticketing at every airport within two hundred miles of Monaco. If he's still traveling under the name Villon, we should be able to find his flight itinerary and have someone waiting on him when he gets off the airplane in New York or Montreal or wherever he reenters North America. It's a long flight and we'll have plenty of time to track him down and set up a welcoming committee. I have no doubt that we'll have him in custody soon."

McGowan was silent as he thought through the possible alternatives. Yesterday his greatest concern was finding the Frenchman—now it looked almost certain that they would have him within a matter of hours. But if the Frenchman were actually taken into custody by the CIA, getting rid of him for good might be more problematic than McGowan had originally thought. It all depended on Rathmann and whether or not he had seen the light.

"Good work, Charles. But have you decided what you will do with the Frenchman after you locate him?"

"Yes, Senator. Are you certain you want to be made privy to that information?"

McGowan posed thoughtfully for a moment.

"I would like to know for certain that we're not going to have these kinds of problems in the future and that the days of Jonathan Traynor-type operations for the Agency are over. So the answer is yes, I want to know your plans for dealing with this loose end."

Rathmann hesitated briefly, then responded.

"We will take him into custody, we will extract from him as much information as possible and then he will disappear. It will be a special project conducted by a select group working out of the Operations Directorate. Very low profile, no visibility, even within the Agency. Rest assured that we will find him, Senator, and that after we find him, he will never again be in a position to embarrass the Agency or the United States government."

McGowan rose to signify that the meeting was over, then moved toward the front door. Upon reaching the door, he offered his hand to Rathmann.

"Thank you, Charles. I have every confidence that you will acquit yourself admirably in concluding this matter, whatever course you elect to pursue. However, I would very much like to be apprised when the matter is finished. By the way, did you find out anything more on the call Traynor made to Italy?"

"No, that appears to be a dead end and perhaps a moot point. Nevertheless, I've asked our Operations Directorate to look into the matter and see how it was done. They're working on it now."

"Very well, then. Please let me know when this matter has been put to rest."

Rathmann was feeling very pleased with himself. He could see a very promising future in what surely would be a McGowan administration commencing in January, 2001.

"Thank you, Senator," the Director of Central Intelligence replied. "I will do just that."

McGowan opened and the door and watched as Charles Rathmann walked down the sidewalk to his waiting car. When the limousine was gone from sight, McGowan pushed his hands deep into the pockets of his robe and walked back into the house. He couldn't help but think about the future. *Soon the Frenchman will be gone and maybe Traynor as well. If he survives his injuries, I'll have to find a way to deal with him later. Even so, without the Frenchman, it will be hard for Traynor's story to merit any credibility. The Frenchman is the key. Once he's been dealt with, nothing can stop me. I'm home free.*

A smile crossed his lips as he quietly closed the door and walked back toward his dressing room to get ready for another busy day.

Four Hours Later—Hart Senate Office Building

Robert McGowan studied the overnight polling data on allowing oil and gas drilling in the Alaskan National Wildlife Refuge. He knew it made sense to open the ANWR; it was inevitable that America would need its resources to supplant at least part of the country's increasing appetite for fossil fuels. Dependence on foreign oil was becoming more and more a critical matter of national security, but the liberals and the conservationists just would not relent. Unfortunately, according to the polls, a majority of Americans agreed. *Well, if that's what the people want, that's what the people will get. I can feel just as strongly about protecting the ANWR as the next guy, and a hell of a lot more so than the*

Republicans, who never seem to get the big picture when it comes to making smart political decisions.

He was interrupted by his secretary.

"Senator, it's Director Rathmann. He says it's rather important. Do you want to take it?"

Maybe this is it, thought McGowan. *They've got the son-of-a-bitch.*

"Yes. Put him on."

Then after a pause, "Good morning, Mr. Director. What have you got for me?"

"Good morning again, Senator. We've had a setback."

McGowan could feel a tingling sensation on the nape of his neck. This deal *had* to go smoothly. Setbacks of any kind were not acceptable.

"Explain."

"Are you certain this line is secure?"

McGowan exploded into the handset. "Yes, Charlie, the damn line is secure, now tell me what the hell's happened."

"We appear to have lost Villon, at least temporarily."

"What do you mean, *lost* him?"

"He checked out of the Hermitage Hotel at noon, which was about the same time Fahoud was shot. That initially presented a bit of a problem. We weren't sure, still aren't sure, how he could have been at two places at the same time. But subsequent events seem to indicate that the shooter had to be Villon. He took a charter bus from the hotel to the airport in Nice where he purchased a ticket on a Delta flight to New York, connecting with Air Canada to Quebec City. Our plan was to watch the flight upon its arrival in New York, to make sure he didn't miss the connection, then pick him up upon his arrival in Quebec."

"So, what's the problem? Did he board the flight in Nice?"

"No. The airline reports that while he was issued a

boarding pass, he never boarded the airplane. Our contact in Nice reported an incident at the airport this afternoon, and when we checked, it turned out to be Villon. From what we can determine, it appears that two men who identified themselves as Interpol agents contacted the local police and asked for assistance in arresting a Monsieur Villon on an international warrant. The arrest was made at the gate as Villon was about to board the airplane. The Interpol agents had arranged transportation to take Villon into custody and transport him to an undisclosed location. Evidently there was a scuffle just outside the front door of the airport, shots were fired and witnesses reported that the prisoner, Villon, was shot in the back, then taken away by the Interpol van."

McGowan held his head in his hands, his eyes closed in thought.

"Okay, Charles, that's not the end of the world. They couldn't have been that far ahead of the Fahoud assassination, so Interpol must have wanted Villon for some other reason. Don't you have some contacts at Interpol that can provide information on Villon and what the hell they wanted him for? Maybe they'll be willing to turn him over to you."

When Rathmann hesitated in answering, McGowan knew something was very wrong.

"We *have* checked with Interpol, Senator, and that's the problem. Unless they are lying to us, and I have no' reason to believe they would do so, the men who arrested Villon and took him away were not Interpol agents. Interpol has no record of any such operation. No Interpol agents have been in contact with Nice police officials within the past twenty-four hours and no agents were sent to the airport to arrest someone named Villon. The name doesn't even show up in their computer."

McGowan was confused. *What the hell is going on here?*

"So who were they? Who's got the Frenchman and is he alive or dead? You said he was shot."

"That's the problem, Senator. We have no idea who has him or why, and certainly no idea of his physical condition. He has literally disappeared. We've got people looking for him and more on the way. This was a well-organized operation by someone who had the confidence to impersonate Interpol officers and enlist the local police to help them. It has all the marks of an operation run by a sophisticated intelligence organization, but I'll be damned if I know who did it. But we're investigating and I'm confident we'll find out. Keep in mind that this is just a few hours old. Give us some time and we'll get the answers."

"Charles, if whoever has him ties this back to the CIA, you're going to have a great deal of explaining to do. I'll try to help you, but this is your problem. You do understand that?"

McGowan waited anxiously as Rathmann considered his answer.

"I think we both understand the situation, Senator. I'll appreciate your continued support."

Then without waiting for a response, Rathmann added, "By the way Senator, I have some other news as well."

His foul mood evident, McGowan growled, "What other news?"

"Jonathan Traynor died at nine-thirty this morning without regaining consciousness. Goodbye, Senator. I'll keep you advised."

Before the report of Traynor's death had fully registered, the call was over. McGowan heard a click and a dial tone. At least he didn't have to worry about Traynor any more. Now if he could just get rid of the Frenchman.

13

BERMAN

22 July 1999—Collioure, France

Aaron Berman sipped his tea as he stood at the window of the upstairs flat, looking out over the beach at Collioure. The beach was crowded with vacationers on summer holiday. The sun was high and the water was clear and warm. The brightly colored fishing boats just across the harbor looked like props on a movie set, bobbing in the water, waiting for someone to take a picture or set up a canvas for a watercolor painting.

There were a few foreigners here, but the crowd consisted mostly of blue-collar French families enjoying a week on the sheltered beach inside the protected bay that was the focal point of the picturesque little town. Many of the women on the beach were topless, even the ones with their husbands and children in tow. No one seemed to take notice. Kids were screaming as they played at the edge of the water, most often with one or both of their parents. Old ladies, probably grandmothers vacationing with the family, were sunbathing alongside young girls who looked like models, and men of all ages were lying on the sand with their dark glasses and white bellies shining in the hot afternoon sun.

Waiters from the bars and restaurants across the narrow street from the bay front were carrying trays of cold drinks and wine in plastic glasses to discrete areas opposite their respective establishments where they had set up chairs and tables for those who wanted to have some refreshment without really leaving the beach.

Unlike the fashionable coastal resorts of the Riviera, there was little pretense here. No one seemed preoccupied with anyone else. That was one of the many things Berman liked about Collioure. And best of all, it was a great place to disappear.

Collioure lay on the southwest coast of France, only fifteen miles from the Spanish border. Berman had first come to Collioure in 1974 while he was still trying to decide what to do with his life after Vietnam and the loss of his left arm. Flying had been the only love in his life, the only thing he knew he wanted to do forever, but that was no longer a possibility. Modern civilization had made great strides in accommodating the handicapped, as he was often called by well-wishers, but there was one thing he knew for certain: there were no one-armed F-4 pilots. And at that time in his life, he was not sure if he ever wanted to do anything else.

It was during that first visit to Collioure that Berman had decided there was something he *might* be able to do, some way he *might* be able redirect his energies to something productive and important, and something that *might* be almost as exciting as tying up with a MIG-19 over Haiphong. He thought back on that time, some twenty-five years before, when he had made the decision of a lifetime, right here in Collioure.

Berman had spent almost a year in the hospital after the shoot-down and rescue. After being officially separated from the service, he had gone home to see his mother in Chicago and had wasted two months lying around the house, watching television and passing time without direction, allowing the housekeeper to wait on him hand and foot. Sometimes he would go out to a liquor store for a bottle of vodka, then sit in his room and drink himself unconscious. He never went to bars or restaurants, afraid he would see someone he knew and would have to go through the entire ordeal about the empty sleeve tucked inside his shirt. He became a recluse, and despite the constant words of encouragement from his mother, he fell deeper and deeper into the pit of self-pity and despair.

He realized that he had to get away—if for no other reason than to give his mother a break. She was dying watching him rot in the big, empty house. He had some money left over from the military pay he had accumulated while in the hospital and from the modest trust fund his father had left for him, so he decided to travel for a few months.

He spent three weeks in Canada, then almost a year in southern California, living in a beachfront rental near Laguna Niguel. Life among the hippies and the dropouts who had adopted the beach cities south of L.A. seemed to be the best environment for someone who did not want to be noticed, so Berman stayed there longer than he originally intended.

After that he went back home for a while, then off again on month-long trips here and there. But by that time he was deep into the trust fund and could see that his lifestyle was quickly going to outstrip his resources. But he didn't care all that much. He figured an impoverished cripple probably would not be any less happy that a moneyed one.

He decided to use what cash he had left for one final fling. He packed one small bag and took off for Europe, telling his mother that he probably would land somewhere on a beach in the south of France, and if everything went well, he would call her once a month. He ended up in

Collioure. It was pleasant and less expensive than some of the other places he had been, and no one seemed to notice him there.

After a few carefree months in Collioure, Berman came to the realization that it would not be long until his money ran out and he could no longer pay the rent. He knew he could always call home—his mother would wire money for a ticket back to Chicago—but he desperately did not want to do that. He was about at the end of his rope when Uncle Efrem found him.

Aaron was totally surprised when his only uncle, who he had not seen in years, showed up one day at the small boarding house where he had been living in the old part of Collioure. Uncle Efrem said that he had been in Marseilles for a meeting, and being so close, he had decided to drive down to Collioure to see Aaron. But he never explained how he knew Aaron was in Collioure. Aaron did not recall telling his mother, or anyone else for that matter, where he had holed-up. It was a mystery how Uncle Efrem had found him, but Berman was preoccupied with wasting his life, so he hadn't given the matter a great deal of thought.

Berman had always liked his uncle. He was witty and gregarious, but at the same time intelligent and under-standing. And early in his visit, Aaron discovered that Efrem had an uncanny ability to get him to talk about things he had no intention of discussing. Aaron spoke freely about his college days at Cal Poly, about his decision to join the Air Force in 1964 and about his complete immersion in flying. He told Efrem that he'd had his career all planned out—what assignments he had wanted, what billets he had wanted to fill and how he had planned to make general by the time he was forty. He talked about the missions he had flown during his two tours in Southeast Asia, missions over

Hanoi and Haiphong and close air support for ground operations in the south.

As he and Uncle Efrem shared a second bottle of wine,
Aaron told in great detail the story of how he had been shot
down in Laos on March 21, 1971, how he had lost his left
arm and very nearly his life, and about the miracle of his
rescue by a man he had never been able to identify. And at
the end of the story, he told Uncle Efrem that he had pretty
much concluded that at that point in his life, he was totally
useless and without a future. Every morning he wondered if
there was really any reason to get out of bed.

Efrem spent two days with Aaron in Collioure, and
during dinner on the second day at a beachfront restaurant
near the jetty, he got to the point of his visit.

"Do you intend to go back home?"

"No, there's no reason to go back, except to see Mother.
I have no other ties and no plans. I think I'd rather stay
here and live on the beach than go back to Chicago and try
to start over."

"Aren't you interested in finding a job?"

"Yes, but I can't think of anything productive that I can
do with one arm. I certainly can't fly, and that's what I
know best."

Efrem paused, deep in thought as he swirled the soft red
burgundy just under the rim of the plastic wineglass.

Still looking at the wine, he asked, "Would you be
willing to work in Israel?"

Berman's family had spent five years in Israel when he
was a child. He had fond memories of the friends he had
made there, and had never lost his mastery of the language.
It was a possibility to consider, but he wasn't sure the offer
was serious.

"Yeah, I suppose so. But hey, Uncle Efrem, I don't want

to be a charity case. You don't have to take me to raise."

They sat there for a minute in silence, then Berman said, "What kind of job do you think I could get in Israel that wouldn't require two good arms?"

"I have a government job in an agency that's always looking for bright people with special talents. You have an engineering degree from one of the best schools in the States, you speak excellent Hebrew, you know about airplanes and have wartime military experience. I know we'd have plenty for you to do and I think you'd find it interesting. How does that sound?"

Berman said he would think about it, and he did—all that night. His first inclination was to turn down the offer, but then he found himself intrigued by the qualifications Efrem had mentioned. It did sound interesting, so the next morning he told Efrem that he thought he might like to pursue the offer. That was when Efrem told him about the condition that made the decision irreversible.

"Aaron, I want to level with you. Normally we'd wait until an applicant was well into the process before springing this on him, but you're my only nephew and I want to save you the pain if it turns out you don't want to go forward. The question is this. Would you be willing to become an Israeli citizen and commit your loyalties totally and unequivocally to the State of Israel, even against the United States if a conflict of interest should ever arise? If you don't want to or can't commit yourself entirely to Israel, that's okay. I'll understand and we'll let the matter drop right now. That doesn't mean I'm going to abandon you and go home—I still want to see if I can help you somehow, but it *will* mean that we can forget talking about Israel."

Berman thought about the condition for a few minutes while he made himself a cup of coffee. He also thought about what Uncle Efrem's offer implied. A government job with those kinds of conditions indicated either a position with the military or some kind of intelligence agency. That piqued his interest unlike anything had since his first day in flight school. He thought about home and about what he would be giving up, which at that red hot moment in time was absolutely nothing.

After thirty minutes of considering all the consequences he could identify, Aaron said, "Yes, I'd like to further pursue the offer. And if it turns out the way I think it might, I'll have no problem with the condition. But I've got to know what I'm getting into before I take the job. Fair enough?"

"Certainly. In fact, I'd have been disappointed if you'd committed yourself without finding out more. Now start getting packed. We leave for Israel tomorrow morning. If you find you don't want the job, I'll get you some travel expense money and you can go wherever you want to try to find whatever it is you're looking for. But I think you're going to find it in Tel Aviv. Let's go."

Berman *did* find what he was looking for. And as it turned out, the special condition didn't bother him at all. As a matter of fact, in just a few short months he became so committed to Israel, its people, their security and their future, that he felt like he'd been there all his life. And the fact that he had only one arm didn't make any difference at all. He found himself capable of making contributions in ways he had never imagined. He was happy and content with his life for the first time since punching out of his burning F-4 over Laos. He was entirely at peace. And more than anything else, he found a sense of self-worth once again in his new position with the Israeli Institute for Intelligence and Special Tasks, more commonly known as the Mossad.

★ ★ ★ ★ ★

Berman was called back to the present by the noise of someone opening the door to the small bedroom that he had converted into a makeshift office. He turned to see the youngest member of his team enter the room and close the door behind him. The young man, still nursing a severely bruised sternum, winced as he walked toward Berman,

Berman waited for the report he was expecting.

"Chief," he said. "Our guest is showing signs of waking up. Do you want to be in there when he comes around?"

"What does Dr. Cohen say? How much will he remember?"

"Not much at first, then it should start coming back to him quickly. He'll definitely remember being shot, but not much after that. Of course, he won't know where he is and probably will be panicked by the fact that he's bound and in a strange place."

"Don't underestimate him. No matter how he acts, our friend will not be panicked. I want to keep him restrained until he understands exactly who we are and why he's here."

"Yeah, Chief, and by the way, I'd like to know why he's here too, and for that matter, I'm curious as to why *we're* here."

Berman stared a hole in the young man, but did not respond.

"Let me know when he's awake enough to talk. But once again, do not underestimate him. No matter what he says or how he acts, keep the restraints in place. I'll make the explanations when the time comes."

The young man turned and walked out, his instructions clear. While Aaron Berman ran the division in an informal manner, it was clear you did not argue with him and you did not press him. He would tell them what was going on when they needed to know.

Berman wasn't sure what he was going to tell his team or how he was going to justify this operation. But that would come later. Right now he had an account to settle, one that was almost thirty years past due.

14

REUNION

22 July 1999—Collioure, France

He was vaguely aware of regaining consciousness. He realized he had been studying the movement of the thin gauze curtains that hung unevenly from a tarnished brass rod above the open window near the foot of his bed. The curtains were swaying gently from side to side in the warm breeze that carried the pungent scent of saltwater mixed with the sweet smell of fragrant flowers. For some reason he was unable to move his arms and legs. He wondered if he was paralyzed, or maybe tied down. That was it. He was spread-eagled on the small bed, his arms and legs tied to bedposts with some kind of plastic bindings. His back ached, his head throbbed and his mouth was dry. He searched his memory, trying to remember how he had gotten here, where he had been.

Things started to clear up. Memories started coming back. He remembered Monaco—staying at the Hermitage, killing Azbek Fahoud. He wondered if he had been caught, maybe by Fahoud's henchmen.

No, he didn't think that was it. There was something else. Yes, he had been at the airport in Nice. There were four men, two uniformed police officers and two plain-clothesmen, who had arrested him at the boarding gate, taken him into custody and led him out of the airport.

And that was when he remembered being shot in the

back. It was not a dream. It *had* happened. It was real.

He mentally took inventory of his physical condition. The recollection of being shot was clear and he could still feel a stinging soreness in his back. Although he had a strong memory of feeling as though he were dying, he also had a sense that he was not badly hurt. He had been shot and hospitalized a few times in the past, but this was different. He was okay, badly beat up and groggy, but physically okay. He wondered how long he had been out.

Then he started wondering who had him and why. What was coming next? Was the Agency behind this? Only Traynor knew about Monaco and Fahoud.

What were his options?

He tested the bindings on his wrists and ankles; no way to break those. He would be patient. Soon someone would come to talk with him. He would let them believe he was too groggy to be dangerous, maybe ask for help to go to the toilet—then he would make his move. He needed to get out of there so he could figure out what had gone wrong. Then he would deal with the situation, do whatever needed to be done.

The stained, cream-colored door to the small room opened. Staley quickly closed his eyes and waited. A man shuffled toward the bed. He was wheezing and smelled of stale smoke. Staley sensed the presence of another man as well, a man who stayed back, near the door.

The first man placed his fingers on Staley's upturned wrist and took his pulse. After thirty seconds or so, he put his clammy palm on Staley's forehead, as if to check for fever.

Staley could feel the man back away from the bed. He then spoke, in English but with a discernable Middle-Eastern accent.

"I suspect you are awake, my friend. If so, please open your eyes. I am a physician and I would like to see if you have recovered as expected."

Staley didn't move.

"*Please,* open your eyes and talk to me. It is important that I know you are conscious. No one is going to harm you and, I can assure you, until my friends have had a chance to talk with you, no one is going to release your bonds no matter what your needs or condition. So, it will be in your best interests to let me examine you and to let me tell my associates that you are awake and ready to talk. Do not make this more difficult than it needs to be."

Staley rolled his head toward the voice and slowly opened his eyes, feigning grogginess and an inability to focus. Through half-closed eyes, he scanned the room. There were two men. The older one, probably the man who had identified himself as a doctor, was standing a foot or so from the bed, looking down at Staley with a concerned expression. The other man, much younger and carrying a 9-millimeter Beretta in shoulder holster over a loose-fitting white shirt, was standing near the door, watching.

In a weak voice, but remembering to disguise his nationality with a heavy French accent, Staley asked slowly, "Where . . . where am I? Who are you?"

The doctor approached him, obviously exercising an inordinate amount of caution. Staley remembered the plainclothesman at the airport saying, "We know who you are." They were wary of him as well. It was disconcerting that his captors knew so much about him and his capabilities. It took away the edge he always counted on in tight situations.

"I am going to listen to your heart and lungs, take your blood pressure and check your reactions. Please lie very still and do not attempt to resist. I promise you that I am not going to hurt you or administer any drugs. I just want to ensure that you are alright."

Staley realized that he was wearing a large, knit shirt over the slacks he had worn to the airport in Nice. He could feel bandages taped to his back. He didn't move as the doctor slid the stethoscope under his shirt and listened to his chest, then wrapped the cuff of a sphygmomanometer around the upper part of his right arm and took his blood pressure. The doctor checked his pupils, shining a small penlight in each eye.

When he was finished, he looked at Staley and smiled.

"You are going to be fine. Probably a bit groggy for a while yet, but otherwise fine."

As the doctor put his instruments back into the small black bag lying on the table next to the bed, he turned to the young man standing near the door.

"I need to take a look at the wounds on his back. Please call me when it will be possible to loosen the restraints on at least one arm and leg so I can roll him over. The wounds will need to be dressed once a day for the next two or three days, then will heal nicely on their own."

The young man nodded, then opened the door for the doctor. Staley watched as both men left the room and closed the door, locking it behind them.

Staley realized that he was still exhausted from the ordeal—an ordeal that somehow had brought him from Nice to a small room somewhere near the ocean, a captive of men whose identity and motives were a complete mystery. He rolled his head toward the open window and closed his eyes, and in a few seconds, he was asleep.

A car horn honked nearby and the unexpected noise caused Staley to jump, awakening him from a sound sleep.

He knew immediately where he was and the situation he faced. The bonds were still in place, but the brightness of midday was gone. Staley sensed a presence nearby and opened his eyes. Shadows of twilight played on the thin curtains. The corner of the room beyond was dark.

Staley turned his head toward the door and, as expected, found a man sitting next to the bed, watching him intently. Even in the dim light, there was something familiar about the man, but Staley could not place him.

The man smiled, then reached out and patted Staley gently on the outside of his right leg—an act of kindness that seemed inappropriate under the circumstances.

"Good evening, my friend. The doctor says you are recovering nicely and will be able to get up and around any time now."

The man spoke perfect English—no accent of any kind. Staley tried to recall the voice, but he couldn't make a connection.

Staley spoke softly but with the heavy French accent of François Villon, his voice tinged with affected discomfort and confusion. "I have to use the toilet. Will you please cut me loose just for a few moments so that I can use the toilet? I will not cause you any trouble."

"Yes, I will cut you loose, as soon as we make our introductions and you understand who I am, who *we* are, and why you are here."

The man was alone in the room. This might be the only time this opportunity would present itself and Staley had to act quickly.

"Please, I have to go *now*. I cannot wait. I will not give you any trouble."

The man smiled—a knowing smile and not the least bit threatening.

"Monsieur Villon, or Captain Delon, or whatever your real name is, I have no doubt that if I were to free you at this moment, you would do a great deal of damage to me and probably to several of my men before we could stop you, assuming we *could* stop you. I do not want that to happen and I do not want to have to take steps in our defense that might cause you harm. So please, listen to me for a few minutes. Then we'll talk about releasing you."

Staley was stunned. The Villon identity was the one he had been using on this trip—even the police at the airport had called him by that name—so this man referring him as Villon made sense. But the Delon identity had been dead for years, except for occasional use in Canada as the name on a post office box or for a package delivery. This guy *must* have been briefed by Traynor. But if Traynor were involved, wouldn't his captors have cut through all the cover identities and referred to him by his real name?

Staley looked more carefully at the man beside the bed. He appeared to be a few years older than Staley but in good shape—like an office type who went to the gym a couple of times a week. Then Staley noticed the empty sleeve where the man's left arm should be. Something about that rang a bell.

Still using the French accent, Staley said, "My name is François Villon, but obviously you know that. And who are you?"

Berman smiled again. "I am *very* pleased to make your acquaintance, Monsieur whoever-you-are. I have wished to do so for a very long time. My name is Aaron Berman. In another lifetime, I was an F-4 pilot in the United States Air Force, and one fine morning in March of 1971, I was shot down in Laos and left for dead. *But,* I had the good fortune of having been found by a young mercenary, presumably a

Frenchman, named Jack Delon, who treated my wounds and carried me out. Although I suspect that you have had many exciting experiences since then, I also suspect that you remember that incident. Am I correct?"

Staley looked at Berman, remembering every detail of the two days he spent in the jungles of Laos finding and recovering the badly wounded pilot. Twenty-eight years had taken a toll, and the face was now clean and free of cuts and scrapes, but Staley was certain it was the same man. And the missing arm cinched it.

"I'm very glad you survived, Captain Berman. I wouldn't have given you much of a chance when I left you at the aid station at Khe Sanh. I see you lost your arm. I was certain you would, but I'm sorry nonetheless."

Berman absent-mindedly rubbed his shoulder near the point where his arm had been taken off. "It was very difficult at first, but I've grown accustomed to it. No more fast movers, I'm afraid. In fact, they won't let me fly *anything* these days without a copilot. But I'm managing just fine."

The two men sat in silence for a moment, then Staley broke the ice by asking, still with the French accent, "How did you find out about me? What is this all about?"

Berman leaned back in his chair and studied the gauze curtains across the bed, as if trying to decide where to begin a long and complicated story. He then turned back to the Frenchman.

"In January, 1972, I was in rehabilitation at an Air Force hospital in Mississippi. One day I had a visitor, a man I didn't know. It was a retired Army colonel named Jonathan Traynor."

Berman was impressed that the man who called himself François Villon showed no reaction whatsoever to the name. The Frenchman was very good.

"Colonel Traynor seemed to know a great deal about me and about my shoot-down and recovery from Laos. He was interested in how I was progressing with the rehab and what I planned to do after my discharge from the Air Force. He told me that he too had been discharged from the military, also due to wounds received in Southeast Asia, and that he was finding other interesting things to keep him occupied. It sounded like a pep talk to me and I had had enough of that by then, so I didn't pay much attention to him.

"But then he started asking more pointed questions, particularly about the details of the day I was shot down. He wanted to know how I found cover, how I kept myself alive as badly wounded as I was, and how I and my back-seater found each other on the ground. He wanted to know if I could recall anything at all about the time I spent on the ground before I was rescued and brought out.

"Well, I of course couldn't remember a thing after I punched out. Still can't for that matter, but I found it very curious that this retired Army colonel wanted to know all about the experience. I started wondering if he was still working for the government, or writing a book, or what he might be up to, and I rather belligerently told him to mind his own damn business and leave me alone.

"He said he understood my reluctance to talk with him about the incident and said he'd probably check in on me later. I never saw him again after that.

"Sometime after my eventual discharge from the Air Force, I left the United States and took a job working for the government of Israel, which is what I'm still doing today."

That last statement really got Staley's attention, although he did not visibly react. Something very strange was happening here and he needed to understand it, all of it, and quickly. But first, he had to get free of the straps that had him tied to the bed.

Remaining in character, Staley grimaced as though terribly uncomfortable and interrupted Berman's train of thought.

Still affecting the French accent, Staley said, "I am relieved to know you are not a criminal or a terrorist. Neither am I. But more importantly, right now I need to use the facilities or I'm going to make a mess here. Please untie me and let me go to the toilet. You can call one of your men to watch me."

Berman was exasperated by Villon's continued efforts to gain his freedom. He had no doubt that if he freed the man Traynor had spoken of, there would be violence and someone would get hurt. He had to finish his story.

"Monsieur, please. I know that you are a dangerous and experienced field agent and right now your only objective is to free yourself. After you have heard everything I have to say, I will free you. I promise. In the meantime, please have the courtesy to lie still and be quiet. Believe it or not, I'm trying to save your life."

Staley acquiesced and relaxed on the bed. He might as well listen to the entire story.

"After almost twenty years in Israel," Berman continued, "I was relatively certain that I no longer had an active Air Force file and that no one in the United States was keeping track of my whereabouts or had had any interest in what I might be doing. Then one day, the day after I was promoted to section chief, my private telephone rang—a telephone I had been assured was absolutely untraceable and anonymous. The caller was Colonel Traynor. It took me a few minutes to figure out who he was, but soon the memory of his visit to the hospital came back clearly. Needless to say, I was very surprised to hear from him.

"He told me that he had kept track of my career and that he wanted to offer his congratulations on my promotion. I, of course, told him that I had no idea what he was talking about, but that I appreciated the call after so many years.

"Then Colonel Traynor told me something I found remarkable and totally fascinating. He told me that he had served in a special capacity to various directors of the Central Intelligence Agency for many years, and that he had kept up with my activities by utilizing the assets of Agency and through a common acquaintance. Before I could object and divert the conversation, he said something to me that I will never forget. He said, 'Aaron, you have a good life and an important position in Israel, your adopted country, and I have followed your career with great interest. I fancy myself as a good judge of character and I believe you to be a man of great integrity. But you owe your life to me and to the man you first met as Captain Jack Delon, the Frenchman who rescued you from the jungles of Laos in March of 1971. I want you to know that he and I might need your help some day in righting a great injustice, and when that day comes, I want you to think very hard and long about repaying your country, *this* country, America, by providing the help we will need. I will be in touch.'

"And with that, he hung up. Despite my efforts and those of my organization, we were unable to trace the call. We knew only that it came from America and somewhere in the Washington, D.C. area. It was somewhat easier to find out information about Colonel Traynor and confirm the fact that he had, for some time, worked with, not *for*, the CIA. While his personal life was relatively easy to explore, his activities on behalf of the Agency were completely shrouded. There were not even dead ends, because there were no trails to follow to a dead end.

"I also tried to find out about Captain Jack Delon, but soon discovered that there was no such man. That was a dead end as well. We were unable to find any associates of Colonel Traynor who might have matched the Jack Delon persona, so, after a time, I let the matter drop.

"Then, four days ago, I received another call from Colonel Traynor. It was a call to one of the special blind numbers set up for one-time emergency use by our field operatives. At first I could not figure out how he could have obtained that number, but after reading the letter I am about to show you, I realized it was through my Uncle Efrem, with whom Colonel Traynor evidently had been acquainted for some time. The Colonel's voice on the phone was very weak. He told me he had been attacked in his home and was badly injured and he might not be able to complete the conversation before passing out, in which event I was to break the connection immediately. He said that the time had come for me to repay my debt to the Frenchman."

Berman paused to see if anything he'd said had had any effect on the prisoner, but the man most recently known as Villon just returned his stare with no reaction or sign of recognition.

Berman pulled a pack of cigarettes from his pocket, took one from the pack and lit it with a worn silver Zippo. There was a faded emblem on the lighter, his F-4 squadron patch from Vietnam. Then he continued.

"The first thing Colonel Traynor asked me to do was to assemble a field team, one that could not be identified as Israeli or tied back to me. I was to take the team to Nice on July 21 and arrange to intercept and arrest a Monsieur François Villon before he boarded his flight back to North

America. The Colonel did not know the airline but was certain that Monsieur Villon would be on a flight to either America or Canada that day or the next. He told me he assumed we could use our resources to find the airline and flight number. Traynor impressed upon me that arresting Monsieur Villon would not be easy and that the agents would have to sedate Monsieur Villon as soon as possible, otherwise there would be great trouble. He also told me to be gentle with Monsieur Villon, as he was the man who had rescued me from Laos. That bit of information, of course, captured my full attention.

"The second thing he told me was that on the way to Nice, I should stop in Bern and go to the Schweizerische Nationalbank where a package would be waiting for me in a box registered in Colonel Traynor's name. He said the package would have my name on it and he gave me a password that would authorize the bank to deliver it to me with simple proof of identification. He assured me that the contents of the package would explain everything.

"At the conclusion of the conversation, he said, 'Aaron, you must help me now. Please do as I ask without question or hesitation. I am certain the same man who tried to kill you twenty-eight years ago is somehow involved in this attack against me, and I suspect that he or those working with him will make an attempt on the life of the man who brought you out of Laos. We both need your help. The package will explain everything. Do not expect to hear from me again.'

"With that, he hung up.

"After giving the matter a great deal of thought, I did exactly what Colonel Traynor asked me to do, and that is how and why you are here.

"As he was walking you out of the airport, my associate

Hassi injected you with a drug that, when combined with the powder shot into your back when you tried to make your escape while getting into the van, resulted in a condition that simulated respiratory failure and death. I am sorry we had to do it that way, but it convinced the local police and allowed us to take you away, ostensibly to a medical facility operated by Interpol. Instead, we brought you here to recover."

Staley considered all he had heard. *So it was Traynor who set me up. But he did it to save my life. At least that's what he told Berman. But there's more here, much more. What was in the package? And what did Traynor say about someone trying to kill him?*

Acknowledging more than he had to that point, Staley asked, "So what about Colonel Traynor? He said he was badly injured? Did he say how? Have you checked on him?"

Berman hesitated for a moment. "Yes, our representatives in Washington followed his case closely. Colonel Traynor died at Walter Reed Hospital yesterday morning from injuries sustained during an apparent robbery at his home the same night he called me. That does not square with what the Colonel told me on the telephone, but that's what is being reported by the Metropolitan Police Department. In any event, I'm sorry."

Staley lay back and closed his eyes. The Old Man had been someone he had respected and admired for many years. He didn't get to see him often, maybe once every year or so when circumstances would permit, but he really cared for the old guy. Jonathan Traynor was the closest thing he'd had to a family in years. Now he was dead. Staley would miss him.

Staley focused on the contradiction Berman had observed. The official report was that Traynor had died from injuries received during a robbery, but in his call to Berman he said that the same man who had shot and left Berman to die in the jungle was responsible for the attempt on his life. *The same man who tried to kill Berman twenty-eight years ago? That would have to be Berman's back-seater in the F-4, the weapons officer we recovered and my Hoc Bao unit took back to Khe Sanh while I went after the downed pilot. I never knew his name, but I'll bet it will be easy enough to find out.*

One thing was for certain. Whoever had killed Jonathan Traynor would die. Staley would find who did it and personally settle that score, no matter how long it took.

Then Staley remembered the package. He looked at Berman. "Did you get the package from the bank in Bern?"

"Yes."

"What was in it?"

"If you give me your word that you won't try to escape until you have read the contents of the package, I'll release you and you can look at it. I'm not armed, so if you want to hurt me, you'll be able to do so easily. I owe you my life. If you want to take it, go ahead."

Staley studied Berman and considered what to do next. Under the circumstances, it didn't make any difference whether or not he gave Berman his word. That wouldn't stop him if he decided the best course of action was to kill everyone in the apartment and leave. But it appeared that Traynor had trusted Berman, and the fact was that Berman could have killed him at any time over the past several hours. So, Staley decided he'd stick around.

Finally he said, "I give you my word, I will take no aggressive action if you release me. I assume that if I choose to do so, I will be free to go?"

"Certainly, if you wish. Just relax and I'll cut you loose."

Berman cut the plastic bonds that secured Staley's legs

to the footboard of the bed, then the straps that held his hands. He stepped back.

Staley rubbed his wrists, then slowly sat up, still feeling a bit groggy from the drugs.

Berman then stepped forward and held out his hand.

"Once again, I'm pleased to meet you, my friend. What should I call you?"

Staley stood and extended his hand, then smiled. "Michael," he said, dropping the French accent. "I think it would be a good idea if you just called me Michael." It was his middle name, after his maternal grandfather about whom he'd heard so much but never met.

Aaron Berman smiled at the loss of the French accent. "Glad to meet you, Michael. And by the way, thanks for pulling me out of the jungle."

"You're welcome. I'm glad I was there to help."

Then the two men, whose paths had crossed twenty-eight years earlier on the other side of the world, shook hands for the first time.

15

FINAL INSTRUCTIONS

25 July 1999—Hartsfield International Airport—Atlanta
John Holt had worked for the United States Immigration
and Naturalization Service for more than twenty-five years.
He was very good at his job and had spotted more than a few
unsavory characters trying to enter the country with bad papers, and once had been instrumental in nabbing a drug
dealer who had been on the watch list for six months.
Anyone who had the poor judgment to try to bluff his way
past John Holt was likely to get caught. He could read people
like a book. Those who tried to beat the system always made
a mistake. There was always something just a little bit off
about their paperwork, or about the way they looked, or in
the way they answered the seemingly innocent questions
Holt had developed over the years to separate the good from
the bad. He knew he had a sixth sense about travelers step-
ping up to his booth who were not who they claimed to be.

Holt finished with the husband and wife from Great
Britain and motioned to the next passenger behind the wide
yellow line to step forward. A nice-looking, well-tanned
man wearing a business suit and carrying a worn leather
briefcase approached the booth and presented his passport
and visa. Holt quickly scanned the arriving passenger, then
flipped through the middle-aged man's heavily-used passport. His name was Beneficio Alterez, a Spanish national
from Càdiz.

"What is the purpose of your visit to the United States, Mr. Alterez?"

In almost perfect English, but with a touch of an accent that would be recognized as Spanish only by someone with a sophisticated ear, Beneficio Alterez replied, "Business. I have business in Alexandria, Virginia, then Memphis and then Dallas."

Holt looked again at the passenger before him. He was slightly nervous. That was a good sign. Anyone with any sense who goes through passport control should be a little nervous. It was the ones who were totally calm and played it cool that you had to watch out for. Either they or the ones who were *so* nervous they constantly looked around and could not stand still. This guy was just the right amount of nervous.

"What business are you in?"

"I am in the commercial construction business. I have contracts with specialty suppliers in the United States and come here about twice a year to renew acquaintances and check on the status of important relationships."

Holt looked up and smiled. "How's the weather in Càdiz this time of year? Is it as hot as it is here?"

"Very warm. Not as hot as Dallas, but warm. Thirty-one, thirty-two degrees during the day, but the sea breeze cools things off at night. Very pleasant, really."

Holt had never been to Spain, but it was one of the places he had always wanted to see. Maybe he would go to Càdiz one of these days.

He stamped Señor Alterez's passport and handed it back to him. *This guy's legit, no problem. Just another European doing business in America. Good for the balance of trade.*

"Thank you, Mr. Alterez. Go to your right to claim your bags, then continue on though customs. Keep your customs declaration form handy. Welcome to the United States."

"Thank you very much."

Hackler Staley slipped his Alterez passport back into the pocket of his jacket and walked toward the baggage claim. He was always surprised at how easy it was to get past immigration. *And the American people think we have border security. Amazing.*

Four hours later Staley, still using the Beneficio Alterez identity, checked into the Four Seasons Hotel on Pennsylvania Avenue in the Georgetown section of Washington, D.C. He chose the hotel because of its location near Traynor's home.

Continuing with the Alterez identity was probably unnecessary, but Staley didn't have any details about Jonathan Traynor's death—whether he had been interrogated or drugged before being admitted to the hospital or if he had given up Staley's real name. Staley was certain that, if it at all possible, the old man would have gone to his grave without revealing that information. But he also knew that in the end, no one could beat the drugs. Staley *had* to find out what transpired before the Colonel died. But that was just one of the items on the agenda. The principal reason for his trip to Washington was to find and secure whatever information Traynor might have left behind; information that was intended exclusively for him.

Staley was still reeling from the shock of discovering that the cowardly weapons systems officer he had rescued from Laos in March, 1971, the one who had attempted to murder his front-seater, was none other than Senator Robert J. McGowan, the leading candidate for the Democratic nomination for President in 2000. And then to think that with almost his final breath, Colonel Traynor had identified McGowan as the person behind the attack that eventually led to Traynor's death.

It was almost more than he could comprehend, but if Traynor had said McGowan was guilty of orchestrating the attack, Staley would accept the information without question. Now he had to decide what to do about it. For that decision, he needed more facts.

Staley slept through the early evening. Around nine p.m., he called room service and ordered a filet with steak fries and a salad, along with a bottle of ginger ale. He figured he might be up all night and wanted to be sharp for whatever he might encounter at the Traynor mansion.

As he waited for his dinner to arrive, Staley opened the manila envelope he had carried with him from Collioure and pulled out the document he had been given by Aaron Berman—a copy of the letter from Jonathan Traynor that Berman had picked up at the Schweizerische Nationalbank in Bern. The remarkable thing about the letter was that it had been written ten years earlier, five years before the old man had called Berman to congratulate him on his promotion. The letter must have been in the bank vault for a long time, probably most of those ten years, but the message was still current.

Traynor was not one to allow unfinished business to remain unfinished. The letter was his way of ensuring that unsettled accounts would be squared, even after his death. Staley could almost hear the old man talking as he reread the letter.

24 September 1989
Dear Mr. Berman:
My name is Jonathan Traynor (Colonel, U.S. Army, Retired). I was medically retired from the United States

Army in 1967 as a result of wounds suffered during my second tour of duty in South Vietnam. I mention this only because I am fully aware of your service during the Vietnam War and the fact that you too were discharged from the armed forces as a result of wounds you received during a close air support mission over Laos in March, 1971.

Since 1987, I have operated as an independent intelligence consultant working exclusively for the United States Central Intelligence Agency. For many years prior to 1987, I served as special assistant to successive Directors of the Agency. Over the years, I have had access to a considerable amount of sensitive information relating to a broad range of topics, including some remarkable information concerning you and the day you were shot down. You may not recall the occasion, but I visited you once while you were in rehabilitation at the Air Force hospital at Keesler AFB in Mississippi. Although that was the only time we met, because of the link between us described in this letter, I have made a point of keeping track of your whereabouts and activities since your discharge from the Air Force in 1972.

Two years ago while working on a counter-terrorism project here in Washington, I met your uncle, Efrem Zeliger, who I knew to be a career intelligence officer with the Mossad. I spent several days with Efrem and we became friends. In the course of a lengthy conversation over dinner one evening, I learned that you were his nephew. It was a remarkable coincidence. I explained to Efrem my interest in you and he brought me up to date on your progress with the Israeli intelligence service.

I told Efrem that I had important information concerning the day you were shot down in Laos, but that I did not want to disrupt your life by reopening old wounds if the matter could be handled without your knowledge or *assistance. But I also told him that if I should need your help, I would have no choice but to ask, because of the overriding importance of the matter. Efrem agreed that it would be best to not involve you unless absolutely necessary, but because of that caveat, he also agreed to update me periodically on your career and how you might be reached, just in case the need should arise.*

If your uncle is able to do so at the time you receive this letter, he will vouch for everything stated above. If not, I am well aware that in your position you have the capability of accessing my service records and verifying on your own much of the above information concerning me, and I would encourage you to do so.

I must admit that I had mixed feelings upon learning that you had left America to take a position with the Mossad, but after talking with Efrem, I now believe that you made the right decision. I congratulate you on your career. Your uncle advises me that you have done excellent work for the State of Israel. He also tells me that you have proven yourself a man of great courage, ingenuity and honor.

The fact that you are reading this letter means one of two things. Either I am dead and you have been contacted by my personal representative (who, by the way, has no knowledge of the contents of this letter or why it has been left for you) with instructions to retrieve this letter from a designated Swiss bank, or urgent circumstances have dictated that I contact you during my lifetime with instructions for you to retrieve this letter. Your uncle has provided me with information for contacting you in case of emergency and has agreed to update those instructions as circumstances change. If I've called you for help on a secure line or contacted you by utilizing other classified procedures, this will explain how I obtained such access.

In any event, I sincerely hope that you will consider the information I am providing with this letter and then act reasonably and decisively to ensure that the proper action is taken.

I have harbored the information I am about to pass along to you for well over a decade, and I must admit to you that as the years go by, it becomes more and more difficult for me to abstain from taking action to remedy the injustice of which I am aware. Since you are reading this letter, I have either died without addressing the situation or find myself unable to do anything about it. In either event, I have made the decision to provide full details to you and allow you to take whatever action, if any, that you believe should be taken. Keep in mind that while Israel is your adopted county, America is the country of your birth and that if those who are unsuitable to lead it should ever be in a position to do so, action should be taken to ensure that they do not accede to the highest offices of this government. Again, I am certain that you will take the appropriate action to prevent that from happening.

I know from talking with you that morning in Mississippi and from reports I've collected from various sources that you have no recollection of what happened after your F-4 was shot down in Laos on 21 March 1971. The following is a substantiated account of the events of that day, based on an unimpeachable eyewitness account and considerable physical evidence (a description of the physical evidence with copies of laboratory tests is enclosed). All of the evidence supports the inevitable conclusion that Robert McGowan, your former weapons systems officer and now a United States Senator, attempted to murder you while you lay grievously wounded that morning in the jungles of Laos and then callously left you for dead. Here are the details . . .

The letter related the substance of Staley's initial and follow-up reports to Traynor describing the events of 21 and 22 March 1971. While the letter identified Berman's rescuer as a Frenchman named Captain Jack Delon, it disclosed that Captain Delon was secretly working for Traynor and had been sent to Vietnam for the specific purpose of retrieving downed aircrews during the invasion of Laos, due to the restrictions imposed by the Cooper-Church Amendment. The letter also included follow-up analysis by Traynor, including lab tests on the slug extracted by Staley from the log behind Berman, comparison with the cartridges removed by Staley from McGowan's .38, and detailed parsing of the after-action statements made by McGowan, which were irreconcilable but overlooked in the heat of the moment.

The letter chronicled McGowan's career as a rising star in the Democratic Party and his election to various state and federal offices, culminating with his then-recent victory in a race for a second term in Senate. That event was the catalyst that caused Traynor to write the letter: the possibility that some day McGowan would be in a position to make significant policy decisions for the United States government. It was a prospect that Traynor could not abide. He stated that he suspected the time would come when McGowan's story would have to be told, and when that time came, it would be necessary for someone to have the information to substantiate the allegations.

Staley stopped reading and walked over to the window of his room. He looked down toward the garden below, not really seeing anything beyond his own reflection in the glass. He recalled how shocked he had been the first time he read the letter and realized that the cowardly lieutenant he had rescued from Laos that morning was Robert McGowan. He had not known the weapons officer's name when making his initial report to Traynor and the face seemingly had been gone from his memory for years. But now he remembered the incident clearly, and in so remembering, he aged in his mind's eye the dirty, frightened face of the young lieutenant into the clean, bright, confident face of Senator Robert J. McGowan.

He wondered why Traynor had never told him—surely the old man knew that Staley had not made the connection. Maybe he was concerned that Staley would blow the lid off, or worse yet, directly confront McGowan. It was Traynor's habit to handle matters in his own way, and Staley could see that while the Colonel had not acted for years, he would never allow McGowan to take a pass on what he had done that hot morning north of Highway 9 in Laos. Justice would not permit it.

Staley walked back to his chair and continued reading. At the close, the letter became personal to Berman. First, there was an unqualified endorsement of the man identified to Berman as Captain Delon, including the revelation that Delon was not his real name and that the Frenchman had continued to work for Traynor long after American troops had left Vietnam. Traynor told Berman that the Frenchman was the most trustworthy, dedicated and efficient field agent he'd ever known, and that his identity was known only to Traynor himself.

Despite the seriousness of the situation, Staley chuckled to himself at Traynor's compulsiveness about security. He was too smart to give up anything he did not have to reveal, even to Aaron Berman. Staley was glad for that. He did not intend for Berman to learn his true identity either. Wallace and Marie would have approved.

In the last paragraph of the letter, the old man offered

these words of recommendation and advice:

> *Remember that you owe your life to the man once known as Jack Delon. If he should ever need your help, you must give it to him. I have trusted him with my life and you can do the same. And if by some chance you have occasion to meet him under circumstances where you are the one that needs assistance, rest assured that you can count on him as well. Just use my name and show him this letter. But until you have his confidence, be very careful. He is extremely cautious and not easily approachable. To those he perceives as the enemy, my friend is a very dangerous man. Get to know him and he will be a worthy ally. Godspeed to you both.*

Staley refolded the letter and slipped it back into the envelope. As he did so, he remembered the deal he had made with Aaron Berman before they had parted the previous day in Collioure. Staley would return to the United States, investigate Traynor's death and, taking the old man at his word, try to determine how and to what extent McGowan might have been involved. Berman would make discreet inquiries in Europe in an effort to ascertain who might be looking for François Villon and what involvement, if any, McGowan might have in that operation.

Berman had given Staley a small laptop computer that looked like an off-the-shelf model, but had been configured to send and receive secure e-mails with a similar laptop retained by Berman. The two men agreed to keep in touch by e-mail on a regular basis. If for some reason Staley failed to check in with Berman at least once in each forty-eight-hour period, Berman would come looking for him, and for Robert McGowan.

* * * * *

Staley, wearing black jeans and a black turtleneck and carrying a small backpack, hunkered down next to the rusted dumpster in the narrow alley behind Traynor's house. He had left the hotel wearing a tan knit shirt, but had slipped it off in favor of the turtleneck shortly after stealing into the alley.

He checked his watch. The luminous dial read two-thirty a.m. It was cool and quiet in the alley. He had been in position for almost thirty minutes and had not heard a sound other than a single car passing in the street at the end of the alley and the whir of the compressor on a neighbor's air conditioning unit.

There was no sign of a police stakeout or other surveillance anywhere in the area. He had been concerned that the Agency would have someone in place to watch the Colonel's house, but apparently no one was there. The absence of surveillance was troubling. *Why isn't the CIA interested?*

Moving quietly, Staley pulled himself up on the six-foot high wall and checked out the small back yard of the mansion. The area near the rear wall was landscaped like an English garden with flowers and tufts of decorative grasses among a few small fruit trees. Staley hiked one leg up to the top of the wall, then dropped down silently on the other side, alert and waiting for some kind of reaction, but none came.

After checking the grounds for surveillance equipment and studying the doors and windows facing the back yard, he was relatively confident that no one was watching the house—no one lying in wait. Again, he wondered why the Agency didn't have a team in place. *Maybe they already knew everything they needed to know about the burglary and the attack on Jonathan Traynor.* That was a disconcerting thought.

Staying within the shadows, Staley quietly approached the back door. He slipped on a pair of tight latex gloves and tried the door handle, finding it locked as expected. After checking the jambs and lock with a small penlight, he easily picked the lock and eased the door open. The house was just as dark inside as it had appeared from the back yard.

Staley made his way through the familiar rooms of the ground floor, stopping here and there to take a look at those areas that had been disturbed by the police investigation. He didn't expect to find anything down here. His visit had a singular purpose. He knew that if at all possible, the Colonel would have left something for him, and only he would know how to retrieve it.

As he walked up the stairs to the old man's study, he remembered the day some ten or eleven years earlier when Traynor had shown him the diary safe. It was a safe that had been built solely for Staley's benefit. There was no one else as close to the old man and no one else for whom the Colonel intended to leave information on active projects in the event of his death.

The safe was in the inside wall of the small alcove that once had served as the shaft for a dumbwaiter that came up from the kitchen. The polished oak door to the dumbwaiter was always open, part of the room's décor. An old brass key protruded from the ornate lock cover. The mechanism that operated the dumbwaiter had been removed, the shaft to the kitchen having been closed off years before, but the appearance of a fully functioning service elevator had been preserved.

Inside the alcove on a distressed wooden platform that complemented the polished oak door sat a sterling silver tray covered with antique crystal stemware and a unique blue glass decanter. The alcove was not quite deep enough for the tray, so the door could not be closed with the tray in place.

Recalling the instructions he had been given years before, Staley carefully removed the tray, then closed the door and turned the brass key first to the right, then to the left, a sequence that had to be completed in less than three seconds. When he reopened the door, the back panel of the alcove had disappeared, revealing a small gray safe behind the false wall.

The combination to the safe was the last six numbers of Staley's original service number, the one he had been assigned and memorized before the Army switched to using Social Security numbers in 1969. After dialing in the 18-22-05 combination, Staley turned the handle and opened the safe, but only a half inch or so. He had to disarm the burn trigger before continuing or the contents of the safe, and possibly his face and hands, would be caught up in a fireball.

Traynor had installed the burn trigger as a final security precaution to ensure that anyone who successfully opened the safe without authorization would never see what was inside. The back wall of the safe had been inset with three small cylinders of compressed propane that were set to release into the arc of an electrical current if the safe were opened without disarming the trigger. There was enough propane in the cylinders to cause an initial explosive reaction and then burn furiously for several minutes; enough time to ensure the contents of the safe were completely incinerated.

Staley slid a forefinger under the lip of the barely-opened door and found the burn trigger switch near the top right-hand corner of the door seat. He pushed the switch up as far as it would go, then stepped back and carefully pulled the door wide open.

Inside the safe were several document-size manila envelopes, each labeled with Staley's name and the name of an operation. One had McGowan's name on it and included something heavy. Staley opened the clasp and found the cartridges he had removed from McGowan's pistol in Laos, along with the spent slug and Berman's gold pen and spiral notebook—all the physical evidence Staley had returned to Traynor upon his return from the Laos operation. Staley slipped the envelopes in his backpack to be examined later.

There was also a small cardboard box in the safe, a box containing a number of audiocassettes, each labeled with a beginning and ending date. And there was one VHS videocassette marked simply: McGOWAN. The cassettes were exactly what Staley was looking for. If Traynor had remained consistent in his practice of recording information he would want Staley to have, the tapes should reveal the circumstances that resulted in the old man's death, and perhaps some final instructions from Traynor as to how he would want Staley to proceed.

Also in the safe was a copy of Traynor's will, a small collection of gold coins, an old Rolex watch with the initials "HMT" engraved on the back and a few miscellaneous papers that did not appear to relate to Traynor's relationship with Staley or his work with the CIA. Staley decided to leave those items in the safe. The old man had never mentioned the will or the personal items, and if he had wanted Staley to take them, he would have left specific instructions to that effect. Perhaps someone else knew about the safe. While that was a possibility, Staley doubted it. But the old man had left these things in the safe for some reason. Staley did not have time to figure out what it was. If need be, he could come back for them.

Staley checked the safe once more to ensure he had not

missed anything important, then closed the door, turned the handle and spun the dial. He closed the door to the dumbwaiter, turned the lock and reopened the door. The back panel of the alcove was once again in place, with no evidence of the safe it concealed. Staley replaced the silver tray, leaving everything as he had found it, and after making a cursory check of the old man's study, walked down the stairs and out the back door of the house.

After returning to his room at the Four Seasons, Staley first watched the videocassette. It was prepared as testimony in the never-to-be-filed case of The United States of America versus Robert J. McGowan. On the tape, Traynor detailed all of the evidence he had assembled regarding the incident in Laos. Staley was surprised at the extent and completeness of the evidence, and Traynor's videotaped testimony was convincing and compelling.

Staley listened to two of the most recent audiotapes, then turned off the machine. He needed time to think.

The Colonel's voice on the final tapes had been crisp and clear, as strong and unequivocal as the first time Staley had heard it more than thirty years earlier. But it sounded different somehow, maybe because Staley knew that the old man was dead and that he would never hear that voice again in person. But more than that, it sounded different because for the first time Staley could remember, Traynor sounded angry. He knew what was happening and that there was little he could do to stop it.

On the last tape, recorded the evening of the burglary, Traynor spoke directly to Staley. He said he suspected that McGowan and Rathmann might take steps to have him eliminated. He also warned that they might try to find and eliminate Staley. He figured it would be Rathmann because he did not believe that McGowan had either the gall or the means to carry out such an operation. But, in any case, it would be for McGowan's benefit, to further McGowan's political aspirations.

Because Traynor knew Staley would not be hearing the tape unless he were dead, he admonished Staley to be careful in his investigation concerning the circumstances of his death, keeping in mind that all of the resources of the CIA might be marshaled against him. But even so, and with a steely conviction in his words, he passed on to Staley his final instructions. Robert J. McGowan must never be allowed to become President of the United States.

Staley accepted the assignment, as he had always done before. But with it, he added a project of his own. If he became reasonably convinced that Rathmann had had Traynor killed, the Director of Central Intelligence would not live long enough to reap whatever benefit he had in mind when he had decided to help McGowan kill Jonathan Traynor.

The following day, Staley contacted Berman using the laptop and they exchanged information. Berman would continue to monitor developments on the Continent and Staley would follow leads suggested by the Traynor diary tapes.

In his final message that day, Berman wrote, "Michael, I hope that it is not your intent to kill Robert McGowan for what he did to me all those years ago. While he deserves to be held accountable for his actions, killing him would not serve a valid purpose. That is my unsolicited advice. Take it or leave it."

Staley replied, "Thank you for your comments, Aaron. I have not yet decided what I am going to do, but I will make sure that you are in no way implicated. Remember, no one knows who I am and no one will ever find out. I will do nothing to jeopardize my anonymity or take any action that will lead to you. But rest assured of one thing. Before this is over, Robert McGowan will remember and regret what he did to you and will suffer for what he did to Jonathan Traynor. You have my word on that."

16

COSTANZA

27 July 1999—Washington, D.C.
Several telephones were ringing at the same time, a constant demand for the attention of the busy workers in the hot, crowded office. Men in short-sleeved shirts, some with ties pulled down from unbuttoned collars, many with sweat stains under both arms, walked among the labyrinth of desks, shuffling papers and looking harried. At several spots across the large, bustling room, recently arrested suspects and innocent witnesses sat virtually next to each other, looking at their shoes and answering routine questions posed by overworked detectives who pecked at dirty keyboards jammed onto crowded desktops amid impossibly stacked mounds of paper, leftover sandwich wrappers and Styrofoam cups half-full of cold coffee.

One particular telephone rang again, then again, the chirp of the ringer almost lost in the din that was as much a part of the squad room as the plainclothes police officers themselves.

After the third ring, just before the call was automatically routed to another desk, the well-dressed detective picked up the receiver and said in a tired voice, "Homicide, Sergeant Costanza."

"Hey Vic, it's Quarles."

"Yeah, Eddie, what have you got?"

"The crime scene detail went through Traynor's house

again, just like you asked. They dusted everything from the furniture to glasses in the cupboards to the mayonnaise jar still in the refrigerator. They vacuumed the carpets a second time and went through the bag with a microscope. They didn't lay down on this one, Sarge. They gave it the best shot I've seen in a while. But they came up with the same stuff as before—nothing new. Our best lead is still the blood we found in the kitchen the first time around. The old man got a piece of the assailant before the guy finished him off, but unless we get lucky on another collar, or take a blood sample of every guy in the District, it's gonna be hard to use that evidence to nail the perp."

"Okay Eddie, come on back in. I want you and Chico to follow-up on Traynor's known associates, his family, friends, whatever. I'm going to take a harder look at this 'intelligence consultant' business. The fact that the Feds hauled off a stack of the victim's papers before we had a chance to look at them and now want to limit our access under a claim of national security smells bad to me. I'll continue working that angle while you guys focus on the more traditional stuff."

"Okay, Vic. I'll be there in about twenty minutes. I'll grab Chico and we'll start runnin' the friends and family traps."

As was his customary procedure, Detective Eddie Quarles hung up without waiting for a response.

Detective Sergeant Victoria Costanza—"Vic" to the men who worked with her in the Washington Metropolitan Police Department's Sixth District—had the reputation of being the smartest and the toughest homicide cop in the District. She was also the most attractive, although it was politically incorrect for anyone to notice, especially her male coworkers. Almost everyone's first impression of

Costanza was that she was a knockout. Everyone's second impression, and one that usually set in after about five minutes of seeing her in action, was that Victoria Costanza was one serious, heavy-duty, no-nonsense detective. It was obvious to all who knew her that the second image was the one she worked hard to promote. There was little she could do about her appearance, but while on the job she did her best not to let it get in the way.

Costanza was five feet nine inches tall and weighed about a buck twenty soaking wet. She kept her raven black hair—a genetic thing carried over from her Italian ancestry—cut short so that she never had to waste time fixing it before heading out at any hour of the day or night to visit a crime scene. While she almost never wore makeup, she was always meticulously dressed, usually in a black suit with a white silk or cotton shirt. Her father, who had retired after thirty years on the force, had impressed upon her that police officers who looked like bums deserved to be treated like bums, especially in D.C., where cops frequently were required to interact with tourists, elected officials and foreign nationals on embassy duty. Whether you were assisting a citizen, interviewing a witness or making a collar, a neatly dressed cop made more of an impact than one who looked like something the cat had dragged in. She had taken that advice to heart, and after twenty years on the force, she still went to work every day looking more like a successful business executive than a gumshoe.

Currently at the top of her work list was the murder of eighty-one-year-old retired Army colonel and intelligence consultant, Jonathan Traynor. Even though the crime scene was in Georgetown, and therefore in the Second District, Costanza had been detailed to lead the investigation. Of the 260 homicides committed in Washington, D.C. during the previous year, only two had occurred in the relatively peaceful, mostly white-collar Second District. The city leader in the homicide category was the Sixth District, with sixty-five. It was the reason Victoria was permanently assigned there. Someone upstairs thought that having the MPDC's best homicide cop stationed in the police district with the highest murder rate was a good idea.

Victoria Costanza was born in D.C. and had lived her entire life there. Her father, Vincenzo Costanza, the son of an immigrant from Lucca, Italy, married his high school sweetheart in December, 1950, just after being called to active duty in the United States Army. He fought with the Second Infantry Division in Korea until being badly wounded in December, 1951. He returned home three months later with a Purple Heart and several citations for valor.

After being discharged from the Army, Vincenzo leveraged his impressive war record to obtain an interview with the Metropolitan Police Department. Despite the opposition of several World War II veterans who had joined the force after fighting in Europe—objections based solely on the fact that Costanza was of Italian ancestry and bore the old-country name Vincenzo—he was accepted for police officer training in July, 1952. He began work as a beat cop walking the streets of the tough area now known as the Sixth District, and after earning his gold badge, became a detective in 1958.

In 1959, when their only child Victoria was just five years old, Elana Costanza died of breast cancer, leaving Vincenzo to raise the little girl on his own. He spent every possible moment with her, sometimes taking her along on overnight surveillance stakeouts, frequently finding an empty desk for her to color or do homework at the office while Vincenzo worked long hours whittling down a never-ending caseload. It was during those years and those times together that Victoria decided that she wanted to be a detective, just like her father.

Vincenzo had a distinguished career with the MPDC, taking official retirement in 1982 at the age of fifty-five. He was in his third year as a part-time security guard at the Riggs National Bank on L'Enfant Plaza when he dropped dead of a heart attack, leaving behind Victoria—the pride of his life.

In 1975, Victoria entered the newly-founded University of the District of Columbia and graduated in four years with a degree in criminal justice. She immediately applied for a job with the MPDC, was accepted, due in no small part to the reputation of her father, and began the police academy training course in the fall of 1979.

She graduated first in her class and was assigned a plain-clothes job at headquarters as special assistant to the Chief of Staff. The assignment was boring—she had asked for a uniformed patrol billet—but at her father's suggestion she agreed to stick with the headquarters assignment without complaint for at least a year.

Three months into the new job Victoria married another cop, and while it was good for as long as it lasted, it lasted only six months. Both spouses quickly realized that they had made a terrible mistake and so they quietly and amicably divorced. The only victim of the divorce was Vincenzo who, in manner befitting his Italian heritage, loudly lamented the fact that the failed marriage would probably take ten years off his life. That statement, while considered hilariously funny when made, was all Victoria could think of during her father's funeral just a few years later.

When her year at headquarters was up, Victoria finally got her wish—a uniform and a patrol car assignment—and was sent to the Fourth District, the northernmost police district in the city. Two years later she rotated to the Seventh District and worked the hard neighborhoods alongside the Anacostia River. Three years after that she took the test for detective and was assigned to the homicide division.

Victoria blossomed as a homicide detective. She seemed to have a sixth sense about crime scenes and could see and hear important clues in witness statements that no one else could pick out. Her case-closed percentage hovered near the top every quarter and her long hours became legendary within the department. In 1985, with her supervisor's recommendation, she attended the prestigious FBI National Academy and through that experience made important contacts within the Bureau. Soon, Victoria was on everybody's short list for the most sought after homicide detective in the District.

Her career continued to build positive momentum until she met Dr. Joseph Witherson in August, 1988. Dr. Witherson had unknowingly treated a gunshot victim who, it turned out, was the perp in a string of drug-related hits in the District's northeast ghetto. At their first meeting in the emergency room at Hadley Memorial, something seemed to click between Victoria and Joe. They were married eight months later.

Joe wanted a wife to stay at home and have children, so Victoria, in an effort to give homemaking and motherhood a fair shot, took an extended leave of absence from the MPDC. Long nights sitting alone, waiting for Joe to come home from the hospital, began to wear on her and soon it affected the quality of their marriage. Once Victoria made it clear that she could not go on in the manner Joe had in mind, things deteriorated quickly. One week short of their first anniversary, Joe and Victoria divorced. Although Victoria refused any kind of property settlement or alimony, saying that the failed marriage was probably her fault, Joe insisted on making a fifty percent down payment for her on a condominium in a yuppie restoration area of the District, and she appreciatively accepted. Two weeks after the divorce papers were filed, Victoria applied for readmission to active duty with the MPDC and soon thereafter she was back on the job.

The hiatus from work and the dissolution of her second marriage cost Victoria in terms of advancement within the department. But that was fine with her. All she really wanted was to be a homicide detective and track down bad guys who had killed other folks in her hometown. By mid-1990, she was firmly back in the saddle, devoting every waking hour to the job.

Because of her black suits and short black hair, her nickname "Vic" and her toughness on the job, many newly arrived police officers joining her unit erroneously believed that Victoria Costanza lacked a personal interest in men. While she at first found that supposition revolting, she finally decided to let them think whatever they wanted. At least no one on the job who held that opinion would try to develop an interest in her. Although she was fairly certain she would never remarry, she dated occasionally, and over the past few years she had carried on a couple of low-intensity, short-term romantic relationships with men outside the law enforcement business. But she always made it clear that she was in it for fun and companionship. Having experienced two failed marriages, Victoria was not yet ready for another serious relationship in her life. She often wondered if she ever would be.

By July of 1999, Victoria was forty-five and still cut a handsome figure. She was in excellent physical shape, was well-schooled in personal self defense and the use of police issue firearms, and she knew her business better than any other homicide detective in the District. And, most importantly, she had the confidence of her superiors in the department. So when an elderly, self-employed consultant with ties to the Central Intelligence Agency was killed during an apparent robbery at his elegant Georgetown home, Victoria was tasked to lead the investigation and find the killer. There were several aspects of the case that had attracted the attention of some very senior MPDC officials, including the prompt appearance of CIA agents at the crime scene and their interference with the gathering of evidence. The implication of a possible connection between the murder and the victim's work for the Agency had resonated with someone up the chain of command. The MPDC wanted their best homicide investigator on the case, and their best was Detective Sergeant Victoria Costanza.

Victoria leaned back in her noisy swivel chair and put her feet up on the slide board pulled out from above the top right-hand drawer of her crowded desk. Her suit jacket was neatly folded over the back of the green leatherette witness chair sitting next to the desk. She liked to keep her jacket on while in the office, but the heat and humidity of D.C. in late July was too much for the building's inefficient air conditioning system.

She reread the reports filed by the responding officers and the MPDC detectives first on the scene at the Traynor home. She knew the reason she had been assigned to handle the investigation was the immediate intervention of the CIA and the implicit possibility that the case was more than a routine homicide. Despite the CIA's apparent willingness to accept the premise that Traynor had been killed as the result of a violent robbery or an interrupted burglary, the arrival of the CIA investigating team so soon after the crime had been called in suggested more. It was almost as though someone at the Agency had expected an attack on Traynor and had positioned agents in place, prepared to respond. If so, then the real motive for the attack had to have been related to Traynor's consulting work for the government. She wondered where that might lead.

Victoria read through the end of the file, then laid it aside and picked up her notepad. She started drawing neat, connected boxes, just as she had years earlier while waiting for her father. She always analyzed things better with a pen and paper in hand.

She absentmindedly drew a number "1" in the first box, with a stylized arrow extending down to an elaborately curved and shaded question mark. The first piece of information in the file, the initial contact report, continued to bother her. The fact that a senior staff assistant at CIA headquarters had called an MPDC station to request that officers check on the victim, just because he was eighty-one years old and had uncharacteristically missed an early morning meeting, was hard to accept at face value. It was so unlike the Feds, particularly the CIA, to request MPDC assistance with any matter, particularly something that apparently involved such a high-level security threat that it was necessary to immediately dispatch agents to the scene. In Victoria's experience, when one part of the picture was out of focus, every other part had to be questioned as well.

Her natural skepticism was one of the attributes that made her a good cop. She did not like conspiracy theories, but there was something very wrong with this particular homicide. The Agency's explanation for its actions was just too neat.

Organizing her thoughts, she scribbled out some questions on the notepad. *Was there some reason the CIA wanted District police to find the victim? Did they need cover to enter the house and search the premises? If so, why? Did they know that Traynor had been attacked before the call was made? Were they involved in the attack? How did they arrive so quickly? When would they have had to leave Langley? Would it have been at about the same time as the call was made to the MPDC? Why would they have done that? Was Traynor currently working on a project for the Agency? If so, what was it? Was there a threat against Traynor related to his work? What was the real basis for the CIA team's insistence on their removal of personal papers and other items from Traynor's home without first allowing the crime scene unit to process such materials? Even assuming that Traynor had access to sensitive intelligence materials, why would the CIA expect him to have secret papers lying around in the open? Why did they take his cell phone? What else did the CIA agents remove from Traynor's home and why?*

Victoria recalled that while in the hospital following the attack, Traynor had been under the protection, or perhaps the guard, of other Agency officers. She needed to find out more about that. Who were they and why were they there? She had asked for an official explanation but so far no answer had been forthcoming. Traynor had not regained consciousness before his death, but the agents at the hospital had made it clear that if he did wake up, no one would be allowed to interview him without a CIA officer present. That had never happened to her before and her questions about the restricted access had never really been answered.

Then there was the matter of the cell phone found next to the victim. The crime scene unit had bagged the phone as evidence, but the CIA team had insisted on taking the phone back to Langley for examination, claiming that something in the memory might involve classified information. Although the phone was later returned to the MPDC, by that time it was clean. According to the report from the CIA lab, the only prints on the phone were the victim's.

The main item of interest regarding the cell phone was a three-minute call than must have been made by the victim shortly after the attack. The call was to a number in Milan, Italy, but the Italian authorities had given Victoria a hard-to-swallow story about how the business to which the number was registered did not exist and, inexplicably, neither did the phone. The CIA confirmed the information she had received from Milan, but refused to answer her inquiries about who Traynor may have called the night he was attacked. She wanted to pursue that possible lead, but she could not do so without CIA or NSA assistance, and she very much doubted that help from either agency would be forthcoming.

While she believed that an Agency connection to the murder was likely, at this point she could not discount entirely the possibility that the crime was just what it appeared to be. The attack had been carried out in street-hoodlum style and it was clear that items *were* taken both from Traynor's person and from the home. The assailant had used a club or a sap—probably a sap—and the old man had been kicked and beaten mercilessly. A professional would have done a better job and, more importantly, a professional would not have allowed the Colonel to get a free shot with that wine bottle. So it probably was an amateur that did the work, but was he acting on his own or doing someone else's bidding?

Victoria decided she would proceed simultaneously

down both paths. Maybe it was a simple robbery. But, if robbery was not the motive, then there were at least two perps to be found: the one who conducted the attack and the person or persons who planned it and set it in motion. Victoria wanted to get them all, even if government agents *were* involved. An old man had been beaten to death in her city and she was not going to go away quietly until those responsible were arrested and brought to justice.

She looked at her watch: six-thirty. No way to make any progress with any Federal agency this late in the day. She would let Eddie and Chico continue to build a file on Traynor—who he was, who his friends and family were and which of them might have wanted him dead—while she studied the government angle. In the meantime, she had put word out on the street that she wanted information concerning a possible robbery-gone-bad in Georgetown and that whoever came in with some good information might earn a get-out-of-jail-free card redeemable at the time of the next drug bust. Snitches were still the best tool available in the fight against street crime in the District, and while this was not a standard street crime, Victoria felt certain that somewhere out there a scumbag drug pusher or two-bit thug was slinking around in the gutter with a few extra bucks in his pocket for services rendered in beating up an old man. Without more evidence, it was about all she could do.

17

RICHARDS

31 July 1999—Paris

Ronald Carlson was working on his twenty-first year in the employ of the Central Intelligence Agency. Over those twenty-one years, he had been posted everywhere from Bangkok to Seoul and Bergen to Saudi Arabia. Although he had done some analytical work, his forte was field operations, often under cover. He had worked with special action teams in Central and South America during the late '70s and early '80s, and had participated in four assassinations— "disappearances" they had called them back then. Carlson was tough and ruthless, but also smart and a career man. He wanted to spend his remaining years with the Agency wearing a white shirt and tie rather than camouflaged fatigues and grease paint.

He had seen many Directors and section heads come and go over the years, and he had survived them all. By this point in his career, he was a true insider, someone who was well known within the Operations Directorate as a guy who could be counted on as a team player, someone who could be trusted to do the job while keeping his mouth shut. As a result, Carlson had been rewarded by being appointed Assistant Commercial Attaché and stationed at the United States Embassy in Paris. It was the best possible job for a career intelligence officer, especially one who enjoyed fine wine and French cuisine.

As he sat at his desk, dealing with routine paperwork, shuffling "read only" folders from the in box to the out box, he was preoccupied with his most recent assignment, one that if not handled in exactly the right way, could cost him more than just his plush job on the Avenue Gabriel.

A week earlier, Carlson had received a call on the encrypted circuit directly from an Assistant Deputy Director of Operations at Langley, a man who had been Carlson's section chief during his years in Central America. Carlson was assigned a delicate and urgent mission and told that the matter was of utmost importance to United States' intelligence operations—meaning the CIA itself—and involved critical national security issues. He was also advised that it was a "black" operation. He was to make no record of the call from his boss and keep no files on the matter. Carlson knew the drill. He had handled operations in this manner before. It was what had earned him his reputation as a team player.

In the brief conversation, Carlson was told everything the Agency then knew about François Villon, including the fact that he had been taken from the airport at Nice in a well-orchestrated operation by professionals who were so bold as to enlist the assistance of the local police in making the grab. He was also told that Villon was considered an imminent threat to the continuing conduct of Agency operations and had to be eliminated, as quickly and quietly as possible. And, of course, he was reminded of the usual black ops disclaimer. The operation had to be conducted without any possibility of a connection to the United States government or the CIA. Anyone apprehended by the local authorities while working on the operation was on his own. The Agency would offer no assistance of any kind and would disavow any knowledge of their actions.

With the formal part of the briefing concluded, Carlson slipped back into the mode of talking with an old friend. "What's really going on here, Bob? I haven't heard of an op like this for a long time. Or have I just been out of the loop?"

"Ron, I'll be honest with you. I don't know all the details, but it looks like this guy Villon was the one who ventilated Azbek Fahoud last week in Monaco. My suspicion is that there is some tie between him and the Agency that the folks upstairs want to break, permanently. It's not like the old days—I don't know everything that's going on around here any more. Hell, for all I know, we may have hired this Villon character to hit Fahoud. All I know is this. The guy sitting up there in the DCI's chair called me into his office and laid it all out for me. He wouldn't get any more specific than I have been with you. You've got all I've got. But he made it clear that this is an important operation and one that needs to be carried out quickly, quietly and with ultimate certainty. And he also told me not to discuss this operation with *anyone,* which I construe to mean my boss included, other than the field agent whom I trust to carry out the job. That's you. So, it's like the question we used to face almost daily back in '82 and '83. We can either call the newspapers and tell them everything we know or we can say, 'aye, aye sir,' do an about-face and carry on with the mission. Obviously, since I placed this call to you, I've decided to do the latter. I suppose it's up to you what you want to do."

Carlson thought about everything his old friend and mentor had just said. He didn't like it, but he would do it. "Thanks, Bob. I appreciate your candor. If you're in, I'm in."

After another moment's thought, Carlson continued. "You know, Bob, I'm not going to be able to do this myself. I'm supposed to be the Assistant Commercial Attaché. I can't go running all over France, interviewing witnesses, asking questions and trying to find some guy. I'll supervise the project but I'll have to use some local talent, just like we used to do in the old days. I'm pretty sure I can get it handled without any comeback sauce. I'll see to it and report back to you as soon as I have something."

"Very good, Ron. I hope to speak with you soon. For God's sake, be careful who you use."

"I will. Talk to you soon."

Carlson hung up the phone, thinking beyond the mission at hand. He knew if he were successful, his star would shine a little brighter back at the home office. This one came directly from the top and, as with any other large business organization, pleasing the men at the top was the best possible way to advance one's career.

The project required careful planning. The most important part was finding the right man for the job. Someone he could trust to handle the matter with efficiency and discretion.

Carlson dug deep in his file of contract operators, looking for just the right man to track down Villon—in France or elsewhere on the Continent—and eliminate him. He came across the name of Bert Richards, a former Philadelphia schoolteacher. After serving in the Gulf War, Richards realized that he had a knack for killing people and the willingness to use his special talents to make things right with the world.

Carlson had a complete file on Richards. Since 1994 he had killed, in contract hits across Europe, at least four—one source gave him credit for five—known criminals who either were on the run or out on bail awaiting trial. One job was commissioned by Carlson's predecessor. It involved a Marseilles gangster who had murdered the daughter of a well-known American philanthropist, and generous political campaign supporter, while stealing her car in downtown Avignon. The French police seemed to be having a difficult time apprehending the suspect. Richards found him in two days and left him lying on the sidewalk just outside a trendy nightspot near the gangster's apartment in Marseilles.

Several law enforcement agencies reportedly had files on Richards, but none of them bothered him since he never left any evidence that could be used in a prosecution, never inflicted any collateral damage, and always limited his targets to scumbags who needed to be killed anyway.

Best of all, Richards was an expatriate American who spoke French like a native. According to the file, he currently was living in Amiens, just one hundred kilometers or so north of Paris.

The same day he received the assignment from Langley, Ronald Carlson made a call to Richards in Amiens. Carlson introduced himself as the replacement to the man Richards had worked with on the Marseilles job and asked about his immediate availability for a contract assignment. Richards indicated an interest and asked to hear more.

Carlson told Richards that the subject was a terrorist who had conducted illegal activities in the United States, then had managed to slip out of the country. While this was not the kind of project Richards had handled in the past, Carlson assured him that the vital interests of the United States and the free world were at stake. The target had to be taken out before he could be apprehended and possibly protected by the French police. Carlson also offered a generous fee for a quick result with no evidence of any connection to Carlson, the embassy or the U.S.

Richards agreed to take the contract.

Carlson passed along the few bits of information he had concerning François Villon: French-Canadian, probably in his fifties, and a professional with extensive field experience. Carlson also told Richards about Villon being abducted from under the nose of the local police in Nice and his disappearance in a white van. Carlson impressed upon Richards the need to be discreet in his inquiries.

Richards accepted the assignment and told Carlson that he would be back in touch within a few days.

Carlson was just about to wrap it up for the afternoon when Richards called. It was not the appropriate protocol. Richards was not supposed to call him at the office during work hours. Something must be wrong, or very important. Maybe Richards had found Villon and eliminated him. Fast work if that was the case.

Carlson flipped the switch under his desk that turned off the tape recorder. He was the only officer in the embassy that had the ability to deactivate the automatic system that recorded every incoming call.

"Bert, this is Carlson. Why did you call me here? I thought we had an understanding that you would call me only at my apartment."

"Yeah, well, since this report ends the project we discussed, I thought I'd go ahead and call."

"What do you mean, 'ends the project'? Did you find Villon?"

"I guess that means I can talk freely on this line?"

"Yes, I've taken care of everything. Go ahead."

"Well, I haven't seen the body, but I have it on pretty solid information that he's dead."

Carlson sat up and grabbed a memo pad from the corner

of his desk. He wanted to make sure he had all the particulars for his report to Langley.

"Tell me exactly what information you have, where you got it and why you think it's reliable."

"First, I confirmed all the info you gave me to start with. François Villon took a room at the Hermitage Hotel in Monaco. He checked out at noon on July 21 and was booked on a Delta flight to New York, but he never boarded the plane. He was arrested at the airport and taken away in a white van. I checked with the police department in Nice. My contact there told me over an eight-hundred-franc dinner that two officers in his unit had been duped into helping some guys grab Villon, believing they were with Interpol. Everybody's pretty embarrassed that they were fooled like that.

"Here's a piece of information we didn't have, or at least I didn't have. Maybe you knew this and didn't tell me for some reason. My contact said that the guys who took Villon shot him in the back when he tried to make a break while they were loading him in the van at the airport. He was unconscious and bleeding when they drove off. The guys posing as Interpol agents told the cops they were taking him to a secure location for medical treatment and interrogation, but one of the cops on the scene said it looked like the guy was dead.

"Consensus opinion squares with what you told me—the snatch was a professional operation run by guys who knew how to set it up and carry it off. Since it was done that way, I figured it was either an organized crime job or a spook operation.

"I checked around in Nice and in the surrounding area, using some contacts a friend gave me, people whose business activities are not fully appreciated by the local gendarmes.

One guy who said he owed my friend a favor said he'd look into it. The next day I got a call from him saying that according to his sources, the operation was run by some eastern Europeans who'd been looking for Villon for some time. He said that even though he'd been shot in the back, which jibes with what the cops said, Villon was not dead when they left the airport. They reportedly took him north to a farmhouse near Larche, a little town on the Swiss border. According to my source, they held him there at the farmhouse for two days under interrogation, then put a bullet in his head and buried him.

"I drove up to Larche and nosed around for an afternoon. I talked with some people who remembered the van and the guys in it, so I'm pretty sure they were there. My guy was absolutely certain that Villon's dead. So that's about it."

Carlson was not pleased. The only way to be absolutely sure was to see the body, feel the pulse. He wanted to be certain when he reported to Langley.

"You think there's any way to confirm the information? Maybe find a grave or a body?"

"No, I don't think so. I can't get much closer without arousing a lot of suspicion. It's not likely I'll find the guys who iced him. I say again, it was a professional job. I did all I could do to find him, but the deed was already done. There's nothing more I can do."

When Carlson didn't immediately respond, Richards continued. "Since I didn't actually take the guy out, I'll settle for half the fee we talked about, plus expenses. I think that's fair. Maybe if I come by your apartment in a couple of days, you'll have my money, okay?"

Carlson really didn't have much choice. Richards had a reputation for being tough and reliable. Carlson had hired him and with that came the inevitability of having to take his word that the job was finished. Without direct Agency involvement, which meant Carlson himself, there wasn't much more that could be done.

"Bert, just to be sure, on a scale of one to ten, how reliable would you say this information is? 'Cause if you're wrong, I'm not going to forget it."

After an uncomfortable pause, Richards said, "Hey, you know yourself you can never be one hundred percent sure on something like this. But I've looked into it enough to say that on a scale of one to ten, I'd have to give it a nine, or maybe even a ten. I think it's solid."

"Then that wraps up the project. You did a good job, Bert. Stop by this weekend and we'll settle up. And Bert, don't forget. This one is very confidential. If you ever talk about this to anybody, it won't go well for you. Do we understand each other?"

"Sure, Ron. I understand. I'll see you Saturday, sometime mid-afternoon. Thanks and goodbye."

Bert Richards breathed a sigh of relief as he replaced the phone in its cradle. The one-armed man standing next to him, who had been listening to the conversation through a small receiver patched into the telephone line, closed the device and handed it to one of the other men standing by. The one-armed man spoke English, the others French. He had been in their custody for several days, but he didn't know how long for sure.

Richards looked up, perspiration glistening on his forehead. His voice weak and barely audible, he asked, "How was that?"

"That was fine," Aaron Berman replied. "Just fine."

"What happens now? Are you going to let me go?"

"I want you to stay with us for one more day to make sure there are no related matters for which we might need your assistance."

Richards looked down at his large, calloused hands. There was an IV port taped to the back of his right hand. The area around it was blue where blood had collected under the rough skin.

In a very matter-of-fact manner, he said, "Are you going to kill me?"

"Not if you keep your part of our agreement. It is important that you believe every word I've told you. If you do as we require, neither you nor your family will be harmed."

For dramatic effect, Berman took some pictures from his pocket and tossed them on the small table in front of Richards. The pictures were of his sixty-year-old mother sitting on her front porch in Altoona, Pennsylvania, his sister and her family at the zoo in Philadelphia, and his younger brother walking out of an office trailer on a construction site near Akron.

Berman continued, "But if you fail to keep the bargain, then . . . well, you *do* understand what will happen, don't you, Mr. Richards? You'll be alive to attend each of their funerals, but only for a short time. Then you'll follow along. You have a reputation for being exceptionally proficient at what you do. Perhaps at some point you will decide that you can avoid us or perhaps even get to us before we get you, but if so, you will be very wrong. Our reach is worldwide. You will never escape us, no matter what you do. And if you run, your actions will result in the immediate death of everyone who's ever been close to you. Believe me, we do not make idle threats."

Richards had no doubt that the men who had kidnapped him would do just what the one-armed man said they would do. He had heard snippets of their conversation about Villon. They apparently did not know he spoke French. Evidently this Villon had really pissed off an international syndicate, maybe some Russians, and these guys were the enforcers.

The truth was, Villon was still alive somewhere and they were looking for him. But for some reason they wanted him to tell the people who had hired him that Villon was dead. Villon was their problem and they didn't want any competition. That was fine. Richards didn't have any trouble with that or with keeping quiet about it for the rest of his life.

The break Berman had been looking for had come four days earlier. In his brief phone call the night of the attack, Traynor had warned Berman that someone would come looking for the Frenchman, probably to kill him. And it was likely that whoever came would be sent either by Senator Robert J. McGowan or by Charles Q. Rathmann, the Director of Central Intelligence. Berman's first order of business was to watch for whomever might be coming, then use that person to uncover whatever treachery McGowan or Rathmann might have planned.

Berman had assigned one of his agents to follow the Villon investigation in Nice. The agent, posing as a journalist, was a beautiful young woman with striking features and an easy smile. It had not taken her long to make friends within the police department and those contacts paid off when an American showed up and started making inquiries about a Monsieur Villon. The American was Bert Richards. The female Mossad agent found out more about Richards, then called Berman with a report.

The next day, as Richards was on his way from Nice to Monaco, Berman's people picked him up, sedated him, then took him to a safe house in Toulon. There he was introduced to Dr. Cohen.

After a couple of hours under the influence of the first round of drugs, Richards told the interrogators his life story, including detailed information about his family. It was clear from the tone of his answers that Richards' family was important to him. He supported his mother and was close to his siblings. It was the opening Berman had hoped for.

A Mossad contact in the United States obtained photographs of Richards' family. The pictures were scanned and e-mailed to Berman in Toulon. The entire process took less than thirty-six hours.

Berman continued to question Richards. Who were his contacts? What was his assignment?

He broke easily. His mission was to find François Villon and to kill him, covertly and without a trace of CIA involvement in the operation. The man who had hired him was Ronald Carlson, the senior CIA officer in France.

The fact that Carlson was directly involved in the matter and personally hired Richards was revealing. The orders had to have come straight from the top, and that meant Charles Rathmann.

Using the synchronized laptop, Berman contacted Staley that afternoon.

Berman related the entire story of Richards and the fact that he had been hired by the CIA to kill François Villon, probably on orders direct from Langley.

Staley asked a few follow-up questions, thanked Berman for everything, then added, "Aaron, I've asked you to do enough now. There will be no more. I am going to destroy the chip that enables us to have these secure communications and dispose of the laptop. I want to ensure there is no possibility that any of this can be traced back to you. I hope to see you again one day, but it will probably be quite some time. Be safe and enjoy your life."

He signed the e-mail, "Very best regards, Michael," then broke the connection.

The first part of Staley's plan was now complete. Rathmann would inform McGowan that Villon was dead. They would believe themselves to be in the clear, particularly McGowan. That's exactly what Staley wanted. He had plenty of evidence to implicate the CIA—namely Rathmann himself—in the conspiracy to murder Traynor and to eliminate any ties between Traynor, the mysterious Frenchman, and Senator Robert J. McGowan. He would check one additional angle, then begin work on the plan to implement Jonathan Traynor's final instructions.

18

LaCLERC

2 August 1999—Washington, D.C.

Staley had decided it was time once again to use the practiced French accent. He needed more information from the police, and more importantly, he needed to provide the police some information they might not have in order to get the investigation of Jonathan Traynor's death moving in the right direction.

It took four phone calls to various offices within the Washington, D.C. Metropolitan Police Department to get the name and phone number of the chief investigator assigned to the Traynor case. Staley was surprised to learn that it was a woman.

It was just after ten on a Monday morning. Victoria Costanza had decided to start the week by concentrating on Traynor's personal life, tying to find a suspect or a motive not related to the governmental involvement theory she felt so strongly about, a theory based mostly on instinct. Some cases were solved by instinct, but most were solved with nose-to-the-grindstone detective work. She was poring over a list of Jonathan Traynor's financial holdings when the telephone chirped.

"Homicide, Sergeant Costanza."

A male voice with a strong French accent responded.

"Sergeant Costanza, I am a former associate of Jonathan Traynor. I understand that you are in charge of the police

273

investigation into the attack that resulted in his death, is that correct?"

Victoria had a standard response for these kinds of inquiries. She took a pen and flipped to a clean page on the white tablet on her desk.

"What is your name, sir?"

The response was unexpected. "Sergeant Costanza, let me be very frank with you before we start this conversation. I do not intend to give you my real name, but for purposes of our interaction, you may call me LaClerc. My occupation is such that giving you my name would serve no useful purpose. Can we proceed on that basis for the time being?"

Victoria leaned forward in her chair and checked the caller ID. No number was shown. She made a note of the fictitious name the caller had given. In an ordinary investigation, she might have written the guy off as a nutcase. But she had already concluded that CIA involvement, or perhaps even the involvement of a foreign power, might be at the core of this case. So she decided to go along for the time being.

"If I don't know who you are, I will not be able to properly evaluate what you have to tell me. I assume the purpose of your call is to provide information concerning Colonel Traynor's death?"

"In one respect, yes, and in another, to perhaps assist you in your investigation. You see, Jonathan Traynor was a very good friend of mine. I knew him well over the years and we worked together from time to time. Because of the nature of his work, I find the circumstances of his death suspicious. Let me ask, do you have a suspect in the case? Or if not, have you developed a theory of what happened?"

Victoria hesitated. She had no idea who this guy was. He refused to identify himself, and it was not her habit to discuss the status of a pending investigation with anyone but her detectives. By the same token, she did not want to dismiss the caller out of hand.

"I cannot discuss the status of the investigation, but I can tell you that we do not have a suspect in custody at this time. Do you have any information concerning the attack on Colonel Traynor?"

Staley paused as if considering a response. So far the conversation had gone as expected. He knew he would have to give Costanza something in order for her to become more forthcoming with information concerning the investigation, and he knew what that something was going to be.

He continued with the thick French accent. "Perhaps if I give you some assistance, tell you things you do not know or might not have guessed by now, then you will become more cooperative."

Victoria was interested. While she had some ideas, some theories, there was nothing concrete. "What can you tell me?"

"I will tell you some things now, you check them out, and then perhaps we can share additional information later. Okay?"

"I'm listening."

"As you no doubt know, Colonel Traynor retired from the United States Army in the late nineteen sixties. Following his retirement, he provided certain specialized consulting services to a number of private concerns and governmental agencies, including the Central Intelligence Agency. If you file a request in an official capacity with the office of the Director of the CIA, they may be willing to confirm the fact that Jonathan Traynor had a special relationship with the Agency. However, whether or not they confirm it, I can assure you that it is true. Traynor was a very cautious and deliberate man. I am aware of some things he was working on recently that involved the Agency, and I also know that certain elements within the Agency were not enthusiastic about a continued relationship with Colonel Traynor. A week before his death he confided in me that his work for the Agency would be over soon and that following that break, he was going to retire. I find it very coincidental that just when Colonel Traynor was about to break off his relationship with the CIA, he is robbed in his home and beaten to the point of death. It is very important that I know exactly how the robbery occurred and what kinds of injuries Colonel Traynor sustained. I have some knowledge of how certain, shall we say 'special action teams,' work within the Agency. Some leave a signature, some use other methods. If I could have access to your reports on the incident, I might be able to help steer you in the right direction."

Victoria was impressed with LaClerc's knowledge of Traynor's activities and of his connection with the CIA. She wished she could interview him in person, take a statement and try to put some pieces together.

Still was suspicious of his motives, she said, "Those are very interesting observations. I would very much like to meet with you and discuss this matter further. Perhaps between the two of us we could make better progress than either of us working independently. Would you be willing to come in and meet with me, or perhaps meet at a more private location outside the office?"

"No. As I said, I will not identify myself and I will not meet with you. But in the interest of earning your trust, I will give you some very confidential information that may be helpful in your investigation. I will ask that you check out the information and, if confirmed, that we talk again later today. Will you agree to these terms, or would you rather I hang up and never contact you again?"

Victoria thought about the offer. It would not do any harm to listen to what LaClerc, or whatever his name was, had to say and, if reasonable, to check it out. If there was something there worth a follow-up, she would not be opposed to sharing some information. But at this point, it was still too early to know what or how much.

"Very well, then. What do you have for me?"

"I assume you still have access to Colonel Traynor's house?"

"Yes, but we've been through it twice, very thoroughly, and some government investigators have been through it as well."

Victoria winced after making that last remark. Any information that was not public knowledge was considered part of the confidential case file.

"When you say 'government investigators,' I assume you mean CIA. This is very important. Were they CIA and did they claim exclusive jurisdiction of the crime scene in order to search Colonel Traynor's home?"

Victoria became defensive, disappointed with her lapse. "I won't answer that at this time. What is the information you wish for me to check out?"

"You do not have to answer now, perhaps later. But if CIA agents appeared to search the home, it fits nicely with what I believe happened. We can discuss this in our next call. In the meantime, I would ask that you return to Colonel Traynor's home. Upstairs in his study there is a hidden safe that I suspect your investigating team did not discover. Am I correct?"

Victoria could not remember finding a hidden safe. She couldn't believe they had all missed it.

"What about the hidden safe?"

"Sergeant Costanza, please. I assisted Colonel Traynor in designing the safe. I am confident that you did not find it, and if by chance you did find it, there would have been nothing left inside by the time you got it open. Am I wasting my time here, or do you wish to have the information?"

Victoria took a deep breath. "Yes, I want to know about the safe. What can you tell me?"

"The safe was designed to be a security safe for keeping documents that could not be allowed to fall into, shall we say, the wrong hands. It is located inside the shaft for the dumbwaiter on the south wall of the Colonel's study. The shaft appears to be an alcove in which the Colonel often displayed goblets of fine crystal on a silver tray. Now, in order to open the safe . . ."

LaClerc explained in detail the procedures for opening the diary safe and disarming the burn trigger. Costanza took careful notes, stopping him occasionally to ensure she had the sequence correct. When he was finished, she considered how to proceed.

"What do you believe might be in the safe?"

"That I do not know, but there is a chance that if Colonel Traynor felt threatened, some clue as to the source of that threat might be locked inside."

After a pause, he continued. "I am sure you must be asking yourself why I have not gone to the Colonel's home and checked the contents of the safe myself, but unfortunately I cannot get around as well as I used to. An occupational injury has limited my mobility. I suspect I would need to employ physical skills that I no longer possess in order to break into the house undetected while presumably under the surveillance of the police department and possibly the CIA."

Victoria made a note on her tablet. *Check house surveillance.*

"In any event, *you* should examine the contents of the safe. Perhaps you will find something useful, perhaps not. But whatever you find, I hope my assistance in giving you the safe will be sufficient for you to share with me more of the information in your case file. I will call you at two o'clock this afternoon. Will that be satisfactory?"

"Yes, that will be fine. I'll be here."

"Goodbye, then."

Victoria hung up the phone and slipped on the coat of her pants suit as she yelled across the aisle for Quarles.

"Eddie, find Chico and meet me downstairs in five minutes. We got a lead we need to run down right now. Get moving."

Detective Eddie Quarles spilled his coffee as he hurriedly slammed the cup down on his desk and grabbed his coat. "Right, Vic. See you downstairs."

It was just after twelve-thirty when Victoria and Chico walked back into the squad room. She was carrying a large plastic bag that contained the remaining contents of Traynor's safe. She had not wanted to ruin any fingerprints or other forensic evidence, though as far as she could tell, there was nothing in the safe that might suggest the reason for the assault or lead them to a suspect. The will looked to be the most promising piece of information, and she would have to study it more carefully after the lab boys had a go at it. She had asked them to return to Traynor's house to see if they could find any fingerprints or other forensic evidence in the alcove, the safe or on the documents inside. She had left Eddie at the scene to explain how the burn trigger worked.

The fact that the safe was where LaClerc said it would

be, and his detailed and accurate instructions for how to open the safe and disarm that ingenious burn device, served as indisputable confirmation that he must have been exceptionally close to Traynor. There would have been no reason for the victim to have taken all of those precautions and then been careless with respect to whom he gave access to the safe. LaClerc would have to be cultivated, even if it did require Victoria to bend the rules a bit with respect to sharing confidential information.

At one o'clock, she made the necessary arrangements to have the next call from LaClerc traced. She wanted to meet him, face to face, and find out what else he might know about Jonathan Traynor and his work with the CIA.

At two minutes after two, the call came in.

"Homicide, Sergeant Costanza."

"Good afternoon, Sergeant Costanza. I assume you found the safe."

Victoria could hear crowd noise. She realized immediately that LaClerc was one step ahead of her. He had anticipated that she would attempt to trace his next call.

"Yes, we found the safe just as you described it. Your instructions for opening the safe were precise and correct. You said you helped design the safe for Colonel Traynor. How did you come up with the propane gas device?"

"Please, Sergeant. Let us spare the small talk. You will not locate me with the trace. Do you have a cell phone?"

Victoria was taken by surprise. "Why, ah . . . yes, I do."

"Please give me the number and I will call you back in less than a minute."

Victoria took stock of the situation and gave up. She figured the likelihood of getting a successful trace on the incoming call would be slight, but she had to try. Rather than argue, she gave LaClerc her private cell phone number. He hung up. She told Chico to forget the trace, LaClerc was gone.

Thirty seconds later the cell phone in the right waist pocket of her jacket rang with the first few bars of Beethoven's "Ode to Joy." Victoria answered.

LaClerc got right to the point. "What did you find in the safe that might provide a lead?"

Victoria looked around to see who was in earshot, then shooed Chico back to his desk. He didn't need to be part of this.

She told LaClerc in general terms what was in the safe, although she intentionally did not mention the will. If LaClerc's real interests were in locating Traynor's final testament, he would have to wait for the lawyers, just like everyone else.

Sounding disappointed, LaClerc responded, "None of that would appear to be of much help. But I have complied with my part of the bargain. Now, please answer for me at least some of the questions I asked this morning. How was the Colonel attacked? What was the nature of his wounds? Was there a struggle? Do you believe it was a simple robbery? What did the CIA agents say when they arrived and what did they do? Have you had any cooperation from the Agency thus far? Please, help me with this and I will try to help you. My only concern is finding out who killed Jonathan Traynor and why."

Victoria decided to answer as many of LaClerc's questions as possible, without giving away any information that would be critical to the investigation or potentially damaging to a case against a suspect. He listened quietly, sometimes interrupting to ask for clarification or elaboration of a specific point. He was particularly interested in finding out who called to report the crime, how soon after the crime had been called in by the investigating officers had the CIA agents appeared on the scene and how they had handled the investigation. Victoria told him everything she knew on those points.

Costanza's story pretty much confirmed what Staley had expected, but in order to maintain his credibility as LaClerc, he had to give her a little more help.

"The nature of the attack does not sound to me like the work of a professional," he said. "More like an alley fight or a mugging. If the Agency was behind the attack on Colonel Traynor, here is the way they would have done it. They would most likely have engaged an intermediary, a known criminal or street tough who would have been told to hire someone else to actually do the work. Whoever represented the Agency in contracting for the work would have made contact only with the intermediary, to ensure confidentiality. The Agency man would have offered a great deal more than usual for a job of this nature, with enough down to pay in advance the thug hired to make the hit, with the balance to be paid when the job was completed. Paying half or so up front would evidence good faith and appeal to the intermediary's greed. The Agency contact would have left it up to the intermediary to hire the talent. The intermediary would have found someone he could trust to do the job, most likely an amateur, maybe a mugger, maybe a drug user who needed the cash, and would have hired him for almost nothing. As you know, there are many people out there who will kill a person for a hundred dollars.

"Now, after the job was done, the only person who could identify the agent who commissioned the operation would be the intermediary. The Agency man would not permit the intermediary to go on living with that information, so he would have had him killed. It is a customary way of handling these matters."

Victoria followed the analysis. It made sense.

"So," she began, slowly at first then picking up steam, "we should be looking for someone with a rap sheet who was found murdered shortly after the attack on Traynor. If we find someone who fits the bill, then we need to track down his known accomplices and acquaintances and see if we can tie any of them to the attack on Traynor."

"Exactly. And, if you find a homicide that fits the profile, and if you get lucky in your investigation, you might also develop a lead to the identity of the contractor. If it points back to the Agency, then you might be able to take down both the thug who carried out the attack and the people who sponsored and paid for it. It's not much, but I believe it's worth a shot, unless you have other solid leads to run down before taking off down this rabbit trail."

Victoria looked at her notes and tried to think of other issues to raise with LaClerc while she had him on the phone. She was completely dependent on his willingness to contact her, so it was necessary that she not let him go if there were any unanswered questions. Finally she said, "Do you have anything else for me?"

"No, not at this time. But if I come up with something, I will give you a call. And I may call you in a few days anyway, just to see if all of this has led to anything profitable."

"I'll be interested in hearing from you, Mr. LaClerc. I want you to know that solving this crime, no matter where it leads, is my highest priority right now."

"I am pleased to hear that. *Au revoir*, Sergeant Costanza."

Staley hung up the telephone. His principal objective, that of finding out all the police knew about the attack on Traynor, had been accomplished with positive results. Maybe he had provided some help to Sergeant Costanza that eventually might lead to finding Traynor's killer, but if so, that would just be icing on the cake. After learning that the police had been asked to check Traynor's house by an executive assistant at the CIA who ostensibly was worried because Traynor was uncharacteristically late for a business meeting, and that CIA agents had appeared at the crime scene shortly after it was called in, he was more certain than ever that Rathmann was behind the murder of Jonathan Traynor.

Victoria sat hunched over her desk, reviewing her notes while absentmindedly rubbing her temples. For the first time in the case, she had a lead. If it panned out, fine. If not, she had run down a lot of dead ends before. It was part of the job.

Five minutes later she summoned Quarles, who had just returned from the Traynor mansion, and Ramirez, and the three detectives started to work on the investigative strategy laid out by LaClerc.

19

MOMENTUM

5–6 August 1999—Washington, D.C./Aspen
"Good morning, Senator McGowan's office."

The young, cheerful voice on the telephone was unfamiliar to Rathmann. He figured there were probably several new faces in McGowan's already crowded office now that the announcement everyone had expected for weeks finally had been made over the weekend.

"This is Charles Rathmann, may I speak with the Senator, please?"

"Who are you with, Mr. Rathmann?"

Rathmann bit his lip, suppressing the urge to scream at the foolish little girl on the other end of the phone line. *I know it takes a while to train these eager kids, but for God's sake, you'd think she'd know who I am.*

"I'm not *with* anyone, young lady. I'm the Director of Central Intelligence. Will you please tell Senator McGowan that I'm holding?"

"I'm sorry, sir. The director of what?"

Like most self-important politicians, Rathmann did not like to go unrecognized, even by a naïve young volunteer. Speaking very clearly, he replied, "Charles Rathmann, the Director of the Central Intelligence Agency, the CIA. Have you ever heard of the CIA?"

The receptionist, flustered at what was obviously a major breach of protocol, said, "Oh, I'm sorry, Mr. Rathmann.

I'll connect you to Mrs. Farnsworth."

Before Rathmann could shout that he did not *want* to speak with Mrs. Farnsworth, he wanted to speak with McGowan, the phone clicked and he found himself listening to a "McGowan For President" commercial, soon to be released to radio stations across the country. By that time, he was livid.

After a full minute, Hazel Farnsworth, now elevated several notches in the McGowan entourage, answered.

"This is Mrs. Farnsworth, may I help you?"

"Mrs. Farnsworth, this is Director Rathmann. Would it be possible, in light of all the extremely important details the Senator is obviously seeing to this morning, to speak with him directly for five minutes?" His patience exhausted, the last few words of his request were louder and more forceful than he had intended.

Unfazed, Hazel Farnsworth replied curtly, "I'll see, Mr. Director. Please hold."

Rathmann fought the urge to slam the phone down and wait for McGowan to call *him* back, provided the Farnsworth woman gave him the message. The radio commercial started playing again.

After another full minute, McGowan came on the line, his voice bright and optimistic. "Good morning, Charles. How are you this morning?"

Still angry, but stifling a sharp response, Rathmann said, "I'm fine, Senator. I just thought I'd call to congratulate you on your announcement and to wish you the very best in your campaign. And, if you have some time, to see if you might be available for lunch to talk about some old business. How does tomorrow look?"

McGowan knew what the "old business" consisted of: the Agency's efforts to locate and neutralize Villon and, possibly, the status of the D.C. police investigation into Traynor's death. He had convinced himself that he had nothing to do with that. It had been all Rathmann's doing.

Having not heard from Rathmann for two weeks, McGowan had begun to feel that the loose ends were wrapping up nicely. But even so, in the pit of his stomach he still had a nagging feeling that the Traynor matter was not completely behind him. Maybe Rathmann was inviting him to lunch to confirm closure. That would be a welcome relief. Despite his busy schedule, he had to make time to hear what the Director had to say.

"Certainly, Mr. Director. Tomorrow looks fine. How about twelve-thirty at Etienne's?"

"I'll be looking forward to it, Senator."

McGowan turned and looked out his wide office window overlooking the Capitol grounds below. Things could not have been better. Everything was running smoothly and right on schedule. His announcement the preceding morning, at a well-choreographed news conference held on the front steps of the Capitol building, of his candidacy for the office of President of the United States had been well received across the country. Because the announcement had been timed to coincide with the highest-rated time slot for the morning talk shows, the networks had covered the event live. As a result, the overnight poll results were overwhelmingly supportive of the McGowan candidacy.

The major newspapers had applauded the announcement as well. Most of them, like *The Washington Post* and *The New York Times*, trumpeted that he was, "the man of the hour," the one Democratic candidate who could continue the positive policies of the current administration without the taint of all the scandals that had so diminished the Clinton presidency. The *Chicago Tribune* said that he was, "the one candidate who could bring honor, intelligence and experience to the office." The *Los Angeles Times* went so far as to say that he was "unbeatable."

The response within his own party had also been encouraging. While the White House had remained mum in deference to the Vice President's undeclared candidacy for the office, several leading members of Congress had immediately jumped on the McGowan bandwagon.

Robert J. McGowan was on top, instantly the front-runner in a field of lackluster Democratic candidates. The nomination of his party appeared to be a foregone conclusion. With any luck at all, the Republicans would nominate the sitting governor of Texas as their candidate and that mistake would ensure victory for McGowan in November, 2000. The White House was his for the taking.

McGowan smiled broadly as he returned to the matters on his desk. He harbored no doubts, no misgivings, no concerns. In just over a year he would be elected to serve his *first* term as President of the United States. The dream of a lifetime was about to become reality.

Victoria Costanza was in a meeting with two detectives from the Seventh District. One of them, Tyrone Jefferson, a large black man with massive hands, was speaking. Costanza had worked with Jefferson before. She regarded him as a good cop and a smart investigator.

"The punk's name was Toby Markham. He had a fair-sized distribution business that he worked out of an abandoned warehouse down by the river. His sheet would take Carney here all day to read." He nodded at his partner with a grin. "Although you could probably get through it in about twenty minutes, Vic."

Victoria smiled at the sleepy-eyed Carney, playing along

with Jefferson's jab, then turned back to Tyrone.

"But the shooting took place in an apartment building, right?"

"Yeah. Shot him in his living room. He had an apartment just off the 295 on Eighth. Old building, bad plumbing, lots of problems. I guess a life of crime hadn't been too good to Toby. He was dead for probably a day before anybody found him. The medical examiner made the time of death sometime during the evening of July 21 or the early morning of July 22."

Same night as the attack on Traynor. Interesting.

"How do you figure it went down?"

"Well, it had to be somebody he knew. Toby was into a lot of deals and had a rep for not taking unnecessary chances. He had a gun in the apartment and he took it to the door with him, but it wasn't even cocked when he got tagged. He had one of those peepholes in his door, and he probably looked outside before letting the shooter in. From the blood spatter pattern, forensics says he probably was shot at close range just inside the front door. It was a cold son-of-a-bitch that shot him. A guy knocks at his door. Toby looks through the peephole and sees a guy he knows *and* that he isn't afraid to talk to. So he opens the door and . . . *wham.* The guy pops him one time, right in the middle of the forehead."

"Did you get a make on the murder weapon?"

"It was a 9-millimeter. The slug was too badly torn up to get much in the way of a match, although we sent it over to the Bureau lab just in case. There were several neighbors at home that night and nobody in the building reported hearing a gunshot. Some of those folks know gunshots when they hear 'em, so I'm inclined to believe the shooter may have had a silencer of some kind."

"Any evidence of motive—was it a hijacked deal, maybe a turf war?"

"So far we haven't been able to turn up any evidence of Toby being on the outs with the local drug czar, a guy named Fat Benny. Only a few guys in the business would have the muscle to handle a job like this if it was payback for a busted deal. The apartment itself was pretty clean. We didn't find any big stash of inventory, just a couple of bags and some coke that looked like it might have been for personal use. We didn't find any cash lying around or in a stash somewhere. But guess what? Toby had a hundred and fifty bucks in his jeans pocket. Didn't figure."

"Any suspects?"

"As we ran down the known associates, possible enemies, competitors, the usual bunch, we identified probably ten people who would have liked to have seen Toby bite the big one. We even talked with Fat Benny. I personally don't believe he was behind it. The problem is, there's no way Toby would have let any of them into his apartment, at least not without his piece in his hand ready to fire. According to several *business associates* we talked to, Toby was really paranoid about personal security. It doesn't seem to add up that he would let a guy into the apartment who had a reason to kill him."

"Where do you stand right now?"

"It's in the stack. We're still working the case but we don't have any good leads. To be real honest, Vic, we have other dead bodies that command more of our attention, if you know what I mean."

"Yeah, I do know. But this one might be related to a homicide over in Georgetown that I've been working."

"Oh yeah? How?"

"My theory of the case isn't tight enough for me to lay it

all out yet, but if you have the time and wouldn't mind giving me a hand, I'd like for you and Carney to see if you can make a connection between Markham and some amateur muscle that Markham might have hired to beat up the victim in my case. If I'm right, Markham may have been killed to keep him quiet. I may be way off base, but I'd appreciate it if you'd take a look at that angle. I'd do it myself, but since you and Carney are working the Markham case, I don't want to get in your way."

Jefferson and Carney had more on their plate than they could possibly say grace over, but they could not refuse Victoria's request, and besides, having Costanza owe them a favor could be a valuable chip someday when *they* needed help.

"Sure, Vic," Jefferson said. "We'll take a look. I'll let you know if we find anything interesting."

Fifteen minutes later, Victoria was back at her desk, working yet another angle on the Traynor case, trying to arrange an interview with the Director of the Office of Public Affairs at the CIA.

Staley had left Washington on August 3, the day after his informative telephone conversation with Victoria Costanza, and had arrived late that evening at his small house on Hallam Street in Aspen. He had been gone for almost a month. At least it was summertime. The streets were clear and there was no danger of coming home to frozen pipes or a snowed-in driveway.

He had three calls on his machine from Arnold Brightman, a New York attorney who was Jonathan Traynor's personal lawyer. Staley knew that Brightman was also Traynor's best and most trusted friend and had heard the Colonel speak highly of him on many occasions, but of course Staley had never met the man. He was certain the calls from Brightman had something to do with Traynor's death.

Arnold Brightman was seventy-eight years old and a wealthy former partner in a small Wall Street law firm that specialized in tax-advantaged mergers and acquisitions between multi-national corporations. Brightman had met Jonathan Traynor's brother Harmon in connection with the negotiation and consummation of several large business deals in which Harmon's company had secured the investment banking engagement. The two men had become close personal friends, and following Harmon's untimely death, it was Brightman who helped Jonathan through the morass of settling Harmon's estate, including the very difficult task of determining a buy-out price for Harmon's interest in his investment banking firm.

It took two full years to close the estate, during which time Jonathan and Arnold became friends as well. Jonathan stayed in touch with Arnold after the probate was completed and the two men met occasionally for dinner when Arnold's business brought him to Washington.

During one of those dinners, Jonathan told Arnold that he had always been interested in commercial real estate development and that he would like to start a company that would buy, hold and eventually sell undeveloped real property in potential resort areas in Colorado, Arizona and California. He also told Arnold that because of his position as Special Assistant to the Director of the Central Intelligence Agency, he wanted to conduct the business through an investment company that could not be traced back to him. He said that he didn't want prospective sellers or buyers to know that the company with whom they were about to do business was owned by someone who worked for the CIA, and that he didn't want his associates at the Agency to know about his investment business. While Arnold thought Jonathan's rationale for creating an untraceable investment entity was a bit paranoid, he nevertheless agreed to accept the engagement and help his friend.

Arnold's idea for shrouding the ownership of Traynor's real estate investment company was brilliant, in that it utilized in a very effective manner one of Jonathan's more obscure holdings.

About five years before his death, Harmon Traynor had discovered the Cayman Islands and had spent several vacations there, usually a week at a time whenever he could get away from the investment banking business. During one of those trips he stayed at The Mainstay Inn, a small luxury hotel located on the south shore of Grand Cayman. Harmon fell in love with the place and on his second visit to the resort just three months later, decided to buy it. Arnold handled the transaction. Although Harmon paid entirely too much for the old, eight-room hotel, owning it and spending time there was one of the great pleasures of his life.

With planning help from Arnold, The Mainstay Inn was contributed by Harmon to a new Cayman Islands corporation formed by Brightman called Mainstay, Ltd. Another of Harmon's companies, one that had been formed to hold his offshore real estate investments, owned all of the stock of Mainstay. The stock of that corporation, with Mainstay, Ltd. as one of its holdings, was distributed to Jonathan upon Harmon's death.

In was Arnold's idea to form Brownstone Investments, Inc. as a U.S. subsidiary of Mainstay, Ltd., thereby completely obscuring the ultimate ownership of the company.

All of the operating profits from the resort operation conducted by Mainstay, Ltd. were sent downstream as a capital contribution to Brownstone, its wholly-owned subsidiary, which used the funds to purchase select parcels of undeveloped real estate and to service the retainer agreement with its sole investment consultant, Hackler Staley. When additional funding was required, Jonathan would make a capital contribution to the real estate holding company, which in turn would make a capital contribution to its wholly-owned, Cayman Islands subsidiary, Mainstay, which then would make an identical capital contribution to its U.S. subsidiary, Brownstone. Based on instructions received from Arnold, Jonathan handled every transaction with sufficient complexity to discourage even the most diligent researcher, if one should ever surface, who might try to identify the origin of the funds or the ultimate owner of Brownstone Investments.

Brownstone turned out to be a very successful enterprise. Hack Staley was diligent in locating and acquiring for Brownstone at least one attractive piece of undeveloped real property each year, sometimes two or three. Over the years, Brownstone acquired properties in the Phoenix/Scottsdale area, in and around the beach cities of southern California and in Aspen, Vail and Telluride, Colorado. Arnold was pleased that Jonathan's idea worked out so well, and more importantly, as per Jonathan's original request, that no one ever made the connection between Jonathan and Brownstone.

Staley listened to the few other messages on his machine. Most were local calls—solicitations for local charities, questions about routine matters such as lawn care or reminders of upcoming activities in which he had participated in the past. Staley had no real friends, so it was unusual for him to receive many calls, even when he was home for extended periods.

He then went back and listened once again to the calls from Arnold Brightman. Each was the same, asking Staley to call him at his office in New York. Staley made a note of the number, intending to call later in the week.

On Wednesday, August 5, Brightman phoned again.

"Mr. Staley, this is Arnold Brightman. I left several messages over the past week or so. It's very important that I speak with you."

"What can I do for you, Mr. Brightman?"

"I assume you've heard about Jonathan Traynor."

"Yes. It was a real shock. I'm sorry I was unable to attend the funeral. I was out-of-pocket and didn't know Jonathan was dead until after it was all over. I assume you handled everything?"

"Yes, I did. It was very private. Jonathan had no living relatives so there was no family present, although a number of his old Army friends came to pay their respects."

Staley had wondered if anyone from the Agency or the police department had attended the funeral. "Anyone else? The Colonel was well known in certain government circles. Any official representatives make an appearance?"

"No, although there were two individuals I did not recognize and they did not appear to be together. One was a tall, dark-haired woman, quite attractive, and the other a young man, mid-thirties. Neither of them introduced themselves."

The woman was probably Detective Sergeant Costanza. At least she's on the ball. The other guy may have been from the Agency, checking to see who might show up.

"I feel really bad that I missed the service."

"I'm sure Jonathan would have understood your absence. But that's not the reason I'm calling. Let me try to summarize this for you. It was Jonathan's wish that upon his death, Brownstone Investments be liquidated and dissolved. I have already begun that process. Because of that, the retainer payment you received from the company at the end of July will be your last."

Staley didn't need a great deal of money, but he did live on the monthly paycheck he received from Brownstone. Now he would have to take a hard look at his investment portfolio, which he had neglected for so long, including the tax-exempt bonds where most of the money he had inherited from Wallace and Marie was still parked. He also might have to start thinking about a budget.

"I understand. That's fine with me."

"Well, as they say, that was the bad news. The good news is that under Jonathan's will, his entire estate passes to a testamentary trust. Terribly inefficient for federal estate tax purposes, but that's the way Jonathan wanted to do it. I am named as the sole trustee of the trust with absolute discretion to pay principal or interest to whomever I choose during my lifetime. Jonathan's wishes, while not expressly stated in the will, were that I am to make regular distributions to you out of the trust in the amount of fifty thousand dollars per month. The law requires that the will be filed as part of the probate proceedings. Jonathan did not want your name to appear anywhere of record; that's why the distribution instructions were conveyed to me verbally."

Staley was surprised and touched by the Old Man's generosity. Fifty thousand a month was more than twice his current retainer from Brownstone. He had never thought much about Traynor's wealth or how he would dispose of it upon his death, but looking back, Staley supposed that he was about as close to the Colonel as anyone. It was thoughtful of the Old Man to make it possible for Staley to retire without worrying about how he would pay the bills.

"Thank you for letting me know, Mr. Brightman. It sounds like the Colonel had a great deal of confidence in you. That means something to me as well."

The lawyer continued. "There is one aspect of the plan as directed by Jonathan that you may find inconvenient. In order to avoid disclosure of interim payments to you during the pendency of the probate proceedings, I will not be able to make any distributions to you until after the estate is closed. However, Jonathan's affairs are in very good order. He had no significant creditors and I do not anticipate any other claimants, so I expect to be able to close the estate within six to nine months. At that time I will make a lump sum distribution to you, retroactive to August 1. I hope that will suit your needs. I can personally loan you funds in the meantime if you require cash for any purpose whatsoever."

Once again, Staley was moved by the Colonel's detailed planning for his benefit. He was certain that Jonathan had suggested to the lawyer that he offer to loan Staley any money he might need until a completely private distribution could be made from the trust.

"Thank you, Mr. Brightman, but I believe I can make it for a year or so without a paycheck. If something unexpected comes up, I'll let you know. Thanks again for the offer."

"There's one more thing, Mr. Staley. The trust set up by Jonathan provides that on the fifth anniversary of Jonathan's death, the entire corpus of the trust is to be distributed to a company called Bong Son Holdings Limited, a Bahamian corporation. Jonathan had me set up Bong Son about a year before his death. I assume that name means something to you?"

Staley remembered only too well. "Yes, it was near the village of Bong Son in Binh Dinh Province, South Vietnam, where Colonel Traynor received the wounds that resulted in his forced retirement from the Army. I was with him when he got hit and helped him to the aid station. Why do you ask?"

"Because, Mr. Staley, you are the sole stockholder of Bong Son Holdings. I am having the original of the stock certificate sent to your home by Federal Express. Jonathan did not want you to know until he was gone."

Staley was stunned. The Old Man had left essentially everything to him, and in the process had gone out of his way to ensure that Staley's name would not appear in any public record. The five-year delay was intended to avoid any notoriety. As usual, the Old Man had ensured that everything was wired perfectly.

Staley stuttered uncharacteristically while trying to respond, "Oh, uh, okay, that sounds fine. Uh, Mr. Brightman, can I retain you to look after things for me, the Bahamian corporation and whatnot, just as the Colonel did?"

"I have already been engaged to do all of that, Mr. Staley. I was the incorporator and am the sole director of Bong Son Holdings. Of course you can change that at any time you wish. Jonathan's will provides that I am to continue to perform legal services for the trust and for Bong Son Holdings until the assets of the trust are distributed. For these services, I'll also receive the sum of fifty thousand dollars per month. After the trust is closed, I will be pleased to work for Bong Son Holdings if I'm still capable of doing so and you determine that you wish to continue to engage me. I wanted to make sure that you are aware of the trust provision designating me as counsel and providing that I am to receive monthly payments out of the trust, especially since I will be making those payments to myself. That part is explicitly set out in the will. I can send you a copy of the will if you like."

"No, that won't be necessary, Mr. Brightman. Thank you for calling and for handling all of these matters, both for the Colonel during his lifetime and now for me. I look forward to meeting you some day. I'll give you a call next time I'm in New York."

"Yes, please do. I have heard some very nice things about you from Jonathan over the years. He obviously felt very close to you."

Staley did not respond to that comment, wondering just how much Arnold Brightman really knew about him and what he did for Traynor.

Before he could respond, Brightman spoke again. "Mr. Staley, if I may. I find it interesting that you have not asked how large the estate is. That is usually the first thing a legatee wants to know. Do you wish to know?"

"Well, yes, I guess I do. I'm still trying to digest everything you've just told me. Do you have an estimate yet?"

"Yes. After liquidation of all the hard assets and the payment of all death taxes, the net value of Jonathan's estate should be about twenty million dollars. It's an impressive amount of money, but Jonathan assured me that you would find a way to put the money to good use."

Staley was stunned. *Twenty million dollars.* "Thank you very much, Mr. Brightman. I'm certain we will have occasion to speak again soon."

The two men who had never met said their goodbyes and hung up. Staley realized that while the enormous amount of money Jonathan had left him would ensure his financial independence for the rest of his life, it also created an unexpected burden. He would have a substantial responsibility in determining what to do with his inherited wealth. Traynor expected him to do something important with the money, and he'd have to figure out what that was. But first, he had two more important and immediate issues to take care of: Charles Q. Rathmann and Robert J. McGowan.

Clearing his mind of the phone call from Brightman, Staley returned to the business at hand.

McGowan was already seated and sipping on a glass of sparkling water over ice when Rathmann entered the restaurant. Unlike most politicians whose rise to national prominence caused changes in their public behavior, McGowan's personal habits had always been as non-controversial as one could imagine. No martinis with lunch, no cocktails before dinner. He was a poster boy for abstention from every kind of questionable activity.

Etienne guided Rathmann to the comfortable table at the rear of the restaurant. Rathmann gave whispered instructions to his security detail at the front door, allowing the two bodyguards to sit at a window table and enjoy a soft drink while keeping tabs on the Director. No one expected any trouble in Etienne's.

Rathmann sat down heavily, found the sweetener for the glass of iced tea Etienne had immediately brought to the table and started the stirring ritual while McGowan waited.

"Sorry I'm late, Senator," Rathmann finally said. "I just came from a meeting with our Public Affairs Director concerning the Agency's response, or stated more accurately, our *lack* of response, to several, *several* mind you, MPDC inquiries in the Traynor matter. Somehow, one of our internal security supervisors got the brilliant idea that it would be appropriate to stonewall the police by giving them no explanation of why we were interested in Traynor's death or why we thought it necessary to search his house before any documents were examined or removed by the investigating officers. Sometimes I wonder if the Peter Principle operates as efficiently in the private sector as it does in government. How do you suppose a supervisor in my agency could form the rational thought that it would be good idea to obstruct a police investigation?"

A cynical smile cracked the corners of McGowan's mouth. "Perhaps you didn't get the word to the right people."

"No, Senator. I got the right word to the right people at the right time. They simply dropped the ball. But it's fixed now. Everyone now understands that Traynor was involved in some highly classified work for us and that we needed to ensure that no documents reflecting the nature of that work were in his home after he was attacked. And they also know that we can tell the police as much, with the understanding that they will keep the information confidential to the extent possible. It's always amazing to me how easy it is to obtain the cooperation of a mid-level functionary, or a police officer for that matter, if you act like you're letting them in on a secret. People revel in the notion that they know something others don't. Human nature, I suppose."

"What is the status of the police investigation, or do you know?"

"They have no suspects and no hard evidence. It's one of those cases that is going to be very hard to break. Of course, the Public Affairs Director has been instructed to tell the chief investigating officer, a woman named Costanza, that we found only a few things of interest in our search of Traynor's home and that we would be pleased to give them a redacted version, leaving out the classified information, if they so chose. I'm sure they will so choose, and we are working on some superficial redactions right now. We have already returned Traynor's cell phone, along with a lab report on fingerprints and a listing of the calls he made before his death, including the one to Italy. That's a confirmed dead end, by the way. There is absolutely no way to trace the call beyond Milan."

Etienne then appeared with the headwaiter, and after some small talk, the two diners ordered lunch: sea bass for Rathmann and a braised chicken breast for McGowan.

When Etienne and the waiter were gone, the Director continued. "While the status of the Traynor investigation was one of the things I thought you might be interested in, the real purpose for this meeting was to confirm to you that according to our sources in Paris, François Villon is dead."

McGowan suddenly looked very interested. He leaned forward in his chair and said, "How do you know he's dead? Who killed him?"

This was the part Rathmann wanted to gloss over. He had spent several days trying to get more background, trying to identify the group that had snatched Villon and then killed him, but Agency inquiries to every friendly intelligence service had turned up nothing. It was another dead end, but he wanted McGowan to feel comfortable that the matter was handled.

"Quite frankly, the details don't make a lot of sense to me yet, but our information concerning his death has a very high degree of reliability. You may recall that our initial investigation revealed that immediately after assassinating Fahoud, Villon traveled from Monaco to Nice in a chartered bus, and that while he was waiting for his flight back to New York, someone took him into custody at the gate and led him out of the airport, presumably for police questioning. However, he apparently was shot just outside the airport while trying to escape and supposedly was taken to an Interpol medical facility for treatment. And, as you know from our last conversation about this matter, Interpol was not involved in the operation and had no knowledge of Villon. The men who shot Villon and then carried him away in a van have not been positively identified."

McGowan pursed his lips, obviously dissatisfied with the report. "As you said, Charles, that's *old* news. What have you learned since our last conversation that leads you to the conclusion that Villon is dead? What evidence do you have? Has anyone seen the body?"

"No. To my knowledge, none of our people have actually seen the body. However, the contractor we engaged in France, a very reliable asset we have used in the past and found to be quite efficient, picked up the trail in Nice, worked though Interpol and other confidential sources known to him, and eventually tracked the kidnappers and Villon to the town of Larche, on the Swiss border. He confirms from eyewitness accounts that Villon was interrogated there and eventually executed. He was buried in an unmarked grave near Larche. Our asset said that based on his investigation, he is certain that Villon is dead."

McGowan traced lines in the tablecloth with his salad fork. "Charles, let me ask you this. Do you even have a *theory* as to who might have taken Villon and then killed him? I'm going to have a hard time believing this story unless I can find a plausible explanation for why."

"Yes, our asset provided the following explanation. According to his sources, Villon was killed by a group of eastern Europeans who had some unsettled business with him. I would not be surprised to find out that some operation that Traynor had run in the past, using Villon, was the reason for what happened. Europe is a small place. If Villon carried out many operations there, it was inevitable that someone eventually would recognize him. The asset said that he had a high degree of confidence in the conclusion that certain eastern Europeans, maybe Russian, maybe Serbian, were responsible for the kidnapping, interrogation and execution of Villon. Maybe someone spotted him in Monaco, found out his travel schedule and laid the trap for him in Nice. While the 'who' or 'why' is not yet confirmed, the bottom line is this, Senator—Villon is dead. We won't have to worry about him showing up and disclosing what he knows about Jonathan Traynor or the Agency-sponsored operations run by Traynor. Villon no longer presents a threat. And with Traynor dead, I'm confident this entire matter is closed."

Before McGowan could respond, the waiter appeared with the lunch entrees. McGowan and Rathmann exchanged a few pleasantries over the meal, but the business was concluded.

McGowan resolved to give the matter more thought, but in the end he desperately wanted to believe that Villon was dead, and so he accepted the Director's assurances with only a modicum of lingering doubt.

For his part, Rathmann continued to worry that the information he had received concerning Villon was not correct, and that some day he might have to face a potential scandal for authorizing the assassination of Azbek Fahoud. But if that day came, he was confident that with Robert McGowan in the White House, the administration would bend over backwards to furnish all the public support and Congressional arm-twisting necessary to sweep the matter under the rug, and that in the long run, he would be protected.

20

MASON

It was just after eight o'clock on a warm, late summer evening. Staley stood in the shadows of his fourth-floor hotel room and looked out across Lafayette Park to the White House. The bright spotlights hidden in the manicured shrubs fronting the north portico competed with the low sun for reflection off the stately white columns of the presidential mansion. It suddenly occurred to him that a hotel so close to the White House was a fitting location for the role he was about to play.

He sipped a decent Chardonnay from the room's mini-bar while watching the activities below. There was the normal gathering of demonstrators parading in front of the high iron fence surrounding the White House grounds, many calling for the President's resignation, others carrying signs in support of the ailing administration. A mother walked twins in a stroller on the north side of Pennsylvania Avenue, while a young black man, wearing a tie-dyed T-shirt and baggy jeans, leaned ominously against a tree on the edge of the park and smoked a cigarette. In the middle of the park were two leftover hippies sitting on a blanket, one strumming a guitar and ignoring the other, who seemed to be looking frantically for something that most likely was lost years earlier.

Staley took deep breath and turned back to the business at hand, butterflies in his stomach for the first time in years.

In a few hours he would set out on a very difficult and unpredictable mission, starting in motion a chain of events that hopefully would result in one of the worst scandals in the history of American politics. Orchestrating the desired result would be tricky, but he believed that if he was convincing enough, and if the targets reacted as he expected they would, it just might work.

Staley had spent most of the month of August at his home in Aspen, working on a plan. After his telephone conversation with Detective Sergeant Victoria Costanza confirming his suspicion that Charles Rathmann was involved in the murder of Jonathan Traynor, Staley's first instinct had been to simply kill Rathmann: to break into his home some evening and put a bullet in his head, then send a letter to *The Washington Post* with details concerning Robert McGowan's treachery in the Traynor matter and in the attempted murder of Aaron Berman almost thirty years earlier. But while simplicity was appealing, that course of action presented several countervailing considerations. For one, killing Rathmann without making sure he understood why he had to die did not seem to be enough. For another, there was always the possibility that McGowan could pull enough strings and spend enough political capital to avoid any real damage based solely on allegations made in an anonymous letter. And finally, it was personally risky. Staley did not intend to spend the rest of his life in a maximum security federal prison if there were other, less perilous ways of accomplishing the objective. Killing Rathmann in an apparent "hit" would cause the entire weight of the FBI *and* the CIA to be brought to bear in finding the murderer. While in his experience a simple plan usually was the best alternative, in this case a simple plan might not guarantee success while permitting an untraceable exit. As far as Staley was concerned, in this matter both were absolutely essential.

During the four weeks he spent in Colorado, Staley grew a beard and allowed his hair to grow longer than it had been in years, coloring in a considerable amount of gray in his sideburns, across his temples and over his ears. He started parting his hair on the right side instead of the left, and his natural cowlick caused the part to run more toward the middle of his forehead. He also purchased some clear eyeglasses, round with thin wire frames, that added to his almost professorial appearance: a stark contrast to his normal cover as a clean-cut, serious businessman. The disguise would be temporary. He would lose it soon after he arrived at his destination. In case anything went wrong during the initial phase of his plan, he didn't want anyone to be able to obtain a physical description or a photo by reviewing security camera tapes or through interviews with flight attendants or counter clerks.

Finally, on Saturday, September 4, Staley left home early in the morning, drove northwest to Glenwood Springs for breakfast, then made the long drive east on I-70 all the way to Kansas City. Staley never flew out of or into the Denver airport under an alias. There were too many opportunities for a chance encounter with an employee who remembered him as Hackler Staley. He spent the night in an inexpensive motel near Kansas City International Airport. The following day, using one of his many assumed identities but with a new picture to match his current appearance, he took a United flight to Washington's Dulles International Airport. There he caught a taxi to Reston, Virginia, and checked into a Motel 6 under the same name and identification documents he had used for the flight. He paid cash in advance and told the desk clerk he would be leaving very early the next morning for an appointment in D.C., so he did not want to be disturbed for the remainder of the evening.

That night, Staley shaved his beard and trimmed his hair to a more respectable length. While he intended to use a moderate disguise in his initial meeting with Rathmann, if things went as planned, Rathmann's ability to identify him would not be a problem.

The next morning at seven o'clock, Staley took a cab from the motel in Reston to Alexandria, Virginia. He gave the driver the name and address of the La Bergerie restaurant on North Lee Street, explaining that he was supposed to meet an old friend there for breakfast.

Staley knew the restaurant would be closed at that hour, but acted surprised when the driver noticed a sign in the window stating that La Bergerie opened for lunch at eleven a.m. Sulking about the apparent confusion in plans, Staley sent the cab on its way, telling the driver that even though the place was closed, he was absolutely confident that this was where he was supposed to meet his friend.

After waiting in front of the restaurant for five minutes, Staley walked two blocks and hailed a passing cab. He asked the driver to take him to Reagan National Airport.

Upon arriving at the airport, Staley carried his bags inside, found a coffee shop and ate a light breakfast while reading the morning *Post*. When he was satisfied that no one had taken an interest in him or noticed that he'd carried his bags in from the street instead of from an arriving flight, he paid the tab and visited the restroom before walking to the Hertz desk and renting the car he had reserved under the name Carl Bonner, a businessman from Kansas City, Missouri.

Staley loaded his bags in the trunk of his car, turned out

of the airport and onto the George Washington Parkway, then drove northwest along the Potomac. He took the exit for Highway 123 and continued west into the low hills of McLean, Virginia, where the rich and powerful maintained luxurious homes on large lots with tall trees and manicured lawns. It was the traditional enclave of those who served in government but were sufficiently wealthy to have little need for a government paycheck.

When he was close to Rathmann's house, Staley pulled out a map he had been given at the car rental counter and spread it out over the steering wheel, as though using it to find his way through the unfamiliar and winding streets. If noticed, he was a visitor trying to find a particular address, or perhaps just a tourist on a sightseeing trip.

Rathmann's large, two-story house was set back in a stand of towering, old oak trees, completely shaded by a full canopy of high-spreading limbs. A traditional concrete walk lined with garden lights extended down from the dark-stained front door to the sidewalk, with an intersecting pavestone path leading to a curving driveway that wound around the side of the house to a hidden garage. Hedges, foundation plants and flowers surrounded the house, complemented by smaller beds throughout the yard, including one with an ornamental concrete bench at the base of one of the magnificent trees.

There were no cars in the drive or in front of the house, and no sign of life from within. Staley assumed that Rathmann had already left for his Langley office, even though it was the Labor Day holiday. The Director's habit of working long hours was well documented. Since he lived alone, it was unlikely there was anyone else in the house at this hour, and there appeared to be no full-time security. That was encouraging.

The area behind the house was heavily wooded and over-grown with natural vegetation. Staley knew from his research that another house stood some two hundred fifty feet behind the Director's on an adjacent lot, but the neighbor's house was not visible through the thick copse of underbrush and decorative trees lining the backyard.

Satisfied with his reconnaissance, Staley continued through McLean, turned north on I-495, drove southeast down the George Washington Parkway along the south bank of the Potomac and finally crossed the Key Bridge into the District.

Staley checked into The Hay Adams Hotel, situated just across Lafayette Park from the White House, at around three in the afternoon, using the Carl Bonner identity and credit card. As he signed the registration form, Staley wondered if this would be the last time he would ever have to check into a hotel using an assumed name. He desperately hoped so—he wanted more than anything for *this* to be his last mission.

At eleven o'clock that night, Staley walked out of the Hay Adams with a backpack casually slung over one shoulder. With a smile and a wink, he confided in the doorman that he was going to meet a lady friend for a late-night glass of wine. The valet brought his rented Ford Taurus up from the parking garage and Staley climbed in after tipping both the doorman and the driver. He tossed his backpack in the front seat and drove east into the heart of the capital.

Six blocks later, Staley turned south and retraced his route from earlier in the day. He passed McLean and turned off I-495 just beyond the Dulles Airport exit. After several attempts, he finally found a gas station with an outside access restroom. He parked near the darkened door of the restroom, disabled the dome light in his rented Taurus, gathered his backpack and quietly slipped into the restroom.

He made certain the door to the restroom was securely locked, then set the backpack on the sink where its contents were more accessible. He pulled on a black turtleneck, then fitted a dark gray wig over his streaked hair. The wig had a ponytail that he threaded though the hole above the headband adjustment at the back of a plain black baseball cap. He used theatrical glue to hold in place a thick gray mustache that matched the wig. Although far from being an accomplished makeup artist, Staley had become proficient with simple disguises over the years.

Satisfied with his physical appearance, he made a final inventory of his equipment. First was his "breaking and entering kit," as he called it, comprised of two black leather pouches fastened to a nylon harness that strapped over his shoulders and under his arms. Inside were lock picks, screwdrivers, insulated and uninsulated lengths of wire, pliers, clamps, mirrors, tape, a flashlight, a circuit tester, a small voltage meter, and a Dremel with various attachments. He had never encountered a security system he'd been unable to breach with these simple devices. Satisfied, he replaced the harness and pouch assembly in the backpack.

Next he turned out the light in the restroom and checked his night vision goggles. He flicked a switch and the dirty bathroom sprang to life in two-dimensional, fluorescent green. He removed the goggles and turned on the light. Satisfied that the device was working properly and the batteries were strong, he placed the goggles in the backpack.

Finally, he took a silenced Colt .22 automatic from the

backpack, pulled back the slide far enough to confirm that a round was in the chamber, engaged the safety and slipped the pistol into his belt at the small of his back.

Staley turned off the light, then cracked the door to the restroom and checked the parking lot. Seeing no one, he opened the door and walked quickly back to the rental car.

From there he drove into McLean and, finding the spot he had selected earlier in the day, he parked the car and worked his way into the wooded area that led to the back of Rathmann's house. It was twelve-fifteen in the morning and a light was still on in an upstairs room, probably the Director's bedroom. Staley settled in for a long wait, as he had so many times over the past thirty years.

At one o'clock, the light went out. Staley made note of the time, but did not change his position. He decided to give Rathmann another thirty minutes or so to make sure the Director was comfortably asleep before he entered the house.

At one forty-five, Staley conducted an area reconnaissance of the house and grounds. He was concerned about the possibility of sophisticated sensors in the yard, but those devices usually didn't work well in residential areas where security fences were prohibited by restrictive covenants. Dogs and other animals roaming the neighborhood at night would set them off constantly. He was relieved to find no evidence of any kind of electronic perimeter security. He was also relieved to find that Rathmann did not have a security detail guarding the house. That level of protection most likely was reserved for times when there was concern for a specific threat against the Director. Fortunately, there was no such threat that evening, at least not that anyone at the CIA could have expected.

Satisfied that the likelihood of discovery between the

woods and the house was minimal, Staley donned a pair of thin latex gloves and cautiously approached the door leading out of the garage and into the back yard.

After locating and disabling the surprisingly simple alarm system, Staley picked the lock on the garage door and slipped inside. He waited there, with the door open, for fifteen minutes, just to be certain there was not a second system that had sent out a silent alarm. If the police were on their way, fifteen minutes should be enough time for the patrol cars to arrive. Staley knew he could escape through the same door and avoid the responding officers, who almost certainly would announce their arrival with flashing lights and blaring sirens. After fifteen minutes, all was still quiet.

Staley closed the door through which he had entered the garage, then went to work on the door into the house, again checking for additional alarm systems and finding none. He was through the doorway in less than a minute.

It was totally dark inside the house. Staley pulled the night vision goggles from his backpack and, occasionally changing to the infrared mode to check for motion detectors, made his way through the downstairs level.

He made a cursory search of several rooms, but paid particular attention to the wood-paneled study. The large desk in the well-appointed study was mostly bare, with the exception of an old brass lamp on one corner, two multi-line telephones on the right side and three neat stacks of paper arranged in perfect order beside an expensive leather desk pad. There was a gold pen set on a marble base at the front of the desk with a brass plate bearing an inscription Staley did not bother to read. He checked the various papers meticulously organized on the desk and found them to be bills and other routine household mail.

He then checked the drawers to the desk and discovered that none of them were locked. He quickly examined the contents of each drawer, finding little of interest, with two exceptions. In the middle drawer on the right-hand side of the desk, he found a cassette tape recorder wired to operate with a remote switch capable of being triggered by the knee of someone sitting at the desk. He'd thought it possible that the Director would have some kind of audio or video equipment in the study for secretly recording meetings in his home. Staley studied the operation of the recorder and the remote. It would work perfectly. His plan contemplated the use of a tape recorder, and he was prepared to obtain and wire the recorder himself. But that would not be necessary. Rathmann's desire to surround himself with cloak and dagger vestiges of his office would be very accommodating.

In the bottom drawer on the left-hand side of the desk, Staley found a 9-millimeter Glock wrapped in an old white T-shirt stained with gun oil. He checked the automatic and found that it was loaded, with a round in the chamber. He wondered what Rathmann expected to do with a loaded weapon in the bottom drawer of his desk. He suspected that Rathmann's real motivation for having the Glock, which appeared to be an Agency-issue model, was to complement his cachet as the Director of Central Intelligence, perhaps allow him to identify with the field agents under his command. That, too, would fit nicely with Staley's plan.

Staley spent several more minutes going through the study. He checked for other surveillance or recording devices in the bookshelves and for the existence of a safe, but found nothing of importance. Satisfied with his examination of the study, he moved on.

In the small paneled bar between the study and the living room, he found a bottle of twenty-year-old scotch, one of his favorites. On a whim he picked up the bottle and two small, cut-crystal glasses and placed them carefully in his backpack. He thought it might help gain the Director's confidence if they shared a drink while getting to know one another.

Staley crossed the living room and climbed the stairs, carefully watching every step as illuminated by the macabre green fluorescence of the night vision goggles.

Just to the right at the top of the stairs, he found and entered Rathmann's bedroom. The Director was lying on his back in the middle of a large bed with a high oriental headboard. A white cotton duvet was pulled up under his chin. Staley watched and listened carefully as the Director breathed with the rhythm of someone sound asleep.

Staley moved quietly through the room, checking for weapons, panic alarms and other matters that required attention before waking and confronting Rathmann. When he was satisfied, he removed his night vision goggles, clicked on the small lamp on the nightstand beside the bed and, holding the silenced Colt in his right hand just inches above the Director's face, shook Rathmann gently.

At first, Rathmann unconsciously resisted being awakened, then stiffened as he opened his eyes and looked into the barrel of the small automatic. Staley held the Director's shoulder with a iron grip. It was important to maintain control until the still-groggy Rathmann had a chance to work out what was happening.

The Director slipped into near panic, his eyes bulging and his voice cracking in fear. "What . . . what . . . what's going on? Who are you? What do you want?"

Staley continued to hold Rathmann's shoulder, rendering him completely immobile under the duvet.

Staley spoke quietly and confidently. "Mr. Director,

please. I'm not here to harm you. I'm here to give you some very confidential information and to ask for your help with an important project. I apologize for doing it in this manner, but when you hear what I have to say, perhaps you'll understand. Okay?"

Rathmann nodded, still terrified but trying to regain his balance. Staley purposely kept his voice quiet and reassuring, not threatening, and it had a calming effect. He continued in a very matter-of-fact tone. "I'm going to take the gun away in just a moment. I want you to sit up against the headboard and put your hands on top of your head until we get better acquainted. The only way I will use the gun is if you attempt to trigger an alarm, make a ruckus or otherwise present a threat. In any of those events"—Staley smiled ever so slightly—"I will put a bullet between your eyes before you can complete whatever it is you're trying to do, and then I'll leave."

Staley allowed that to sink in for a moment, then said, "Just to make certain we understand each other, Mr. Director, please respond verbally."

Rathmann's gaze alternated between Staley's face and the Colt. His voice was still shaking and almost an octave higher than normal as he replied, "Yes, I understand."

Staley relaxed his grip on Rathmann's shoulder and motioned for him to sit up. Rathmann squirmed out from under the duvet and braced his back against the headboard with his hands on top of his head as instructed, his eyes riveted on Staley. As he did so, Staley backed up and sat down in a high, wingback chair that he had repositioned to the side of the bed. He laid his pistol on the edge of the nightstand, well out of Rathmann's reach, then produced the bottle of scotch and the two glasses from his backpack. His hands still protected by the rubber gloves, he poured two fingers of scotch in each glass and handed one to Rathmann.

"It's okay, you can take your hands down now. But please, be very careful of making any movements that I might misunderstand. I've been doing this kind of work for a very long time, Mr. Director, and I don't take even the slightest risk. So bear with me."

Staley smiled again as he gestured for Rathmann to accept the scotch.

Rathmann slowly dropped his hands and reached for the glass, his fear being overtaken by confusion. Staley silently offered a mock toast, and to his credit, Rathmann managed to return the gesture and join Staley in a sip of the whisky.

Breaking the silence, Rathmann spoke, this time his voice more controlled. "May I ask who you are and why you are here?"

Staley answered very politely, "Yes, you may. If the intent of your first question was to learn my name, it's not important. In my line of work, I really don't think much about my real name anymore. But if giving me a name makes you more comfortable, for reasons we'll discuss in a minute, you can call me 'Mason.' If, on the other hand, your question was more general in nature, I can best be described as what in your agency would be known as a 'field operative.' For the past seven years I have worked on a most secret basis—'classified' would not be an appropriate adjective because there is no security classification suitable for what I do—solely for one principal. That principal is the Office of the President of the United States. Not the President himself, but the *Office* of the President. You appreciate the difference, I assume? You would be surprised how many people in government do not."

"Yes, I appreciate the difference," Rathmann replied,

sounding more confused than ever.

Staley continued, "Mine is a strange job. I am very rarely called upon to take direct action on behalf of my principal, and frequently when I am called upon, I am not required to report the success or failure of the assignment I've been given. But then, my success or failure usually is reported in the media."

Staley smiled for effect and took a sip of scotch. "I've never met the President, by the way. I'm what you might call a 'deniable asset.' My direct employer is a former business executive who deals only with one person in the administration, and that person is very close to the President. Not even the White House chief of staff knows of my existence. But let there be no mistake, whether or not the President himself knows about me, or that someone *like* me is working behind the scenes, ultimately I am implementing *his* desires and *his* agenda. And once in a while, I have to clean up a mess. Am I being too vague here, or do you understand what I'm saying?"

Charles Rathmann had been involved in Washington politics long enough to understand exactly what the intruder was alluding to in his cryptic explanation. And he was well aware of all the problems that had surrounded this administration from its inception. The fact that someone like the dangerous-looking man now sitting in his bedroom was working behind the scenes explained a lot of unanswered questions. But even so, they had no business treating Rathmann in this manner. He was, after all, the Director of Central Intelligence. Gradually he found his fear turning into anger.

"I believe I understand what you're saying. But if I am correct in my understanding, why has the President, or as you put it, the *Office* of the President, sent you here to break into my house in the middle of the night and confront me by putting a pistol to my head? I meet with the President and the chief of staff on a regular basis. Surely any information the President wants to give me or any assistance the President might need from me could be handled in a face-to-face meeting. Quite frankly, Mr. Mason, or whatever your name is, I find this outrageous. Your explanation better be good or both you *and* the President will find yourselves in very serious trouble. Surely you know that."

Staley took another sip of the scotch, then picked up the Colt, cocked the hammer, and rested it on his lap.

"Let's get something straight," he said. "While threatening the President can be dangerous, threatening me is always a very bad mistake, one that most people don't get to make twice."

Staley leaned slightly forward. "I want to make sure you understand, Director Rathmann, that my personal security is extremely important to me. As a matter of fact, it is at the very top of my list. I am also very protective of the security of my principal. If I were to become convinced that you are or might become a threat to that security, I would have no compunction whatsoever about killing you. As a matter of fact, that is frequently the best way for me to ensure that people who meet me in the course of my duties cease to be a security threat. I have been assured that you are bright enough to cooperate in what I am about to ask and, more importantly, to not provoke me. My principal would prefer that you remain alive and in your current position for the foreseeable future, but if there is any doubt about your willingness to do so on a guaranteed confidential basis, without threats and without causing any trouble whatsoever, I have the discretion to terminate your engagement in whatever manner I deem necessary and appropriate."

Then, in a fluid motion executed with almost unbelievable speed, Staley simultaneously raised the Colt, leaned across the bed and touched the barrel to Rathmann's right temple. The Director was instantly rendered speechless and immobile.

"So, Mr. Director, what do you say? Do you want to continue to posture and threaten me, or do you want to listen and, if everything works out well, stay alive? Believe me, it's your call."

Feeling the terror of being close to certain death, and without moving his head so much as an inch, Rathmann cut his eyes sharply to the right and looked at Staley down the length of his outstretched arm, all the while feeling the cold steel of the automatic pressed against his skull. He swallowed hard, unsure of what to say other than, "Please . . . wait a minute. I didn't mean that comment as a threat. I'm just trying to understand what's going on."

Staley held the gun to Rathmann's temple for a few more seconds, as if considering whether or not to pull the trigger, then sat back in his chair, released the hammer on the small automatic and replaced it on the nightstand. He took another sip of scotch, hesitated, then continued.

"The matter for which my principal needs your assistance involves Senator Robert J. McGowan."

Rathmann tried his best to control any visible signs of the jolt of electricity that ran through his body. His dealings with McGowan had been kept secret from even his closest associates. Could this somehow involve Traynor or the Fahoud matter? "What about Senator McGowan?"

"In the interest of time, I will tell you what we know. First of all, we know about the connection between the Agency and the late Jonathan Traynor."

Rathmann started to protest, but stopped when Staley raised his hand.

"We know that Colonel Traynor was engaged by the Agency, specifically by you, to eliminate Azbek Fahoud. And we know that Senator McGowan was apprised of this operation and, with your cooperation, was in some way involved. We also know, and this is very troubling to me since I knew and respected Colonel Traynor for many years, that Senator McGowan, possibly with Agency assistance, was responsible for Colonel Traynor's death."

Staley avoided any indication that he believed it was Rathmann who was personally and directly responsible for Traynor's murder. He had to leave the Director an out on that score or he would never buy into the plan.

Rathmann's stomach twisted with fear while his mind spun through every detail of his meetings with McGowan. *How could anyone know so much? But even so, thank God he doesn't know that I was the one who had Traynor killed. As for my dealings with McGowan, there was no security leak on my side. Was it McGowan? Was he careless or is he trying to set me up? No, that doesn't make any sense—if I go down, he goes down. What's the agenda here?*

Staley continued. "We also know that you employed the assets of the Agency to hunt down and, if found, to kill Traynor's associate, the Frenchman named Villon, who assassinated Fahoud. It is our belief that you did so at the urging of Senator McGowan. Are we correct in that belief, Mr. Director? I remind you again that you must be very careful in answering my questions. Do not attempt to mislead me."

Rathmann hung his head and tried to compose himself before answering. He was afraid to lie, afraid his eyes would give him away or that that the intruder already knew the answer and was trying to trap him.

Finally, he said, "Yes, everything you've said is true, except for one thing. While we did employ Agency assets to find the Frenchman, it was all McGowan's idea. He more or less threatened me with exposure of my approval of the Fahoud operation if I didn't go along. But our agents did not find the Frenchman, at least not alive. We received a report that Villon was killed by eastern European gangsters and buried near the Swiss border. That's all I know about the matter."

"The real issue here, Mr. Director, is not the Agency's involvement in the assassination of Fahoud, or for that matter, any assistance the Agency may have rendered in the murder of Colonel Traynor. Rather, the issue that interests my principal is, why did McGowan want Traynor killed and why did he want Traynor's man, the Frenchman, killed as well? Have you ever seriously wondered about that?"

Rathmann paused, then answered. "I've always accepted the notion that for political purposes, McGowan wanted to eliminate any connection between himself and the Fahoud operation. He was aware of it and tacitly approved it, you know. Oh, I knew that he had some problem with Traynor, something they argued about in my office one day, but I didn't know what that was about or how serious a matter it might become." Then Rathmann decided to take a calculated risk. "I never thought McGowan might attempt to *kill* Traynor because of it."

Staley let that one pass. He knew Rathmann was lying about his involvement in Traynor's death, but having Rathmann believe that his story was being accepted at face value was important.

"Mr. Director, we *know* the answers to those questions and we have the proof to substantiate those answers. But as with much of the information known to us about a number of politicians at every level of government, the real question is, is there a reason to use this information, either by disclosing it to the person who has the most to gain by keeping it secret, or by disclosing it to the public where political careers are made and lost? In this case, there is a very good reason to use the information we have on Senator McGowan. Simply put, my principal does not want Robert McGowan to be the nominee of the Democratic party for the office of President, whether next year or any year in the future.

"I have no idea why my principal wants to thwart Senator McGowan's presidential aspirations, nor do I care. But whatever the underlying reason, someone has deemed it sufficiently important to engage me to get McGowan out of the race and, consequently, for me to enlist your assistance toward that end. And even more importantly, all of this must be accomplished without any possible connection to the administration."

Rathmann looked shocked. "Surely to God you don't expect me to, to . . . *eliminate* him? He's a United States Senator, probably the most high profile United States Senator. I can't possibly arrange for something like that. There's no way I could ever get away with it, I mean, even if I were to agree to try."

Staley smiled. "Relax, Mr. Director. We don't want you to terminate Senator McGowan. We want you to confront Senator McGowan with certain documents and physical evidence that my principal believes will make it very difficult for him to continue his campaign. We will want you to confront the Senator with these materials and advise him that you believe the information to be so damaging that it would present a risk to our national security if the Senator were to be successful in his bid for the presidency. Now listen carefully to the instructions I am about to give you.

"You will meet with Senator McGowan, at a time and place of my choosing, and show him the evidence we will provide. We want you to be thoroughly familiar with the evidence so that you can walk the Senator through each item. It is important that he understand exactly what you have and how it may be used. We trust you can handle that aspect of the project."

Rathmann continued to sit quietly, wondering where all of this would lead.

"Developing a story for how you obtained the evidence without the knowledge or assistance of anyone in the Agency is the tricky part," Staley continued, "but we have a plausible scenario. You will tell the Senator that you obtained the evidentiary materials from a man who identified himself as a former associate of Jonathan Traynor. You will tell him that this former associate had the materials delivered to your home in a locked briefcase by a local courier service. Tell him that the man obviously intended to keep his identity secret, since he referred to himself only as 'Mason.' "

Rathmann looked confused. "Mason? But I thought you . . ."

"I don't want this to become too complicated, Mr. Director. One name for all the mythical characters in this story will simplify things, don't you agree?"

He smiled, then continued without waiting for Rathmann to respond. "You should tell McGowan that you ran a complete background check on Traynor and found no relatives, business associates or friends named Mason, first or last name, so you believe 'Mason' is an obvious cover for someone who does not want to be found. You will tell him that this Mason called your private line two weeks ago and insisted that he speak with you concerning a matter involving Jonathan Traynor. Since only a few people have your private number, and since you were concerned about the Fahoud matter, the death of Traynor, and the subsequent search for Traynor's French assassin, you took the call. Explain that Mason told you that two days before Traynor was attacked in his home, he gave Mason a locked briefcase with instructions to deliver the briefcase to you, and *only* to you, in the event of his death. Tell McGowan that Mason said he had waited a month to call you because of concerns for his own safety. Tell him that Mason appears to be an amateur, someone who probably became involved only because Traynor trusted him. Suggest that Mason may be a long-lost cousin or nephew, or maybe the son of one of Traynor's old Army buddies. At any rate, tell McGowan that Mason sounded scared and seemed to just want to get rid of the briefcase.

"Tell McGowan that after talking with Mason, you were anxious to see what information was so important to Traynor that he entrusted it to a third party with instructions to deliver it to you upon his death. So, you mentioned nothing about Mason or the briefcase to anyone at the Agency. The next day, the courier delivered the briefcase to your home, just as Mason described.

"Again, it is important that you assure McGowan that other than yourself, no one at the Agency knows about Mason or has seen the contents of the briefcase. It is also important that you tell him that according to Mason, Traynor's instructions were that Mason should not try to open the briefcase. Tell McGowan there was an old fashioned wax seal across the latch, that the seal hadn't been broken and that Mason told you he had not opened the briefcase. Any questions so far?"

"No, I understand."

Staley continued, "Good. Now, here's the heart of the

matter. You will tell McGowan that you have reviewed the contents of the briefcase, made certain confidential inquiries at the Pentagon and elsewhere, and based on your investigation, you find the story to be credible. You will also tell him that in your opinion, if the contents of the briefcase were ever to become public, it would be politically catastrophic for McGowan. Express your concern about whether or not Mason or anyone else has actually seen the contents of the briefcase. Maybe Mason broke the original seal and replaced it with a new one before giving the briefcase to you. Or maybe Traynor hadn't sealed the briefcase at all. Maybe it was Mason's way of trying to hide the fact that he had seen what was inside, worried about the consequences of someone discovering his identity. Tell the Senator that because of the uncertainty of who *might* know what is in the briefcase, you believe it would be very dangerous for him to continue his campaign, since if he were elected president and the information found its way into the wrong hands, there would always be some doubt as to whether or not he was subject to blackmail. Therefore, you think he should seriously consider terminating his candidacy.

"That's it, Mr. Director, a very simple operation. My principal believes that when faced with the prospect of disclosure of the information that will be provided to you, or possible blackmail if he should win the presidency, the Senator will opt to withdraw from the race. That's what we want."

Rathmann sipped his scotch while considering the proposition, if you could call it that. He was fairly certain he didn't have much choice. This guy Mason was not likely to accept no for an answer.

"Do you really believe the information you are going to furnish about Senator McGowan is sufficiently damning to convince the Senator to withdraw?" Rathmann asked. "Is it that bad? Moreover, is it true?"

"I'll let you be the judge. The circumstances surrounding our obtaining the information are not important; however, we have a high degree of confidence that the information is true. And, we are certain it would be politically devastating if disclosed."

Rathmann turned and looked at the digital clock on the nightstand on the other side of the bed. It was three a.m. He tugged at the sleeve of the Yale T-shirt he wore as a nightshirt, contemplating a response. He also was thinking ahead. *Who can I contact in the White House to confirm this Mason's identity and his story, or should I assemble an Agency team to find out who he is and where he came from? What person close to the President might be ruthless enough to be involved in an operation like this? What if Mason is right and McGowan withdraws from the race? How is all of this going to affect me long term?*

That was the most important question. After all, up to this point he had been counting on McGowan being in the White House for the next four, probably eight, years. This very well might change all that.

Finally he spoke. "All right, I'll do as you ask. How will you get me the information?"

"I will leave it for you in a secure place sometime within the next few days. I will call you either here or at your office to confirm the time and the location. I will then call you periodically after that to get current updates on the status of the operation. I expect you to be very forthcoming in response to those calls."

"How will you identify yourself?"

"Again, let's keep it simple. I'll just say it's Mr. Mason calling."

"Fine," said Rathmann.

Staley handed the Director a small pad and pencil.

"Please write down your private office number, and Mr. Director, do not attempt to trace or record my calls. Believe me, I'll know. I understand that your private number also rings to your secretary's desk. Her name is Kathy, I believe? Please advise Kathy to immediately put through any calls on that line from a Mr. Mason."

Rathmann took the pad and wrote down the number as requested. He then handed it back to Staley.

"Is that all I have to do, then?" Rathmann asked. "Nothing else?"

"That's all, Mr. Director. Either nature will take its course from there, or perhaps we will have to help it along. But in any event, after you confront McGowan with the information, your role in this matter will be finished. And incidentally, Mr. Director, my principal will be very pleased to hear of your complete cooperation in this rather unusual project. At some point, you will be appropriately rewarded for your efforts."

Rathmann seemed relaxed, though pensive, probably considering the relative merits of all the possible alternatives, including a decision to ignore the request and go after "Mason" with all the awesome power at his disposal.

As he finished the last of the excellent scotch, Staley studied Rathmann, as if reading his mind. "Before I leave, I have a few very important caveats for you to consider. First, do not attempt to confirm the instructions I have given you with anyone in the White House, and do not attempt to determine, directly or indirectly, howsoever clever you might believe the means of the inquiry might be, my identity or my connection to the White House."

Staley picked up the Colt and laid it gently across his lap for emphasis. "Any such inquiry will be denied and the message ultimately relayed to me. At that point I will be forced to take appropriate action to correct what I would consider to be an unacceptable breach of security. Please remember what I said earlier about the importance to me of my personal security and the security of my principal."

The implication of the statement was not lost on Rathmann.

"Second," Staley said, "do not attempt to follow me, locate me or investigate me, through your own Agency, the FBI or otherwise. Once again, if any information of that nature should become known to me, I will consider it a major breach of security.

"Third, keep in mind that by reason of my visit here tonight, you have been made privy to one of the most closely guarded secrets ever associated with any presidential administration. Fewer than a half dozen people have ever known of my connection to the White House, and two of them are now deceased. This mission is considered so important that it was decided to bring you into the fold. Be very careful about betraying the trust that has been extended to you. Keep in mind also that by being included in this exclusive group, you most certainly will benefit both politically and personally in the future.

"Finally, do not fall into the trap of believing that Senator McGowan can help you or that if he is elected President, he will be able to intervene and make things right. You must be convincing in your presentation and you must not let on that your efforts are motivated by any desire other than the welfare of the country and the integrity of the presidency. McGowan will try to convince you to aid him in some scheme to downplay the necessity of disclosure or the relevancy of the information. If he does, simply tell him that you cannot take the risk. If he threatens you with disclosure of the Fahoud matter, tell him that you are prepared for the consequences of such disclosure. Whatever he says or promises, do not allow him to co-opt you. *That* would be a tragic mistake on your part. So, Mr. Director, do we understand each other?"

"Yes, I believe so."

"Good. Do you have any questions?"

"None that I can think of right now."

"Fine. I will go over the instructions with you one more time to ensure there is no misunderstanding as to what we expect. You are reported to have a remarkable memory. It will serve you well to listen carefully so that you will be able to handle this matter in exactly the manner I have described."

When he was finished, Staley paused, waiting for any questions. There were none. Finally he said, "Very well, then, I will be in touch with you soon."

Staley rose, gathered up his gear and replaced the wingback chair against the wall. Still holding the Colt loosely in his left hand, he said, "I will be leaving now the same way I came in. I suggest that after I'm gone you turn off the light, roll over and allow the scotch to help you fall asleep. If I hear you leave the bedroom, or if you pick up your telephone within the next ten minutes, I'll assume you have elected to reject our offer, and that would be a very unwise choice. Good luck, Mr. Director. I believe this operation has an excellent chance of success. I know you will give it your best. Good night."

With that, Staley left the bedroom with the nightstand light still burning. He walked down the stairs and out the back door.

Rathmann lay in bed, thinking about what he had agreed to do and what the consequences might be if he refused. No, he could not refuse. He was quite certain that Mason would kill him. In his six months with the CIA, Rathmann had met a few field agents, both current and former, but none of them were as intimidating as Mason. He had death in his eyes. Rathmann had seen it close up and he believed.

He thought about the meeting he was going to have with McGowan. How would it go? It sounded easy when Mason laid it all out, but *he* did not know that Rathmann had been principally responsible for Traynor's death. When confronted, McGowan would have some unexpected leverage. Maybe he would try to use it. Rathmann knew he had to work through the problem carefully and come up with a plausible approach to McGowan, one that would not result in the Senator taking the offensive. It would all turn on the contents of the briefcase.

What was McGowan's secret? Will the threat of disclosure be sufficient to cause him to withdraw, or will he insist on continuing the campaign? If so, what will Mason do? Will McGowan try to threaten me with the Fahoud matter? Or even worse, the death of Jonathan Traynor? Will the truth about Traynor somehow get back to Mason? Mason said that he and Traynor had been friends. If Mason finds out that I was the one who had Traynor killed, what will he do? Now that could be bad—very bad.

A few minutes later, Rathmann checked the clock. It had been fifteen minutes since Mason had walked down the stairs. Surely he was gone.

As Rathmann started to roll out of bed, the thought of Mason sitting beside his bed, in Rathmann's *own chair,* casually fingering that assassin's pistol with no apparent hesitation to use it at the slightest provocation, began to weigh heavily on his chest. Breathing became difficult and he could feel the burning of the scotch rise in his throat. He knew he was hyperventilating, but he couldn't stop.

Rathmann barely made it to the door of his finely appointed master bathroom before falling to his knees and vomiting his insides out. It was not his best moment as the Director of Central Intelligence. At that instant he wished to God he had never taken the job.

21

PREPARATION

10–14 September 1999—Washington, D.C.
It had been three days since Mason's middle of the night visit, three days to worry and wait. Rathmann was just beginning to feel normal again, finally able to work without constantly being distracted by the thought of looking into the snout of the four-inch silencer attached to the business end of Mason's automatic.

It was ten-thirty on a Friday morning. Rathmann had left his house at four a.m. in order to participate in a transatlantic briefing relating to the discovery of a possibly catastrophic development in Iraq. A high-ranking member of Saddam's Baath Party had defected through Jordan with information about a germ warfare delivery system allegedly furnished to the Iraqis by the Russians. For the most part, no one in NATO believed the report. The general consensus was that the defector was just seeking to curry favor with the West, but in light of the seriousness of the matter, a conference call had been hurriedly arranged. If after fully vetting the matter the intelligence service of any participating NATO member became convinced that the story had some semblance of credibility, further action would have to be taken immediately.

Rathmann, a deputy and two analysts had participated in the call representing the United States. Although the defector's story was still being evaluated, the likelihood that

Russia had given Saddam a means to launch a biological attack was considered highly unlikely. Nevertheless, Rathmann was in the middle of working through a stack of research reports and analyses on the subject when someone rang his private line. He assumed it was the White House, but even so he allowed his secretary to answer.

After a moment she buzzed in, "Mr. Director, Mr. Mason is on the private line."

As instructed, he had advised his secretary that he was expecting a very important and confidential call from a Mr. Mason, and that when he called, she was to ring the call through, no matter what the Director might be doing at the time. In some ways, he was relieved that the call had finally come.

Rathmann closed his eyes and tried to relax. "Thank you, Kathy. I'll pick up."

The Director depressed the touch pad opposite the private line on his telephone console and raised the handset to his ear.

"This is Charles Rathmann."

The hauntingly familiar voice of Mason came through the earpiece, his friendly tone almost overplayed. There was crowd noise in the background. "Good morning, Mr. Director. Were you expecting my call?"

"Yes, just as you indicated."

"So I assume that this call is not being traced and that our conversation is not being recorded?"

"That's correct."

"Very well. Let me ask you, do you plan to be home this evening?"

"Yes, I expect to be home by ten o'clock or so, but I can be home earlier if need be."

Staley hesitated a moment as the volume of a boom box

perched on the shoulder of a passing teenager became intrusive. After the youngster moved on, he continued. "Mr. Director, may I speak freely about the matter we discussed the other night?"

"Yes. The line is entirely secure, there is no one listening, there is no one in my office, and the call is not being taped. You have my word."

"Good. Very early this morning, before you left for the office, I placed a brown leather briefcase on the second shelf of the workbench in your garage. You should find the contents of the briefcase to be very interesting. I will expect you to use the materials to prepare the briefing we discussed."

Rathmann waited for a moment to be sure Mason was finished talking, then responded, "I'll review the contents of the briefcase over the weekend."

"Good. Now the briefcase contains original documents and original physical evidence. I want to emphasize in the strongest possible terms that I want all of the material returned to me in exactly the condition delivered to you, is that clear?"

"Yes, I understand."

"Also, Mr. Director, I assume you understand that you may not enlist any help, secretarial or otherwise, in organizing the materials or preparing briefing notes. You must do it entirely on your own."

"Yes, I assumed as much. I plan to do everything myself."

"Good. I will call you sometime early next week to check your progress, to answer any questions you might have and to give you some final instructions."

"That will be fine."

"Excellent. I will speak with you next week then."

* * * * *

As was his habit, during the entire time Staley spoke to Rathmann, he was constantly aware of everything that was going on nearby, always checking for someone or something out of place, someone he had seen earlier in the day or someone who might be paying too much attention to what he was doing. The small kiosk in Union Station where Staley had originated the call was in a nook on the first floor near the west side of the beautifully restored structure. The two-story, mall-like main promenade was packed on both levels with shoppers, diners, tourists and kids just hanging out. Reopened in 1988 after years of renovation, Union Station was one of the busiest commercial retail locations in the nation's capital, but it was still a major transportation hub with rail service to all the great cities located up and down the Atlantic corridor.

The Station was the perfect place to make an untraceable call. Staley did not like the idea of calling Rathmann at his office, but it was necessary in order to test the Director's compliance with Staley's explicit instructions. The fact that Rathmann had not beefed up his home security system or brought in a full-time security team to watch the house was a positive sign that he was fully intimidated and on board with the project. His response to the call was also encouraging. There had always been the chance that he would try to circle the wagons, launch an investigation and make finding Mason a national priority. But he evidently had taken no such steps. Staley's belief that Rathmann's sense of self-preservation, and his fear of Mason, would keep him in line apparently was being borne out by the Director's every action.

Even so, Staley had kept the call short and to the point. No reason to get overconfident at this early stage of the game. Promptly after hanging up the phone, Staley worked his way into the crowd and out through the main doors to the sprawling complex. Even if the call had been traced, there was no way anyone could find him. Not here.

Rathmann checked his watch for at least the tenth time in the past hour. The afternoon and early evening had passed slowly. The biological weapons scare had turned out to be a hoax, just as everyone had suspected. The would-be informer had finally caved in.

It was still just before seven. Because it was a Friday afternoon and there was nothing in the works that demanded the immediate attention of the Director, he sent his secretary home at five-thirty. He told her that he intended to have a relaxed weekend at home and he did not expect to need her until Monday morning.

It would have been out of character for the Director to leave so early, so he had spent the time between five-thirty and seven working on mundane matters, with his attention divided between a reshuffling of senior staff assignments, a report of new terrorist activity in Malaysia, and thoughts about the future—his future. The mid-morning conversation with Mason had tainted the entire day. Now that he was irrevocably committed to the project, he wanted to get home, open the briefcase, and start to work. The sooner he could put this matter behind him, the better.

At seven-fifteen, Rathmann switched off his computer, returned some documents to the security safe mounted in the wall of the walk-in closet located next to the door of his private restroom, turned off the small lamp on his credenza and took the private elevator to the executive entrance at the ground floor level.

Chester Blaylock, a large black man with silver hair and

smooth face that belied his sixty-eight years, was waiting downstairs along with Carlos Armallo, a member of the Director's domestic security detail. Blaylock had been driving DCIs for over twenty-five years. During that time he had gotten to know them all, enjoying varying degrees of familiarity depending on the personality of the man holding the office. Some were friendly and talked regularly with their driver and bodyguards, while others were more remote. Some were always too busy or too serious, others more self-contained. Nevertheless he had admired and respected most of the men for whom he had worked. That did not hold true for his current boss. He had recently decided that he must be getting too old for the job. Just tolerating the current Director was almost more than he could handle. Blaylock found Charles Rathmann to be arrogant and flippant, patronizing to the staff and his security officers, and worst of all, motivated entirely by political self-interest. As far as Chester Blaylock was concerned, Rathmann reflected all the worst qualities of an administration that had come to Washington on a wave of hope and would be leaving on a pile of garbage.

Both Blaylock and Armallo jumped to their feet as the bell rang, signaling the arrival on the ground floor of the executive elevator. Without speaking or missing a stride, Rathmann walked past the two men and out into the parking garage toward his Agency limousine. Twenty minutes later they arrived at the Director's posh home in McLean. Rathmann had not said two words since leaving Langley. His only communication with the driver and his bodyguard had been a gruff "yes" when asked by Blaylock if he was going home for the evening.

Blaylock remained seated behind the wheel, something he would never have done when delivering previous DCIs, as Armallo climbed out of the passenger seat and opened the back door for the Director. Armallo led the way up the sidewalk to the front door and, after Rathmann opened it, disappeared inside for ten minutes while making an obligatory check of the house.

When Armallo returned to the limo, Blaylock glanced questioningly at his friend, who responded with a simple shrug of his shoulders. Despite their obvious personal feelings, no member of the Director's staff ever said anything disloyal about their boss. It was one aspect of the job that gave Chester Blaylock a sense of pride, a sense of professionalism that kept him on the job and out of retirement.

The two men rode in silence for the twenty-minute trip back to Langley, each wondering how long Charles Q. Rathmann would remain at the helm of the world's premier intelligence service.

Rathmann waited patiently for Armallo to inspect the house, checking for signs of a break-in or other indications of a potential threat. Knowing that Mason had defeated the Agency-installed security system twice in the past week had convinced Rathmann that his first order of business, *after* completion of the McGowan matter, should be to trash the existing system and start all over again.

As soon as the front door was closed and the deadbolts set, Rathmann raced through the kitchen and into the garage. He found the brown leather briefcase exactly where Mason said it would be and carried it, unopened, into the house and into the study. He set the briefcase on the desk and looked at it for a full minute before going to the bar and pouring himself a small snifter of cognac. He finished the cognac before screwing up the courage to open the briefcase and find out once and for all what terrible secrets would be responsible for the political destruction of Senator Robert J. McGowan.

The first two items in the briefcase, lying on top of a thick manila file, were two small plastic bags. He removed them from the briefcase and checked their contents.

One bag contained what appeared to be pistol cartridges, including one that had been fired. Inside the same bag was a smaller plastic pouch containing a dull gray slug, apparently deformed by impact.

The other plastic bag contained a gold Cross ballpoint pen and a small three-by-five-inch spiral notebook. Rathmann's interest was drawn first to the notebook. He removed it from the bag, and as he flipped the pages, he realized that it was a combat pilot's notebook, with notations that appeared to be radio frequencies and call signs, along with other indecipherable notes. He replaced the notebook in the bag, intending to study it in greater detail later.

He set the plastic bags aside and picked up a box containing a videocassette in VHS format. The label on the cardboard sleeve read, "Statement of Jonathan Traynor, recorded July 24, 1989." Rathmann removed the VHS sleeve and found the same description on the label. He set the tape aside for later viewing as well.

He then extracted the manila folder and reviewed the contents. On top was a typewritten memorandum, dated the day before, that included an inventory of the briefcase and a summary of the documents included in the file, some of which were brittle and yellowed from age. The memorandum was addressed to Charles Rathmann, Director of Central Intelligence.

Rathmann read the memorandum twice before fully appreciating what he held in his hands. It was potentially devastating, both to McGowan and to himself. The information concerning Rathmann's involvement in the Fahoud matter and in the subsequent efforts to find and kill the Frenchman seemed to be gratuitous and not necessary for the confrontation with McGowan. Mason was just making sure that Rathmann knew what Mason knew, twisting the knife a little bit deeper to ensure the Director complied with his instructions. It was a not-so-subtle hint that the information could destroy him as well, but not if he carried out his part of the bargain.

The documents included several memoranda labeled, "From: Jonathan Traynor, To: McGowan File," bearing dates starting as early as 1971 and continuing through a day just a week before his death. In addition to the memoranda, there were transcribed witness statements, military medical records, photographs bearing the name, "Berman, Aaron, CPT, USAF," a forensic metallurgy report, and a photocopy of a written after-action report submitted by someone whose name had been redacted before copying, thereby making it impossible to identify the author. There were a few loose papers containing handwritten notes and research references. And finally there was a copy of a United States Air Force Citation for the Award of the Silver Star Medal to First Lieutenant Robert J. McGowan.

Rathmann read though the printed material, examined the photographs and the physical evidence, then inserted the videotape into the VCR sitting on top of his large screen television. The videotape came to life with a scene from a dark wood-paneled study. The first few frames consisted of Traynor walking from behind the camera and around his desk to a large leather desk chair. There was no off-camera discussion and no indication that anyone else was present at the time the tape was made. Papers, some of which probably were at that minute lying in Rathmann's lap, were already positioned on the desk pad. If the date on the sleeve was correct, Traynor had made the tape in 1989, some ten years earlier, and he looked much younger than Rathmann remembered him.

After being seated, Traynor picked up the papers in front of him, looked into the camera and began speaking.

My name is Jonathan Traynor, Colonel, United States Army, retired. Today's date is July 24, 1989. I am sitting in the study of my home located in the Georgetown section of Washington, D.C. There is no one else present. In the event this videotape is being used in a trial or an adminis-trative proceeding, or in a private investigation conducted by an instrumentality of the United States government, I now wish to take an oath that my testimony here today will be the truth and nothing but the truth, so help me God.

The tape went on to set out, in excellent order and much in the nature of a presentation by a prosecutor to a grand jury, the relevant evidence in support of a case against Robert J. McGowan for the March, 1971 attempted murder of fellow United States Air Force officer Aaron Berman. The facts were detailed, thoroughly researched and compel-ling, and when the videotape was finished, Rathmann was convinced that what he had seen was true. Almost twenty-nine years earlier, Robert J. McGowan, now one of this country's most powerful politicians, had shot, then left for dead, the pilot of the F-4 Phantom fighter bomber with whom McGowan had been shot down in the jungles of Laos during one of the last major operations of the Vietnam War.

After reading the file and viewing the videotape, it all came together for Rathmann. That day in his office when

Traynor had asked him to leave so that he could have a few words in private with McGowan, Traynor had confronted McGowan with the knowledge of what McGowan had done. In the course of that confrontation, Traynor had inadvertently revealed to McGowan that the Frenchman who had rescued McGowan from Laos and then found and rescued his pilot, Aaron Berman, was the same man that Traynor had sent to assassinate Azbek Fahoud. McGowan knew that the Frenchman had to have been the source of Traynor's information as to what had really happened that day in the jungle. *That* was why McGowan had been so insistent on getting rid of Traynor and on tracking down and killing the Frenchman. The entire business didn't have anything to do with national security or protecting the Agency or McGowan from exposure with respect to the Fahoud matter. It had to do with eliminating the only two people who knew of McGowan's treachery and therefore presented the greatest threat to his presidential aspirations.

Rathmann felt like a fool. McGowan had played him like a cheap violin.

Rathmann was a quick study. By one-thirty in the morning he had pored over the documents contained in the manila folder enough times to have thoroughly absorbed their entire contents, even to the point of having some portions memorized. He had developed such a complete picture of what must have gone on between McGowan and the pilot named Berman that he felt like he had been there and experienced the event. The videotape of Traynor struck him as eerie. Here was a very intelligent and sophisticated man who for almost thirty years had harbored a burning hatred of Robert McGowan. In fact, it was his hatred of McGowan that had ultimately led to his death. Traynor must have known that the materials in the briefcase would not be sufficient to obtain a conviction in a court of law, but he evidently believed that when the time came, the facts revealed in the file would be sufficient to destroy McGowan—both politically and personally. And he might just have been right.

Rathmann spent most of the ensuing weekend studying the evidence and working on the preparation of an outline for a meeting with McGowan. He knew that his performance in the climactic meeting would have to be convincing. He was certain that his political future, if not his life, depended on it. By late Sunday, his work was finished.

On Tuesday afternoon, September 14, Rathmann was sitting at his desk reviewing the latest information concerning terrorist camps in Afghanistan when his secretary buzzed in.

"Mr. Director, it's Mr. Mason on the private line."

Rathmann put the intelligence assessment aside and answered the phone.

Mason's voice was soft and pleasant. "Good afternoon, Mr. Director. Are you free to talk?"

Rathmann answered with a simple, "Yes."

"Good. Have you prepared for the briefing we discussed?"

"Yes, I have. I finished the work this weekend."

"Are you satisfied with the final product? Do you have any questions?"

"Yes, I'm satisfied, and no, I don't have any questions. I believe I have prepared a presentation exactly as we discussed. Do you want me to preview any part of it with you?"

"No. I don't think that will be necessary. In view of all that's at stake, I have absolute confidence that you'll do an exemplary job."

Rathmann squirmed in his chair, thinking about the possible consequences of disappointing Mason. "What do we do now, Mason? How do you want me to set up the meeting?"

"Here's exactly what I want you to do. Listen to me carefully. My principal is concerned about the momentum that is building in support of McGowan's campaign. We need to act quickly so that his withdrawal from the race does not cause any permanent damage to the party. And by quickly, we mean no later than this weekend. We'd like to see him make the announcement in time for the Sunday talk shows. I want you to call Senator McGowan this afternoon. I checked his schedule. He has an engagement Friday night here in Washington with the leadership of the American Bar Association and some prominent trial attorneys from across the country. There is a cocktail party and reception followed by a dinner. The ABA is not going to endorse any presidential candidate, so the event is just an excuse for face time and personal politicking with some well-heeled potential contributors. Three of the other announced candidates will be there too, but the Vice President has elected to pass, probably because there is no organizational money to be raised.

"I want you to call McGowan and tell him that it is absolutely essential that he meet with you alone, at your home, on Friday night. Let him pick the time. If he balks, tell him it's a matter that cannot wait. If he mentions the ABA event, tell him that it might be better if he attends the reception and cocktail party, then slips out before dinner to meet with you. Tell him it will be better if no one else knows he's meeting with you."

"But what if he won't agree? How much can I tell him to get him here?"

"Give him enough that he can't resist the invitation. Tell him that you have information concerning the day he was shot down in Laos and that you must discuss it with him immediately. Tell him you're concerned that it might become public before he has a chance to prepare for it. If he needs more encouragement, feed him some information from the file, but as little as possible. We want to keep him hooked and we want to him to be surprised when confronted with the evidence. I know it's a short fuse, but it's important to my principal that your meeting with McGowan take place this Friday night."

Rathmann considered the instructions, then asked, "Why my house? Why not my office or somewhere else?"

"You have a tape recording system in your study, do you not?"

Rathmann paused, processing the implications of Mason's statement. *The son-of-a-bitch has probably been through my house from one end to the other.*

"Yes. I sometimes use it when I have a meeting in my home with someone who prefers to meet outside the public glare of Langley. Why?"

"Does McGowan know about the system?"

"No. He's never been to my house."

"Good. He may not be suspicious of your taping the meeting if it is held in your study over a friendly glass of wine, and when he sees what you've got to show him, he'll understand why you chose not to meet in a public place."

Before Rathmann could comment on the rationale, Staley continued. "We believe it could be very important to have a voice tape of the meeting between you and

McGowan, especially the first part of the meeting. I suspect you'll catch him off guard with the evidence from the briefcase and that in his surprise, he'll make statements that he won't be able to disavow later. I want his initial reaction on tape. If it comes down to it, if he later elects to fight, if he tries to discredit the evidence, the tape may be the insurance we need to convince him to do otherwise. As for what you say during the meeting, that's entirely up to you. I have confidence that you're bright enough to confront McGowan without saying anything that reflects badly on you."

"What if something comes up that I can't avoid? Something that might be misleading or that might suggest my involvement in, or even knowledge of, certain activities that might be considered, let's say, questionable?"

Staley paused for a moment, entirely for dramatic effect. Rathmann was responding exactly the way he had expected. "As I said, it's the first part of the meeting that's important—McGowan's unprepared reaction to the allegations and the evidence." Another pause. "Do you have the capability of starting and stopping the recording device without being noticed? Can you do it while sitting at your desk?" Staley also knew the answers to those questions.

"Yes, there is a switch under the desk that I can trigger with my knee. There's not much point in having a recording system if you can't operate it surreptitiously while in the middle of a conversation."

"Good. Whenever you see the conversation heading in a direction that makes you uncomfortable, turn off the recorder. But not during the first part of the meeting. I want that part on tape. Are we clear on that?"

"Yes. I believe I can handle it that way."

"As I said, you can control what you say, and if you handle this right, you can keep McGowan focused on his problems, not yours. Remember, my principal selected you for this project. We do not want to see you taken down. But we do want McGowan's initial reaction to the evidence on tape. When that part of the meeting is finished, turn off the recorder. If something should be said on the tape that puts you in a bad light, we'll edit that out before confronting McGowan. The original tape will never see the light of day anyway, so it won't be apparent that it has been edited. Again, it's the threat of exposing the tape that, if necessary, we'll present to McGowan."

Staley did not want Rathmann to falter on the tape issue. It was an important part of the plan to have a recording of at least part of the meeting with McGowan.

"Okay, Mason," Rathmann said. "I'll call McGowan tomorrow and set up the meeting for Friday night at my house. How will I confirm to you that the meeting is on?"

"There is a door on the north side of your garage that opens onto a sidewalk that winds around to the driveway. Outside that door, almost hidden by the ivy, is a wall light in a decorative black fixture. I will check that light tonight, tomorrow night and Thursday night. When you have the Senator's agreement to meet with you on Friday night, leave the light on all night. If the light is not on all night on any of those nights, I will contact you Friday morning, and I will not be pleased. You must do whatever it takes to get the Senator to your house on Friday night, and he must be alone. Do you understand?"

"Yes. I'll find a way to get him there."

"Good. Now let me make a few suggestions for how you might want to lead the conversation."

Staley walked Rathmann through the proposed meeting with McGowan. When he'd finished, he said, "Thank you, Mr. Director, and good luck. I'll contact you this weekend after your meeting with the Senator. I'll be very anxious to hear how it goes. We're counting on you."

Staley checked the light outside Rathmann's garage door that night, but it was dark. However, the next night, it shone brightly all night long.

The plan was in its final stages. Execution would come soon. Staley looked forward to finishing it at last.

22

CONFRONTATION

17 September 1999—Washington, D.C./Fairfax County, Virginia

McGowan winced at the glare of the oncoming headlights. He was driving south, toward McLean. The night was ominously dark, mostly overcast with just a slight glow of the moon low on the horizon. Although he was alone in the car, he felt a presence there with him—a demon he thought he had exorcised years ago—an almost palpable fear of exposure. It held the promise of a consequence he could not bear to face, an outcome he could not allow to occur.

McGowan swerved the car to avoid a poorly-outfitted jogger. He realized that he had been daydreaming again, his mind replaying over and over the words Rathmann had spoken on the telephone the day before. *"This is a very serious matter, Senator, a matter than cannot be discussed over the phone. It involves what purports to be an eyewitness account of the events of March 21, 1971. We must meet so that I can show you what I have—what has been given to me. No one else has been made privy to this information, but I have grave concerns about how it might affect your future, political and otherwise."*

McGowan glanced at the clock on the dashboard of his Lincoln Town Car. It was ten o'clock. He had told Rathmann that he would meet him between ten and ten-thirty. *What can it mean, "an eyewitness account of the events of March 21, 1971"? There were no eyewitnesses. Berman was unconscious, and besides, he had permanent amnesia after the rescue. It couldn't be Berman. The only other possibility is the Frenchman, and he's dead. Good God, surely there wasn't someone else there, someone hiding in the jungle who saw what happened? That can't be. There wasn't anyone else. There's no "eyewitness account." It's not possible. So what's Rathmann up to?*

McGowan had attended the private meeting with the ABA leadership, then stayed for the reception and cocktail party with the larger group. He had even responded to a request to make a few extemporaneous comments to the two hundred or so lawyers gathered for the event. The remarks had not been specially prepared for the evening. He had simply clicked on the tape that ran constantly in his head: the environment, education, health care, social security, jobs. He could make that speech in his sleep and expand it or shorten it to fill whatever time was allocated. Although the canned presentation had several alternative endings, he didn't even remember how he'd closed. He'd suddenly found himself standing with a glass of champagne, smiling and shaking hands with the well-dressed crowd, all seeking to enjoy a brief moment with the celebrity. He was physically present in Washington, D.C., but his mind was far, far away, almost twenty-nine years in the past and in the remote jungles of Laos.

When the doors had opened into the adjacent hall filled with dozens of round tables for eight, covered in linty white tablecloths, sweating water glasses and hotel flatware, McGowan had made an excuse, bade farewell to his nominal host, the current President of the Bar Association, and slipped away. The other candidates would be delighted that he had left, and although his absence would be noticed, everyone understood that the demands on the time of a presidential candidate were many and that it was perhaps presumptuous of them to expect the Senator to spend the entire evening with their small group.

McGowan had released his driver for the evening, telling him that he wanted to drive himself to the reception, then enjoy the peace of being alone for a few hours before going home. There would be few opportunities to be alone after the campaign swept into high gear.

The size and grandeur of the houses passing by on both sides of the Town Car escalated dramatically as McGowan turned into Rathmann's exclusive neighborhood. The address was just ahead.

McGowan pulled into the Director's driveway at ten-twenty and drove around back to the rear-facing garage door, as instructed. After turning off the engine, he sat in the dark car for a full two minutes, both to gather himself for the confrontation he had hoped to avoid and to ensure that no one would see him walk around the side of the house to the front porch. At least Rathmann had the good sense to leave the porch light off. When the two minutes were up, McGowan took a deep breath, slipped out of the Lincoln and started walking toward the door.

At that exact same time, Victoria Costanza and Eddie Quarles stood outside a second-floor apartment in a run-down tenement building a block west of the Anacostia River in northeast Washington. Victoria was on the left side of the door and Eddie on the right, both pressed against the wall of the hallway. Both officers had their service pistols drawn and held in front of them in the two-hand ready position. Costanza wished again that Chico had been with them. His wife had picked this very night to have their third child—

another boy according to the ultrasound pictures that Chico had proudly shown around the squad room.

Damned inconsiderate of Marguerite, thought Victoria. *I could use Chico right now.*

She looked at Eddie and nodded. Quarles raised his eyebrows as if to say, "Here goes," and then, in his best imitation of Chico, knocked frantically on the door and shouted something in Spanish. Victoria had no idea what Eddie said, or if it really was Spanish, but it sounded good and the urgency in his voice was convincing.

Nor did the detectives know whether or not Wes "the Weasel" Ratowski spoke Spanish, but the frantic shouting of something in a foreign language often had a way of causing a perp to open a door, if for no other reason to threaten whoever was outside making all the noise. It was usually a hell of a lot more effective than standing in front of the door and yelling, "Open up, this is the police."

Victoria had studied the information gathered in connection with the investigation of the Toby Markham case and had discovered that Ratowski had signed on to do a job for Toby in order to work off a debt. Very little happened in the drug underworld of East Washington that remained a secret from the gangs and hoodlums who worked those streets. Although it was usually hard to shake out information, with the right amount of persuasion and a promise of looking the other way on a known score, the weak ones sometimes gave up what they knew. That was how Victoria and Eddie, with a lot of help from Tyrone Jefferson, made the connection back to the Weasel. After that, it had taken only a day to find him.

Wes was asleep on the couch when the shouting and banging on the door started. *What the hell?* He didn't move at first, but then whoever was outside started up again. He didn't need that kind of attention. He needed to get rid of whoever was out there and make sure they didn't come back.

Finally he boosted himself up off the couch, ran his fingers through his long greasy hair, and started for the door. On the way, he picked up the sap, his favorite tool for convincing people to do as he asked. He stopped at the door and listened for a moment. The yelling and pounding started again.

Wes had to stop the noise. "Who's there? Whadda ya want?"

Eddie abandoned the Spanish and slipped into a heavily accented English, just like the boys in the barrio where he had grown up. "Hey, man. Der is a fire in da hallway, man. Ju gotta get out, ju know?"

Dropping the sap to his side, Wes impatiently opened the door. "What the hell . . ."

Victoria immediately recognized the Weasel from the photos in his thick police file. She also saw the sap clenched in his right hand. Before he could finish whatever he'd started to say, Victoria grabbed him by the front of his filthy T-shirt and pulled him through the open doorway, smashing his face against the doorjamb of the apartment across the hall. When Wes tried to turn, Eddie kicked him hard on the outside of his left knee and drove the butt of his service pistol down on Wes's collarbone, crashing him to the floor. The leather sap fell from Wes's hand. In an instant, Victoria was on his back, pulling his hands behind him and cuffing him, while at the same time shouting that he was under arrest.

Victoria rolled him over on his back, then she and Eddie each took and arm and sat him up against the far wall of the hallway. Victoria went through the litany of the Miranda warnings, making sure Wes understood and answered each question.

Wes admitted to knowing Toby Markham, but denied having anything to do with the Traynor murder. After a few more questions, Victoria called for backup to take Wes into custody.

She and Eddie executed the search warrant on Wes's apartment. The Weasel was a sloppy criminal. They found enough to put Wes away for a long time, but nothing directly related to the Traynor case. Except maybe for the sap. She looked forward to getting that to the lab.

When Rathmann answered the door, he found a remarkably composed Robert McGowan standing in the shadows of the front porch. Based on McGowan's reaction to the telephone call, Rathmann had expected the Senator to be rattled when he arrived. Rathmann realized that he should have known better. McGowan was too practiced at controlling his emotions to allow anyone to see him upset, no matter what the news.

Maintaining a demeanor appropriate to the seriousness of the occasion, Rathmann ushered his guest into the foyer. "Good evening, Senator. Thank you for coming. This isn't a pleasant task but one we need to face."

Getting straight to the point, McGowan said, "Good evening, Charles. What's this all about?"

Rathmann guided McGowan through the darkened living room and into the study. "It's a remarkable story, one that I hope isn't true. But I am very concerned that some of it, maybe all of it, might be. Have a seat. Would you like a glass of wine or something stronger while we talk?"

"Not now, Charles. Let's get to it. What have you got?"

Rathmann seated himself behind his large mahogany

desk, and as he positioned himself in the chair, he moved his right knee against a rubber boot on the inside of the well. The rubber boot covered the switch that triggered the recording system.

He took a deep breath and began. "Robert," he said, having decided that there was no longer any reason to maintain formalities, "several days ago I received a call on my private line at Langley from a man who identified himself only as 'Mason.' Mason told me that he was an old and trusted friend of Jonathan Traynor and that shortly before his death, Traynor had given him a locked briefcase with instructions to deliver it to me, secretly, in the event anything happened to Traynor."

Oh my God, thought McGowan. *It* was *Traynor. What has he done?*

Rathmann proceeded to tell McGowan the story, as coached by Staley. McGowan listened attentively, showing no visible reaction. He interrupted Rathmann several times with questions. He asked who Mason might be and what Rathmann had done to find out, and whether or not anyone else had seen the contents of the briefcase or heard the story.

When Rathmann finished, McGowan said, "Okay, Charles, let's see what's in the briefcase."

McGowan watched Rathmann open the briefcase and meticulously place the contents on his desk, organizing the various items for logical presentation. It was one of those habits that made McGowan want to scream. Charles Q. Rathmann—always the bureaucrat, always the pedant.

When McGowan saw the plastic bag with the cartridges and the spent slug, he stood and leaned over the desk, his face close to Rathmann's. "Damn it, Rathmann, can we skip the display? Just let me see what's there!"

Rathmann opened his hands and leaned back. "The first thing you will want to do is read my memorandum summarizing the contents of the briefcase. I think you will find it helpful in organizing the materials. After that, start with the unsigned report from Traynor's agent who gathered the most incriminating evidence. Then look at the medical records, the photographs and interviews apparently conducted by Traynor himself."

McGowan unsealed the plastic bags, dumped out the cartridges and rolled them over in his fingers. His eyes lost focus, as though remembering the last time he had seen them. He picked up the spent slug. *How the hell did the Frenchman find that slug? A million-to-one shot. And how did Berman survive after all the ways he'd been hit? And why in God's name did Traynor make a career of putting together a case against me? I was a nobody in 1971. Why would he care? And why did he wait all these years?*

For the next few minutes, neither man said a word. McGowan read the memoranda and reports and examined the evidence, then looked up at Rathmann.

In a solicitous voice, he asked, "What do you think, Charles? Do you believe all of this?"

Rathmann had not expected that question, so he equivocated in answering. "I don't know, Robert. It's all very circumstantial, but quite compelling. There is one more thing you have to see, as well. It's Traynor's testimony, recorded on videotape."

Rathmann turned toward the television mounted in the bookshelves behind and to the right of his desk, and using the remote control that had been lying on his desk pad, clicked on the power. Jonathan Traynor appeared as he walked from behind the camera and into the center of the picture.

McGowan slumped back into his chair. He watched with fascination and dread as the old man told the story of McGowan's treachery. It was more than he could stand. "Dammit, Charles, turn it off. I don't want to ever see that son-of-a-bitch again."

As Rathmann clicked off the television, McGowan stewed, trying to decide what to do next.

"Are you certain no one else has seen this?" he asked.

"No, I'm *not* certain. That's the point. For all I know, Mason made copies of these documents and is prepared to sell the whole story to the North Koreans or the Iranians. When the briefcase was delivered to me, the wax seal you see there was unbroken and the lock was secure. I had to jimmy the lock to get it open. But who knows, maybe Mason poured the seal and maybe he had a key all along. On the other hand, if Traynor really did seal the briefcase and Mason really didn't have the key, as he said, then maybe no one else has seen it. I can assure you that no one else has seen it since it's been in my possession. And, obviously, some of this material—the bullets and the slug, for example—cannot be duplicated. The bottom line is I don't know, I *can't* know, who else, if anyone, has seen what's in the case."

Rathmann paused thoughtfully, then looked McGowan straight in the eye. "I'm inclined to believe Mason's story that he didn't open the briefcase, but I would not be willing to bet the farm, or the national security of this country, on it."

McGowan cocked his head, obviously not pleased with where this was leading. "What are you implying?"

Rathmann steeled himself for the unpleasant task. It was time to meet McGowan head on. "Under the circumstances, I believe it would be extremely dangerous for you to become President of the United States. And quite frankly, Robert, if all of this is true, I wouldn't want an attempted murderer in the White House. I think you should seriously reconsider your candidacy."

McGowan flared. "Listen to me, you bastard. If I go down . . ."

Before McGowan could complete the sentence, Rathmann jarred his knee against the rubber boot inside the desk well, deactivating the recording system.

". . . then you'll go down with me. Remember, the Fahoud assassination was all your doing. I tried to stop it. And I know that you had Traynor killed, and that you tried to kill the Frenchman. And what's more . . ."

Staley, who had slipped into Rathmann's garage and then into the house when he had seen McGowan drive up, listened to the conversation from the darkened kitchen just outside the rear door of the study. He unconsciously clenched his fists in anger when he heard McGowan acknowledge that it was Rathmann who'd had Traynor murdered. He had hoped that Rathmann's meeting with McGowan would confirm that piece of information. The evidence had been strong, but circumstantial. Now there was no doubt.

Staley refocused again on the conversation taking place in the next room. Rathmann was on the defensive, trying to divert attention back to the contents of the briefcase. Staley leaned against the wall and listened.

When McGowan finally calmed down, Rathmann again pressed his knee against the rubber boot inside the well of the desk. He wanted McGowan's answer to the next question on tape. He knew it would be the one Mason and his superiors would want to hear.

"Listen, Robert. I would very much like to help you find

a way through this, but we can't ignore the evidence in the briefcase and the Traynor testimony. If it surfaces and it's true, or even if it has a semblance of truth, you will be compromised. So you tell me, Robert. Is what Traynor said true? Did you shoot your pilot and leave him to die in the jungle? It's a simple question."

McGowan glared at Rathmann for a full minute before answering, his voice dripping with contempt. "A simple question? What the hell do you know, Charles? You were safely off at college, drinking beer and dodging the draft when I was flying combat missions in Vietnam and Laos. You're in no position to judge me. You're the Director of the CIA. You send agents out all over the world to handle dangerous assignments, and yet you've never heard a shot fired in anger. You can't sit there and tell me what I should have done, or what you would have done in the same circumstances, because you can't possibly know what it was like to be there. I was young and in a life-threatening situation, and I made a decision. A decision based on my belief that Berman was going to die anyway and that both of us dying didn't make any sense. So I did what I did, and do you know what, Charles? Whatever I did under those circumstances all those years ago shouldn't make a damn bit of difference today. It's ancient history. It has nothing to do with my ability to lead this country as its President. It's behind us and it should stay there. So don't ask me if Traynor's story is true or not, because as far as I'm concerned, whatever happened in that jungle never happened at all. It's today, right now, that's important. This is *my* time, Charles. The presidency is mine for the taking, and you know what, I'm going to take it. *Damn* Traynor, and damn his briefcase full of evidence. And as for you, Charles, don't get in my way or you'll regret it. I promise you."

McGowan's articulate dissection of Rathmann was powerful and effective. Rathmann sat silently, slumped in his chair, unable to formulate an intelligent response. He kneed the boot and turned off the tape.

His resolve waned. He couldn't follow through, couldn't press McGowan to withdraw from the race. Not now, not after that. Even when faced with a devastating truth, the Senator's charisma overpowered. On the other hand, there was Mason. But hadn't he done what he was supposed to do? He had the tape. Mason could listen to the tape and know that Rathmann had done what Mason had asked. Surely Mason wouldn't hold him responsible for McGowan's decision.

McGowan again stood and looked across the desk at Rathmann. "Well, Charles, what's it going to be? Are we going to work together on this and try to forget this conversation ever took place, or are we going to be at odds and let the chips fall where they may? It's up to you."

Rathmann mumbled something about working with McGowan and to try to help him. He promised McGowan that the Traynor materials would never see the light of day, and that if Mason ever showed up with copies, threatening an expose, Rathmann would see to it that he was dealt with.

Staley, listening to the conversation from the kitchen, was disgusted by Rathmann's weakness. The man was despicable. The fact that he was in charge of the nation's most important intelligence organization was a travesty. But that was a situation that would be corrected very soon.

McGowan, satisfied that he had Rathmann under control, sat back down in the large leather chair across from the desk. He and Rathmann talked for five more minutes, mostly about Mason and what to do if he resurfaced. Then McGowan pointed to the briefcase. "Charles, I want you to

361

put all that material back in the briefcase and give it to me.
I'll see to it that it's destroyed. You won't have to be involved."

Rathmann had anticipated that McGowan would demand either that the briefcase be destroyed or that he take
it with him. He remembered well Mason's admonishment
that the briefcase be returned intact. He couldn't give the
briefcase to McGowan. He didn't want to face Mason with
that news. He didn't want to challenge McGowan again either, but this time he had no choice.

"Robert, there's been more than one occasion over the
past few weeks when you've threatened me, sometimes directly, as you did a few moments ago, and sometimes indirectly, as you did in connection with the Fahoud matter. I
know you have information that could bury me, Robert.
You've made that clear. I don't like being threatened and I
don't like being at risk. But that's the way it is. You're
holding the cards. And because of that, it is in my best interests to do everything I can to support you. Despite
what's in this briefcase, that's what I plan to do. But just to
make sure we stand on relatively equal footing going forward, I think it would be best if I hold on to the briefcase.

"I'm not making any threats here, Robert. It's just a way
to ensure we keep each other's best interests at heart. As
you said, if I make this information public and you go
down, you'll take me down with you. That certainly is not
in my best interests. I think that in the long run, we'll both
be more comfortable if we're forced to rely on each other's
discretion."

McGowan realized that Rathmann had the leverage he
needed to change their relationship. There was nothing
McGowan could do but accept the situation and make the
best of it. At least for now, his future and Rathmann's

would be tied together. But things change. Someday, he would have that briefcase.

McGowan rose. He took one parting shot at Rathmann. "I understand exactly what you mean, Charles, and I believe we can continue to work together, as we have these past few months. But never forget that I am a politician, and a damned good one. You can't be certain that what's in that briefcase is true or if anyone will believe it. I tell people what to believe, Charles. Most of the time they don't know what's true *until* I tell them. You may hurt my career by disclosing what is in that briefcase, but the worst that will happen to me is early retirement. On the other hand, if I go public with what I know about you, you will spend the rest of your life in federal prison. Think about it. Then lock that briefcase away. I never want hear about it again."

Despite the threat, Rathmann felt an enormous sense of relief that McGowan had agreed to allow him to keep the briefcase. But that wouldn't be the end of the matter. He would still have to deal with Mason. Somehow Mason was going to use the materials in the briefcase to get McGowan out of the race. Rathmann hoped he could convince Mason to be discreet, to use photocopies of the documents and pictures of the physical evidence. He'd have to deal with those issues later. Right now he just wanted to get McGowan out of his house. He needed time to think.

Rathmann stood and walked around his desk. "I understand, Robert. I can't imagine why any of this would ever come to your attention again."

He placed his hand on McGowan's shoulder as the two men walked through the living room to the front door. Rathmann checked outside to ensure none of his neighbors were about, walking a dog or taking a late evening run. When he was satisfied that McGowan could leave without being seen, Rathmann opened the door, the two men shook hands and McGowan walked around the side of the house to his car. Rathmann watched through the window as McGowan eased down the driveway, turned into the street and drove away. It had been an exhausting evening.

When Rathmann walked back into his study to turn off the lights, he was startled to find a man standing in the middle of the room. Rathmann gasped and jumped back, reflexively grabbing his chest.

Then he recognized the intruder. The hair was more black than gray, no baseball cap or ponytail this time, and no mustache, but there was the same black turtleneck and those ominous-looking latex gloves. Mason.

Rathmann spoke first, "Good *God,* man. You scared me half to death. Where did you come from? What are you doing here?"

Mason smiled. "I came in the back door. Hope you don't mind. I wanted to get a report on your meeting with the Senator and check on the tape. You *did* make a tape, didn't you?"

Rathmann's mind raced. *How much did Mason hear?* "How long have you been here? Did you listen in on the meeting?"

"I asked you a question, Mr. Director," Mason asked coldly. *"Did you make a tape?"*

Rathmann started thinking frantically about how he was going to relate to Mason what had happened during his meeting with McGowan. It would take some improvisation, but with respect to the early part of the meeting he could tell the truth. The tape would corroborate what had happened during the initial confrontation. McGowan had essentially admitted that he shot the pilot named Berman.

"Uh, yes. I made a tape of the critical parts of the

meeting, particularly the parts where I confronted McGowan with the evidence, just as you asked. But we need to talk."

"Good. Let's listen to the tape, then talk. While we listen, I'd like to have another drink of that very good scotch you have in your bar. Would you mind getting us two glasses?"

Although infuriated that Mason would have the nerve to ask him to fetch them a drink from his own bar, Rathmann knew that the next few minutes with Mason were going to be critical, so he agreed. He turned and walked back into the living room, turned on the light in the small bar, and poured healthy portions of the expensive scotch in two crystal tumblers. When he returned to the study, he found Mason waiting for him, standing in the middle of the room and holding Rathmann's own Agency-issue Glock. The pistol was pointed at the middle of Rathmann's chest.

Rathmann froze. Looking back and forth between Mason's eyes and the thick gunmetal gray automatic, he stammered, "Wha . . . what are you doing? Why the gun?"

Offering a smile that was more ominous than comforting, Mason said, "Mr. Director, I want you to stand very still. I plan to have a drink of that scotch in just a minute, but I want to get something out of the way first. So please, stand right where you are, do not move, and do not spill my scotch."

Rathmann, uncertain as to what might happen next, but having successfully survived the previous encounter with Mason holding a gun on him, remained motionless. Summoning the courage to speak, he said, "Okay. What is it?"

Mason continued. "First, let me tell you about myself. As I said when we first met, my real name isn't important. You know me as Mason. Over the years I have been known by many other names. I believe you recently have become familiar with two of them. Do the names Jack Delon and François Villon ring a bell?"

"Dear God," exclaimed Rathmann, *"it can't be!"*

"Yep, that's me," Mason said lightly. "I'm the man who, twenty-nine years ago, found Aaron Berman just after your friend Robert McGowan tried to kill him. And I'm the man who, a couple of months ago and on your orders, assassinated Azbek Fahoud. I'm also the man your bureau chief in Paris recently engaged a contract operator to kill. But as the saying goes, the reports of my death have been greatly exaggerated."

Mason's demeanor darkened. "I was also a lifelong friend of Jonathan Traynor. As a matter of fact, I considered Jonathan to be a second father after my own father died."

A cold fear gripped Rathmann. Barely able to speak, he muttered, "I'm sorry about Traynor. It wasn't . . . I didn't . . . ."

Mason interrupted. "No, don't bother. You see, I *know* it was you who had Jonathan killed. And that was a costly mistake."

Suddenly it all became clear. Rathmann understood what was about to happen.

"Because for *that,* you're now going to die."

Rathmann staggered backwards, reflexively pulling his elbows close in to his body. "No . . . please!"

Staley fired six bullets from the Glock, all carefully aimed. The first bullet struck Rathmann in the upper right portion of his chest, the second in his left arm, the third bullet found his left lung and the fourth went cleanly through his heart. The fifth and sixth bullets struck the wall and doorframe behind him, both imbedding after tearing away splintered pieces of wood. By the time the echo of the gunshots died down, Rathmann was on the floor, dead.

Staley was counting on the fact that the thick walls of the study, which was located near the center of the house and had no windows, would suppress the noise of the gunshots. He did not waste time to check. He had to move quickly.

He walked over to the body, felt for a pulse and confirmed that Rathmann wasn't breathing. Staley had seen a number of dead men in his time, including several that had died at his hand, but this was different. This had been personal. He looked into Rathmann's lifeless eyes, still open as he lay at a cocked angle on the floor, one broken glass beside him, the other upturned on the thick Persian rug now running red with blood. As Staley studied his victim, he experienced a deep feeling of satisfaction and closure. Jonathan Traynor could lie in peace now. His murder had been avenged.

Returning to the moment, Staley went to work on the study. He quickly gathered up all of the evidentiary materials and replaced them in the briefcase. He rewound and played the tape, then rewound it again and stopped the tape with the remote trigger at the same spot where Rathmann had stopped it. He used the oily rag he had found in Rathmann's desk to wipe off all fingerprints on the Glock and placed the pistol on the corner of desk. Even though the latex gloves would leave no trace, he wanted the automatic to look as though someone had carefully wiped it clean. He replaced the oily rag in the bottom left-hand drawer of Rathmann's desk, leaving the drawer partially open. He left the spent shell casings lying around the room exactly as they came to rest after being ejected from the pistol as he fired.

When he was satisfied with the crime scene, Staley took the briefcase and left through the garage and out the back door, the same way he had entered, carefully locking the doors behind him.

Once outside, Staley took a deep breath of the cool

September air. The first part of his plan had gone well. He felt no remorse about killing Rathmann—only a sense of vindication. Soon McGowan would be dealt with, too. Then it would be over.

Staley made his way back to his car through the wooded area, using the same route he had followed the week before. He needed to kill some time, so he drove out toward Dulles Airport. Finding an all-night restaurant, he stopped for a late dinner.

After a greasy hamburger and an iced tea that tasted like it came out of a can, he drove south for about fifty miles. Then he turned around and headed back toward the District. He was careful to observe the speed limit and to avoid small towns where a curious officer might pull him over. The last thing he needed was a confrontation with a local constable or a record of a traffic stop.

At three a.m., he passed Senator Robert McGowan's home in an exclusive new development located in the northern part of Fairfax County, near the Potomac. He knew from his research that the McGowans had been in the house for only a year or so.

The house was dark. Concerned that loitering in the area could attract the interest of a security patrol, Staley drove on and exited the neighborhood. He pulled in at an unpaved side road about a quarter mile south. From there he made his way back to the house on foot, stopping from time to time to regain his bearings and to make sure no one had seen him.

McGowan's burglar alarm system was newer and more sophisticated than Rathmann's, and it took Staley almost thirty minutes to defeat the system, pick the locks and make his way into the house.

As a result of his cursory examination of the house

during two drive-bys earlier in the week, Staley believed the attic would be accessible from the second floor. That was his objective.

He moved quietly through the downstairs area, his night vision goggles creating a ghoulish, flat green picture everywhere he looked. The master bedroom was on the first floor, down a wide hallway that led from the foyer, past a side entrance into the large kitchen. He quietly made his way down the hall and checked the bedroom. As expected, both McGowan and his wife Sarah were sound asleep. McGowan was lying on his back, snoring loudly, and his wife was turned away, facing the far wall.

Just as Staley took his first step back from the doorway, intending to slip down the hall into the foyer and toward the stairs, Sarah McGowan sat up, rose from the bed and began walking toward the bedroom door, rubbing her neck to work out the stiffness caused by a restless night.

Instead of retreating into the foyer, which would have been the most visible route, Staley backed into a dark corner near the large armoire that stood gallantly at the closed end of the hallway. He turned off his night vision goggles and stood motionless, just a few feet away from the woman as she ambled past him, into the kitchen. She turned on the ceiling lights, opened the refrigerator and poured a glass of orange juice from a cardboard carton. She made no effort to be quiet, as though she were trying to retaliate for her husband's incessant snoring.

Staley remained in the corner, now partially illuminated by the kitchen light, and considered his alternatives. If she came back into the hallway with the light still on in the kitchen, or if McGowan awakened and followed her into the hall, Staley would be discovered. If that were to happen on a normal mission, under normal circumstances, both

McGowan and his wife would end up dead. But this was different. Staley didn't want to kill the McGowans, especially not Sarah. So he decided to take a calculated risk. As Sarah McGowan stood in the kitchen drinking her orange juice with her back to the wide door into the hall, Staley stepped out of the shadows and silently walked fifteen feet into the darkened foyer, past both the doorway into the kitchen and the open door into the McGowans' bedroom. He watched Sarah carefully as he moved, all the while hoping she wouldn't turn around. He had decided that if he were discovered, he would leave both McGowans unconscious but alive. He would accept the very slight risk that either of them might be able to identify him. He didn't think it likely that they would be able to do so under the circumstances. But the plan would be blown and he would have to improvise on the fly. The prospect of everything coming apart because McGowan's wife—never a factor in the plan—wanted a drink of orange juice in the middle of the night was just too incredible to fathom.

Staley made it safely into the welcome darkness of the foyer. Immediately after clearing the kitchen doorway, he heard Sarah set the empty glass on the granite countertop. If he had waited another five seconds, she would have seen him. He had been very lucky, and so had she. Staley took a deep breath and waited.

Soon the lights in the kitchen went out and Sarah walked back into the bedroom. She made a visit to the bathroom, then returned to bed.

Ten minutes later, Staley switched on the night vision goggles and checked the master bedroom again. Both McGowans appeared to be sleeping.

Staley climbed the stairs to the second level, and after looking in three of the upstairs rooms, found the door to the attic storage area. He stepped inside, closed the door and removed his goggles before turning on a small flashlight.

Five feet from the attic door, with one side against the near wall, was a large gray file cabinet. It was covered with a light coat of dust and one drawer handle was loose. Beside the file cabinet was an old nylon suit bag. He placed the briefcase on the floor behind the file cabinet and covered it with the bag. He then walked out of the attic, closed the door and made his way back down the stairs. He paused quietly near the hallway leading to McGowan's bedroom, but there was no noise other than the continued snoring.

Satisfied with his work, Staley left the house the same way he had entered, reset the security alarm and walked back to the rental car. The telltale thread he had left on the unlocked door handle had not been disturbed, so it was unlikely that a passing police officer had seen the car and investigated.

He climbed in and drove back to the Hay Adams. The night shift doorman nodded and smiled. Staley walked into the lobby and took the elevator to his room. Fifteen minutes later he was sound asleep. His last thoughts were of the operation he had just completed and whether or not Jonathan Traynor would have been satisfied with his performance.

Staley slept until almost noon. Then he packed, checked out of the hotel and, as Carl Bonner, flew back to Kansas City, where he retrieved his car. From there he drove on to Aspen, arriving early in the morning the following day.

He thought about the mission all the way home. He had done all he could do. Now it was up to the system to take care of Robert McGowan.

23

RECKONING

18–19 September—Fairfax County, Virginia

Mike Grady had worked a couple of other CIA-related homicide cases in his twelve-year career with the Major Crimes Division of the Fairfax County Police Department, so he knew generally what to expect. The Agency would offer to cooperate, but would provide no real assistance. They would claim national security concerns as justification for taking charge of the crime scene, withholding evidence, limiting access to witnesses, and monitoring news releases. Every time one of their own was involved in a major crime, either as the victim or as a possible suspect, Grady could count on the folks at Langley to batten down the hatches and set up a defensive perimeter. And those were just the routine cases.

This one was the granddaddy of them all. Somebody had popped the Director of Central Intelligence, and it had happened in his home, right here in peaceful Fairfax County. This case would be on the national news for a long time— probably wall-to-wall coverage by the twenty-four-hour cable news channels. Media types would be everywhere, relentlessly bird-dogging the investigators. While the CIA would be responsible for slowing down the investigation, it would be the Fairfax County Police Department that would take the heat when there were no answers to the reporters' questions. And, as lead investigator, Grady would be right in the middle of it all, trying to solve a murder while at the same time carefully managing the available information and making excuses for why access was being denied here or information limited there.

All things considered, he had been lucky on this one. Rathmann's housekeeper had found the body at seven-thirty on a rainy Saturday morning and her first reaction had been to call 911. If it had been a weekday morning and the Director's security detail and driver had been the first to arrive, they almost certainly would *not* have called the police. More likely they would have called Langley and a CIA investigating team would have been all over the crime scene before the Fairfax County police were even notified.

Because the housekeeper's call came in to 911, a patrol unit responded and the experienced officers first on the scene cordoned off the area and called the Major Crimes Division. Mike was in the middle of fixing breakfast for his wife and two kids, a Saturday morning tradition, when he got the word. He dropped everything and made the fifteen-minute drive to Rathmann's house in just under ten. On his way he called the crime scene investigations unit. One of their teams arrived just minutes after Grady.

He knew that established protocols required that he notify the Agency, but he took his time before doing so. He wanted the CSI unit to take plenty of photographs, check the body, bag the apparent murder weapon, dig the slugs out of the wall, dust for prints, scrape for fibers and foreign objects, and otherwise make a full and uncontaminated evaluation of the crime scene. But he also warned them to stay out of anything that appeared to be a government file or an Agency document. He wanted to be able to assure the CIA investigating team that no breach of security had occurred.

While the CSI unit was going about its business, Grady

tried to work out exactly what had happened. Obviously, it wasn't a robbery or a contract killing. The victim was carrying two glasses of scotch into the study when he was shot. That meant he knew the shooter and was probably having a cordial conversation with the perp just before he was killed. Grady felt lucky. You didn't often get that kind of lead right up front.

He made notes and drew diagrams in his notebook, posing questions and suggesting possible answers for later examination and evaluation. He knew that first impressions of a crime scene were sometimes lost if not recorded, so he was careful to follow the procedures he had developed in over a decade of major crime investigations. He studied the scene and walked around the house, inside and out, looking for signs of a break-in or something else that might offer a lead. Then he used his cell phone to make a call to the contact number at Langley, knowing he was going to get a world-class ass-chewing for not calling in sooner.

Mike had just finished a five-minute call with a very pissed-off supervisor assigned to the Agency's internal security detail when one of the CSI team caught his attention and motioned him back into Rathmann's study.

"Hey, Mike. Look at this." The techie had pulled the victim's chair out from the well of his desk. He pointed to the rubber boot on the right side at knee level. "Bet you a hundred there's a tape recorder here somewhere, probably in a desk drawer. I've seen a switch like that once before. Shades of Tricky Dick, huh?"

Using his handkerchief to avoid spoiling any prints, Grady pulled open the right-hand desk drawers. The recorder was in the middle drawer—a mini-cassette with a tape still in it. The power was on and the "record" button had been pressed. The remote trigger probably overrode the power switch, which meant that the machine was set up to record whenever the contact under the rubber boot was engaged. *Hot damn! Don't tell me we got a recording of a conversation between the victim and the shooter. Nobody catches a break like that.*

This particular piece of evidence warranted the solid gold treatment. Grady turned to the leader of the CSI team. "Okay, here's what I want. Take pictures of the recorder, just like it sits, and the rubber boot trigger. Then take out the tape, dust it, mark it and bag it. I want the original taken back to your lab right now, before anyone else gets here. I want the tape evaluated in every way imaginable, then I want it copied. Send the copy with your report to my office—before noon today. I want limited access to the tape. If anyone in your shop has to listen to the tape in order to evaluate it, I want a list of everyone who hears it and a reason why. That tape might contain more than evidence in this homicide investigation, so everyone who listens to it might end up at the center in a major blowup over at spook headquarters. We need to treat the tape as a serious national security item. If possible, I want to hear it first and by myself. Finally, I want the original of the tape kept in the vault in the evidence room with only one person to have access to it. Namely, me. Got it?"

"Sure, Mike. We'll get a copy and the report over to you ASAP."

Grady and the CSI team continued to work the site, careful to preserve any forensic evidence that might make a difference in identifying a suspect or obtaining a conviction. Ten minutes later, a plain white sedan drove up with three of Langley's finest, as Grady liked to think of them. As expected, they asserted primary jurisdiction over the crime scene, claimed that all of the documents in the house were classified, and demanded an interview with the responding officers, detectives and crime scene investigators before they would be permitted to leave the premises. Mike represented the police contingent in negotiating with the CIA officers, and after much haggling, agreement was reached with respect to what could be taken from the scene and what would remain under the exclusive jurisdiction of the Agency.

When everything was lined out, Mike took the head of the CIA unit aside for a quiet chat.

"Mark, I know you're going to blow a gasket when I tell you this, but we found a remotely-operated tape recorder in the victim's desk. There was a partially recorded tape in the machine and it was set up to operate. I think there is a good chance we might have a conversation between the victim and the shooter on tape."

Mark Johannsen, a former District cop who had been attracted by the glamour of working for the CIA, became visibly upset. "Where is it? I want that tape right now."

"Sorry, Mark. I sent it back with our CSI guys."

Johannsen was livid. With a look of barely controlled anger, he jabbed his index finger into the middle of Grady's chest. "So help me God, Grady, if you've found a tape of a confidential meeting between the Director of Central Intelligence and some third party, and somebody, *anybody*, listens to that tape without being cleared by us, I'll have you fired at the very least, and possibly charged with a violation of a half a dozen Federal laws. Do you understand me?"

Grady glanced down at Johannsen's finger, then looked up at the taller, blond-haired agent. He spoke very softly so as to avoid a scene in front of the other officers. "Johannsen, if you don't take that finger off of my chest in the next three seconds, I'm going to break it and your wrist."

The two men glared at each other. Then Johannsen dropped his hand to his side but continued to scowl at Grady.

Grady, his demeanor calm and businesslike, said, "I've sent the tape for technical evaluation and safekeeping. Right now it is potentially the most valuable piece of evidence in a major homicide investigation involving the Director of your agency. Can you imagine the difficulty the Commonwealth's Attorney might have getting that tape admitted into evidence if it comes out that the CIA—who nobody in the country trusts, by the way—took the tape from the crime scene and held on to it for some time before turning it back over to the police? You were a cop once. Use your head."

It was obvious Johannsen knew Grady was right, but it was equally obvious that he did not like it one bit.

"What do you plan to do with the tape?"

"I was getting to that. I'm going back to my office in about a half an hour. By noon the CSI unit will be finished examining the tape and preparing their report. They are going to secure the original in our evidence vault and send me a copy. No one but me is to listen to the tape except to the extent necessary for a complete workup. If anyone else does listen, I'm to get a list of names. We're treating this as a potential national security issue, but I've got to listen to the tape to see if it provides a key lead in the murder investigation. I hope to have a copy of the tape along with the CSI report within a couple of hours. If you'll meet me at my office around noon, we can listen to the tape together and I'll give you a copy of the tape and a copy of the list."

It was just after noon on what had been a frantically busy Saturday. Mark Johannsen, along with a distinguished-looking, gray-haired man Johannsen had introduced as the

CIA's Deputy Director for Intelligence, were sitting across the desk from Mike Grady. All three men had steaming cups of coffee in front of them. Johannsen and Grady also had notepads and pens. The DDI sat passively, his hands folded in his lap. In the center of the desk was a cassette tape recorder similar to the one found in Rathmann's study and a report from the CSI unit. Grady had reviewed the report before Johannsen and his superior had arrived.

"Well, gentlemen, from your perspective, the good news is that our tech people did not have to listen to the tape to make their tests. There's more they can do, but that *would* involve listening to the tape and with the warning I'd given them, they elected to hold off until we decide whether or not the tape will be useful in the investigation. So, it will be the three of us. Are you ready?"

Johannsen answered, "Okay, Grady, fine. But I'm warning you. If we get into any matter that the Deputy Director believes involves national security issues or internal Agency concerns, we will ask you to stop the tape and we will then insist on having the original and all copies delivered to us before we leave the building, understood?"

Grady sighed. "I understand that's your position. Let's listen for a while before we get into an argument."

Johannsen looked to the DDI, who nodded. Grady took that as indication to go forward and started the tape.

As soon as it became clear that Rathmann was meeting with Senator Robert J. McGowan, the ranking minority member of the Senate Select Committee on Intelligence, Johannsen reached across the desk, stopped the tape, and looked once again at the Deputy Director. Before Grady could react, the DDI nodded to Johannsen and said, "Let's continue." Grady again pressed the "play" button.

From that point forward, neither Johannsen nor the DDI

made any effort to stop the tape. All three men sat transfixed by what they were hearing, sometimes looking away,
unfocused, in an effort to comprehend the meaning, other
times looking at each other in amazement.

When the tape abruptly ended, Johannsen said, "Is that it?"

Grady checked the counter, then the CSI report. "Yep,
that's all of it. Mr. Rathmann had a remote activator switch
in the knee well of his desk and he either intentionally or ac-
cidentally turned off the recorder at that point."

The DDI sat silently for a full minute, thinking about
what he had just heard. As a career intelligence officer with
over thirty years' experience, he was probably the most capable man in the Agency and most likely would be named
acting director until a successor to Rathmann could be proposed by the White House and voted on by the Senate. He
turned to Johannsen. "We get a copy of the tape and of the
evaluation report, correct?"

"Yes."

"Good." Rising from his chair and turning toward
Grady, he said, "Thank you, Detective, and good luck in
your investigation. Please keep us advised if you turn up
anything that directly affects the Agency."

Without so much as a smile, the DDI turned and walked
out of the office with a stunned Johannsen in trail.

After the door had closed, Grady sat quietly at his desk,
trying to fully digest all he had heard and contemplating the
implications. *When was the tape made? Last night? Where are
the materials and the videotape that Rathmann played for
McGowan? Who was Jonathan Traynor? Where was
McGowan last night? Did he have an alibi? Did a prominent
United States Senator kill the Director of the Central Intelligence
Agency over something that happened almost thirty years ago?
Dear God, don't let me blow this one.*

★ ★ ★ ★ ★

By ten o'clock that morning, the major networks had already tapped into the story, with reporters on the scene in front of Charles Rathmann's elegant home. Access to house was not permitted, of course, but the Fairfax County police officials, medical examiner staff, FBI agents and other law enforcement personnel going into and coming out of the house were questioned loudly by the increasingly large gaggle of media representatives that had gathered in the street. As Grady expected, it was a circus with non-stop coverage on all the networks. The only information approved for release to the media was that Charles Q. Rathmann, the Director of the Central Intelligence Agency, had been killed in a shooting incident inside his home. No other information was available.

Early that same afternoon, Victoria Costanza received a call at her condominium in the District. The caller identified himself as Lieutenant Mike Grady. "Sergeant Costanza, I'm with the Fairfax County Major Crimes Division across the river. I'm investigating the death of Charles Rathmann, the Director of the CIA. Have you been following that today?"

Victoria had seen the reports. Because the Traynor case was still at the top of her stack, she had wondered if there was any possibility of a connection between Rathmann's death and the Traynor murder. It was a cop's way of thinking. She knew nothing to suggest a connection, but she couldn't rule it out. She had decided to find out more about the Rathmann case first thing Monday. She knew the investigating officers in Fairfax County would not want to be bothered today; they had plenty on their plate already. The fact that someone, a lieutenant, had taken the time to call her today suggested that there may actually be a connection between the two cases.

"Yes, I've been following it," she said. "Have you got something that points to a connection over here?"

"We may have. As I understand it, you are leading the investigation into the death of a man named Jonathan Traynor, is that correct?"

Bingo! Well, I'll be damned.

"Yes, Lieutenant, I've been chasing it for almost a month. You think there's some tie-in with the Rathmann case?"

"I think there may be. We may be able to help each other. Would you be willing to come over this afternoon and talk for an hour or so? I've got something here I know you'll be interested in hearing."

"You bet. I'll be there in less than an hour, traffic permitting. Give me your office address."

Grady did so, then added, "Sergeant Costanza, there's one more thing. This investigation, if it takes the course I expect, is really going to blow up a storm, including far-reaching political repercussions. I'd prefer that no one other than you and your boss know about my calling you in on this. I've already cleared it with him and you should call him to confirm. Okay?"

The warning got her full attention. *This must be heavy stuff. I wonder if Grady has evidence that the CIA killed Traynor? Only one way to find out.*

"Sure, I'll do that on the way. See you in about an hour."

Fifty minutes later, Victoria was in Mike Grady's office, listening to the tape recording of the meeting between Rathmann and McGowan. The content of the tape was beyond anything she could possibly imagine. She closed her eyes and listened carefully as Charles Q. Rathmann, the Director of the Central Intelligence Agency, confronted Senator Robert J. McGowan, the leading Democratic candidate for the office of President of the United States, with allegations that in March, 1971, deep behind enemy lines in Laos, McGowan had attempted to murder his wounded pilot by shooting him in the head, then had abandoned the pilot's presumably lifeless body in the jungle, *then* had refused to lead a possible recovery attempt.

Even more remarkable, from Victoria's perspective, was that all of the documentary and physical evidence supporting the allegations against McGowan had been compiled and organized by Jonathan Traynor, based on reports from a secret operative who, posing as a mercenary, had led the team that rescued both McGowan and his critically wounded pilot. It seemed almost inconceivable that the story detailed by Rathmann on the tape could have any credibility whatsoever, yet it sounded to Victoria as if McGowan had conceded the truth of the accusation.

She reconsidered her theory that the CIA was involved in Traynor's murder. She didn't believe in coincidences. One of the major problems in her investigation had been identifying someone that might have had a motive. McGowan certainly fit the bill. Maybe he had arranged to have Jonathan Traynor murdered. But that didn't make any sense. While McGowan had a great deal to lose if Traynor went public with the information, it was highly unlikely that McGowan would have engaged Toby Markham to hire Wes Ratowski to kill Traynor, and then taken care of Toby in such a cold-blooded manner. McGowan was too visible to be involved in that kind of plot. And besides, those *were* CIA officers who followed up the murder attempt and worked the crime scene. If the Agency *was* involved in the Traynor murder, then perhaps it was Rathmann working alongside McGowan. But that didn't make any sense either. Rathmann had not received the Traynor file until after Traynor was dead, and McGowan appeared to be hearing it for the first time. It was all too confusing at this point. Victoria decided she'd go back to her office and try to work out possible scenarios that involved both Rathmann and McGowan. Right now, she couldn't quite see the connection.

When the tape had played through a second time, Grady turned off the machine. "What do you think?" he asked.

Since Grady had bared his soul to her, Victoria would do the same. She laid out all of the facts she had uncovered in the Traynor investigation, including the phone call from the man who called himself LaClerc and her suspicion that the CIA might have been involved. She also told Grady that under interrogation, and after blood residue found on his leather sap matched that of Jonathan Traynor, and his own blood matched that found in Traynor's kitchen, Wes "the Weasel" Ratowski had confessed to the crime. He had also confirmed that he'd been hired to make the hit by a small time hood named Toby Markham. She told Grady that they were following up the Markham lead, and that several bar patrons in a dive Markham used to frequent had given statements to the effect that Markham had been sought out to handle an important job by a man wearing khaki pants and a black windbreaker, and that Toby had told several people that he was about to make a big score. Her team was still trying to locate the unidentified man, but he was their leading suspect as the person who'd contracted for the hit.

Grady was interested and took notes. He asked about Traynor's background, where he had come from and what his connection was to the Agency. Victoria told him everything she knew.

The two detectives talked for twenty minutes. Then Victoria said, "So what's your gut instinct, Mike?"

"It all points to McGowan right now, but there are lots of gaps to fill in. We don't know for certain when the tape was made, but alibi is the big issue. The medical examiner makes the time of death last night between ten and midnight. We haven't yet spoken with the Senator, so we don't know where he was at that time. If he was making a political appearance or otherwise has a solid alibi, we're going to have to look elsewhere, at least for the shooter. I've got detectives out right now, talking to Rathmann's neighbors, trying to find out if anyone happened to see McGowan's car in the vicinity last night. I tried calling the Senator at his home just a few minutes ago, but he wasn't in. I talked to his wife. I identified myself and told her I wanted to ask the Senator a few questions related to the Rathmann murder investigation because of their close working relationship. She was reasonably receptive to that explanation and told me she expected him later this afternoon. He's evidently in his office up on the Hill. I'll be waiting for him when he gets home. I'm anxious to hear what he has to say."

"Other than what you've told me, do you have anything solid, like murder weapon, prints?

"There are prints from several different people all around the house, but we haven't matched any of them yet, other than to Rathmann and the housekeeper. We're waiting on the CIA for prints of the bodyguards and expect to find some hits there. One of my detectives is trying to round up McGowan's prints, but we know from the tape that he was in the house at some point, so finding a match there will be no surprise.

"Rathmann's Agency-issue Glock was the murder weapon. It was found at the scene but had been wiped clean. Rathmann evidently kept it in his bottom desk drawer, wrapped in a rag. Looks like the perp removed the Glock from the desk drawer, then shot Rathmann as he came into the room, carrying two glasses of scotch. The bottle was still open on the bar."

"Two glasses? So he was in the process of entertaining whoever shot him?"

"Yeah, it looks that way."

"I'd say that puts McGowan on the short list of prime suspects. Anything else?"

"Well, as I mentioned earlier, we didn't find any of the material Rathmann and the Senator talked about on the tape. It's gone. If it *was* McGowan, he would taken it with him. I mean, hell, that *is* the motive. Presumably he didn't know Rathmann was taping the meeting, otherwise he would have taken that too."

"Sure. I agree. By the way, how did the shooting go down? Anything to indicate a professional?"

"No, and that's interesting, too. The perp fired six shots from Rathmann's automatic, from what had to be very close range, but only four of them hit the target. Rathmann took one in each side of his chest, one in the arm and one in the heart. The other two bullets hit the wall and doorway behind him. Pretty wild shooting."

"Sounds like someone who didn't know what he was doing. Does McGowan own a gun? Any indication he might know how to use one?"

"Good question. No, as far as we can tell from checking registrations, he doesn't own a gun, although as a former Air Force officer he probably had to qualify with a pistol. But that was years ago. A lot of water under the bridge since then. I'd be surprised if he's had much practice firing a handgun lately. You might recall that he gets lots of press for supporting all the anti-gun legislation."

"What about a search warrant for McGowan's house and car? Those are both within your jurisdiction."

"I'd love to have one. But, as you can imagine, no state court judge is going to be too enthusiastic about issuing a warrant to search the home of the guy who everyone believes is going to be the next President of the United States. The Commonwealth's Attorney said he wouldn't even think about going to the judge without first knowing whether or not the Senator has an alibi."

"I can understand that. Some judges across the river would probably require a confession before issuing that warrant. Do you think you can get a warrant if you can show that McGowan doesn't have an alibi? If he has the Traynor materials, he's not going to sit on them forever."

"That's what worries me too. The Commonwealth's Attorney has agreed to stand by until six o'clock this evening. If I can clear the alibi problem by then, he knows where he can find a judge that he believes will issue a warrant based on what we've got."

Victoria processed the information offered up by Grady. McGowan certainly appeared to be the logical choice, but other possibilities could not be ignored. "What do you know about this Mason, the guy Rathmann said gave him the evidence gathered by Traynor?"

"We don't know any more about him than what Rathmann said on the tape. We had Kathy Frazier, Rathmann's secretary, in here just a few minutes ago and she confirmed that a Mr. Mason called the Director on his private line twice in the last week. She had no other information about Mason. I've asked Mark Johannsen over at the Agency to run Mason's name through the CIA's records and let us know if he comes up with anything. After meeting with him and the Deputy Director of Intelligence earlier today, I think he'll cooperate in helping us try to find Mason, but I don't expect much. On the tape, Rathmann told McGowan he tried to identify Mason but had no luck. We'll continue to follow the Mason angle, unless it appears that Rathmann was trying to scam McGowan, which doesn't make any sense to me right now. I suspect Mason is just who Rathmann said he was—an anonymous bag man for a dead Jonathan Traynor."

Victoria agreed with Grady's inclination to discount Mason as a suspect. It was hard to figure why he would give Rathmann the information collected by Traynor and then kill him.

"So," she said, "we've got a perp who knows the victim, was invited into his study, was offered a glass of expensive scotch and, surprising the victim as he returns with the scotch, nearly empties the victim's own automatic all over the room, including four slugs in his host. And, we've got a tape recording of a meeting between Senator McGowan and the victim in which Rathmann tells the Senator that he's got evidence that would almost certainly put to bed for all time McGowan's political career. Then there's Rathmann's strong suggestion that, because of that evidence, McGowan should withdraw from the race. And finally, all of the evidence described on the tape is gone. I guess that leads back to the question at the top of your list. Where was Robert McGowan last night between ten and midnight?"

Grady nodded in agreement. "Yep, that's a pretty good summary. I expect to find out shortly when I interview the Senator at his home."

Victoria stood and offered her hand. "Thanks, Lieutenant, and good luck. I appreciate you bringing me in on this. If I get anything new on the Traynor investigation, I'll let you know. I still think there's a connection here, but I need to give it some more thought."

Grady shook her hand and thanked her for coming, then walked her to the door. As she was leaving, Victoria said, "Would you mind if I give you a call from time to time to see how this thing is shaking out? I'm going to be mighty curious to know what you find out about McGowan: whether he has an alibi, whether you get the warrant and if so, what you find. I'll keep it tight, of course. You can count on me for that."

"Sure thing. Call me anytime and I'll bring you up to speed."

Victoria drove straight to her office. She wanted to make notes of her meeting with Grady while the information was still fresh. She felt certain now that something developed in the Rathmann case would be the break she needed to find the man who paid Toby Markham to kill Jonathan Traynor.

Mike Grady spent the next hour organizing his thoughts and preparing for his interview with the Senator. When he was satisfied with the game plan, he grabbed his jacket, walked to his car and headed north toward the home of Senator and Mrs. Robert J. McGowan.

McGowan was deeply concerned about what might be about to happen in his life. He had arrived at his Capitol Hill office at about eight o'clock that morning and had been working only an hour when a secretary had rushed in to tell him that Charles Rathmann had been killed in a shooting at his home in McLean. That had been hours earlier. Details were not being released by the police, but because of his position on the Senate Select Committee on Intelligence and the close relationship between the Committee and the Agency, McGowan had been informed early on by the FBI that Rathmann had been murdered. The Chairman of the Committee had also called, along with several of McGowan's cohorts in the Senate. The Capitol police had stopped by at mid-morning to advise the Senator that they were beefing up security in the building. Everyone was concerned about what had happened to the Director of the Central Intelligence Agency and why.

Staffers working in McGowan's office that Saturday afternoon were totally preoccupied with the Rathmann story and its possible implications. Not a great deal of work was accomplished on the campaign and very few calls and e-mails were received from constituents and supporters. Most Americans, including the paid staff and unpaid volunteers in McGowan's office, were in shock, waiting for the next shoe to drop.

Throughout the afternoon, as he watched continuous coverage on CNN, all McGowan could think about was the briefcase full of evidence accusing him of shooting Aaron Berman and leaving him for dead in the jungle. The briefcase and the evidence it contained were a time bomb that could destroy McGowan's political future—a time bomb that had to be defused.

McGowan's mind was spinning, but he tried to remain optimistic. *Dammit to hell, why didn't I insist on taking that briefcase? If I'd insisted, Rathmann probably would have cratered. No, that's not true. He wasn't going to give it up. Can't do anything about that now. Okay, so where's the exposure? Rathmann was a careful man. He wouldn't have left the contents of the briefcase lying around. Surely he has a safe somewhere in the house. As DCI, he would have to have a safe. After*

I left, he probably put all of the Traynor materials back into the briefcase and locked it in the safe. If so, the CIA will be the first to open the safe. There's no way the CIA is going to let the Fairfax County police see the contents of the safe until they've gone though it first with a fine-tooth comb.

That, he concluded, was his best hope. The CIA either had or soon would have the briefcase. As soon as they realized the significance of the Traynor materials, they would contact him. They would not accept the contents of the briefcase at face value—they never accepted anything at face value—and they would not release the file to the police or to the public. As a result of his position on the Committee, McGowan had a lot of clout with the Agency. He would work with them closely, denying everything of course, and concoct a story about how someone obviously was trying to harm him politically, maybe even a foreign government. That was an angle he could work for some time. The longer he could keep the Traynor materials locked up within the Agency, the more likely those materials would never see the light of day. If he could contain the problem for a few months, maybe even until after the election, the whole thing might blow over. That would be the best of all worlds.

But what if Rathmann didn't put the materials away? What if he didn't have time to put them in the safe before he was killed? What then? If so, then the cops would have everything by now. They would have read the file and watched the Traynor videotape. Left unchecked, that could be catastrophic. But that scenario is highly unlikely. Just relax. It'll work out. It always works out.

McGowan turned his attention to a proposed campaign trip planned for early October. He tried to stay focused on the papers in front of him, but he couldn't avoid thinking about the Traynor file. He wondered if he would have sufficient political influence in Fairfax County to keep the materials suppressed. Maybe his lawyers could file a lawsuit seeking a restraining order. Or maybe the Agency's security people would require the police to turn the materials over to them. Then he would be back at the first scenario, with just a few more complications. The thought of the Traynor file lying on the desk of some detective at the Fairfax County Police Department made him physically sick.

But if that was the way it turned out, maybe he *still* could explain everything to the American people. He would go on national television and relate how Jonathan Traynor had been a longstanding right-wing political enemy who had manufactured the whole thing. There was no hard evidence that Traynor had had any connection to the mercenary who had rescued him and Berman. The Agency would never acknowledge that story. There were no living witnesses to contradict McGowan's version of the events of that day, as familiar to most Americans as the story of Jack Kennedy and PT 109. It was all a politically-motivated, unsubstantiated attack by a sick, venomous old man. McGowan thought he could make that explanation work if need be, but it would be risky and in the long run probably would cost him some votes. Nevertheless, as long as he secured the nomination, he was fairly certain he could handle the rest.

While not nearly as important as his own problems, from time to time throughout the day McGowan also considered the question of who killed Rathmann and why. *Was it a burglary, or was it something related to his job at the Agency? Had someone targeted the Director of Central Intelligence for assassination? Serious consideration of that possibility would cause the boys at Langley to stop any release of information and lock down the Agency like a maximum-security prison, which could work in my favor. But what if it was a terrorist attack? Who might be next on the list? Or worse yet, what if it was the man Rathmann called Mason? If it was Mason, maybe I'm at risk too.*

McGowan had started wrapping up the final items on his desk when his cell phone rang. No one had that number except his wife, and she never called him on his cell phone. He checked the caller ID. Sure enough, the call was from home.

"Hello, honey," he said, trying to sound cheerful. "How are you doing?"

"I'm fine, Robert." Sarah sounded stiff, as though someone was listening in on the call. "Do you plan to come home soon?"

It was a simple question, yet odd in the way it was phrased. Still, McGowan saw no need to be suspicious or clever. "Yes, I plan to leave shortly, just as soon as I finish up a couple of things. Why?"

"Robert, the Fairfax County police are here. The officer in charge is a Lieutenant Grady. He's very nice and says he'd like to wait here until you get home. He says it's about Charles Rathmann. Evidently, they want to talk with you because you knew and worked with Director Rathmann. Is that all right?"

At first, McGowan could not imagine what questions the police might have about his relationship with Rathmann. He didn't know anything about the Director that would help in their investigation. Then the obvious answer struck him. *Of course. This isn't about my relationship with Rathmann. They must have found the Traynor file. That's what they want to question me about. They're trying to tie up loose ends. At least they came to me first. What am I going to say? I've got to keep a lid on this. Surely I can convince them that no purpose would be served by making the file public. It can't be material to their investigation. Should I call my lawyer? How soon do I need to file some kind of legal action to suppress the file? If they won't commit to keeping it under wraps, I'll call Jerry right away. He won't know what to do, but he has partners who handle matters like this. He'll find someone.*

Then he had another thought. *Wait a minute. Maybe that's not it at all. I wonder if they know I was at Rathmann's house last night? Maybe that's what they want to question me about. Maybe they want to know if I saw anyone else there or if Rathmann told me he was expecting someone. But how would they know I was there? Rathmann and I agreed we wouldn't advertise the fact that we were meeting. Well, whatever they want, I need to think about last night and get my answers down pat before I get home.*

"Sure, honey," he said. "It's fine. I'll leave the office right now and will be home just as soon as possible. Ask the police officers to come in and offer them coffee or a Coke. Tell them I'm on my way. Okay?"

As the wife of a career politician, Sarah McGowan knew how to deal with the unexpected. "Okay, Robert. We'll see you soon."

Mike Grady had positioned himself where he could see out the front window of the McGowan home. When the Senator's black Lincoln Town Car pulled up in the driveway, Grady excused himself and walked outside to meet McGowan. Sarah started to follow him, but he politely asked her to remain inside while he talked with the Senator alone.

McGowan saw the plainclothes officer waiting for him at the edge of the driveway. He climbed out of the car and shut the door.

"Lieutenant Grady, I presume?" the Senator said with a

slight smile and an outstretched hand.

"Yes, sir." Grady shook McGowan's hand, then offered his badge and credentials.

"What can I do for you, Lieutenant?"

"Senator, I'm investigating the death of Charles Rathmann. I suspect you've been following that story today?"

"Yes, of course," McGowan said somberly. "I was informed by the FBI early this morning. As you can imagine, there were security concerns because of my position on the Senate Select Committee on Intelligence. My wife Sarah indicated that you know about my work with the Director and that is why you want to talk with me."

"Yes, sir. That is something we need to explore."

"The report of Director Rathmann's murder was very distressing to me for a number of reasons," McGowan said, "not the least of which is the irreplaceable loss to this country of an exceptional public servant in an extremely important and sensitive position. Beyond that, Charles Rathmann was not only a colleague, he also was a close friend. I simply cannot believe that he's dead."

McGowan paused for a moment, frowning and staring off into the distance, as if remembering a particularly memorable experience with the now deceased Director. He then refocused on Grady. "Can you tell me, Detective, what exactly happened to Director Rathmann? Was it robbery? Murder? I've been concerned all day that it may have been an act of terrorism. That would be devastating. Let me assure you that you can bring me in on whatever you know, even if it's not for public consumption. The Committee will be fully briefed at the earliest opportunity anyway."

As Grady stared into McGowan's photogenic face, he gained new respect for the Senator's ability to lie with an aura of absolute sincerity.

"Yes, Senator, I suppose I can tell you," Grady said. "Charles Rathmann was shot several times, presumably murdered. There was no indication of robbery and it does not appear to have been a terrorist act."

"Do you have any idea of who did it or why? Do you have any leads?"

"None that I am free to discuss with you, Senator. But in order for us to conduct a complete and thorough investigation, it will be necessary for me to ask you some difficult questions relating to the circumstances surrounding Director Rathmann's murder. I hope you understand."

"Fine, but I'm not sure how I can help."

Grady looked directly into McGowan's eyes and in a very formal manner said, "Senator, because we are in an investigative phase here, before I ask you any further questions, I believe it would be appropriate to inform you that you have the right to remain silent. If you chose to give up that right . . ."

As Grady recited the Miranda warnings, the color drained from McGowan's face. Grady had been reading suspects their rights for over twelve years and it never ceased to amaze him how the recitation of that simple litany could take the starch out of the average citizen, even those who started the interview full of bluster and self-confidence. That was the principal reason he had given McGowan the Miranda routine right up front. Whatever McGowan was about to say would be tempered by the fact that Grady was treating him like a criminal suspect, even though the Senator was not in custody.

Grady finished with the obligatory, "Senator, do you understand the rights I've just explained to you?"

McGowan was reeling. "Yes, I understand my rights under the law, but I do not understand why you have formally advised me of my rights. Are you implying that I'm a suspect, or that I'm in custody? For God's sake, what's the meaning of this?"

"No, Senator, I do not mean to imply that you are in custody at this time. But in view of the questions I'm about to ask you, it is important that you understand and acknowledge your right to remain silent instead of answering."

McGowan moved closer to the shorter Grady and in a stern, angry voice said, "I don't know what you think you're doing here, Lieutenant, but I do not appreciate the treatment I'm being given. It is beyond belief that you would suggest my culpability in a crime so loathsome as the murder of Charles Rathmann, a friend with whom I have worked closely for quite some time. What is the basis for these questions you intend to ask me?"

Grady didn't take the bait; this was *his* interview. "For the record, Senator, please give me an account of your whereabouts last night from say six o'clock until two this morning."

It was one of the questions McGowan had expected and had prepared for. *He knows I was at Rathmann's house. They either found the briefcase or some other indication I was there. Maybe Rathmann kept a calendar. That had to be it. I'm certain I did not leave anything that would indicate I was there last night. I didn't tell anyone I was going to Rathmann's house. Did anyone see me? Did I touch anything? Did I leave any fingerprints on anything? What difference does it make? I've already thought through this. I can't risk the police catching me in a lie. I have to tell the truth and then control the consequences.*

McGowan glared at Grady, registering his displeasure with everything that was happening. Nevertheless, he answered the detective's question. "Well, let's see. I was here at home until about six-thirty, at which time I drove to the Mayflower Hotel in the District for a cocktail party and reception with the leadership of the American Bar Association. I did not stay for dinner, but instead left the event at about nine forty-five or so and drove to Charles Rathmann's home in McLean. Director Rathmann and I met for about an hour, after which time I left his house and drove directly back here, arriving sometime after eleven. My wife, Sarah, was still up, watching the last of the eleven o'clock news when I arrived. Shortly thereafter, we went to bed and I slept through the night."

Grady studied McGowan's face intently. It was difficult to lie to a police investigator, no matter how calm the suspect might appear to be. Despite his matter-of-fact recitation, something was troubling McGowan. Grady had to remind himself that McGowan was an experienced politician, a man who could change sides on an issue in the middle of a debate and switch loyalties in a heartbeat without an ounce of compunction. He was known to be a consummate actor in his presentations before the Senate.

Still, he was nervous and Grady thought he knew why. He jotted down a few notes, then once again looked directly into McGowan's eyes.

"Senator, what was the purpose of your meeting with Mr. Rathmann? What did you and he discuss?"

McGowan paused for a moment as if considering whether or not to let Grady in on a terribly important secret. "Detective Grady, I am sure you know that because of the close working relationship between the Central Intelligence Agency and my Committee, a great deal of very sensitive intelligence information is shared with us by the Agency. I can only tell you that Director Rathmann and I were discussing important matters that I am not free to disclose to you at this time. Perhaps if the matter of an appropriate security clearance could be addressed . . . ?"

"In the course of your discussions, was the name 'Jonathan Traynor' mentioned."

"Not that I recall," McGowan replied quickly—*too* quickly. "I knew Jonathan Traynor. Director Rathmann introduced me to Colonel Traynor a couple of months ago. However, I do not recall the Director and I speaking of Colonel Traynor after that, not until his death a few weeks later. I may be wrong about the timing. It's difficult to remember everything Charles and I talked about. At any rate, I had nothing to do with Colonel Traynor or his activities and I knew very little about him. I do recall Charles being quite upset when he learned that Colonel Traynor had been murdered in a robbery attempt. I believe it was at his home in Georgetown. Do you believe there is a possible connection between the two cases?"

McGowan was pleased with his ad-lib effort to divert the conversation by suggesting a connection between the Traynor and Rathmann murders.

"We have nothing concrete on that as yet, Senator," Grady said, "but it certainly is an interesting theory. Nevertheless, you and Director Rathmann did not discuss anything about Colonel Traynor last night, is that correct?"

McGowan was starting to feel uncomfortable. He had decided that he would not lie to the police, but a connection with Traynor was something he didn't want to acknowledge. He could always reconstruct his answers later, if need be.

"That is correct. To the best of my recollection, we did not."

Grady made some notes. "Now Senator, just a few more questions and we'll go inside. Charles Rathmann recently had been in contact with a man named Mason. We know, for example, that Mason called the Director on his private line at least twice during the past two weeks. Did Director Rathmann ever mention a 'Mason' to you? Does that name ring a bell?"

McGowan's heart raced at the sound of Mason's name. *Oh, no. Please don't let them know about Mason. Wait a minute. There was nothing about Mason in the file. Maybe they're just following up recent contacts Rathmann had with persons who can't be identified. That's got to be it.*

"No, I don't recall discussing anyone named Mason. Why do you ask? Is this Mason a suspect in the case?"

Once again, McGowan again was pleased with himself for interjecting another possibility. All things considered, it *could* have been Mason who killed Traynor.

Grady did not answer McGowan's question. He simply said, "Senator, I'm going to make this easy for you, out here and away from your wife. If you know anything about Charles Rathmann's death, I suggest you tell me now. The more cooperative you are early on in this investigation, the more open minded we will be in trying to understand exactly what happened, maybe give you the benefit of the doubt later when it might make an important difference."

McGowan was shocked by the implication of Grady's statement. It was far from anything that he had prepared for or even remotely expected. *Do the police really suspect that I killed Rathmann? Or is Grady just fishing? This is insane!* With genuine astonishment in his voice, McGowan said, "Surely you can't seriously believe that *I* had anything to do with Charles Rathmann's death?"

Grady continued to stare directly into McGowan's eyes. "I'll ask you one time, Senator, then we'll move on. Did you kill Charles Rathmann? If it was in the heat of anger or because you felt threatened, we might be able to help you by understanding the circumstances. But the bottom line is, did you kill Rathmann?"

The accusation was outrageous, way off base. So far off base that McGowan began to wonder if there was a hidden agenda at work here. Maybe a political angle.

"No. Absolutely not. I did not kill Charles Rathmann, and I strongly resent your implication that I did. You'd best be very careful, Lieutenant Grady. False accusations against me will be seen as politically motivated and I will do everything in my considerable power to make you and your superiors pay."

Grady didn't take well to the threat. He nodded his head and pursed his lips into a tight smile. "Fine, Senator."

He then continued. "Senator, we have reason to believe that certain documents and other items were taken from Charles Rathmann's home last night after he was murdered, and we also have reason to believe that you may have taken those items. So I will ask you sir, did you take anything from Charles Rathmann's home following your meeting with him last night?"

"Absolutely not," he answered confidently. "No, I took nothing from Rathmann's house. And again, I want to register my outrage at these inappropriate questions. This is beyond the pale, Lieutenant, and I do not intend to permit this escapade of yours to go unaddressed."

Grady checked his notes, then looked up at a very angry and shaken McGowan. "Thank you, Senator. You may go inside now if you wish. I'll be in to speak with you and your wife in just a few minutes. Then we'll wrap this up."

McGowan glared at Grady, then stepped up on the front porch and walked into the house.

Immediately after the door closed, Grady took out his

cell phone and called Robin Wickham, the Commonwealth's Attorney for Fairfax County, who was still in his office, waiting for the call. Grady related the substance of his conversation with McGowan, the fact that McGowan admitted being at Rathmann's house the night before, and the fact that McGowan lied about discussing Traynor and the man named Mason. The call lasted less than two minutes. It was exactly the information Wickham believed necessary to make a compelling case for the issuance of a warrant.

As soon as he completed the call, Grady walked back into the house. Robert and Sarah McGowan were sitting in silence with the two detectives who had accompanied Grady to the residence. Grady remained standing.

"I know this is uncomfortable for you, Senator," he said, "but in light of your answers to my earlier questions, I have requested the issuance of a warrant to search the premises, including your vehicles, for certain papers and other materials that appear to be missing from Charles Rathmann's home. I expect to have the warrant delivered here within the hour. My detectives and I will remain with you until it comes. I apologize for the inconvenience, but it is simply a matter of police procedure that we are required to follow in conducting a thorough investigation. I hope you understand."

McGowan closed his eyes. A number of disjointed thoughts took off in several different directions. *Why would the Fairfax County police want to search my home? What do they believe I took from Rathmann? What did I say to Grady that gave him reason to call for a warrant? Is there anything in the house that shouldn't be here? Is there a political angle here? Is someone trying to embarrass me? How will I handle this with the media? What will be the effect on my campaign? Who would issue such a warrant and why? What difference does it make what their excuse is? This is an outrage. I'm not going to sit here and tolerate this egregious behavior. I'm going to chew some ass with the Chief of Police and then with the County Board of Supervisors. Someone's head is going to roll for this.*

Sarah McGowan was speechless. She watched as her normally calm husband became visibly angry. He stood abruptly and moved toward Grady, his eyes narrowing in barely suppressed rage.

With his voice rising in pitch and volume, he said, "I will not tolerate any more of this, Lieutenant Grady. I want the Police Commissioner on the telephone right now. You are not going to continue with these unfounded accusations or this outrageous intrusion into our home. I will not stand for it."

Grady replied calmly, "Senator, I realize that this is a difficult situation, but we really have no choice. If you want to call the Police Commissioner, please feel free to do so. But I expect to have the warrant issued within a few minutes, and that is not something within his purview. If there is nothing here to find, then that will be the end of the matter. If you wish to file a complaint about the manner in which you've been treated, you may do so. Again, we're just doing our jobs."

Sarah McGowan regained her composure quickly. She stood beside her husband and gently took him by the arm. "Robert, perhaps it would be a good idea to call Jerry Foss. I think we should have our lawyer present for whatever happens next. Let's go into the kitchen and have a glass of iced tea. You call Jerry and see what he has to say, maybe ask him to come over as soon as possible. We have nothing to hide, so let's just get past this. It may not be in your best interests to make this a major issue right now. It might be better to take a deep breath, try to relax and let things play out. We can deal with this later."

McGowan continued to glare at Grady as his wife tried to reason with him. He finally relented and the two of them walked into the kitchen. A minute later, Grady could hear the Senator talking angrily on the telephone, probably to his lawyer.

Robin Wickham incorporated the information provided by Grady into the partially completed application for a search warrant sitting on his desk, and then called the district judge who had agreed to be available to consider the application. Ten minutes later, Robin Wickham was in the judge's living room obtaining a signature on the warrant and twenty minutes after that the warrant was delivered to Mike Grady, who at the time was sitting on the front porch of the McGowan home, reading over his notes, fleshing out the report of his interview with the Senator and detailing every action he and his detectives had taken since arriving at the residence. If the warrant turned up nothing, he would be responding to departmental inquiries for the next month.

Grady thanked the courier, a young intern working in Wickham's office, then walked back into the house. He gathered up his two detectives and led them into the kitchen. McGowan looked up, slightly more under control than when he had stormed out of the living room some thirty minutes earlier.

"Do you have the search warrant?"

"Yes, sir." Grady handed the warrant to McGowan, who studied it for a moment before handing it to his wife.

"The warrant was issued by the Circuit Court of Fairfax County. It authorizes us to search your home, the surrounding premises, and your vehicles. I am now serving the warrant. Will you permit us to carry out the search authorized by the warrant? I can wait a short while for your lawyer to be present, if you wish."

McGowan spit out the answer. "We have decided that we will not need to have our attorney present for this witch hunt."

"Fine, Senator."

McGowan, still angry, added, "We are not going to resist the execution of your ridiculous warrant, Lieutenant Grady. But if you destroy or unnecessarily disrupt anything in this house, I will hold both you and the Fairfax County Police Department fully responsible. In any event, when you're finished, you can expect to hear a great deal more about this from us and from our attorneys. I do not plan to let this matter drop."

McGowan turned his head away from the detectives and dismissed them with a wave of his hand. It was a side of Robert McGowan no one had ever seen publicly. Sarah was concerned about the image her husband was projecting, but perhaps there was no downside to all of this. Surely everyone in America would be sympathetic to the Senator in light of the horrid mistreatment he and Sarah had received at the hands of the Fairfax County police.

It took Grady and the other officers less than an hour to find the briefcase hidden under the nylon garment bag stuffed behind the file cabinet in McGowan's attic. Grady opened the briefcase, took a quick look at the contents, then carried it downstairs to the breakfast room where McGowan and his wife had remained during the search.

McGowan had explained to Sarah what the questions and the search warrant were all about—nothing, really, according to his rendition of the story. Yes, he had gone to see Rathmann the night before, and no, he didn't know anything about the murder until he received the news this morning. He and Sarah commiserated with one another. They made plans for how they were going to handle the media exposure and, eventually, make the county government pay for this unconscionable intrusion.

The tension between Robert and Sarah had just about melted when Grady unceremoniously walked into the breakfast room and placed the briefcase on the table between them. When McGowan saw the briefcase, he slumped in his chair and closed his eyes, shaking his head almost imperceptibly. "Oh, dear God," he said quietly, a reaction that would be very important some months later at his trial.

It took the Senator about thirty seconds to regain his composure and become defiant. Standing, he jerked his head toward Grady and pointed a finger in an accusatory manner. "*You* did this, didn't you? You planted it. Who put you up to it? I did not bring that briefcase into this house and you damned well know it. I have no idea how it got here."

He looked at Sarah, who stared at the briefcase, then her husband. McGowan tried to ease her obvious concern. "Sarah, surely you don't . . ."

"Robert, what is this?" she asked, confused by his guilty reaction. "What's going on?"

McGowan tried to find some way to explain, but he didn't know where to start.

The silence was broken by Mike Grady, whose words cut through McGowan's heart like a knife.

"Robert McGowan, you are under arrest for the murder of Charles Rathmann."

Grady turned to one of the other officers standing by. "Cuff him, Zach. Take the Senator downtown and I'll meet you there."

To Sarah McGowan, he said, "I'm sorry, Mrs. McGowan, but your husband will have to go with us now."

Sarah, barely holding back the tears, pleaded with her husband. "Robert, what's happening? What should I do?"

As the detective guided him toward the front door, McGowan talked over his shoulder, instructing Sarah to call his attorney and have him meet them at police headquarters. Consistent with police procedures, McGowan was not allowed to stop and have a conversation with his wife, so she trailed along, asking questions as McGowan was led down the long driveway toward the police car. The exchange between Robert and Sarah became more urgent as he neared the patrol car. Several neighbors looked on in surprise as the Senator was ushered into the back seat and driven away, his wife staring after him in shock.

The scene was chaotic. It always happened that way when a white-collar suspect with no priors and a good reputation was taken from his home, handcuffed and charged with a serious crime. Some cops thought it depressing, others felt sorry for the guy who had been caught, others empathized with the family.

But for Mike Grady, the feeling could not have been better. He had taken down a murderer less than twenty-four hours after the crime. The fact that the suspect was wealthy, had a lovely wife, lived in an exclusive neighborhood, was a well-known United States Senator and aspired to become the next President of the United States, made no difference to Grady. He had heard the tape of the meeting between Rathmann and McGowan and had seen the documents in the file. In his mind, McGowan was lucky to have been on the outside for the last twenty-nine years. It was justice delayed, but not denied. Robert J. McGowan finally would be doing the time he deserved.

★ ★ ★ ★ ★

Just a few hours later, in an extraordinary Saturday evening court session, Robert McGowan was brought before Magistrate Amelia Cramer, who had agreed to preside at the defendant's initial appearance and bond hearing so that the Senator would not have to remain in custody through the remainder of the weekend.

Reporters crowded the courtroom, but cameras and recording devices were not permitted. Robin Wickham, the Commonwealth's Attorney who had taken a huge risk in seeking the issuance of a search warrant for the Senator's home, represented the Commonwealth of Virginia in the proceedings, and a visibly uncomfortable Jerry Foss, McGowan's personal lawyer, entered his appearance on behalf of the defendant.

The case was called and Magistrate Cramer asked Wickham to explain the nature of the charges against the Senator and the circumstances of the arrest. After a brief presentation by Wickham, during which the Senator continually interrupted to protest his innocence, Magistrate Cramer generously offered to release the defendant on his own recognizance on condition that he surrender his passport and that he agree not to leave the state, except to attend to his duties as a United States Senator in the District. Foss conferred quietly with his client, then announced that the terms of release as outlined by the Magistrate were acceptable to the defendant.

The proceedings were over in less than ten minutes. Reporters rushed from the room to file their stories while McGowan and his lawyer followed the bailiff out to finalize the arrangements for his release.

The next morning, all of the Sunday talk shows scurried to reshuffle their programming. Frontline reports from stalwart journalists traveling with the troops recently sent to East Timor were relegated to the back burner, as were live interviews with shaken victims of the deadly hurricane that had ravaged the coast of North Carolina and overseas feeds from sister networks covering a major earthquake in Turkey. As far as the major news outlets were concerned, there was only one story: the arrest of Senator Robert J. McGowan in connection with the death of Charles Rathmann, the Director of the Central Intelligence Agency.

Speculation ran rampant as to exactly what had happened. At Robin Wickham's direction, very little information concerning the Rathmann murder had been made public by the Fairfax County Police Department. The facts that formed the basis for McGowan's arrest had been presented by Wickham in scant detail at the initial appearance. The television commentators, undeterred by the lack of hard facts, filled the information gap with conjecture. While many appeared preoccupied with a possible political angle, others were more imaginative. One talking head suggested that agents of an international terrorist organization might have killed Rathmann and framed McGowan for the crime in order to destroy his chances of becoming President. Another, a self-described former CIA insider, reported that Rathmann and McGowan had worked together often and that there was some friction between the two. Yet another, a prominent criminal defense attorney still basking in the afterglow of the O.J. Simpson trial, postulated that self-defense might be an issue in the case. Soon the network anchors ran out of fresh material and began repeating themselves.

Meanwhile at "McGowan for President" headquarters, the reaction of volunteers and paid staffers vacillated between shock and concern, with some still hoping for news that would exonerate the Senator and breathe life back into what now appeared to be a seriously threatened candidacy.

By late Sunday evening, a pall of disappointment seemed to hang over the entire country as America watched and waited to find out what would become of Senator Robert J. McGowan.

Across the Potomac River, Victoria Costanza followed the action on CNN. Late that afternoon, she called Mike Grady at home, congratulated him on the good work and received a complete update.

Two time zones away in Aspen, Hackler Staley relaxed with a freshly brewed cup of hot coffee in the living room of his small house on Hallam Street. He watched the continuing live television coverage of phase one of the personal destruction of Robert McGowan. The plan he had conceived to bring McGowan down was working better than he could possibly have expected. So long as the system continued in its relentless pursuit of the truth—or in this case, Staley's manufactured version of the truth—the final mission that was Jonathan Traynor's legacy would be completed without the need for his further involvement. It would be Hackler Staley's final mission as well.

He sighed and sipped his coffee. It was over at last.

EPILOGUE

23 March 2000—Fairfax, Virginia

It was a quiet Thursday afternoon in Fairfax, Virginia. Staley walked slowly along a seldom-used pavestone path that led away from the front entrance and around to the side of the Jennings Building Judicial Center. The grass was beginning to green and the lawn maintenance company workers, bundled up in hooded sweatshirts, were pruning trees and turning over beds on the grounds of the courthouse. It was the best spot he had found to take a break from the stuffiness of the courtroom while avoiding the area in front of the courthouse that had been set aside for live television reports and interviews.

The afternoon was unseasonably cold for an early spring day in northern Virginia. The trial of Robert McGowan was in its fourth week. Staley had followed the proceedings on Court TV and the twenty-four hour news channels and was well aware that the overwhelming evidence against McGowan, while circumstantial, had been accepted as gospel by a vast majority of Americans. According to the polls, public support for the disgraced Senator had declined into the low teens. Regardless of the outcome of the murder trial, not even the most diehard political partisan would want to be identified as a supporter of a man shown to be guilty of the despicable conduct McGowan had engaged in, and then covered up, some twenty-nine years earlier.

Staley shoved his hands deeper into the pockets of his charcoal worsted slacks and turned up the collar of his black herringbone sport coat against the bone-chilling breeze. He wished that he had brought a topcoat along on this trip. A mackerel sky overhead portended the oncoming frontal system predicted by local weather forecasters.

He hoped the case would go to the jury soon so that he could return to Aspen and catch some spring skiing in the deep powder on the west side of Snowmass or on the tough, ungroomed trails at the top of Highlands that were for the most part avoided by spring break skiers. He had traveled east to see the last few days of the McGowan trial in person, having remained in Colorado for most of the past six months. He wanted to hear closing arguments, wanted to see McGowan squirm in his chair as the prosecutor recounted the evidence for the jury. But Staley did not intend to stick around for the verdict. Whatever the outcome of the trial, he and Traynor had already won.

The truth about Robert McGowan had been laid bare at the preliminary hearing where the Commonwealth's Attorney had played the tape recording of the meeting between Rathmann and McGowan on the night of the murder and then had meticulously identified, described and presented to the Court each item found in the briefcase recovered from McGowan's home. The Senator's new lawyers—dark-suited, serious men from a large Washington, D.C. law firm—had aggressively tried to suppress the contents of the briefcase, claiming irrelevance, prejudice, no foundation, hearsay and every other conceivable basis for exclusion of the Traynor materials, but the Court had denied every motion, overruled every objection.

In a failed effort to preserve some sense of personal dignity, McGowan had called a news conference the day after the grand jury returned an indictment officially charging him with second-degree murder in the death of Charles Rathmann, an offense punishable by a term of imprisonment from twenty-five years to life. In that news conference, McGowan announced with a heavy heart that in view of the unfortunate and unfounded troubles that had been visited upon him, he had no choice but to withdraw from the race for the office of President of the United States. In fact, the money had dried up and there was no continuing support for his candidacy. Throwing in the towel was more symbolic than substantive.

The leadership of the Democratic Party heaved a collective sigh of relief, then refocused their attention on the next logical front-runner, the sitting Vice President. There was talk of initiating proceedings to expel McGowan from the Senate, but with a two-thirds vote required and the Republicans still smarting from the dramatic defeat suffered during the impeachment debacle, the unspoken consensus was to wait for the outcome of the trial. It was widely believed that following a murder conviction, a Senate vote to oust McGowan would be unanimous.

The news anchors and the print media editors who had glorified McGowan prior to the announcement of his candidacy had been shattered by the revelation of what the charismatic Senator had done all those years ago on one remarkable day during the Vietnam War. Early on, some had tried to make excuses, others had sought justification, but the would-be defenders soon gave up the cause. Even his father-in-law, the esteemed Randolph Winston, had refused to rally to his defense, stating only that, "Sometimes things happen in life that we cannot understand." McGowan's Silver Star citation, the springboard for his political career, had been highlighted on every network, the deception reflected there described by some as the worst kind of lie. By the time the Iowa caucuses rolled around in January of 2000, instead of being headlined as the leading presidential candidate, McGowan was little more than an unsympathetic defendant in a sensational murder trial.

By the close of the Commonwealth's case in chief, McGowan's guilt appeared to be a foregone conclusion. The evidence had been compelling, the defense unable to place in question the most damning elements of the prosecution's case against the accused—the tape recording of the Senator's meeting with the victim the night of the crime, the lies to the police during his initial interrogation, the briefcase full of evidence found in his home, and most of all, the Traynor videotape. Motive, means and opportunity were proven beyond a reasonable doubt. All that remained was the inherent uncertainty of a jury verdict. The country sat back, unmoved by the defendant's emotional assertion that he was innocent, and waited for the ugly affair to come to an end.

Victoria Costanza had been forced to take a week of vacation. She had not missed more than a day or two of work for over three years. Her boss had called her into his office and ordered her to take off for at least a week—ten days would be better—with no arguments. Since she did not have anywhere else to go, she had decided to drive down to Fairfax and watch what was being billed as the last week of the McGowan trial. While her boss may have thought she was on vacation, in reality she was still working the Traynor case and would continue to work it until she found out who was behind the old man's murder.

Victoria had only one remaining lead: a police artist composite of an average-looking, middle-aged man in a black windbreaker who had met with Toby Markham a few days before the Traynor murder. She felt confident that the guy in the sketch was her man, but so far nothing had turned up. The drawing had been widely circulated in the District and she had received a few calls, but none had led to anything. She also had left copies with the Public Affairs Director at the CIA, with a request to circulate it through the various offices at Langley, but that was a dead end. The PAD had shown little interest in trying to identify a CIA employee as the man in the composite. Nevertheless, Victoria was not about to let the matter drop. She had the sketch in her purse and carefully looked at every man entering the courtroom to see if she might spot the face in the drawing.

Victoria had seen the well-dressed, middle-aged man sitting quietly in the back of the courtroom for the past few days. She had discounted him as a match for the man in the composite, but he had continued to attract her attention. He had dark hair with just a touch of gray at the temples, a mid-winter tan and rugged good looks. He had been doing his best to go unnoticed, slipping in and out of the last row of seats, not speaking to anyone and avoiding eye contact. She had wondered what his interest in the trial might be. He did not appear to be a reporter or media type, and he certainly didn't look like some guy who attended high-profile murder trials just for kicks.

She found herself intrigued by the mystery man. He was much too withdrawn to be a reporter and he did not appear to be taking notes as a writer might do. He was dressed like a successful businessman, but what kind of businessman would take a week off work just to watch a trial? Although he tried very hard to hide it, he had a subtle "look" about him—Victoria was not exactly sure what kind of look, but a look nonetheless. She began to wonder if he was some kind of law enforcement officer, maybe a Congressional investigator or perhaps FBI, or maybe even a CIA agent come to keep tabs on the damage being done to the Agency.

Whatever his story, she found herself curiously attracted to the dark-haired stranger.

During a recess on Wednesday, Victoria met briefly with Mike Grady, who had checked in to see how the trial was progressing. The two of them discussed the McGowan case in general and the connection she continued to believe existed between the Traynor and Rathmann murders. During the conversation, she had asked Mike if he knew the nice-looking guy in the dark suit who had been sitting alone at the back of the courtroom. Grady said he hadn't noticed the man she described, but after taking a good look at him as he reentered the courtroom following the break, Mike told Victoria that he'd never seen the guy before. Her interest piqued, she decided that she was going to meet the curiously handsome man in the back row.

As the judge gaveled the proceedings to a close that day, she rose quickly to try to "inadvertently" bump into the mystery man as the spectators filed out of the building.

By the time she made her way to the back of the courtroom, he was gone.

Staley continued to watch the gardeners as they labored with their early spring chores. But his attention was not so focused that he failed to identify, catalog and evaluate every possible threat in his surroundings—the passersby on the sidewalk near the street, the cars and SUVs moving slowly through traffic and those parked at the curb. He scanned the windows of the surrounding buildings, unconsciously checking for the best place to conduct long-range surveillance or establish a sniper's perch. He had tried on many occasions not to do it, but he couldn't help himself. It was a habit he would never shake, borne of too many years of living on the edge of danger.

In the midst of it all, Staley was surprised to realize he was thinking about Detective Sergeant Victoria Costanza. He had been giving a lot of thought lately to what he was going to do with his life. The prospect of growing old alone had begun to weigh on him in recent weeks. Over the long, dark winter in Aspen, Staley had for the first time in years felt the stirrings of a need to talk with someone, to spend time with someone he cared about—but he had not been able to overcome the burden of his self-imposed isolation. Because of his background, he wasn't sure he had the capacity for meeting people, making friends or building a relationship. And because of his natural aversion to social situations generally, a predilection he would never be able to conquer, he wondered how he could *ever* expect to meet someone that he might find interesting.

Yet that that was the very reason he was thinking about Costanza. She was here and now. He had seen her in the courtroom every day that week and had been quite taken with her. She was striking in appearance and yet did not seem to notice the attention she attracted. She seemed very much at ease with herself and comfortable when speaking with others, not the least bit pretentious or self-absorbed.

Staley had recognized her from the research he had done following the telephone call he had made to the MPDC, posing as the French-Canadian named LaClerc. He had been impressed with her willingness to pursue the Traynor case beyond the arrest of Wes "the Weasel" Ratowski, the scumbag who had killed Jonathan Traynor. Rather than closing the file, as most detectives would have done, she had kept the investigation open, continuing to look for the person who had contracted with Toby Markham for the hit. Little did she know that the man ultimately responsible for Traynor's death had already been tried and convicted, and that the sentence had been carried out.

Costanza was definitely in his head. Standing there in the cold, looking out across the courthouse lawn and thinking about the loneliness that lay ahead upon his return to Aspen, Staley decided he'd try to find a way to meet Victoria Costanza. But he would have to do it as himself—as Hackler Staley—not some invented personality with a carefully constructed past. He had been so many different people and played so many different roles over the years that being himself was not that easy anymore, especially when dealing with strangers. The thought of meeting her, maybe spending time with her sharing thoughts and conversation, made him uncomfortably nervous. He questioned his ability to actually go through with it. *Let's say that by some chance I did find myself in a position to meet her, how would I start the conversation? What would I say? What could I tell her about myself, about my past or my family? If I were able to get to the point of asking her out for a drink or maybe even dinner, what would we talk about? And if by some miracle something clicked between us, how could I ever become close to someone that I could never trust with the secrets I've carried for so long? How could it possibly work out?*

Staley was still mulling through those thoughts when he heard someone walking on the pavestone path behind him. He turned his head slightly toward the front of the courthouse as if looking at something interesting on the street. Just at the edge of his peripheral vision he saw her, Victoria Costanza, casually strolling toward him along the path, ostensibly watching the gardeners and the passersby, just as he had been doing. As soon as he recognized her, his determination waned. Instead of turning to meet her, he looked away; a retreat into the comfort of anonymity.

Victoria watched the handsome stranger closely as she walked slowly toward him along the path. He was taller than she expected, at least six feet, and his shoulders were broad, suggesting an athletic build. His hands were in his pockets and he stood confidently erect, with his head up but still, as though staring straight ahead but at nothing in particular. His clothes were expensive and well tailored. His shoes were traditional in style and well polished. She saw a flicker of reaction the moment he heard her coming. She smiled as he casually glanced to one side, apparently at something in the street but just as easily taking in whoever was walking toward him along the path. He looked relaxed and contemplative, preoccupied with private thoughts, but the subtlety of his awareness suggested that he was wound tighter than he appeared. She wondered if she had been right, if he was some kind of cop.

This is going to be awkward, she thought. *What am I going to do? Walk up to this guy, introduce myself and tell him I'd like to meet him? I'm definitely no good at this.*

She walked on slowly, trying to decide what to do. When he was just a few steps ahead, she resigned herself to finishing what she'd started. *Oh, what the hell. Here goes.*

She came abreast of him and stopped, looking out across the grounds of the courthouse, vaguely following the progress of a squeaky wheelbarrow.

Almost simultaneously, they turned to acknowledge one another.

Staley nodded his head, offering a thin smile before turning his attention back to an Hispanic worker tilling a flower bed twenty feet away.

"Cold out here, isn't it?" Victoria said, immediately feeling insufferably stupid for attempting to start a conversation in that manner.

"Yes, it is," Staley replied, fighting the impulse to slip into another character—to continue the conversation as someone else.

Well, let's try that again, Victoria thought.

"I've seen you in court the last few days. How do you think the trial is going?"

Staley turned back to Costanza, still uneasy but working hard at being himself. "Looks to me like McGowan will probably be convicted," he replied matter-of-factly. "What do you think?"

"Yeah, looks that way to me too. Do you have a particular interest in the trial, or are you just spectating?" *Spectating? Hell, I don't think that's even a real word.*

Staley's immediate reaction was to concoct a story, avoid admitting anything, divert attention, make up something that sounded plausible, then end the conversation and walk away. But when he turned and looked into Costanza's dark, interesting eyes, he could find no reason not to tell the truth. By the same token he could not allow her to know that *he* knew who she was.

"No, not spectating," he said. "I have an interest in the case because of an old friend." *That wasn't so hard, and it's the truth. But I'll have to be careful with her. I have to keep in mind that she's a cop and I've recently committed a half a dozen felonies here and in the District, including the murder of Charles Rathmann.*

Before she could inquire further about the connection, he asked, "What about you? Why are you following the trial?"

"Well, it's a long story, but the bottom line is, I'm a police officer."

Victoria studied the man's face, searching for a reaction to her statement. There was no change in his demeanor. He continued to look into her eyes, waiting. *Well, at least he's not mortified by the fact that I'm a cop,* she thought. *That's good.*

She continued, "If you've been following the trial, you know that the evidence compiled by a man named Jonathan Traynor played a key role in the McGowan case, and that Traynor was murdered in his home a couple months before Rathmann was killed."

"Yes," he said. "I know about that."

"Well, I'm a D.C. homicide detective. For the past seven months I've been investigating the death of Jonathan Traynor. I believe there's a connection between the two cases and I'm down here, on vacation actually, to see if something comes out in the McGowan trial that might give me a lead as to who had Traynor killed."

Victoria's explanation gave Staley an opening to continue the conversation on a subject with which he was more comfortable. Raising his eyebrows in feigned surprise, he said, "Really? Now that's interesting. Jonathan Traynor was the old friend I mentioned a minute ago. Ever since I learned about his secret files being involved in the Rathmann murder, I've wondered if there's a connection between the two cases. I'll be anxious to hear if you turn up anything."

Victoria wondered why she had never encountered the man standing next to her during the course of her investigation. Who was he and what did he know about Traynor? Her interest in him was more than just personal now, but the attraction was still there. She also sensed that he was never going to make the first move for the two of them to get acquainted.

"Sure," she said. "If you'll give me your card, I'll call you if I find something."

Suddenly feeling pressured, Staley tried to buy time. He made a production of checking his pants and coat pockets, apparently not finding what he was looking for. "I guess I don't have a card with me," he said. "Why don't you give me your office number and I'll call you in a couple of weeks to see where things stand?"

He immediately regretted the conditioned response. But the thought of giving someone accurate information about himself cut deeply against the grain. He had spent too many years living in the shadows, doing everything in his power to remain unidentified. He hoped Costanza wouldn't take it as a brush-off line.

Rather than being discouraged, Victoria became more determined than ever to move the conversation forward. Although she was nervous about appearing to be aggressive, she decided to make the first move. Instead of responding to his request for her office number, she studied the interesting stranger for a moment, then said, "I've got an idea. Since you were a friend of Colonel Traynor, maybe you can help me with my investigation. How about if we get together sometime to talk about the case? I'd like to know more about you, more about your relationship to Traynor, I mean, and . . ." She shrugged her shoulders helplessly. "You know, whatever . . ." Her confidence faded and she lost track of how to end the sentence. She turned away, trying to regroup. *Oh, hell. That was smooth. Now he probably thinks I'm an idiot.*

Seeing her embarrassment, Staley managed another smile. After an uncomfortable pause, he said, "Yeah, I think I'd like that."

He turned back toward the gardener for a moment and

fidgeted with the keys in his pocket.

The two of them stood silently, trying to think of what to do next.

Victoria turned and started to say something, but Staley interrupted her.

They both stopped, waiting for the other to continue, then laughed nervously at the awkward moment.

Finally, Staley looked directly into Victoria's eyes and said more confidently than he felt, "I know it's the spur of the moment, but why don't we try to have dinner some-time? Maybe this evening? If you're free, of course."

Victoria smiled her best smile and said, "I'd love to, and tonight is fine. But if we're going to have dinner together, I think it would be a good idea if we introduced ourselves."

Holding out her hand, she said, "Hello, I'm Victoria Costanza."

She could see that for some reason this strangely attractive man was uncomfortable with the prospect of introducing himself. She wondered if he had something to hide or if he was just really that shy.

But then, as though a monumental decision long-considered had finally been made, he smiled warmly and took her outstretched hand.

"Hi, Victoria," he said. "I'm Hack Staley."

And with those few words, a simple introduction, his new life had begun.

About the Author

DAVID STINSON is a business lawyer with a large Oklahoma City law firm. He lives with his wife Becky in Edmond, Oklahoma. In February 1971, as a helicopter gunship pilot with a United States Army air cavalry squadron, he flew daily missions across the border in support of Operation Lam Son 719, the failed ARVN incursion into Laos that is the backdrop for *The Traynor Legacy*.